FIREWEED AND BRACKEN

FIREWEED AND BRACKEN

A Novel

JENNIFER COFFEY

Library and Archives Canada Cataloguing in Publication

Title: Fireweed and bracken : a novel / Jennifer Coffey.

Names: Coffey, Jennifer, 1953– author.

Identifiers: Canadiana 20190154748 | ISBN 9781988098883 (softcover)

Classification: LCC PS8605.O3378 F57 2019 | DDC C813/.6—dc23

Printed and bound in Canada on 100% recycled paper.

Now Or Never Publishing
901, 163 Street
Surrey, British Columbia
Canada V4A 9T8

nonpublishing.com
Fighting Words.

We gratefully acknowledge the support of the Canada Council for the Arts
and the British Columbia Arts Council for our publishing program.

For Don, and for my children.

PROLOGUE

I WILL KILL AGAIN, *six inches high, red ink, not felt pen, not blood (barely enough anyway), scrawled out on the white vertical slats of the bedroom wall, and the Labrador retriever whirling around and around, frantic.*

His master hardly looks disturbed, at least not from this distance. You can see him through the opened front door, beyond the living room and straight across into the privacy of his bedroom. He is lying on his bed facing the wall, fetal position, not dreaming and soon to become famous in a way that will make his mother inconsolable and the rest of his family angry and confused.

The howling dog has alerted a neighbour (well, three or four neighbours, but that is the way on Prince Edward Island), and before long a spirited competition arises over the layman's duties of this insurrection. Who will phone the police? Who will examine the body to determine if it is indeed a body and not, after all, a shallow-breathing victim of . . . what?

Some, of course, are more privy than others to the tales of greater gore, but all in all the quality of the details proves satisfactory to almost all who hear them:

Male, thirty-three, five feet eight inches tall, brown hair, brown eyes, school teacher, immaculate, reserved, infectious laugh. Dead. Murdered. Bashed over the head with a baseball bat and choked with the sleeve of a size fifteen SC Walker blue-and-white striped dress shirt, although many contend that a dress shirt doesn't have enough strength, which causes a whole other argument about silk worms and fibres that has nothing to do with science or shirts or with anything related to his death at all. Following the choking—the absence of substantial bleeding supports this—a wooden-handled nine-inch knife stamped "Old Nick" was shoved up his rectum, the blade wide enough to slice muscle and fat on either side, separating the buttocks and creating an asymmetrical Betty Boop protuberance. What many never learned, however, is that the butt of a du Maurier Special Mild cigarette had been jammed into the dead man's navel.

CHAPTER I

The Northumberland Strait stretches ahead from Cape Tormentine across to Borden, beads of silver rippling across the tips of small blue waves. When she was twelve, Effie had been given a vial of mercury from the Consumer's Gas man who lived in her apartment building. A pretty treasure for a pretty girl, he had said, black rot showing between his bottom teeth when he smiled. Her mother had warned her, of course, about the dangers of lecherous men, which was ironic, Effie thought, given all. Years later Effie poured the mercury down the toilet in a fit of Minimata terror, poisoning the very fish, and people, she was hoping to save.

Now, sitting on the edge of a picnic table, waiting, she imagines the quicksilver surfing from her bathroom toilet, down through the sewer lines and out into the sea. The memory of the bubbles rolling on her palm brings unexpected tears. Up close, she could be anyone's daughter, practically dressed and prepared, leaving home for the first time. From a distance she resembles a painting by Modigliani, melancholic and unadorned. She shifts her shoulders forward, the hollow in her collarbone deep and unforgiving. Her tailbone aches.

She stands up, eager to return to the bus that will take her onto the ferry, relieved by the beckoning arm of the driver. She makes her way back onto the carrier, dumping her purse, a faded copy of *Anne of Green Gables*, and a packet of cherry licorice onto the seat beside her. She pushes up her sleeves, frowning at the pattern of freckles on her long arms, hating summer. She straightens her knee socks and checks her skirt for wrinkles, inspects her hands and adjusts her ring, perpetually annoyed by her elongated fingers, grateful that no one can see her bony toes. She tamps down her anticipation, her eagerness for a life more contained;

life in a smaller place where people know one another, where they stop on the sidewalk to say hello and how are you. The place where her mother comes from.

A mammoth, pop-eyed woman is lumbering toward her, varicose veins resistant against knee-highs, massive breasts swaying, barely contained by her floral shift. Hurriedly, Effie spreads her belongings across the empty seat beside her. She picks up her book and raises it to her face, the pages so close that the lines blur.

"Hello, dear. Is this seat taken?" The woman drops a travelling case on the floor and clamps one hand on each armrest, lowering herself slowly. A piano at the end of a crane.

Effie reaches for her items as an elbow plunges into her rib cage. She smiles weakly, swallowing a wash of *April of Paris* perfume as the woman fans her legs with the hem of her dress.

As soon as the bus is parked in the ferry's hold, Effie squeezes by her seatmate and forces her way to the front, two boys clambering past her, the trio disembarking in a heap.

Up on deck, alone, knees pressed together in the cold ocean air, she follows the horizon, eyes swooping upward with a seagull as it lifts into the air. Fat clouds bloat the sky. She pictures blowing laundry and placid, square-shaped cows. Hay drying in the sun. She is a Dutch farm girl folding her linens. Sea spit, smelling like kippers, squirts her face. She shuts her eyes and inhales. *Alabaster*, her mother had said. *The colour of your skin.*

Effie opens her eyes to a German Shepherd. He is walking toward her, his nails tapping across the deck. He stops, lays his chin across her lap, eyebrows raised. She strokes his forehead, his fur unexpectedly downy between her fingers, the light in his eyes tender and expansive. She's always wanted a dog. As the dock comes into plain sight, a loudspeaker instructs passengers to return to their vehicles. Effie stands up. The dog stifles a whimper.

The heels of her shoes clang all the way down the metal stairs as she makes her way onto the bus and up the aisle, her ponytail flapping against her back. Forced to once again climb over the mammoth woman, Effie stumbles slightly, her skirt stretched to its limit. She falls into her seat, then reaches into her purse to retrieve her novel. She snaps open the book. The woman dozes beside her.

Anne Shirley is speaking to Matthew Cuthbert. *'My life is a perfect graveyard of buried hopes.' That's a sentence I read in a book once, and I say it over to comfort myself whenever I'm disappointed in anything.*

The two boys jostle across the aisle, one tugging on his suspenders, the other pulling strands of bubble gum from his mouth, attaching it to the window beside him.

As the bus rumbles down from the ferry, Effie takes in a prolonged view of Prince Edward Island. She remembers none of it from her childhood, except for a brief memory of being on the ferry when she was five, the sunlight reflected in the tips of her patent leather shoes, her mother bending to kiss the top of her daughter's head. They are on their way to visit Effie's uncle who, her mother said, could hypnotize lobsters.

What she expects today—tidy frame cottages with gables and white picket fences, apple blossoms and lilac bushes, climbing English roses—is not what she gets. Instead she is welcomed by a sparse display of buttercups and scrubby colourless stalks she can't possibly name.

She prefers the approach to Montreal. Kayakers paddling upriver. Red brick buildings and hydro towers. Glorious church steeples. Blowing flags emblazoned with fleur-de-lis, and lofty grain elevators that nudge sibling silos. Cargo lots waiting for sailing ships that float in and out of the harbour. The flour factory, the enduring train bridge, the buildings of Old Montreal. And Notre Dame—its hugging, dark interior—glowing in the late afternoon light.

But now what she sees are stunted trees and flat-roofed houses. Rust-coloured soil. A yard swarming with ornaments— caterpillars, ants and dragonflies—clinging to artificial daisies and dirty lilies, antennae and wings twisted from the wind. Some of the flowers are bent over backwards, others labour with broken stems.

This is not the island of Anne.

Effie suppresses a laugh then looks beyond the sleeping woman to the boys, the one with the suspenders reminding her of Huckleberry Finn, orange hair sticking up, blue jeans rolled at the cuffs. *Got my Sunday boots on, got my Sunday pants, goin' to the barn dance tonight.* She wonders if he has a father.

The boy catches Effie's gaze. "Whaddya lookin' at?" Mucous clings to his nostrils, remnants of a summer cold.

"*Excuse* me?" She fixes her eyes on him, her arched brows signalling contempt.

"I'm askin' ya roight now—whaddya lookin' at?" He screws up his face and crosses one eye.

Effie puckers her lips to keep from laughing. "Nothing," she says.

"What's that supposed to mean, huh? *Stick woman.*"

"Nothing," she repeats. "I don't mean anything." And then, sharply, "Mind your business."

The boy glares at her, his eyes little sparks of fire. "You mind *yer* business, *insect.*" And as he turns back to his friend he says, not quite under his breath, "*Khunt,*" aspirating the h.

Effie's cheeks blaze. She stares at him, eyes distended. As he begins to gyrate side to side, she knows that he is mocking her.

Consider the source.

The fat woman sleeps on.

Effie wipes at a smudge on the glass and reassesses the landscape. Where are the tall oaks, the lush maples? Effie hates conifers. They remind her of Christmas and unhappy families. Presents delayed, parties unattended. She catches sight of her face in the bus window, her reflection staring back.

She looks out of touch with her generation; a wooden doll, slim and very white. Her hair, tied back in a black ribbon, stops abruptly just above her shoulder blades. Her arms and legs hang down like hinged sticks, her chest concave. At twenty-eight, people seldom guess her for more than twenty-three despite the shadows under her eyes. Her head, always too large for her body, embarrasses her, the act of trying on hats more tedious than fun.

Cheesehead.

Then again, the people on the bus also seem years out-of-date, like characters in a movie. One-strap Ikeda overalls and wide-striped rugby shirts; feathered bangs, mushroom cuts and mullets. *Deliverance,* she muses, or *Cape Fear.* Don Messer rubes and greasy, insolent teens. She doesn't see herself as anachronistic at all.

She turns again toward the sleeping woman, following her hairline, examining the shape of her ears and her broadened nose, lips curving upward. Her eyebrows are black, the way her hair must have been when she was young. Her character has worked its way through her. It is in her wide doughy face and open pores, and in her laboured movements. Like a river and its tributaries.

The bus rolls on, rising and falling with the tarmac, and the scenery improves, tidy quilted farmland shooting off from the main highway on either side, the Northumberland Strait fading from view. Black-spotted cows graze undisturbed, surrounding colourful clapboard farmhouses that show little sign of wear. Pink and purple lupins choke the roadside, miniature against the layered clouds that bank the far-reaching sky. What a change! Effie half expects the Virginian, Horseman of the Plains, to come riding by.

As the bus approaches a village, Effie counts the church spires that dot discrete points along the side roads. One, whitewashed with black gloss trim, is unlike any she has ever seen.

Effie's companion stirs beside her, sensing that they are slowing down in preparation for a stop. Giving herself a shake she moves forward in her chair, grips the armrests, and hoists herself up. She smiles at Effie and holds out her hand. Effie hesitates then places a moist palm in the woman's cool grasp.

The woman walks swiftly down the aisle and emerges into the sunlight, clutching her travelling case. She turns and looks back. Effie feels a familiar tightening in her chest that presses into her left breast and leaves as fast as it comes.

As the bus pulls away from the curb, Effie spies another church, its velvet-red brick flecked with sticky milkweed that has attached itself to the chapel in a magnificent floral spray. *Talcum powder for the soul*. She spots the side-length of a gated fence and wonders if it is the entrance to the graveyard. She imagines all the families buried there, the first and second cousins, the aunts and uncles, the brothers and sisters who died decades ago from Spanish flu or winter staphylococcus or some other careless misfortune.

Here is the church, here is the steeple, open the doors and see all the people. This was how it began. And ended.

A memory of her mother's near-death—the way the church had abandoned her—came back to Effie yesterday in the train station: ten years earlier, sitting in her Borg coat waiting in Union Station for the train to Montreal, called back home by the stationmaster. An extended family of Mennonites passed by in their round black hats and collarless coats. Scuffing across the marble floor, the small flock smiled chastely at their feet, bombarded by the thousands of daily travellers making their way into the city.

Effie's eyes followed their shoes, every pair of them black, shuffling past the clock tower, turning right toward the ramp, subsumed by an ocean of footwear that skimmed across the furbished tiles, owners toting duffel bags, purses and cold weather beverages. And somewhere at the other end of their journeys, mothers, friends, husbands and wives waited with warm, hearty lunches and freshly made beds.

Despite the call, Effie had lingered a full ten minutes before making her way back out into the freezing night air wondering if, like the church, she too would abandon her mother.

The driver informs the passengers that they are approaching Charlottetown. Effie opens her purse. She splits the wrappers of two Band-Aids and winds the bandages around her bitten thumbnails. Licking her middle finger, she runs it across the arch of her eyebrows and takes stock of her face in her compact mirror, disparaging her blemishes and her slightly crooked bangs. Rifling in her purse for her mother's green-handled comb, she wonders if her uncle is anything like her mother, or perhaps even her father, a man about whom she remembers only dribs and drabs, all of little consequence.

She recalls that her father's hair was so black it looked blue in the sunshine and under the soft light that was clipped to the metal headboard of her bed. She can see him leaning over to kiss her goodnight, his hair shining in strips of sapphire, how he smelled of lime-scented aftershave and how his day-old whiskers tickled her in a way that wasn't unpleasant. She can't see his face exactly but she remembers his fleshy skin, not fat, but the sort of face you wanted to touch, eyes like charcoal, slashes of warm light deep inside. She remembers him cleaning his fingernails with the cardboard end of a matchbox and that he wore his socks higher than most of the women she knew and how, when he laughed, his stomach flattened. But in her memory, her father is always slightly out of reach.

Her uncle she remembers mostly as a pair of brown pants and oversized shoes, and calculates his age at fifty-two, five years younger than her mother would have been. She figures that any-one who hypnotizes lobsters before boiling them has to be kind.

As Effie steps down from the bus, the orange-haired teenager elbows her in the side and surges in front of her. He sticks his tongue between his teeth and makes a sucking noise. "See ya later, khunt." His friend pushes into Effie from behind and for a moment she stalls, sandwiched between them.

Chapter 2

Bill Cambridge paces the VIA bus station on University Avenue. Passenger trains stopped running on the island years ago and the old brick CN building by the Hillsborough River has been replaced by what a visiting architect once described as "a throwback to Melmac dishes." Bill hopes the bus will be on time. He has to get his wife and kids off to Friday Bible worship and there's a school board meeting to attend. A dozen or so people mill around. Bill knows everyone. And everyone knows him.

He stops pacing and stands in the emptying depot, lifting his legs alternately to wipe his Florsheim shoes on the back of his pant legs. As he unwinds a paper cigar band he sees a fidgety woman at the far end of the terminal. She is sitting next to a paisley suitcase. He has only a graduation photo of Effie to go by. The last time he saw her she was a scrawny, gopher-toothed kid. He isn't fussy for kids, not even his own, and sometimes he wonders how far he has veered from what he should be. (What that is he doesn't know.) He scrapes a match on the side of his belt and lights his cigar, sizing her up through the first energizing puffs. She is skinnier than a barometric bird and pale as parchment, her eyes enormous and blank. Nothing like her mother, he thinks, and he shudders as he walks toward her.

"Effie?" His eyes narrow, a biologist examining his specimen. "Effie *Cambridge*?"

"Uncle Bill?" Effie stands up, smoothing her skirt. She puts her arm forward to greet him. "How do you do?"

He doesn't take her hand. "Goodness Effie, it's been a long time." He looks helpless, his eyes darting aimlessly, and his helplessness seems to distress him. Effie raises her outstretched hand to her face and fans herself as if she is hot, trying to blow away the cigar smoke.

Moving closer to her uncle she again offers her hand and smiles. *Mr. Potato Head.* "Thank you very much for inviting me to Charlottetown." Her voice is strong. She feels armed.

Bill topples toward her and curls the ends of his fingers into hers. He shakes her hand limply like the elders who had confirmed her when she was twelve. Bill, looking around, bellows, "The pleasure is all mine, my dear. Wonderful to see you!" He smiles out into the empty station. "A chip off the old block—like looking in a mirror!"

In truth he believes that she is no chip off anything, and he wonders if bringing her here is a mistake. He had hoped that by inviting Effie to fill the position at the high school he would expiate his guilt in the matter of his sister, but Effie's diffidence offends him. He picks up her suitcase abruptly and nods toward the parking lot.

Effie, clutching her purse, follows her uncle outside. His scruffy shoes and sloppy suit irk her. She can tolerate a lack of style, but nothing about him is agreeable. He looks oafish, cartoonish, an embarrassment to her mother's memory. She restrains a laugh and feels immediately ashamed. He has, after all, offered her a job and a place to stay, and he had picked up her suitcase without asking.

Uncle and niece walk in silence to a royal blue Pontiac and Bill drives to a neighbourhood he calls Brighton. The choppy roads of the downtown pavement disappear, patches of black tar signifying recent touch-ups.

Effie studies the houses, remembering the passengers on the bus, wondering if any of them live here. "Have you lived in this neighbourhood long?" She glances sideways at her uncle then back to the houses. *Leave It to Beaver.*

Pressing his foot harder on the gas pedal, Bill speeds through the side streets, taking some of the corners up over the curb.

Effie grabs for the door handle as her uncle swings the car into a driveway and lurches to a halt. "Send the wife and kids out, wouldja? I'm dropping them at church."

"Shall I get my suitcase?" She says this nervously, as if asking whether her leg needs amputating.

He has a vague sense that he has been unkind. "No, no. I'll bring it in. Go on. Make yourself at home."

Effie climbs out of the car and walks up to the split-level house. She knocks before tiptoeing in. Her aunt stands in the kitchen doorway, her cousins straggling up the hall toward Effie. Fifteen-year-old Martha, a girthy and petulant-faced girl, scuffs along the carpet trailed by Willie, who is one year older than his sister and a decade surlier. The girl zigzags, blocking her brother's attempts to move ahead, the odour of stale menstrual blood following her.

Effie's aunt, short-legged and pinched, moves like luggage on a conveyor belt. Everything about her seems tight—nose, lips, arms pinned against her body.

"You must be Effie," she says, pointing upstairs. "The pink room, top right. If you're hungry the kitchen's in back. But don't touch the stew. That's for supper." And that is all. Effie's uncle steps into the house and drops the paisley suitcase inside the doorway.

Effie watches them file out, two cloche hats and a baseball cap. She takes herself upstairs, thankful for the brevity of this first family meeting. She walks flatly toward the bedroom and gasps.

The walls are pinker than bubble gum. Ice white sheers billow from either window, side panels tied up in opulent bows. A four-poster bed stands against one wall, fishnet slung across the top and hanging down the sides, sections scooped up and fringed with beaded tassels. On the bedside table sits a ballerina lamp. The little dancer wears a tickle-me-pink tutu, porcelain with an asymmetrical hem. Her chin points down assuredly, as if she can support any weight, her head and upraised arms protected by a polka-dot shade. Early Maritime Rococo.

Effie sits down, hugging her calves to the chenille bedspread. Dead ahead on a raised surface and set in a plastic frame hangs a bas-relief of Jesus. He is attending the Last Supper. She stands up and inches toward the picture. Jesus' arms are open, palms up, resting on the table. He cranes his head to the left as if he is looking for something, his hawkish nose obstructing his peripheral view, long ginger hair neatly parted and shaped, shiny with a bit of a wave. His right eye, painted blue, turns inward toward his nose. Even with strabismus, Jesus looks no different than many of the boys she had gone to high school with.

Effie laughs out loud. This would kill her mother all over again. Effie does not hear her aunt mounting the stairs.

Aunt Shirley glares from the hallway, a sprig of hair escaping from beneath her hat. "Something amuses you?" Her wire-rim glasses slide carelessly across the top of her nose. Her tiny eyes bulge.

"It's Jesus," Effie begins, timid. "Jesus, you know, was a Capricorn. I was just wondering where his ascendant was."

"What are you talking about—His *ascendant*? He was raised in Jerusalem and He died in Jerusalem. Everyone knows that— or they *ought* to."

"Jerusalem? Wasn't he raised in Nazareth?" Effie points at the bas-relief.

"That's where He grew up, not where He ascended!"

"Oh—*that* ascendant. Oh no, I mean astrologically. I was wondering about his ascendant because, well, Capricorns are easily led astray and, after all, Judas betrayed him horribly." She hopes to divert her aunt with her knowledge of Jesus and ancient astrology. "I thought that maybe he had Libra rising."

"I don't know what you're talking about." Snatching her Bible from the hallway table, Shirley turns and heads off to church, with leather pumps squeaking and the added burden of praying for Effie's soul.

Effie lies down on the bed, slides under the covers and pulls the bedspread up over her head. Her mother, a Capricorn like Jesus, had widely encouraged goodness. *Though I speak with the tongues of men and of angels, and have not charity, I am become as a sounding brass* had been copied out and taped to their refrigerator before Effie was old enough to read. And also like Jesus, her mother had suffered.

Once upon a time her mother had a beautiful voice, a rich contralto with an expansive range, the sort of voice that people in smoky bars paid money to hear. In their church-going days, Sundays almost always found the two of them together, sitting side by side, fingers entwined, and singing—*Rock of Ages, Nearer My God to Thee, Jesus Bids Us Shine*—her mother's honeyed notes rising toward the vaulted ceiling. Between hymns her mother whispered in conspiratorial tones that everyone—the fur-hatted and the gloveless among them—must pay a tithe, no matter what their annual income. This seemed like hypocrisy to Effie, that her mother should have such stringent rules for others, as well as for herself, when her mother had so much trouble keeping herself upright on the couch and when her salary barely kept them fed. On these occasions, Effie clasped her mother's hand harder, struggling to love her better, to tamp down resentments, to protect her mother from imperious, hateful authority. And her mother, newly appeased, consoled herself, believing that a like-minded daughter would be lenient and therefore less likely to betray.

Effie, exhausted, falls asleep.

Garfield sits at her mother's kitchen table while Effie prattles on about the Democratic Convention. But Garfield doesn't want to hear about the convention. "Supply and demand, supply and demand," and he bangs his fist on the table.

"Where's your accent?" Effie asks.

"What accent?"

"Your Ja-mai-can accent. What did you do with it? You can't sing Rock of Ages without your accent."

Garfield runs his hand inside Effie's cotton underwear along the outline of her buttocks and then up again, following her spine, tickling her shoulder blades, reaching around to fondle her breast. "Come away from the stove," he coos. "Come, come, come away." He sits naked on the chair, his penis erect, white spill showing at the tip. Effie drops to her knees and feathers her tongue along the shaft. "It tastes like copper pennies," she says. She wants Garfield to insert his long soft fingers and find that place that makes her feel turned in on herself. She doesn't think about the loneliness.

"Supply and demand," he murmurs, and bends toward her, gliding his tongue along her lower lip. "All pennies are made of copper, Effie." He pulls her to him and cups his hand against her pelvis.

Effie wakes up, crying.

CHAPTER 3

"You can't influence the board, John. You know they're all idiots." Donnie Fitzgerald pulls on his moustache, his round face soft in the filtered light of the bar. He looks over at his best friend and smiles, wondering how many times they have had this argument and what, if anything, he can do to mitigate it. "You've taught at that school as long as I have. For Christ's sake, it's 1988. You ought to know better." He shakes his finger rapidly like a toy gun—*rat-a-tat-tat*.

John MacDonald swats Donnie's finger away. "I can accept degrees of nepotism, I'm that much of a hypocrite." His voice tightens. "But to bring in a niece from Toronto? I just don't know." How many times have they had this argument he wonders, as he scans the empty bar, his eyes black.

The Morning Dove had once been Carter's Apothecary, for seventy years boasting the pharmacy's black leather stools where customers once nursed milkshakes and ice cream floats. Next to a Regency mirror hangs a life-size photograph of Irish revolutionary, Michael Collins, below him in three long rows decanters of scotch, rye, rum and liqueur.

The bar's owner, a woman everyone in town referred to as the Matriarch, died seven months ago, suffering a brain stem hemorrhage. Her six boys, diligent sons of a formidable mother, inherited the business and keep her memory alive in the front picture window where a crowd of porcelain dolls, their faces coated in asbestos dust, line wooden tiers. Angus, her youngest son, works the bar.

"Oh that's right. It's pure coincidence that your uncle, the Honourable Evers MacDonald, Minister of Public Works and Government Services, continues year after year to secure the contract for paving the ever-sinking parking lots of this Garden of the Gulf for whomever he pleases." Donnie laughs, breathless. "Johnny, what are the degrees and layers of nepotism in *that* hardy perennial? Besides, what if it turns out that Effie Cambridge is attractive?" He cocks his head like a rooster.

John grimaces. "Evers MacDonald is my *great*-uncle and I see him maybe once every five years. And you know what *you* can do with attractive."

"My point exactly. Babies and bathwater, John."

John and Donnie have been friends since early childhood, drawn together in catechism class where John's tendency toward belligerence and Donnie's desire to make people laugh sparked a tantalizing attraction. Even as a boy, John's habit was to ask difficult questions—questions the priests found combative, non-contemplative.

If the Holy Spirit approves of marriage as a way to get rid of lust, then why can't married women use birth control? If we are meant to love the sinner and hate the sin, why do we not approve of anyone who isn't Catholic? It's all right for priests to be homosexual as long as they are not having sex with one another, but everyone knows that priests have sex with one another. . . . With God, aren't all things supposed to be possible?

Most of the children shied away from John, not wanting to be contaminated by proximity, but Donnie moved in the opposite direction, finding himself in awe of a kid whose defiance went straight to the heart of the church's hypocrisy. Supported by open-minded parents and adoring siblings, Donnie reached out to this angry only child.

Donnie raises his empty beer glass. "If we had any sense we'd be at the beach. Angus," he yells. "two more, please!"

"Ah yes," John scoffs. "The beach. The last refuge of hick-town heathens."

Donnie unfurls his arm and sweeps his hand like a ringmaster. "As usual, that distinguished sweater and pant set you're wearing is *perfect* for the seashore."

"Why don't you ask Alice Montgomery how funny things are for her? How would you feel if some import supplanted *you* at school?"

"Jesus John, you're owly. The whole bloody island is the size of Manhattan, as you yourself love to spout more fervently than anyone I know. How much more self-sufficient would you have us be? And no one is getting rid of Alice." Donnie puts his face in his beer glass, his moustache lathered in foam. "She's pregnant. And so what if the new teacher is from away? We do have an entire longstanding Lebanese population here, as you might recall. I know they're not black but it's something."

"No. The blacks came here as slaves. And where are they now?"

Donnie bats John away. "And so what if her ridiculous uncle has something to do with it? She'll get by on her own merits or not, just like the rest of us. I'm gobsmacked by your sanctimony and surprised by your hypocrisy. You're the one always railing against island insularity."

Angus deposits the beer on the table.

"Alice Montgomery happens to be—"

"Oh oh," Donnie groans. "Speak of the devil and he doth appear. And that must be his niece. Interesting."

Angus echoes, "Interesting."

John shakes his head. "Imagine having *that* for an uncle."

Bill Cambridge ambles toward the corner booth, Effie at his side. She has traded her practical shoes for a pair of imitation Prada sandals that she bought on sale on Queen Street in Toronto. Her halter dress hangs just below her knees.

"If it isn't the Cat and the Yammerkid." Effie's uncle swerves his gigantic head toward his niece. "Effie, say hello to your coworkers—Donnie and Johnny." He pumps out his chest, his belt riding up, his socks exposed.

Donnie's mouth widens into a broad smile. "How do you do?" He leaps up. "Angus, bring this woman—" and turning to Effie, he asks, "What will it be? Wine? A beer?" He holds out his hand.

Effie steps back like someone about to be bitten by a large insect. "Something less heady, please. It's too early in the day for yeast." She peers into Angus's face. "Have you any root beer?"

Angus shakes his head no, smiling. Donnie sits down.

"I'll take a Coke then, please. If you're sure you've no root beer."

Donnie drums the seat beside him. "Take a load off."

Effie sits down slowly.

"Diet or regular?" Angus asks.

"Are you sure you won't have a beer? It's never too early for a little eye opener." Donnie nods in the direction of Bill Cambridge. "Just ask your uncle."

"Regular, please. Aspartame causes brain tumours."

John leans forward and offers Effie his hand. "How do you do? John MacDonald. I work in the music department." His voice sounds sombre, ministerial. "What was that about aspartame?"

Since puberty, Effie has been attracted to ecumenical men. She glances at the hair on his knuckles, at the thickness of his fingers. "Effie Cambridge," she says, and her neck reddens. His hands remind her of Caravaggio's St. John the Baptist, tending his sheep.

"I was just saying to John that it's too nice to be indoors. At least until now." Donnie cups Effie's hand. "Don Fitzgerald. Chemistry explosions. How do you like the island so far?" Donnie is dazzled by Effie's eyes. They are as big as pancakes.

She withdraws her hand and fastens it over her wrist. "My mother grew up here. She planned to come back some day."

"And did she? Will she?"

"Oh no." Effie keeps her voice low. "My mother is dead."

"Oh, I'm so sorry." Donnie glimpses down at his beer.

"It's not your fault," she replies. She nods at Angus, who is setting a tumbler on a coaster in front of her. She smiles at the tropical umbrella stuck through a slice of lime, a tiny pink sail on a little green boat.

In all her years as a waitress, Effie had never put an umbrella in a non-alcoholic drink. She can hear her boss at the Port Credit diner, Hippolytos Houlis running his fingers through his thick hair, his eyes crackling. "What kinda fancy drink is that? *Trimalakas!*"

Angus, a pleasant but halting pony, mutely accepts her thanks and walks away.

"What will you do at the school? What will you teach?" John asks as if he doesn't know. The edge slips away from his voice. She *is* attractive, he concedes. Her eyes are as round as pies.

"Grade ten English." A small green spider shoots down from the high ceiling, braking inches above her head. "Apparently, I'm also directing the spring play."

John laughs and blots his beer glass with a bar napkin. "That's brave." He glances up and spots the spider. "So, you're an English teacher. . . ."

"Yes. Originally I was hoping to teach art." Effie halts. "The subject," she says. "Not the person."

Donnie grins appreciatively.

Bill plods toward them, pulling a cigar out of his shirt pocket. "I was takin' Effie over to Dr. Bob's," he says. "I've arranged an apartment for her." He smiles and winks. "Perhaps if you boys—"

"Nine holes or eighteen?" asks Donnie, glad to be getting rid of Effie's chaperone. "We'd be honoured to keep her."

Effie recoils. "I'm not chattel."

"Eighteen. Jesus, thanks boys." He hauls out a wad of bills from his pocket, raising his leg to wipe his shoe on the back of his pants. He slaps two twenty-dollar bills on the table.

John shakes his head. "We can pay our own tab, thanks just the same, Bill."

Bill Cambridge hustles out of the bar, ignoring John and bawling "Good day!"

Effie watches her uncle leave then drops her gaze from door to window, scanning the dolls, distracted and enthralled by their antiquity. Little dolls, she says to herself. Little dolls all in a row.

Fifteen years ago her best childhood friend had made Effie a snug West Indian beauty, long hours spent sewing and primping. Pink peppermint dress, folds of material fashioning breasts; looped chain draped around her neck. A pair of hoop earrings. The doll was the most beautiful gift Effie had ever received. That same summer, Kathleen's stepfather pressed his stepdaughter's palms into the red-hot elements of the stove.

Donnie snaps his fingers playfully in front of Effie's face. "Hello? Effie? Are you on the planet?"

Effie nods, embarrassed, her eyes following a long line of white webbing. "The cobwebs go all the way up to the second floor," she says. "Is Miss Havisham up there?"

"Oh, not to worry." Donnie laughs. "Only muckety-muck Conservatives and off-island guests of the privileged are permitted to dine up there."

John searches above Effie's head for the spider, but it has disappeared. "It's not the place for schoolteachers," he says. "To go against the order would be tantamount to revolt, and there's already enough of that festering below the hemlines. Although they do let us up there once a year at Christmas."

Effie canvasses her new companions. She wonders why John wears a sweater in July, but she likes his bearing, his anachronistic comportment, and she hopes she has made a solid first impression. She has a thing for angry men, as long as they aren't angry with her. He seems intense—melancholic but loyal—and she suspects he has a big brain. Like Voltaire or Leonardo da Vinci.

"So you're moving into Dr. Bob's building?" Donnie slurps at his beer. "That's only a five-minute walk to my house."

Effie toys with her straw. "Apparently somebody died and there's an apartment free. Death liberates everyone, in the end."

"Father Timothy and his sister lived there for years," John says, bypassing Effie's comment. "His sister outlived—"

Donnie interrupts. "His sister *the* Sister you mean."

John turns to Effie, ignoring his friend. "Sister Shannon Margaret."

"Turns out," Donnie begins, "the sister and the brother were rumored—oh, stop rolling your eyes, John. It isn't as if this is news to you."

John smirks. "Donnie's the good Catholic at this table. He'll have all the prurient details. More than you can shake a stick at."

Donnie stands up. "Why don't we finish off here and take Effie over to the good doctor's? After that, let's go to Stanhope. Have you been to the beach yet, Effie? You'll love it." He imagines her wet in her summer dress, the outline of her body clinging to the cotton. He points at Bill's money and says to John, "What'll we do with that?"

"Let me worry about it." John refolds the twenties and tucks them into his pants pocket.

The threesome cross Richmond Street and cut through the churchyard, Donnie walking close to Effie's side. Years of trespassing have worn a hard path into the grass. The overhanging leaves of the trees reach down so low that Effie can touch them. She smells salt coming up from the harbour.

Effie looks past Donnie and over at John. The sun flashes across his high forehead, shimmering down one cheek, the other side of his face in silhouette. His eyes arc like half moons, generous lids folding under his brow. Silken hair rims his forehead, softening a receding hairline that betrays the inevitable loss, a vulnerability Effie finds seductive. He reminds her of a boyish Rembrandt.

"Look, there's Dr. Bob." Donnie points toward a reedy man reclining against the hood of a station wagon. "Hey, Doc! Come on, guys," and he reaches for Effie's forearm.

Effie rushes out ahead and hurries across the street, ignoring the traffic. She announces herself from across the road, thrusting out her hand in introduction. "Hello. I'm Effie Cambridge." The strap of her dress loosens at her shoulder.

"Hello doll! Hello boys!" Then back to Effie, "I hear you're hunting for digs." Dr. Bob sways back on his heels and then forward again, like a bamboo tree. A bronze plaque behind him reads *Cornelius Kilbride, 1869*.

"The apartment is pretty spacious, and you can find a roommate, yes? But the rent's reasonable, even for one." Dr. Bob's eyes sparkle. "Pays to be shone down on by Sister Shannon— God's lengthiest tenant—and the blessed provincial government who have put a roof on things like your rent, Missy." The doctor places his hand on Effie's elbow, guiding her forward. "Come on upstairs and tell me what you think." He herds the trio through a glistening foyer and up a wide flight of stairs, flinging open the first door he comes to. "It's furnished, $330.00 a month with an annual 4% increase. All-inclusive. Are the terms satisfactory?"

"It sounds perfect, but might I look first? I ought to know what I'm renting." Effie blushes and rights her shoulder strap, wondering how it is she has spent twenty-eight years in Ontario with dispassionate, ordinary people (except for her neighbour who ate coal) and now this.

She crosses the threshold warily, gaping at a tall crown-moulded room that unrolls into a long central hallway—honey-coloured hardwood planks—and flush against the living room wall a century-old piano, painted gold.

Dr. Bob slides in behind her. "Do you play?"

"Badly," Effie says, imagining herself sitting at the piano, her fingers feathering the keys.

"If by badly you mean seldom, then that's just as well. The other tenants might not appreciate the noise."

Effie, mildly offended by the word *noise*, looks away, her eyes landing on an amber chandelier—ostentatious by Port Credit standards—suspended from the ceiling on a three-foot chain. A circle of leaping foxes is etched into the perimeter of the glass, their ears pointing upward, mouths open as if they are singing. Or hungry. In the corner of the room beside one of two tall windows an oak dresser, childish letters carved into the side of the wood, leans humbly. Effie can read **DAVID** from across the room. Kitty-corner to the dresser a rocking chair, its arms missing spindles, beckons haplessly, and in the centre of the spacious room a teak coffee table rests on a frayed Moroccan rug. A red velvet sofa, columns of thick white threads exposed like peg teeth and visible at the gaping seams, hunches along the wall next to a nonworking fireplace.

"This is what is meant by eclectic," Donnie whispers in Effie's ear.

They edge forward, converging at the end of the hallway.

"Can I paint?" Effie asks.

"I don't know," the doctor replies. "Can you?" He breaks into convulsions of laughter. "Whatever you like, my dear. I leave it with you. When you've had enough looking around come downstairs and we'll discuss the particulars."

As he walks down the hallway a petite yellow-haired woman jostles past him, sneezing violently. "Has anyone seen Pistachio?" Dr. Bob pats her head.

"Hey there, chicken legs." Donnie smiles at the woman. "How are things over at the newspaper?"

"Fancy running into you here. I don't suppose"—she sneezes again—"you've seen Pistachio?" She runs the back of her hand across her watering eyes.

"You're the only person I know who sneezes when she's *away* from her cat. Have you looked in Rutherford's apartment? Mr. Kitty's probably up there being hand fed shrimp." Donnie puffs up in imitation of someone too engorged to move, pointing above their heads. "Hard to believe they let that woman work in a hospital."

"She's not *that* fat," John and Mary speak simultaneously.

Donnie shrugs. "Perhaps he's up there smothered in Béarnaise."

John turns to Effie. "I seem to have lost my manners. Effie Cambridge, meet Mary Rose. Mary, this is Effie—your soon-to-be neighbour."

Effie steps back as Mary extends her right hand. The two women smile uncomfortably, and as Effie squashes her clammy hand into Mary's child-size palm she spies a patch of orange. There, curving his potbelly around the edge of the opened door, stands Pistachio. He sashays down the hallway, heading directly for Mary.

"Oh, you devil!" Mary reaches out for her pet. The cat purrs loudly.

Effie studies Mary as Mary bends down, her long blond hair falling around the contours of her cat. Mary gathers up Pistachio like the Madonna cautiously lifting her baby out of his cradle. Effie fingers the fine ends of her own hair. "Handsome is as handsome does," she says. Her pupils retract.

"Pardon *me*?" The cat continues to purr in Mary's arms. John runs his hand across his forehead and closes his eyes. Mary and Donnie stare at Effie.

"Oh nothing." Effie feels the red rushing from her neck to her cheeks. "It's just something my mother used to say."

"It means that you are only as attractive as you behave," says Mary. She touches her fingers to her lips and glances toward the window and the sunlight, then lowers her eyes in deference to Effie. The wool of John's sleeve brushes against her arm.

"Exactly!" Effie croaks, volleying for a recovery. "Exactly."

"Oh for god sakes," Donnie says, "enough of this." He raises his hands in mock supplication. "Let's go to the beach." He turns to Mary. "Are you coming with us?"

John rests his hand on Mary's shoulder. "Yes, do come Mary."

"Let me put Pistachio away, and then, yes, I'd like that. Thanks."

"I'll come upstairs with you," John's voice is light and cheerful. "Donnie, why don't you take Effie down to Dr. Bob?"

"Always the bridesmaid," Effie mumbles.

Three heads turn to look at her.

"Oh, I'm only kidding," she says. "Completely kidding."

They walk out of the apartment in single file, Effie behind Donnie, Pistachio riding high on Mary's small shoulders.

Effie sits in the passenger seat of Donnie's Honda Civic as they drive north, away from town. Mary and John share the back seat. Donnie had retrieved his car, bathing trunks, and towels while Effie stood in Apartment 1 signing a twelve-month lease and accepting two gold-plated keys from Dr. Bob. Effie wishes she owned a bathing suit, momentarily forgetting about her skinny legs and arms.

"Effie," Donnie points out the window enthusiastically, "see that school? John and I went to junior high there. And John lives right over there, down that street."

Effie waves away gas fumes. "Which one?"

"You can't see it, but it's there. Keep looking right. It's three houses down on the left."

"You own your own home?"

"He's a spoiled brat, Effie. Mr. Money Bags."

John juts forward and grabs the back of the passenger seat. "Don't listen to him, Effie." He pokes his finger into Donnie's back. "I'm thirty-two, Buster. I worked hard for that house."

"Yup. Him and his dad. They worked hard." Donnie's head keeps time to a radio ad. "I'm thirty-two and I don't own a house."

John pulls down hard on Donnie's ear. "Listen, there's nothing wrong with a little parental support. I paid him back over a year ago. I might still be at home too if I had a family like yours."

"You mean poor?" Donnie turns up the radio and begins to sing. "*My name is Luka. I live on the second floor. I live upstairs from you. I think you're a big fat bore.*" He takes one hand off the wheel and snaps his fingers. "God, I hate this song."

John eases back into his seat.

Donnie looks at him in the rearview mirror then puts both hands on the wheel and leans forward, forcing John out of sight.

The car bumps and bangs over the uneven pavement. Mary and John chat in the back seat. Donnie hums tunelessly. Effie watches as the rows of colourful houses dwindle into a network of farms. Seagulls glide in and among thick clouds piled high like mounds of mashed potatoes. Effie smells salt again.

She fans her toes through the white sand and stares out into the endless Gulf of St. Lawrence, the ocean a sheet of flickering blue and silver.

"Where is it that you are, Effie? Awandering afar, inhaling caviar, a motion picture star?"

Effie feels Donnie's hot breath on her face.

"Olands or Schooner?" A tidy roll of fat hangs loosely over the waistband of his boldly patterned swimming trunks.

She hugs her knees. "No wonder the Greeks thought the earth was flat. Look at it—you can't know that it just doesn't fall off somewhere, can you? You have to be much higher up to see a curve in the horizon, and even then it would be hard to tell." A white-rimmed jellyfish floats in the lap of a wave, bobbing like a lifeless suction cup.

In truth, this water frightens her, falling off the way it does beyond any visible horizon. How could anyone possibly believe that drowning was a peaceful way to die. Any minute a belt of water longer than Hadrian's Wall could rise up and wash away everything. She'd heard this about pregnant women, their capricious hormones and lack of restful sleep, their dreams about water—flooding rivers; intractable whirlpools; bottomless swamps where a person had no defence—and she can't imagine how anyone would want to spend their days confronted by the interminable sea. Lake Ontario provided at least an idea of the other side, the strands of northern New York lined with pretty fishing vessels even when you couldn't see it, or them. But here, what was there to imagine? Seven days on a vertigo-inducing ship? As many hours flying in an airplane that at any minute could careen into the freezing ocean waters, its passengers lost forever, their passports and holiday shirts and party dresses strewn about the shark-infested waters?

"What's *he* doing here?" John jerks his head toward a muddy-faced man who is tramping along the beach. "Look at those sunglasses and that hair. God, if that doesn't say everything about him." The man's thick heels sink into the sand, his feet pointing out like a duck's. "His head's shaped like a television."

"My shit for brains cousin," Donnie sniggers. "It's a wonder the Charlottetown police hold onto him." He whips out an imaginary six-shooter from the waistband of his swimming trunks.

"He failed high school but still got the job over a barnyard of graduating students, thanks to his older brother."

"Isn't that nepotistic? Or do all relatives enjoy a free hand?" Effie asks.

"Yes, it is nepotistic, Effie." John squints and raises his arm to his brow against the sun. "You can run a police station any way you like, at least here." He pauses, modulating his voice. "Not to offend, but didn't *your* job come through your uncle?"

Donnie turns on John. "Who died and made you God?"

Effie blushes. She had gauged her question pertinent; hadn't seen her mistake. She opens her mouth to speak but no words come out.

Mary has been sitting calmly, invigorated by the sharp sea. She flirts with a bumblebee that persists in making contact with her hair. She lowers her sunglasses and looks at Effie. "Frick and frack, Effie. That's all it is." She enunciates each syllable carefully and softly. "It's hard to believe, but when they're not together they actually sound like adults." *Ak-chew-a-lee.* "It isn't that John doesn't know better, he just needs to be contrary."

John laughs, hoping his laughter will prove he isn't mean, that Effie will understand he didn't intend any unkindness. He likes her. She is odd. He understands odd.

"On the other hand," Mary points over at Donnie, "that guy has clay for brains."

Donnie pokes his friend in the arm. "Yeah. Red clay. And there goes my cousin—Moby Dork. Look out, John. Thar he blows!"

Effie looks back at the water. An image of Diddy Wishingwell floats through her head.

John digs his toes into the sand, brushing away a horsefly. He sidles over to Effie, self-conscious in his short-sleeve Polo shirt and cut-off denim shorts. "Are you with us?"

"Oh yes. I was just thinking of the ways that people fit together. Or don't."

"You mean like a jigsaw puzzle?" Mary asks.

"And not like Siamese twins?" Donnie teases.

"Yes," Effie says, "and magnets."

John wiggles his toes. "Symbiotic, co-dependent or healthy? Although I suppose symbiotic *is* co-dependent, so perhaps that's redundant." He cannot seem to extricate himself.

Mary and Donnie laugh. "*Perhaps?*" they ask in one voice.

"It's funny," Effie says, "the way you all bicker. And yet any-one would know you're not angry with one another." Her eyes burn in the sun's glare.

As Effie lies on the sand she imagines the look on Hippolytos' face when he learned that she was permanently gone—how angry he must have been and then, later, how sorry. She pictures her town at night in the blue-grey streetlight, the faraway cries of the common loons, and the church bells on Sunday morning.

CHAPTER 4

Effie stares down at her patent leather shoes. *I can buckle these all by myself*, she says out loud. *I am three years old*, although she deliberately pronounces it *phree* and she is, in fact, four. She can't tell time but she knows, because the television is still on and the screen is black, and because no sound comes at her from anywhere, not even a set of tires rolling faintly along Lakeshore Road, that it must be very late.

Instinct tells her to head across the street and follow the road behind the grocery store, not too close to the lake but toward the only hotel Effie knows. Her mother has pointed it out with that familiar tone in her voice, the one she uses when she tells Effie to stay away from the man in Apartment 3 or when she complains that the cost of their favourite tomatoes is too high.

Because she is only four, Effie doesn't understand terror as much as she possesses a strong sense of pragmatism (years later, she will occasionally lapse into a momentary diversion, a game of nature versus nurture that she uses to console herself; to remind herself that either way, there isn't much a child could have done to change things). The feeling at the core of her stomach as she goes hunting for her mother is swallowed up by a flash of indignant little girl fierceness and the sort of reassurance that fairy tales with happy outcomes provide.

The pavement is wet with dewy frost, a reminder of the homemade popsicles back home in the freezer box. Soon summer will be here and the flowers will bloom everywhere. She loves white daisies and pink gladiolas the best. Effie longs for her mother.

A colony of milk-white seagulls bob gently down by the pier. Momentarily distracted, Effie wonders if their bottoms are cold from the water. Her chubby fingers clutch at her sides as she marches alone in the dark listening to the sound that her heels make—clack clack clack clack—ushering her along and reconfirming a sense of purpose and physical safety.

It is only when she nears the hotel's front door and sees the man standing behind the desk that she feels herself on the verge of crying. She doesn't want trouble. *We don't want trouble*, she hears her mother saying in her head. *Please darling, not now.* And just as Effie is about to turn around and retrace her steps back to the apartment building, she hears a voice cry out to her from the bushes.

"Effie, my pet, is that you? What are you doing out here in the dark?" The words come at her tired and tumbling, their syllables faltering, looking for places to hide, and Effie knows her mother is drunk.

Hands on her hips, already impatient with the rippling consequences that will come from her mother's inebriation, the little girl shouts, "Mummy, get up!" and she shivers as the cold night air slides up and under the oversized sleeves of her gabardine coat, an Easter gift from her mother. She has no complex idea about coincidence or calamity, or that the thing adults sometimes call synchronicity is often linked to an innate knowledge of who, and what, we come from. Effie merely wonders what her mother is doing there sitting on the damp grass, her hair sticking out like chicken feathers and, visible even in the dark, with what looks like a bruise forming in a semi-circle beneath her eye. And where is her purse and why is one of her shoes not on her foot?

"Mummy, get up!" Effie repeats. And this time a feeling she does recognize creeps over her. "You have to come home with me now!"

Effie's mother slides her fingers up the side of the wall, gripping a hedge with her other hand, trying to leverage herself. Like a genie out of a bottle, slowly she rises, until she is able to reach for her daughter's small hand. "Where is my shoe?" she asks, shocked and imploring all in one instant.

Effie feels her lower lip quavering and she holds her breath while she looks in the brush for her mother's high heel. Finding it she presses the shoe to her chest, her bottom lip curving down as the tears pour from her eyes, clinging to a black-coloured hope that her mother will somehow get better.

The next morning Effie knows there is no point in trying to wake her mother or even to see if her mother's corneas are intact, a yardstick Effie sometimes uses to judge whether there is life in the still body lying on the bed. Prying her mother's eyes open (a prodding that would typically waken all but those closest to death), and observing the glassy cones of her mother's eyes staring back at her, Effie consoles herself with the incontrovertible evidence and climbs back down to go about her day.

But today there is no need for climbing and Effie pads straight out to the kitchen, the soles of her pre-schooler feet scuffing across the linoleum floor as she grabs the back of a chair and pulls it over to the counter. Once there, she extracts the bag of bread from the corner of the cupboard and weighs her options between toast—a procedure that always initially frightens her before giving over to proud feeling of accomplishment—or ketchup sandwiches.

From the living room she hears "Once upon a time not long ago and not far away" and Effie knows if she hurries to eat her breakfast and wash her face and brush her teeth she won't miss the Friendly Giant, a character who makes her smile and clap her hands and encourages her belief in talking roosters and giraffes. The cow jumping over the moon is her favourite part, and she is sorry that her mother isn't here to share this ritual with her. She loves the magic of the castle, too, and the tiny village where farmers and their children and wives live and work together and where nobody ever gets sick or dies.

If someone were to ask Effie, "What does death mean?" she would think of a place behind a locked door where the cowboys and Indians kill each other. She would remember the morning she saw the shadows of leaves move back and forth across the wall and how she crouched down in her snapping pajamas, very afraid. Death was where an absence of time was, where you couldn't get back the people you love or make your thoughts work in order.

CHAPTER 5

The weeks that followed that first day at the beach had not played out as Effie expected. She assumed that her warm introductions to Donnie and John and Mary promised easy friendships and a blithe continuity. Even romance. But she was wrong. They weren't her friends. In fact, they were barely acquaintances.

At first she blamed her loneliness on the claustrophobic town, stifled further by this cavernous apartment. What does she know about stripping wallpaper and painting perfect edges? Her muscles hurt from hunching over the steaming teakettle and from driving her arm up the wall, shearing away a century of layers. Ladders terrify her—she borrowed one from Dr. Bob—and she worries about inhaling toxic glue. She furrows the metal scraper into the plaster, gouging out weaker portions of the wall, fretting over lead and asbestos, mildly afraid her I.Q. will drop insidiously, like Charlie in *Flowers for Algernon*.

Her luck and expertise vary depending on the tapes she plays on her Sony cassette recorder. She weeps over Emmylou Harris and Tom Waits, swings her hips widely to Paul Simon in South Africa, and goes wild over Eddy Grant and *Electric Avenue*, jumping and gyrating around the coffee table. She wonders if John has given her a second thought. He certainly seemed to like Mary well enough, but someone as attractive as Mary surely has a boyfriend. Effie wishes now she'd had the foresight to ask.

During paint-drying intervals, Effie rearranges the furniture. She wheels the piano around like a fat kid on a sleigh. After sitting in every corner of the room, it comes back to rest in its original position, quite pretty against the pear-green walls. She rolls up the Moroccan rug and hides it in the hall closet, replacing it with a braided mat she has found on sale at Zellers. She patiently stitches closed the open seams of the couch, wondering, while she sews, if she is wrong about John—perhaps he already has a girlfriend, another teacher who spends summers away. Someone polished and refined. *Like an apple.*

A local secondhand store provided affordable accessories— scarves for draping, a lace tablecloth reduced in price because of a nickel-sized blob of wax, a magazine rack, a deep-green corduroy armchair that she boosted up the stairs, two framed photographs of unknown families, and a pair of binoculars. (She wants to break away from her mother's decorative themes, hav- ing once declared that she would throw up if she saw another lobster trap. Her mother had refined taste despite their lack of money, but the seashore exceptions stand out in Effie's memory as a grotesque personal embarrassment.) She wonders whether John would appreciate her decorating style.

When she isn't painting and repairing, Effie sits on the deep window ledge that overlooks the churchyard and the better part of downtown. Heady from fumes, she watches the anonymous passers-by, wondering who they are and where they are going. Their lives march by in horizontal lines, from the Morning Dove on her extreme left to the offices of the Department of Veterans Affairs on her right, St. Paul's church standing soundly in the centre, its windows glistening luminously. In late afternoon, gov- ernment workers scuttle by in pairs, small groups or singly. Effie eyes the human traffic enviously, and waits to catch a glimpse of John.

She wants to go out, to meet people—colourful, local people who are warm and interested in her—but from her window the town feels impenetrable. Her uncle has called twice to ask her to dinner but she cannot make herself go. The thought of seeing her aunt and their children—the smell of their children—gives her stomach pains.

When she is hungry for more than bakery bread she orders take-out from a Lebanese restaurant around the corner. At first she chooses healthy meals—hummus and pita, or a tofu garlic platter—charmed by the island's acceptance of foreign food, hoping that this might bode well for all outsiders. Later, as her loneliness becomes more pervasive, she asks shyly for a hot hamburger with French fries and gravy, or a two-piece order of fish and chips with vinegar, the fat content offset by a generous side of coleslaw and a slice of orange. She longs for a bowl of Bavarian cream that her mother used to make on special Sundays. When her loneliness overtakes her, she rolls small balls of Wonder Bread into her palm and eats them.

From time to time rain falls inaudibly, blotching the sidewalk below her. There are no August thunderstorms; here the rain scarcely moistens the trees. Effie misses the metallic scent of earthworms, the trill of songbirds after a downpour; the choral chirping of robins and sparrows replaced by screeching, hungry seagulls. A parcel of crows, nesting in the oak trees in the churchyard, caw incessantly.

One crow sorrow, two crows joy, three crows a letter, four crows a boy.

Sitting on the ledge she wonders if coming to Prince Edward Island was the right thing to do. Perhaps she should have looked for work in Toronto, or gone to Jamaica with Garfield. She yearns for the warm neon lights of Sam the Record Man, and her stomach tightens. The heavy salt air filters through the windows, reminding her of rancid herring. She misses the lake.

Sometimes she sits stiffly at the piano, her left hand following the keys of the bass clef, her fingers hovering above the black and white strips of ivory but not touching them. Carefully, she presses her right index finger on middle C, pleased to hear the note speak back to her. She gently taps the keys, finding as she goes that she prefers the black ones over the white, their sounds reminding her of the Chinese restaurant on Lakeshore Road and its mural of hand-painted bridges.

One Thursday evening Effie lounges in bed, *The Magic Mountain* face down on her chest, an open root beer beside her on the floor. An army of shoes march up the stairs to the third floor amid cackles and snorts of laughter. Pistachio meows plaintively in the outer hallway as the shoes move forward overhead, clumping their way to the back of the apartment directly above her. Voices cascade down, sliding between the plaster and brick and spilling out through open windows.

"I thought she looked dreadful, didn't you?" *Smoky, like Marlene Dietrich.* "I never liked her anyway, and besides—"

Effie reaches over and picks up her pop.

"She's a troll." *Higher pitched. More strident.* "That's not very charitable of me, I suppose. But her mother was such a pie-faced bitch, and all that talk about her father—" She crops off the end of her syllables. Fath-*ther. Vader.*

Effie sits upright, *The Magic Mountain* slipping to the floor. She climbs out of bed and scuffles into the kitchen where the voices are even clearer. She sits at the table, her lips to her bottle, and listens hard. She feels like Mata Hari, cloistered, her cotton nightgown cool against her skin. Above her, Mrs. Hitler rants on and Effie toots long, deep notes across the top of the bottle. She can't believe her good luck.

A third voice speaks. "Oh, I don't know. Remember when I worked with her? I figured she meant well, at least." *Cajolery,* thinks Effie, like someone coaxing hot pie out of a pan.

Dietrich counters. "Oh, who cares what she did or didn't do?"

Effie wonders which one is her neighbour, Mildred Rutherford.

The smoky voice continues. "I would rather be caught *dead* than be seen in that flimsy red skirt and those stupid blue heels. She looked like Minnie Mouse." (Ear-splitting laughter)

"Minnie's blue period." (more howls)

Effie laughs too, passing root beer through her nose. She grabs a corner of her nightgown and swipes it across her face. The inside of her nostrils burn.

The last speaker continues. "What? Who told you *that*?"

"He *what*?" The Dietrich voice rises up—"He put it *where*?—then sinks back down. "Oh, for heaven's sake, you're having us on."

The cajoling woman whines, "He has a *problem*, like I said to you before. Do you think I should see him again?"

"Are you out of your *miiiiind*?" The smoky voice hangs onto the last word as if it were a musical note.

"He's having a libidinous conflict. As a means of control."

Effie pictures this woman in a khaki uniform and an arm-band.

"He feels appropriated. Completely emasculated." Effie laughs loudly and then, afraid she has been overheard, covers her mouth.

"The only way he can ejaculate—let's call a spade a spade here—is through de-sublimation. Yours *or* his."

Another voice emerges, this one pleading, sweeter. "I wish I understood why we always fall into these traps. It's lonely for people. It's even lonely for me sometimes."

Effie wants to tell her that she agrees, that the world is selfish and unkind.

A new voice replies. "Everyone has problems. It's simply a matter of how we deal with them."

Effie spirals in her chair, waiting anxiously for the woman's next words.

"Confession has saved me."

Aunt Shirley.

"Maybe if you stopped thinking about the kind of man you want and prayed more for goodness and *God*ness, better things would happen to you."

Mrs. Hitler interrupts. "Last week I shat beet butter clusters. I am perpetually warning my nurses against discolourations and non-digestibles, and I am *always* forgetting myself. Let's eat!"

Rutherford.

A rush of shoes scrape across the floor like industrial sandpa-per. Effie yawns and grabs another root beer from the fridge. She skitters up the hallway, brushing against the wall. The joints of the hardwood creak beneath her bare feet. She flops onto the couch in the front living room and waits, hoping their words will filter as easily through the fireplace. But all she hears from above is an occasional laugh. She is too far from an open window. On her way back to the bedroom someone yells, "*Gross!*"

That night Effie dreams of a barren cemetery, empty except for a terrace of lopsided monuments and three lilac trees in full bloom. The smell of the purple flowers overwhelms her and she drops down on her knees in front of a gravestone. The inscription reads, *There but for the grace of God go I.* In the stillness of the lonely yard, the clucking of a hundred chickens comes up from behind her. Effie turns her head to see them. Some of the birds are pudgy, others thin. A few wear aprons, the rest arrayed in starched housedresses. Effie hears her mother's voice all around her whispering, *"Pinny, pinny, pinny!"* Effie scans the churchyard but can't see her mother anywhere. The voice disappears, lost in the congregation of birds that walk toward her, each one wearing blue high-heeled shoes. They pass Effie without notice, waddling into the grove of trees beyond, a river of discarded eggs in their wake.

At four in the morning Rutherford rolls over and falls out of bed. Effie sits up dazed, wondering if her ceiling is about to cave in.

CHAPTER 6

Effie sits at her desk in a classroom on the second floor of Minegoo Senior High, the school name adopted from a Mi'Kmaq Indian legend. Effie knows this story from her mother, who told her that after the Great Spirit completed the task of creation, a portion of red earth remained in the sea, yet to be named. The Great Spirit decided to form a crescent-shaped island and inhabit the territory with red people, his people. Here, he said, they would be out of harm's way, free to inhabit the land as they wished. The island would be named Minegoo. *Made in heaven.* The last thing Effie remembers her mother saying about the legend was, "If only the Great Chief had thought to tell the red people about it."

John MacDonald steps into the classroom, smiling. "How are you?" A sliver of sun sparks off his tie clip.

Effie stares at his nose. It grows out of his face like an upside-down carrot.

"Where have you been?" he asks.

"Where have *I* been?" Effie crosses her ankles. "*I* haven't *been* anywhere. Painting the apartment, mostly." A small pain jabs her lower back.

"You never came back over to the bar. Not once. We looked for you." John stresses the word *looked*. "And you know we drop by the bar pretty near every day. We're not very exciting."

"I was busy settling in." Effie stares at the blotter on her desk, pretending to be preoccupied with important things. The ribbon in her hair peeks out from behind her, curled edges of a perfect figure eight.

"Mary wanted to stop by and see you, but she didn't want to intrude." He smiles again. "Are you busy today after class?" He turns his head and his nose becomes a different shape, sharp and aquiline. Roman.

How like a Caravaggio painting, she thinks—a study in light and dark. "Not especially busy," she says.

"Okay then, meet me out by the water fountain. Do you know where that is?" She watches the sparkles of light scamper along his sleeve. "We'll be closing up early today, around two." And he is gone.

Effie stands up and massages the sore spot on her back. Outside the classroom students rustle like restless steer, an avenue of blue jeans and logo t-shirts, shoulders pushed back into the lockers of the technical wing, not unlike the boys in Effie's high school where the girls had kept to their own quarters, convening around bathroom sinks, waving away cigarette smoke and admiring their makeup in streaky mirrors. Effie had loved high school—the classrooms, the lessons, the smell of chalk—but she had hated the kids.

Minegoo Senior High feels similar in design and upkeep, built in the 1950s and framed by a network of century-old trees; in need of minor cosmetic attention (plaster and painting) and desk replacement, blue ink scarring the laminate surfaces.

She examines the desks for perfect alignment then walks to the far end of the classroom and tightens the coat hooks. She checks the blackboards for smears and can't decide if she should write out her name. Ms. Cambridge? Ms. Effie Cambridge? Miss E. Cambridge? And what colour of chalk should she use? A butterfly flutters in through an open window then floats back out again. Effie glances out into the schoolyard and sees that some of the leaves have already turned orange and yellow and red.

"Oh, Miss! Miss! Come look, Miss." A slit-eyed giant of a boy barrels into the room and shoves out his hand. "Look Miss. It's a froggy, eh?" His skin folds like accordion pleats when he smiles. *Of Mice and Men*, thinks Effie. *Lenny*.

Effie clamps her hands together. "Yes, I can see that. Where did he come from?" *Where did you come from* is what she wants to ask.

"Outta my pocket, Miss." The boy shows Effie his flattened palm and nods toward his pocket. "Nothin' else in there." He beams at the frog and then down at his teacher.

"No, I mean before that. Before your pocket. Where did he come from?"

"From the mother frog, Miss! I'll put him out, eh Miss? I just wanted you to have a look at him. Thought it might bring you luck on your first day, that sort of thing." He brushes the frog's head with his own as he wanders out of the classroom.

"Don't put your lips on him!" Effie yells after the boy.

Her eyelid quivers.

A rush of activity occupies the morning. Thirty students arrive at the first bell, no one early and no one eager to sit at the front of the room. Effie shushes the class and points to the black-board.

Effie Cambridge.

"Good morning, class. My name is Ms. Cambridge. I am your homeroom teacher and, for some of you, your grade ten English teacher." A handful of boys continue to speak in low tones. Over her shoulder she adds quietly, "Disruptive behaviour will not be tolerated." She turns and faces the class. "Daily announcements will begin in ten minutes." They stare, baiting but silent. A few girls giggle. She takes roll call. *Acorn, Arsenault, Bynon, Callbeck, Dalziel, Gaudet*—"That's pronounced Goody, Miss!"—*Halfpenny, Jarvis, Kenny, Lowther, MacBride, MacFayden, McWade.* . . . On the last "*Here, Miss!*" the principal's voice comes over the PA system.

Good morning, girls and boys. Several students laugh. *Welcome to your first day at Minegoo High.* "Welcome to you, too!" *While many of you are returning to us, some of you are here for the first time. Welcome.* The frog boy smiles at Effie, showing a row of small teeth. *There will be no formal classes today* (more whoops) *but the teachers will remain in their homerooms until 2pm should any of you need help sorting out your timetables. I recommend that you try to do this in class today and not at home as you will encounter some difficulty otherwise. Please pay special attention to the section in your handouts on behaviour and take notice of what will and will not be tolerated.* Dalziel sticks up his middle finger at Arsenault, and the two boys laugh. *We have a new dress code in place and starting this year there will be no smoking on school property.* Arsenault lets out an elongated *f* sound. *For those of you bringing children to school, we have day care set up and ready to go in Room 18.* Halfpenny looks down, hiding her eyes behind long black bangs. *Please read your booklet for specific instructions. Also, if you are driving a car and you park it in the teachers' area, you* will *be towed. Be kind to your teachers and to each other and we'll see you back here bright and early tomorrow morning. Have a good day.* "You too, Sir!"

Effie folds her arms across her chest. "So much for diligent behaviour." She inserts as much authority into her voice as she can manage.

The boy with the frog raises his hand. "Miss, can I open another window? It's some hot in here." He lifts off before Effie has time to answer. "Not to worry Miss. I know what I'm doin'."

One of the boys calls out, "Yeah Miss, ol' Brucie Jarvis. He's been here before."

The boy lets go of the window crank and turns to Effie. He speaks clearly. "Three times, Miss." He faces the students. "There. I said it myself."

At ten o'clock the classroom empties and Effie gets down to her paperwork, transferring names onto marking sheets and reviewing the term requirements. She puts her hand to her forehead when she reads the words *content, analysis, structure, medium, form.* She opens the boxes that are stacked beside her desk, sorting books into piles, pleased to see that copies of *Lives of Girls and Women, Twelfth Night, To Kill a Mockingbird, The Wars* and the anthology of poets she requested have all arrived safely.

By noon, when it seems unlikely that anyone else is going to come by, Effie wanders outside for a break. The schoolyard is uninhabited except for a man holding a measuring tape and pacing out a plot of grass. He doffs his railroad cap at Effie. "Hullo," he says. "Hot day for this time of year."

"Yes, I suppose it is." She scratches her arm. "Can I help you?" she asks and immediately realizes the inanity of her question.

"Not unless you can give me a permit." He stops pacing. "I feed the kids here at noon but there's some consternation over the space I'm to be allotted."

"You feed the kids?" Effie pictures him holding a bag of peanuts out to a herd of elephants.

"I have a snack car." He gestures toward the empty space. "Hot dogs—steamed, not fried—pudding, milk, yogurt. Only the things their mothers would feed them." He laughs, taking his hat off and holding it by the brim. "Were those the things your mother fed you?"

Effie throws up her arms in mock despair, and the man laughs again. As she turns back toward the school he calls out to her, "See you later."

"I don't like Mondays—tell me why I don't like Mondays." John pushes through the school's double doors and out into the vibrant afternoon. "How about you, Effie?" He nods to a group of students.

Effie looks away from the teenagers. "I *hate* that song. I don't understand why we gratify adolescents by writing kill-the-teacher songs. Even if it is a true story." She clasps her books to her chest. "Anyway, this isn't Monday, it's Tuesday." The grass sinks like plush carpet beneath the soles of her new shoes. "Does the first day of school always bring out the singer in you? That seems more like your friend Donnie."

"Ha! You should see the mad scientist today. Or worse, you should see his students." John plucks a leaf from a tree. "No, the first day generally makes me think of *Lord of the Flies*. But we do what we have to. And as a music teacher, I think my life is easier, if somewhat noisier." They walk along a path away from school property.

"How was your first day?"

She pauses, smiling, trying to anticipate where this is headed, if anywhere. "And what is it we have to do?"

He pinches the stem of the leaf and waves it in front of her face like a tiny flag. "Have dinner with me. Help me atone for my sins." A carful of students roll by and honk. John raises his hand and the car weaves down the street, smoke spitting from its tailpipe.

"Atone for what sins?" Effie examines his profile coolly, noting that his face is faintly pocked and his lips are tumescent.

"But since it's too early for dinner, come to the framing store with me. I need something for my camera." They walk past the street where her uncle lives.

"Why not go to a camera store then?"

"We haven't got one. Not what you mean, anyway." He bats the leaf to the ground. "Do you know the story about the man who spent twenty years in prison? The day of his release they give him back his jacket and he finds a ticket stub in the pocket for a shoe repair. The man thinks, oh well what the hell, so he takes the bus into town, walks into the shop and shows the ticket to the fellow behind the counter. The shoe repairman looks at the ticket and says, "They'll be ready Tuesday.""

Effie rolls her eyes. "Hysterical."

"Anyway, that's kind of what life is like in Charlottetown. Here, we go to the framing store for camera supplies. But you haven't answered my question. How was your day?"

"Strange, I think, but not definitive." She notes again his deep-brown eyes. "Some of the kids are abysmally naïve for their age and others seem far too old."

"Fortunately for me, that's less of a problem," John says. "Most of my kids are blowing and fingering all day."

Effie smiles at the image of faces puffed out and fingers stopping up holes and wishes she had been able to take music classes when she was young, resenting the time restraints put upon her by her after-school job at the restaurant. Mostly, she had signed up for serious classes, which she hoped would propel her into a prestigious university.

And in Effie's memory, Kathleen Raminsky sits beside her in biology class watching Effie cut into the rubbery flesh of a fish belly and trying not to cry. Effie looked at her helplessly. It was an assignment after all, and Effie was already ticked because Kathleen had left all the hard parts up to her. It wasn't as if slicing through flesh was Effie's idea of a good time. In fact, she thought it was cruel. As she completed the splitting she peered into the open flesh, disbelievingly. "This fish has swallowed a pen!" she cried, as Kathleen runs from the room, the class roaring with laughter behind her.

Effie's shoe heel catches on the curb. She falls forward, lunging for the pavement. Textbooks fly out of her hands and she grabs for John's arm. He hooks her under her armpit, slipping on *The Elements of Style*, banging his head into hers. They slide down to the street together, laughing.

Effie doubles over, snorting. Blood dribbles from her knee. "Oh my God, my books! There's blood on my notebook." John wets his index finger with his tongue, then reaches across Effie's splayed books, wiping blood from below her knee. As his finger moves across her flesh, Effie feels a familiar pull. She stands up quickly and flattens her skirt. "It's okay, John. I'm fine. Which way is the store?" She cushions the books in her arms and watches him rise and brush off his pants.

CHAPTER 7

Effie is unaware of the comments that circulate the staff room, teachers indicating their horror that any child should live in such squalor, with such a mother. They borrow their observations from novels penned during the Industrial Revolution and from salacious American paperbacks, never having actually been to Effie's apartment. But they have seen her mother around town, waxing and waning between dishevelled and decorous, and they cluck their tongues over Mrs. Cambridge's obvious inability to find a balanced centre.

In class, Effie's dimpled legs dangle from her chair, her feet barely touching the floor. Her skin shows signs of waxy porousness caused by a diet rife with carbohydrates and sugar. During difficult periods, bread, potato chips, popsicles and cereal make up the bulk of her meals and, throughout favourable spells, and when her mother isn't carrying goods home from the bakery— date squares, chocolate éclairs, sausage rolls, pork pies—a steady supply of loose change affords Effie a wide selection from the Dairy Bar: candy necklaces, black balls, chocolate cigarettes, licorice pipes, ice cream sandwiches, wax whistles—the array seems endless. Her wrists have become so engorged that she can no longer fasten her plastic party watch comfortably.

Her classmates seem aware that Effie is not quite like them and, on account of this, they either stay away from her or try, because their parents have told them, to be extra kind. And because she is an adept student, often the first child in the room to put up her hand despite an overwhelming shyness, another aspect of what the kids feel for her is admiration, a quiet astonishment that will turn to jealousy and, sometimes, outright mockery. Only later on, after Effie has stopped making herself fat, does she figure out how to silence people with a look.

Here, in grade one, Effie doesn't understand herself as anything but beautiful, a word she hears almost daily from her mother, drunk or sober. "You have such a beautiful nose, darling." "Effie, your beautiful eyes have come from God." "I always wanted a beautiful daughter, and look how lucky I am to have one." No mere epithets these, but offered up with tenderness and wet-eyed love from a voice that vacillates between whispery awe and shamefaced regret. Effie carries these words and phrases with her; clings to them like a castaway looking for salvage.

At school she is comforted by the things around her. Brightly coloured letters of the alphabet that run on a Bristol board railway track around the upper edges of the room. A tankful of goldfish resting on the window ledge and cared for by Miss Erb, who has brought them in from home. The spinning globe beside which, during rainy recesses, Effie stands and memorizes the countries, her greatest challenge Europe and its capitals. To her, Belgium seems like the name of a city and Brussels the country, and the same holds true for Romania and Bucharest, and so on down the line. She loves staring at the coat rack too, and tries to match the footwear with its garment, striving not to envy the special sets; ensembles that look like presents from places Effie's mother can't afford. She has no idea that most children her age can't pronounce or even read such difficult names or that when she smiles she has the sweetest face of everyone in grade one, despite her haunted eyes.

At home, some form of company almost always prevails, either in the presence of her mother or issuing out of the Monarch radio or from the TV screen or in the voices emanating from the record player. She knows all of "El Paso" and "He'll Have to Go," along with "Catch a Falling Star" and "Take These Chains from My Heart," visualizing herself in a Dale Evans cowgirl dress and boots, a red Western-style hat plunked upon her head, singing from a rodeo stage. *All my faith in you is gone but the heartaches linger on, take these chains from my heart and set me free.* Her eyes light up as she sings, and she smiles sagely down upon the imaginary crowd, proud to be sharing her gift; to be making the onlookers happy.

But sometimes the long ashes of her mother's cigarette slip off and fall into a glass of vodka. Black diamonds and red hearts decorate the rim, reminding Effie of gambling and *Gunsmoke*, of Miss Kitty sitting in the saloon, black ankle boot hoisted up on the wooden rung of a neighbouring chair, the moled queen of Dodge City licking peanut butter from her lips.

Boyfriends pay visits to her mother, usually on weekend nights. The first wave consists of educated men—professors, lawyers, accountants—that her mother had met at the University of Toronto where she once worked in the insectory, dissecting and bisecting potato beetles and cinch bugs. The men—guests, her mother had called them—come as far as the entryway to the living room, interchangeable and suited, with creamy skin and even teeth. Sometimes they offer Effie a quarter and she smiles, showing off her kiss curls. After they escort her mother out, Effie reaches up and locks the door behind them. At eight o'clock she goes off to bed and turns her back to the dark. In the morning the bitter smell of Nescafé fills the little kitchen, a can of Carnation Evaporated Milk sitting faithfully on the counter. Effie dubs these suitors the "coffee men." Later, long after her mother no longer works at the university, the suits are replaced by uniforms: cab drivers and bartenders and veterans from the Legion. Many are Maritime migrants, people whose accents and attitudes her mother understands. They do not take her mother out. They take her on the couch or the bed or on the hardwood floor. Sometimes they lie there all night. Effie tiptoes past on her way to school.

On Sundays, sobriety permitting, Effie and her mother trail off to the First United Presbyterian Church where another species of song captivates both mother—the music creeping up from a dark past—and daughter, who is looking toward the future. Effie loves especially the Christmas hymn, "Twas in the Moon of Wintertime," and "Jerusalem," the first because she is reminded of the baby Jesus being born under a great star and of all the birds watching from their nests, and "Jerusalem" because even though Christ wasn't born there the city is close to two seas, and on account of the fact that her mother said this isn't a song that truly belongs in the Presbyterian church and therefore they should love it all the more, as if it were an orphan. Effie worries for the orphans and tries not to think how near she is to becoming one of them.

The minister preaches what her mother calls fiery sermons, which Effie is permitted to sit through. He speaks of a tall tower and evil cities and how the prodigal son was welcomed back even though his brother didn't understand why that was fair, and how Abraham almost cut off Isaac's head at the altar but in the end didn't have to because an angel said no. Sometimes the spit flies out from underneath the minster's moustache and straight across the top of the lectern.

In the Bible anything seems possible, and the words cast a spell over Effie as she ponders the light holiness and the blessed trinity. Her mother grabs onto her hand, their fingers thickened by their gloves, the feeling soft and comforting.

And when the service ends, Effie feels exhilarated exiting the church, gazing down from the hilltop, God's love spreading all over the world. Surely from here her mother will be safe, at least for the short walk home.

At the end of grade one, when Miss Erb hands Effie the diligence award—a copy of *The Golden Book of Fairytales*—Effie senses her first real inkling of hope; an assurance that life offers something that, although she can't yet fully understand, will fulfill a promise as large as that delivered by the mighty Gitchi Manitou. She carries her book home proudly, its tall edges digging into her bloated belly.

CHAPTER 8

When John and Effie arrive at the Morning Dove they find Donnie in the corner booth with a mugful of beer. "There she is! What took you so long? Christ, what a day." He slouches in his seat. "Why are you limping, Effie? Those bastard kids!" Angus canters toward them, tray balanced, white towel draped over his arm.

"First we went to the framing store, but they were out of film, so," she laughs slyly, "we took the long way around the park. Jo—"

Donnie bolts up. "Sorry, Angus, we've changed our minds about dinner." He shrugs an apology. "Let's go," he says to Effie and John. "I just remembered that Mom's making stew. She makes the best stew on the island, doesn't she John?" He gives a thumbs up to Effie.

"How do you know Ruth's making stew?" John fishes a ten-dollar bill from his pocket.

"Because it's Tuesday, you idiot. Where have you been for the past twenty years?" Donnie watches John slide the money under the saltshaker. "It's a beautiful day," he says. "We'll be walking."

"It's *three* blocks from here. How else would we get there? Steam engine?" John taps Effie's shoulder. "Just ignore him."

Outside of the bar they veer left, away from the churchyard and Effie's apartment, stopping briefly at the Co-op on Queen Street so Donnie can pick up a jug of milk. A few feet farther, they round the corner onto King Street. "I've lived here all my life," Donnie says.

Donnie's family home pitches toward the road, a slim margin of soil separating the house from the sidewalk. Paint peels away from the clapboard in chocolate curls, revealing bleached yellow chips underneath, and the screen door sits cockeyed on its hinges, puncture wounds poking through the silver netting. A boy with hay-coloured hair waves at them from an upstairs window. He has a winsome, open face.

Donnie, John and Effie enter through an enclosed porch, a pot of lupins perfuming the air. Three cats saunter toward them, two black and sleek, the other a fat brown tabby. The aroma of beef stew and dumplings floods out from the kitchen.

The house feels small and self-contained, and the ceilings, which are low, lend to an atmosphere of intimacy, the warmth enhanced by a pleasant dampness that permeated the walls long ago and settled in for good, the harbour only two blocks away.

Donnie steers Effie into the living room and onto a worn sofa. "Mom! Get out here. Come meet Effie!"

John plunks down in an armchair and a grey-haired woman putters into the room.

"Effie's teaching with us at the school," Donnie explains. "She's from Ontario." He winks over at Effie. "You know. From away." He sits down on the couch beside her. Effie pulls her skirt over the scrape on her knee.

"*Howdjuyado,* Effie?" Donnie's mother wipes biscuit dough from her pants. The boy from the upstairs window appears behind his mother's back. "*Howdjuliketheeiiilun?*" the woman asks.

Marezeedotesanddozeedotes.

"Pardon me?" A ginger cat stares over at Effie from his perch on the piano. His whiskers furl upward.

"How *do-you* like *the-island?*" The woman's words collide in cadent clusters. She half-whispers when she speaks, as if everything were a pleasant mystery.

Effie hears a trace of her mother's voice, the lilt and the accent. "Oh," she says. "The island? It's lovely, thank you." She sits back down and folds her hands in her lap like a polite child.

The boy hurries over and introduces himself as Gordy.

John sets his sock feet up on the coffee table. "Where are the rest of the boys, Ruth? Are they coming home for supper?"

"I expect them shortly, John." She smacks her hands together, disrupting the flour. "Donnie, for the love of God, get your feet off the cushions. You'll ruin them."

Effie spots two kitchen plates secured to the wall, the words *Parva Sub Ingenti* etched into their borders. She looks over at Donnie's mother, who is laughing with her son. "Would you like some help, Mrs. Fitzgerald?" Gordy waits beside the couch, his mouth hanging open in admiration, his eyes barely blinking, hoping to escort the visitor wherever she wants to go.

By the time supper is laid out on the table a half-dozen men aged thirteen to thirty-two have come home, followed by Donnie's father, Abel, who has jet-black hair and a face that hangs down like a hunting dog. Black suspenders fastened to a pair of black woollen pants hang loosely over his white shirt.

Effie fields questions from every chair at the table.

"How long have you been here?"

"How long are you staying?"

"Do you like teaching?"

"Do you like dumplings?"

"Are you Donnie's new girlfriend?"

"Cambridge. I've heard of your people, but unfortunately I don't think I've ever had the pleasure of meeting them." Ruth looks up, trying to remember.

"Not so sure that my uncle and his wife are exactly a pleasure," Effie laughs. "But—"

A thundering *bang bang bang* rattles the front door.

"For goodness sake." Ruth excuses herself from the table, striding toward the hallway. "Do they have to pound on the door like that? They'll take it off the *rest* of its hinges."

Donnie leaps up. "Wait, Mom, I'll go. You stay put." He sprints toward the front of the house.

"This used to be the bootlegger's house," Abel explains to Effie. "People wandered in here all hours looking for liquor." He snaps a strap on his suspenders. "I got up one morning and found a fellow sleeping in the hallway. We had to start locking the front door."

"It's cousin Jimmy," Donnie yells to the back of the house. "John, can you come here for a minute?"

John excuses himself from the table and trudges through the living room toward the front door. He can see the policeman's square head. "What is it?"

"We've had a complaint." Donnie's cousin thrusts his hand through his mown hair. "From the Murphy boy." He wedges his back into the porch wall and vacantly flexes his arms.

"*Which* Murphy boy? There are at least five hundred."

"This is hardly the time or place." Donnie frowns at his cousin. "We're just finishing supper." He takes a step closer to John. "I can just imagine the quality of complaint, if it's the boy I'm thinking of."

"He says you harassed him." Jimmy hooks his thumbs under his belt.

"How so?" John stares at the officer's belt buckle, a two-headed serpent in the shape of an M. "In what way, exactly?" The serpent stares back.

Jimmy detaches his thumbs and rubs his hands along the sides of his pants, his uniform shiny from wear. "Tommy Murphy said you said inappropriate things about his family."

"Inappropriate things—about his family? What would that be? Such as who taught him that it was okay to smoke in the hallway at school? Unless he's taking after you. Or that he can't wear only an undershirt in class, even when it's hot?"

"He said you were badgering him."

"Which is it, James—harassment or slander?" John's voice is precise. "Listen to me. You had better get your story straight before you come around here menacing me with litigious mumbo jumbo." He leans in closer. "And how did you know where I was?"

"Where else would you be? Everyone knows if they want to find you they just hafta look for Donnie."

"Jealous?"

"Listen you creep, you might be able to talk to your students that way but it doesn't work on me."

"You're an idiot." John looks at him, unflinching, his voice moderate.

"You think I don't hear what some of those kids say about you?" Saliva spurts from Jimmy's mouth and lands flatly on John's shoulder.

John continues to stare at him, his tone steady. "Get out of here, you abhorrent piece of shit."

"Yes, it's time you were leaving." Donnie holds the door open.

Jimmy walks out into the night, turning briefly to look at John. "Faggot." He jerks his shoulder to straighten his coat. The streetlight illuminates his back.

"Keep at it, Jimmy, and you'll find a cop at *your* door," John calls out behind him.

"Asshole. Who in the hell does he think he is?" Donnie turns the lock on the door and smiles half-heartedly. "He's got a face only a mother could love, and even then. . . ."

John sweeps his arm around his friend. "Handsome is as handsome does," he says, the quaver in his voice only slightly betraying him.

CHAPTER 9

Effie walks west along Grafton Street toward the high school. Content to find herself alone, her eyes follow a band of burnt orange bleeding across the horizon. She has spent hours sitting in her window evaluating the Gothic architecture of the Anglican Church, contrasting it with the modern simplicity of Veterans' Affairs, but she hasn't taken in much else.

Here, past the north side of the church, a stately red brick building rises up from among the trees and Effie wonders if this might be a courthouse or a natural history museum. Beside it surges another beauty, its imposing columns a miniature Pantheon. This must be where the Fathers of Confederation met. She envisions thin, mutton-chopped men approaching from the stairs, a thicket of tall black hats and morning coats, tapered pants on burnished shoes. A long line of Abraham Lincolns. She pictures John among them, making his way toward her, his face serious but loving. His hands are clasped solemnly—but not creepily—and his eyes flash a hint of that twinkle she saw on the beach. He laughs as he touches her hand, happy; indifferent to protocol.

A Labrador retriever darts out in front of her, covered in soap bubbles, his tail wagging joyfully, wetly, as he makes a back-legged leap for Effie's shoulders. Effie jumps back. "Shoo! Get away!" She flicks her hand at him. His eyes sparkle good-naturedly, as if he might speak. "I can't play with you," Effie pleads. "I'll get dirty." The dog prances and circles, eager for her company. "There now, please. Go away."

An empty bottle of dish soap floats in the fountain beside them, hundreds of tiny bubbles drifting up from the water past the heads of three stone soldiers and into the leaves of the trees. Behind her a man's voice scolds, "Bob!" and the dog lopes off. Effie wonders why dogs are so attracted to her.

She walks on, occasionally glancing down at her tartan skirt and angora sweater, pleased with their classic lines and kittenish fit. She likes the sound of her penny loafers striking the sidewalk, admiring their practicality and polish. She has always wondered why more teachers, more schools for that matter, didn't insist on uniforms. In fact, Effie had argued feverishly on the university debating team for this very change. "We must address," she had said, "what has become a ghastly injustice to destitute children everywhere—an injustice to those children who cannot *afford*, for example, brand-named clothing. More critically, we must investigate the imprint that affluent children leave upon their less fortunate peers—*rich* children who flaunt their status strutting about in Sergio Valente jeans and Sky Jordan sneakers. Why only last year a child in Baltimore *died* because of a pair of high-top Adidas."

Tommy Murphy makes his way to school from the opposite end of town. Despite a sizeable glob of gel, the hair on the back of his head pokes out like a nest of matted straw. When he was a child his mother would set him on her lap and, closing her eyes, inhale. *My boy smells like a barnful of hay. He's a wonderful baleful boy.* Now fifteen, Tommy dresses without labels or brand names in a way that Effie would champion. But the rim of his baseball cap is shredded and thin, and his plain white t-shirt has been washed a hundred times. His blue jeans are short and mis-shapen—girls' jeans—and his tennis shoes break open in tiny fissures and veins at the sides, their cracks and slices exposing gauzy grey socks.

Tommy scuffs at things as he walks up the street: bottle caps, cigarette butts, can lids, bits of remnant paper. His legs shoot out like hockey sticks, *whoosh, bam, clunk*. With the back of his bare arm he swipes mucous from the crease above his upper lip and wipes it on the front of his jeans. He moves mechanically up the sidewalk, a mass of clattering bones. He looks small and hunched, like a crooked letter *k*, his eyes constantly shifting. Typically he is late for school, except when his father's fists send him out of the house early.

He crosses the road to the deserted schoolyard, the leaves on the trees blowing soundlessly in the soft wind. Tiny goose bumps rise on the back of his neck and along the surface of his skinny limbs. He thrusts his fingers up through his hair, rearranging the strands. Stepping onto the sidewalk that borders the school he nods at Jimmy Fitzgerald, who is sitting in the front seat of his police cruiser, drinking coffee from a Styrofoam cup. Both boy and man look over at Effie as she approaches from the other side of the field. Tommy glances back at Jimmy, who is making a face. Neither see John MacDonald watching from a window above.

As Effie makes her way across the grass, Jimmy turns the key in the ignition and backs out onto the road. The tires of his car spit gravel as he drives away. Effie sees the boy from behind. He moves like a frightened rat, and she feels sorry for him. The teenager sharpens his pace, angling for the school's side door. He steals a quick look at Effie, pulls back the handle, and disappears.

At nine o'clock Effie stands in front of her homeroom class. She recognizes two new faces: her cousin—what is her *cousin* doing in this class?—and the boy from the schoolyard. She shivers.

"What is your name?" she asks the boy.

Students crane their necks in anticipation of trouble.

"Murphy."

"Is that your first name or your last?"

"Mind yer business," Tommy Murphy grunts, sliding his middle finger along his cheek.

"Ex*cuse* me?" Effie folds her arms across her chest and grips her sweater. Angora sticks to her damp hands.

He stares blankly at her. "You heard me." The corners of his mouth turn up like a ventriloquist's dummy.

From the back of the room Martha Cambridge puts up her hand. "Why don't you ask me who *I* am?"

Bruce Jarvis runs into the classroom. "Sorry to be late, Miss!" He slides down into an empty seat, panting, the corner of his jacket catching on the back of his chair. He starts to laugh.

"Sorry, Miss." He signals toward his arm, which is trapped inside his sleeve. "It's kind of like a straitjacket. See?" He pokes his elbow aimlessly into the air, and someone mumbles, "Fitting."

"Yes, I can see," Effie says, and turns back to Tommy.

"I want your full name please, and I want it *now*."

"Oh, that's Tommy Murphy, Miss." Bruce Jarvis disentangles himself from his sleeve.

Khunt.

"Why are you here, Tommy?"

"Home room, *Miss*." Tommy holds down on the *s*. *Missss*.

"And why were you not here yesterday?" She stares at him, frozen.

"I was."

"*Where?*"

"Mr. *MacDonald's* class."

Effie opens her mouth to speak but finds she cannot. As she heads toward him, the ten minute bell rings.

Tommy squirms out of his chair and away from his desk, his bony shoulder blades jutting up through his t-shirt, tennis shoes sliding along the buffed floors.

Effie turns her back on the class and begins to speak. She hopes the students cannot hear the quiver that is lodged in her throat. "As you can see from the blackboard, I have outlined this semester's schedule. We will begin by looking at a cross section of American poets, including two of my favourites, Robert Frost and Edna St. Vincent Millay." She pivots and faces the class. She tries to remember some of their names. *Jarvis, Callbeck, Arsenault, Halfpenny.* "After that we will take up Timothy Findley's *The Wars* and Alice Munro's *Lives of Girls and Women*. Do any of you know these books?" She smiles at Halfpenny, feeling absurd. "Following this, we will study one of the most penetrating novels ever written, Harper Lee's *To Kill a Mockingbird*, and then end the year with Shakespeare's play, *Twelfth Night*, which I think you will find a great deal of fun." Someone (Dalziel?) carps, "More like a great deal of *work*."

"And for those of you with an interest, I will be directing the spring play, also *Twelfth Night*. I hope most of you will come out and audition." Halfpenny grins up at her from under the fringe of her bangs.

"I want to help all of us become better acquainted with one another, so I propose an informal session before we get down to work. Bruce, would you mind closing the window? And you boys—Dalziel, Arsenault, Lowther and Callbeck—each of you please take one corner section of the room and start placing the desks in an L-shape." They stare at her. She explains. "So that the desks form a square." Dalziel and Callbeck grimace.

As Effie speeds to the back corner to demonstrate, Virginia Halfpenny comes up from behind holding a desk in mid-air. "Like this, Miss?"

"Exactly." She smiles at the girl. "Virginia, yes?"

From the corner of the room somebody catcalls, "You mean *Vagina*."

Effie turns swiftly. "How dare you? One more word from any of you and I will send you out of this classroom and have you put on suspension. Is that abundantly clear?" She rests a hand on Virginia's shoulder. "You mustn't mind them. They have no manners."

"I know all about them," Virginia says. The tip of her nose wiggles when she talks. "Island boys are pigs, Miss." She says this as matter-of-factly as if she were saying, "I don't like egg salad sandwiches."

First days share similar features. They are filled with an idea of energy, either too much or too little. First days are not fluid, but are joined by events, blocks of time, frameworks. First days stand out in memory, overexposed vignettes. They paint little portraits, small pictures that drop in our laps when we don't expect to see them. Their memory is static: evocations that must, because of their novelty, be absent of taste and smell and speech. First days, therefore, tell lies. This much Effie feels but cannot articulate.

At the end of her first full day of school, Effie takes the long way home through the baseball diamonds in Victoria Park. She sits down on a low row of bleachers behind two chatty women, the autumn sun warming her face and hands. She can smell hot dogs and fries.

Three innings later Effie gets up from the bench, strolls across the field and wends her way along the short road that cuts through to the water. She wants to manoeuvre past the distractions of the day. It isn't enough that she has managed to sidestep the teachers by staying out of the lunchroom (although the principal will not accept the deferral indefinitely). She saunters toward the shore, craving a hot dog. The wind rustles through the trees, leaves blowing inside out, their white undersides waving.

Sitting down on an incline next to a cannon, she looks out at the blue-green liquid as it breaks across the rocks, water shearing into land, a level plane. When Effie's mother was pregnant with Effie she had a dream—a seaside cottage set high into a cliff, the ocean hanging like a wall of slow-moving curtain. "Portentous," she said, every time she repeated the story.

With her mother, there were always omens and superstitions.

Shoes on the table, *bad luck.*
Hat on a bed, *bad luck.*
Eating from a knife, *bad luck.*
Stirring with a fork, *bad luck.*
Passing on the stairs, *bad luck.*
Misbuttoning a shirt, *bad luck.*
Spilling salt, *bad luck.*
Ladders, *bad luck.*
Cats, *bad luck.*
Crows, *very bad luck.*

"Hey you." Mary's voice comes up behind Effie soft and soothing, not a surprise at all. She lays her bicycle on the grass and carefully removes a raft of papers from the wicker basket. She is dressed like an African explorer—khaki shorts and a diaphanous heart-sleeve blouse, attractive but utile boots. She sits down.

Effie eyeballs the wad of paper. "Writing a book?" she asks, and leans against a tree.

"Practically." Mary brushes grass stubble off her shins. "I'm working on a series of articles about a proposed—potential—bridge between Borden and Cape Tormentine." She enunciates carefully. *Po-tent-she-al*.

"Oh yes," Effie says. "John and Donnie were fighting about that."

Mary laughs. "Frick and Frack."

"What do you think about it?" Effie is distracted by the blueness of Mary's eyes, which are as lustrous as marbles. "The link, I mean."

"It isn't so much what I think about it, but what islanders want."

"Aren't you an islander?"

Mary shrugs. "I suppose I am." She looks down at the papers in front of her. "But as a journalist I'm required to be impartial."

"Well then," Effie grins. "Which side are you rooting for?"

"I'm actually (*ak-chew-a-lee*) on the side of the pro-link group—Islanders for a Better Tomorrow. Their opponents, the Friends of the Island, believe that the island culture will be destroyed."

"That's funny," says Effie. "The pro group call themselves islanders and the anti group call themselves friends of the island. You'd think it would be the other way around."

"Some islanders are near hemorrhaging, which I think is ridiculous. I don't believe the ecology is at risk if they opt for a bridge, and it would be way easier to buy decent clothes. As it stands I have to go to the mainland to shop." She points to her socks and giggles. "Not that I'm a spectacular dresser or anything."

"But wouldn't you miss the ferry?" Effie remembers the German Shepherd clacking toward her across the gangway. She wonders if the dog's owner is an Islander or a Friend of the Island.

"There's always the one at Wood Islands, during summer, but if you ask me the link is the only smart thing Brian Mulroney ever supported." Mary pushes herself up off the grass. "We voted in a plebiscite in January and, so far, it looks like a better tomorrow." She dusts off the back of her shorts. "It's usually so much colder this time of year." She sets her papers back into the basket of her bicycle and rights her bike. "Coming?"

Effie straightens her skirt. "Why are marbles called marbles if they're made of glass?" She walks with Mary along the path.

"Pardon me?" The bike wheels click.

"You know. Marbles. They're not made of marble, they're made of glass."

Mary pauses. "I suppose that's true. Just the way some ruby isn't ruby at all but rose quartz, and jade can be soapstone or jasper or garnet. And not all ivory is ivory."

"How do you know all that?" Effie asks.

"When my father was diagnosed with leukemia, he retired early and took up some quiet hobbies. He loved gemstones and wild animals. And word games. He especially loved oxymorons."

Effie wags her finger playfully at Mary. "It was vaguely obvious that the larger half of the praise would go to the least favourite, who was pretty ugly."

"Say, you're good."

Effie extends her hand to help steady Mary's bicycle. "What happened to your dad?"

"He lived for nine years after the diagnosis. He missed his job something terrible, though. He drove a school bus." The wind blows her hair across her face.

"So then he died?" Effie hesitates, unsure how to proceed.

Mary gestures past the paved drive that winds through the park. "Do you know what that is?"

"It looks like the Guv'nah's house." Effie glances at Mary to see if she is smiling.

"You're close," Mary says, and keeps on walking. "It's the home of the Lieutenant Governor. Fanningbank."

Effie sighs. "Why would one family need all that space? It's immoral. Do you write about places like that, too?"

"Sometimes I do."

"And what about immorality? Do you write about that?"

"If only they'd let me. It used to enrage my father—that the most newsworthy stories were always given to the men. Still are, actually."

"Such as?"

"Homicide. Homicide made to look like suicide." Mary slows down. "Political machinations. Things like that."

"You must miss your father terribly."

Mary wipes her hair away from her cheeks. "You have no idea. He was everything to me. To us." She glides her fingers gently over the bicycle horn. "Is your father alive?"

As they walk toward home Effie replies slowly, hesitantly. "I really have no idea."

CHAPTER 10

Effie times it accordingly, knowing that on Sunday morning John will be returning the family dog to his parents before church. He made a joke about it on Friday after school, citing the universal Blessing of the Animals. "Trust the Anglicans to do them all at once," he said.

The neighbourhood reminds her of an upscale Maycomb County, insular and treed, the religious dutiful but ambling, not a black person in sight, however; shuttered windows and capricious front porches set off by semi-tidy lawns and picket fences, cats roaming aimlessly.

She waits by a tree near the end of his street trying not to look obvious, hoping her lie will be believed, hoping he will walk from this end down, and not the other. Either way, she has a quick stride and is confident she can catch up. Charlottetown is small, and no one will suspect their run-in as anything more than a minor coincidence, especially since she hinted that, as a rule, she likes to take a Sunday morning walk. John even teased her about her weekly constitutional. People might wonder about her strolling in the rain, but she has an excuse for that as well. Besides, given the weather, she is less apt to run into anyone at all. Except John.

Within fifteen minutes four more people have walked by, three of them students, calling out, "Morning, Miss Cambridge!" and "Hey there, Miss," and she is about to give up entirely when she spies him about thirty feet away, coming around the corner. What should she do? Walk toward him? Cross the street? Bend over and pretend to tie her shoelace?

As a waitress in Port Credit, Effie would glide past her boss and the customers like a ballerina, capable and confident in servitude. But here, on equal footing, she has no idea how to proceed. Deciding instead to go for bold, she stands and waits.

"Hi there," she shouts, grateful to the mist for masking her perspiration.

John cranes his neck forward. "What are you doing here?" A receding line of oak trees fans out behind him in v-formation.

"Stalking you," she laughs.

He approaches her quickly, like a man on a mission. A good sign, Effie thinks.

"You do know it's raining?"

"This isn't rain. The angels are spitting," she says. "You people wouldn't know rain if it fell on you." She closes her umbrella. "Seriously, I was waiting for you. I remembered that you said you were returning your dog early, so I took a chance. I thought you might like to join me in my constitutional. Show me the sights."

"In the rain?" John shakes off water from the leash. A damp cat dashes in between them and runs onto a porch, seeking shelter.

Effie grins. "You're not made of paper."

"I suppose not." He nods obliquely toward the houses on his street. "I would ask you in for coffee but my place is a mess."

Effie doesn't believe him, but she isn't eager to find herself trapped in a house with last night's evidence—dirty wine glasses, melted-down candles, flimsy underwear lying across the arm-chair, a small lace bra tucked hastily underneath the couch cushion.

"I wish I could offer you the special tour but would you accept the discount instead?" he asks, seeming to Effie oddly out of place in his surroundings.

Effie weighs her reply, hoping his option might lead to more expedient intimacy. "I'll take the discount if you leave me room to ask some questions." She longs to touch his sleeve.

"Okay, follow me." John spirals back in the direction from which he has come, down Longworth Avenue.

"Over there," he says, pointing to a beige two-storey clap-board, "is where my grade one teacher used to live."

"Where is he now?" Effie asks, excited by this promising beginning.

John slides his index finger across his throat, instantly regretting the action.

"Sword fight?" she asks.

"Not exactly. He drowned. Volunteer fireman. Humane Society board member. Father of five. Fell through a hole in the ice." He speaks flatly, as if to dare more would risk him speaking at all, and he regrets more deeply his cavalier decision to talk of this man at all—as if a lost life could be reduced to caricature.

"We take the yin with the yang," Effie says, realizing too late how callous that sounds. "Sorry. That's not how I meant it. I have Tourette's," she explains. "Of the tongue."

John hurries to change the subject. "Is it genetic?" he asks.

"It was either that or the drinking." Effie slows her pace. "That isn't fair. My mother drank but she was also protective and kind, qualities I am not sure I inherited."

"What did your mother like to do on Sundays?" John touches Effie's shoulder as they saunter around the corner.

Effie shivers. "Besides church and housework? Well, for one thing, she liked to soak her feet in warm water and bleach and shave off the hardened edges of her calluses with a razor blade." She wonders why she feels compelled to tell him this.

"Industrious," John says. He frowns down on Effie fondly, but she doesn't see him.

"And sometimes we'd argue." A drop of rain rolls off of Effie's nose.

"About what?"

Effie shrugs, wishing he would take her hand. "Oh, stupid things. Latin pronunciation. Hemlines. Clokey Productions."

"Clokey Productions? You are a woman of mystery."

"My mother insisted that the people who produced *Davey and Goliath* were Mormons. But my mother was wrong. Clokey Productions is a Lutheran organization, not Mormon." Perhaps if he would take her hand she could stop talking nonsense.

"How do you know that? Or should I say why do you know that?"

"Because I was a Mormon when I was eleven. The show was made by the same people who made *Pokey and Gumby*. Why

would the Mormons involve themselves with plasticine figurines?" I've known him for a month, she thinks. *Shut up. Shut
up. Shut up.*

"For the same reason they own shares in Coca Cola."

"That's what my mother said. But I don't think that's true."

Effie can almost hear her mother's feet glide across the hardwood floor, the whir of the vacuum cleaner aimed at dust
bunnies and infinitesimal cigarette ash. But Effie isn't eager to
relay the finer details of some Sundays to John.

"And apple crisp," Effie says.

"The Mormons made apple crisp?"

"My mother made apple crisp. On Sundays." She looks at
him quizzically. "You knew what I meant."

"When I am out walking with the queen of non sequiturs I
take nothing for granted."

They round another corner and walk quietly past several
houses.

Effie sighs longingly. "What a beautiful street." She pretends
she hasn't come this way before. Granted, it was only once and
in the dark, but she is eager to impress John with her opinions
and responses.

"Fitzroy. It's my favourite."

"Who do you know that lives here? Any girlfriends?" Her
voice rises with her level of curiosity.

"Hardly. But my mother's best childhood friend lives in that
one."

John indicates a modest Cape Cod beauty and Effie thinks,
Miss Maudie Atkinson.

"The yellow's so pretty." Effie wishes it were hers.

"They paint the exterior every five years. Religiously."

"I love the dormers and peaks. And so many stoops and
verandahs." She sees herself sitting in a white wicker chair holding a chilled glass of lemonade, a plateful of molasses cookies balanced on one knee.

"The owner of that one—she's in her nineties—has managed the property on her own since her husband got shipped
off to prison twenty-some years ago." John arches his

eyebrows, knowingly. "You know—the guy with the ticket in his pocket."

Effie laughs. "How gothic. What did he do?"

"He killed someone. There were also rumours that he was inappropriate with young girls, but no one ever produced any proof." The wind rattles a street sign as they walk by.

Effie steps aside as if she's seen a ghost. "Good thing he's locked away, then."

"Yes, but doing bad things, even horrible things, doesn't mean you're incapable of rehabilitation. Or that you're necessarily immoral." John worries he's upset her, aware that he is often caught out saying the wrong thing, his intentions misunderstood.

"Murder and pedophilia aren't immoral?"

"I was thinking more along the lines of a bounced cheque. Or stock market fraud."

Effie feels this topic is going nowhere. "Have you ever dated someone who was morally reprehensible?"

"Only if you count Judy Connolly."

"Why? What did Judy Connolly do?" Kill someone, too?

"She stole three rolls of dimes from her father's desk drawer. Fifteen dollars, all of it spent on candy. And I helped her eat it."

"Co-conspirators. That's even worse than stock market fraud. What did she look like?"

"Well, she had roly-poly legs and a dumpling face and fat blond ringlets. I was seven and smitten. Funny thing, though. Her father was a judge. Makes you wonder."

"What happened to her?" Effie imagines a cartoon character. Little Lulu.

"You're like a dog with a bone."

"Bow wow."

"Judy went to Dalhousie to study law. Last I heard she had married some legal beagle who looked just like her father." John tips his head toward a house on the corner. "That symmetrical beauty over there is relegated to the university president."

"Anyone else besides Judy Connolly, immoral or otherwise?"

"Nosy little thing, aren't you?" John slings the leash around his neck. "Let's see. In grade four I had a crush on my music teacher, who let me play the triangle in the Christmas concert. I stood over the baby Jesus at the inn, tinkling out 'We Three Kings.'"

"She must have had an ear for talent."

"Clearly he did." John smiles. "And then in grade eight I saw *Rosemary's Baby* and fell in love with Mia Farrow."

"Oh, so creepy."

"Better than falling for Linda Blair."

Effie raises her closed umbrella, using the handle as pointer. "That house over there looks like a mansion. I had no idea there were mansions in Charlottetown."

"You live two blocks from here and this is the first time you're seeing these houses? You *must* be an islander." Rain channels along the corduroy creases of his pants. "That house is called Fairholm. A Father of Confederation used to live in there."

"Weren't there any real girls?" Effie asks. "Besides Judy?"

"There was one girl in high school. Her name was Natasha Davidoff. Natty for short." Nearby church bells signal the end of Sunday service.

"Was she pretty?" Effie pictures a Russian spy.

"Not by modern standards, perhaps. But I liked her. She was kind. And modest."

Effie holds her breath.

"She went on to become a physicist and moved back to Boston with her mother a few years ago." A steady stream of churchgoers set off up the street.

"Modesty is such a desirable quality," Effie says, exhaling. "And of course scholarship." A *learned* Russian spy.

"I don't think she would have had time for me. She had a lot of discoveries to make and—"

"Why not you? You seem as good a catch as anyone I know."

"Thank you, Effie. But what makes you so sure?"

Effie opens her umbrella against a new onslaught of rain. "From the little I know, you appear super smart, not just bookishly but in the way that you understand people's motives. And you clearly aren't afraid to have opinions. Everyone says so."

"Really? Like about the Mormons, you mean." John steps in closer to Effie, out of the rain.

"Mormons? What about them?"

"I have opinions about them, too," John says. "Like those little cars they drive."

"Ramblers."

"Yes. Kind of like us. Ramblers. And speaking of rambling, I ought to be getting back. We're right smack dab in the middle of our two homes, which I think makes us egalitarian."

Effie steps back. "Thank you for the tour. But you're a liar. I live closer."

"Next time I'll make it longer. I have to shower and get ready for my parents and their Sunday roast. I'd ask you along—"

"Oh, I couldn't," Effie protests, her stomach in knots. "I have a date with a hot hamburger."

"Oh really?" John raises his eyebrows. "Do I know him?"

Chapter 11

The librarian offers to help Effie find the novels she is looking for, books her mother has sent her daughter off to locate because, for the past three weeks, Mrs. Cambridge has been hiding from the world, having lost another job and trying to keep herself away from the liquor store, knowing that soon she and her daughter will be without money for rent.

Effie walks to the fiction section, pausing to look through the wide panes of glass and over at a softball game in progress in the field by the Credit River, half-wishing she could join the group of kids, half-resenting that, for the most part, they don't want her on their team. She pulls down on her sleeves, aware that she is growing taller and, with the stamina of a resistance fighter, skinnier. Her mother has stopped bringing home bakery goods, which has helped, and the spare coins, once easily accessed, have dried up with not so much as a nickel buried beneath a couch cushion. Out of necessity, Effie's mother, whose hands tremble with the transactions, has seen that every penny has been relegated either to bills or groceries so that the pair aren't in debt or hungry.

But Effie wonders how long her mother can hold out; how many days, or hours even, before she slips out of the apartment and down the street to the LCBO. Lavinia Cambridge has been dry for three solid months—a new record—and their home has been absent the visitors who, even and often when friendly, make Effie's stomach churn. But her mother needs to work, and who will have her now?

In her hand Effie holds a list: Pearl Buck, *The Good Earth*. John Steinbeck, *The Grapes of Wrath*. Somerset Maugham, *The Razor's Edge*. Anything by Leon Uris. The note gives her permission to take out a book from the adult section.

Compelled by a red background and bold lettering, Effie picks up a copy of *Uhuru*, written by a man named Robert Ruark. She examines the cover, the black silhouetted arms raised in what looks like rebellion, and she sees the words 'best-seller' and 'POOR NO MORE.' Cradling the book in her arm she walks on, hoping to inspire her mother with new writers instead of the usual fare—Effie replays the names in her head like an incantation: *Buck and Steinbeck and Maugham, Buck and Steinbeck and Maugham*, not doubting their appeal but worried because their stories never seem to cure her mother of the sadness that sits heavily on her slight shoulders. Besides, her mother is as interested in world geography as Effie is, and this *Uhuru* sounds and looks like a book about Africa, which Effie would know is true were she to read further.

She pauses again, spying Kathleen Raminsky coming into the building. The two girls smile at one another, each of them too shy to make further advances, and Kathleen heads off to the children's section, hoping that *Bonfires and Broomsticks* is on the shelf. Effie wonders if she and Kathleen might become friends, although she doesn't go as far in her head as best friends because best friendships are for children who come from homes where cupboards are well-stocked, sleepovers are a regular part of the weekend routine, and mothers and fathers take Polaroid snapshots of family outings and holidays.

It isn't that Effie exactly envies them either. Not exactly. Her mother is one of a kind. A woman who carves vegetables into shapes of smiling faces and flowers. Someone who slips beans from a delicate copper ashtray and tucks them under her daughter's pillow for wish-making. An out-loud reader of sonnets—*How do I love thee? Let me count the ways*—and fairy tales. A cheek nibbler. A hugger. A red lipstick kisser. A mother who reminds her child that no one on earth is quite like her, or is loved any more than this mother loves her little girl. Who tells her that all people, at heart, are good. And that Effie mustn't judge all lives by her mother's failures. Effie's mother relays life lessons through stories, too, some of which relate back to her own childhood.

"It's like fireweed and bracken," she explains. "When the young shoots of fireweed are peeled they can be eaten raw or cooked like asparagus. But if you eat too much, it will give you diarrhea. And with bracken, you have to be sure not to eat the adult plants, which are poisonous." Here Effie's mother pauses, taking a minute to remember the days when she, as a young girl, would lie down in the roadside gullies and look up at the sky, picturing heaven before eventually coming back down to the earthly pleasures of tactile vegetation, ignoring the tedium back home.

"They're beautiful plants," she continues, "one like a fern, the other with four-petalled flowers. I picked them and ate them as a child. It's the same way with people. You have to know who's going to be good for you, and at what time of their life, and yours. Otherwise you will sicken yourself, just the way I have sickened myself at times. And when I sicken myself, the trouble rubs off of my skin and right onto you. And we don't want that for the people we love, or for anybody."

Effie appreciates her mother's parables. She hauls them out as lessons when she wants to admonish other children, either in person or in her fantasies, and she cleaves to them when life becomes unbearable.

Three weeks after Effie carries home *Uhuru*; one week after the book and the rent are overdue, and two nights after her mother has failed to return from a late-afternoon walk, Port Credit Social Services show up at Effie's door, demanding answers. Even a child of ten can spot the absurdity in that.

CHAPTER 12

Embarrassment, anxiety and annoyance compete in Effie as she walks up to her uncle's front door. His fossilized Pontiac sits in the driveway covered in wet leaves. The porch light droops sadly from a wire, its globe cracked and dirty. That she had not noticed this detail before perplexes her, even irks her, as if the absence of observation means a lack of responsibility. As she reaches for the doorknocker two men come up from behind, talking loudly. She turns to look at them.

"Hey there, honey."

In the dim glow, Effie is still able to see that the man's shirt clashes with his jacket.

"Here for the party?" He plays with the magnet on his bolo tie. "You're the one from Ontario, aren't you?" He elbows the man standing next to him and grins. *Pistol Pete.*

"Is that any of your business?" She wants to strangle him with his tie, but reaches for the knocker instead.

"No need to get your skirt in a twist, honey." He leans into her, legs and arms akimbo. "Just trying to be friendly."

The second man slides up beside her. "And no need to be rude. If you weren't Bill's niece, I'd insist on an apology."

"For *what*?" Her heart races.

"I'm on the board that gave you your job." He speaks smoothly, breezily. "If you want to maintain the status quo, don't dick with my friends."

Effie exhales. "If this is what passes for status quo, I'll opt for radical action any day."

She grabs the door handle and steps in quickly, shoving it closed behind her and turning the lock. Steaming toward the kitchen, she ignores the heavy *thump thump* of the door-knocker.

Effie's Aunt Shirley stands facing the kitchen sink, her hands flapping, the garbage disposal grinding. Bill Cambridge stands next to her, the cuffs of his pants resting loosely on top of his leather slippers. He wears a mustard-coloured shirt.

"It *burnt*, Bill." Shirley Cambridge's curls bob spastically. "Let it *be*." She raises her arm to her brow, her hand speckled with chocolate. The sampler on the wall above her reads, *Cleanliness is next to Godliness*.

"And what do you propose we do now?" Bill Cambridge points to two wax-candle numbers, a 1 and a 6, lying on the counter, remnants of chocolate stuck to their stems.

"It's her own fault. She wouldn't clean the bathroom when I asked her to and I couldn't hear the oven timer from up there." Shirley licks icing from her fingernails. "She'll just have to make do without. There are plenty of other things to eat in this house."

Willie Cambridge darts into the room, aiming for the refrigerator. Bill, turning to face his son, stares blankly at his niece then nods. Shirley spots Effie in the window's reflection but does not move. Effie mouths a quick hello then spins around, coming face to face with the men from the front porch. She steels herself, but they muscle past her and head up the stairs. Her uncle follows.

Effie makes her way to the living room and drops down in one of the chairs. Willie returns with a cupful of pop and rejoins three friends who are hunched in front of the television playing *Warlords* on an Atari. A barrel-shaped woman sits in the far corner of the room nibbling on raw cauliflower and carrots, flipping their ends into the stand-up ashtray beside her. Creamy vegetable dip oozes from her lips onto a small paper napkin. Beside her, two women stand head to head whispering. Purple party balloons pepper the wall and a turret of conical hats layer the mantel. Martha is not in the room. What sort of a sixteenth birthday party is this?

Not the sort she remembers—Effie and Bernie Hughes playing Spin the Bottle, kissing in the rec room closet, his dry tongue jammed into her mouth, her shoulder pressed into the panelled wall. Kathleen was late for the party and Effie wondered why, and how she would escape Bernie's clutches without her friend there to save her. Maybe Kathleen's stepfather was up to his usual tricks, or Kathleen had walked her mother to work as she often did. Effie pushed back on Bernie's heavy chest, the fibres from his sweater itchy against her throat. He had persisted. The Beatles were singing "Hey Jude" and overtop of *take a sad song and make it better,* Effie heard Sam Squires shout across the room, "Wow. The alkie's daughter got herself a date."

Rising from her chair, Effie goes off in search of her cousin. As she climbs the stairs to the second floor, conversation spills down from the landing. Effie stops and flattens herself against the wall.

"What do you mean, he *killed* himself?" Her uncle's voice sounds raspy.

"They think it was because of his wife. Because she's sick."

Effie pictures the speaker twirling his tie.

"But why would he shoot himself in the head . . . it doesn't make sense. Neither does the location."

Effie's heart pumps harder.

"Maybe he was moved." *The Marlboro Man.*

"The guy was clearly desperate."

Effie imagines her uncle, hands in his pockets fiddling with loose change.

"I guess." A pause, then, "Who found him?"

"Jimmy Fitzgerald. He pulled round back and bang. Door open, gun on the ground."

Effie's head tingles.

"Straight out of a movie."

"Bloody strange, if you ask me."

"So much for our golf dates."

"Jesus."

"Poor Fitzgerald."

"If you believe him."

"Why wouldn't I? He's done no wrong by me."

"The guy's crookeder than a three-dollar bill."

Bill Cambridge smothers a laugh. "Crookeder? Don't you mean—"

"What's up with your niece, Bill? She got a large pickle stuffed up her arse?"

"You leave my niece alone."

"No worries there."

Effie's aunt calls out from the downstairs hallway. "Bill! Where are you?"

Effie forces her way up the remaining stairs. Brushing past the men, head down, she rushes to her cousin's room. She doesn't knock before opening the door.

Martha Cambridge sits on her bed between an open box of cookies and a jumbo bag of potato chips. A transistor radio plays faintly from the headboard, and slack against a pillow lolls a full-grown Raggedy Ann. Martha hikes up her dirty ankle socks and wriggles uncomfortably in her dress. The room smells stale.

"What are you doing here?" Chocolate rims her upper lip. "You've got your coat on."

Effie tries to erase the men from her head. "It's your birthday and you're not downstairs," she says. "How come?" Potato chips straggle out of the bag onto the bedspread and Effie feels suddenly, irretrievably, sick at heart.

"It's hardly a party for me. Did you get a load of who's all down there?"

Effie eases out of her coat and lays it across the bed. "But I was down there, waiting for you." She opens her purse. "Here, I have a present." Effie places a small package gently beside her cousin and perches on the edge of the bed. "Open it."

Martha swivels from side to side then picks up her gift. Holding the parcel away from her, she plays at untying the ribbon.

"It's not a bomb, Martha." Effie forces herself to smile, the word *suicide* echoing in her head.

"It's a book." Looking up at her cousin, Martha speaks cautiously. "Is it a romance?"

"Just open it and see," Effie says. "You like romance novels then?"

Ripping at the paper with stubby fingers, Martha halts when she reads the book's title. "I'm too old for fairy tales." She slumps and sighs. "You can have it back. I'm not a kid."

Effie grimaces. "But these are the complete fairy tales of Oscar Wilde. It's a wonderful book." She softens her tone. "I have a copy myself, right beside my bed." She sees the tears forming in Martha's eyes. "You'll love it."

Martha examines the book as if it were a jarred specimen.

"You and Oscar Wilde share a birthday. I thought it might be nice for you to have one of his books and to see how talented October 15th people are." Effie looks around the room to see if anything has changed since her first, and last, visit. "Is that a new picture?" she asks, pointing to a provincial scene of shepherd and sheep.

Martha scoops up one of the chips from the bed and eats it. "Wasn't he a fag?"

"That's a terrible word, Martha. Decent people don't use words like that." Effie presses her hand to her forehead. "Homosexual is what you mean. Or gay."

"All the kids at school say fag. Or homo. What's the difference?"

"First of all, not all the kids say fag or homo. That's not possible or even likely." Effie isn't sure on this point but she carries on. "Second of all and even more important, name calling isn't kind or fair or right."

Martha sizes up her birthday gift. "*Fairy* tales?" She ekes out a smile.

Effie can see that Martha is being playful and not mean-spirited. "Yes. Fairy tales," she says.

Martha slides over to the edge of her bed. "I'll go downstairs with you if you like."

"In a minute, okay?" Effie says. She wonders if the men have left the house. "I have another small present for you. Something special for your sixteenth."

Martha, her mouth hanging open, watches as Effie retrieves a jeweller's box from the side pocket of her purse.

"Close your eyes," Effie says. "Don't peek." Approaching Martha from behind, Effie unclasps a chain and loops it around her cousin's neck. The underside of the girl's hair feels sticky with perspiration.

"Do you like it?" Effie asks.

Martha stares at her cousin and then down at the teardrop pendant.

"It's a fire opal. From Mexico." Effie watches as the girl runs her fingers across the surface of the stone. Martha has a look on her face that Effie can't decipher. "The fire opal symbolizes love," Effie says. "It's also the stone of the bird of paradise." She pauses. "It's your gemstone."

"It doesn't go with my dress," Martha says. "It's so red."

"No. It doesn't." Effie has already steeled herself for rejection. "Would you like me to undo it?" She knows the trouble here is with Martha, for Martha. A heavy feeling pushes its way into Effie's chest nevertheless.

No!" Martha swings her thick legs over the side of the bed. "I'll change my dress is all I meant." She stretches the synthetic material away from her neck. "I hate dresses anyway."

As the cousins walk into the living room, one of the chatting women calls out, "Oh, it's the birthday girl!"

Martha's cheeks flare. "Hello Miss," she says.

And then Effie remembers where she has seen this woman. Minegoo High.

Martha locks eyes with her mother from across the room and then says to the teacher, "Thank you for coming to my party."

"You are most welcome." The woman steps away from her friend and the mantel, toward Effie. "I'm Jill Hannebury. We haven't been properly introduced although I've seen you at school." The ceiling light casts diamond patterns across her heart-shaped face. "Your young cousin is one of my best students." Jill Hannebury sparkles like the Queen of the Stardust Ballroom.

Martha stutters, "I'm I'm—"

Shirley Cambridge appears at her daughter's side.

"Hello again, Mrs. Cambridge. I was just saying to Effie that your daughter is one of my best students."

Shirley Cambridge squints over the rim of her eyeglasses. "How so?"

"I hope this is all right with you, Martha, my talking about you in this way." Jill averts her eyes away from Martha's mother and replies, "Because she tries so hard."

Bill Cambridge booms from behind, "How's my girl? Are you having a nice party?"

Effie looks toward the landing.

Jill Hannebury inches away from the family group and resumes talking with her friend. Effie scrutinizes her uncle, searching for signs of anxiety. She wonders what has become of those men.

Shirley Cambridge pushes back her shoulders. "Where have *you* been?"

"How's my girl?" Bill repeats. He smiles winningly at his daughter. "Pick a hand," he says.

"The left one."

"Pick another hand," Bill says.

Martha giggles. "The right one."

"Voila!" Bill winks at Effie. "Is that how you say it?"

Martha's father produces an envelope from behind his back. He hands it to his daughter.

The boys have stopped playing their game and lie on their backs, watching the show.

"Voila!" Bill repeats, pointing at Martha. "Now open it."

Martha shakes it then rips off one end and tips the envelope. A thin gold object slips out into her hand. "It's a key," she says.

"A key to *what*?" Shirley Cambridge pitches toward her daughter.

Bill points at the window in the direction of the driveway, shooting a sidelong glance at his wife. "I was going to trade the old Pontiac in, but I've decided it should be yours."

Martha's cheeks blotch pink and her eyes fill with tears. "May I go out and sit in it?"

"Sit in it? It's your birthday! Take it for a spin around the block. Just drive like I showed you and don't go too far."

As Martha walks to the hallway and out the front door, Willie rises scarlet-faced and strides out of the living room alongside his mother, shoulders taut, necks rigid. Their feet barely make a sound on the wall-to-wall carpeting.

Willie's friends, familiar with these sorts of interruptions, get up from the floor and put on their shoes. Crouching to tie their laces, they mumble good night. One of the boys yells to Martha as she pulls out into the street, "Happy birthday!" his voice disappearing down the driveway.

Jill Hannebury nods to her friend and crosses the room. "Thank you for having us over this evening, Bill." Then turning to Effie, "It was a pleasure to finally meet you." She smiles like someone grateful for escape. The other woman joins her and they deliver their thanks while securing their scarves.

As Bill and Effie watch the guests depart, their eyes sweep across the room and land on Shirley's seated friend, now left alone.

The heavy woman brushes bits of carrot and cauliflower from her lap onto the rug. "I can see you've no use for me here." She pushes herself up and wipes her wet lips with a balled-up napkin. "Invited to a party and everybody leaves before cake. Terribly rude."

"Why don't you stay and have a drink?" Bill waves his hand toward the credenza. "We've got a boatload of punch." He looks over at his niece. "Effie, you must know your upstairs neighbour, Mildred Rutherford?"

Effie puts her hand to her throat. "*You're* Ru—Miss Rutherford?"

"I have a busy schedule at the hospital tomorrow," the woman says. She inspects her Wallabees for vegetable remnants. "Peggy Trainor is being released next week and there's a lot to do before that happens." Rutherford shudders.

Effie watches the colour drain from her uncle's face. She is surprised by her sudden maternal feelings toward him. She asks conversationally, "Who is Peggy Trainor?"

"Only the police chief's wife!" Without warning the heavyset woman clomps over to the door. "Are you coming? It's a long walk and it's *late*."

Effie shrugs at her uncle. "I have to go upstairs and get my coat." She wonders which would be worse—running into her aunt or those men again or walking home in the dark with Mildred Rutherford.

CHAPTER 13

Effie presses the heels of her hands into the blackboard ledge, facing her students. "Good afternoon, class. I am so pleased to see that many of you took up my challenge and dressed for Halloween." Noting Martha's empty chair she wonders if her cousin's absence has to do with reluctance or with that nasty mother of hers.

Effie pokes a book bag that is lying bloated on her desk. "As promised, I've brought candy. Now let me see if I can guess who you are."

She scans the room and writes on the board—

> *Popeye*
> *Scout*
> *Wonder Woman*
> *Alice*
> *Long John Silver*
> *Sherlock Holmes*
> *Superman*
> *Snow White*

"I am gratified to see that many of you like to read fiction. Even if some of it comes in the form of comic books."

"Or cartoons," Gary proffers.

"Or cartoons, yes," says Effie. She walks through the room and stops at Gary's desk. "And for those of you who didn't participate—for example, Mr. Lowther here—I am going to ask that you offer up, to the class, a synopsis of Timothy Findley's *The Wars*, which I expect all of you to have finished for today as requested." She checks the time on her watch. Tomorrow night the students will be putting on the Autumn Airs concert for their families and today's recital is intended to be a less nerve-wracking trial run. "We have twenty minutes before assembly. Gary, the floor is yours."

Danny claps his hands. "Nice one!"

Gary shrugs. "That's easy, Miss. Robert Ross is the main character of the book and he is nineteen years old. He's from Toronto. When the story starts out he is caught up in the ravages of World War I."

Effie takes a deep breath. A psychiatrist had once described her mother's life that way. *The ravages*, he had said, and Effie immediately understood the magnitude.

Gary continues, his voice growing unsteady. "He had a good relationship with his Dad." He looks at Danny. "Like what you have with your Dad." He hesitates. "And you too, Griffen." He looks back at Effie. "Robert Ross's mother was an alcoholic. Or at least she became one after her daughter died." Gary picks absently at a scab on his elbow. "The daughter had pet rabbits."

Effie waits for Gary to go on.

"And Mrs. Ross gets depressed and tells Robert that everyone is a stranger to one another, even people in families."

"And do you think that's true?" Effie feels her throat muscles tighten. She puts her hand up, stroking the front of her neck.

"It can be true." He stares at the surface of his desk. "Every day is different."

"Whom do you most admire in the story?" Effie is afraid she is going to cry.

"That's hard." Gary looks up at her and soothes his scab with the palm of his hand. "I really like Robert. A lot of people might think he wasn't a hero, but I do. In the end I think he felt like the horses. And I think he was strong—the way he ran around the block twenty-five times, how he survived in the trenches and in the mud. But mostly, I admire the mother."

"The mother?" Ruthie Acorn plants her hands on her hips. "Why the mother? She was just a drunk."

"Because she looked at what was hard and knew what she'd lost. It just got to be too much for her." Gary peers out at the class, narrowing his eyes. "It would have been too much for anybody."

"Indeed it would, Gary." Effie turns her back on the class and erases the blackboard, grateful for the interruption over the PA.

As the assembly begins, Effie folds her arms tightly across her chest, from behind her the sound of trooping feet as the senior jazz band, a parade of white shirts, black pants and fedoras, stride by. Saxophones, trumpets and clarinets swing up the aisle, a stream of gleaming brass and silver and gold. At the tail end of the procession John lugs a bass trombone, walking stodgily behind his students. Effie hopes she isn't blushing.

The musicians file onstage, whisking dark glasses from their shirt pockets as they sit down. The laughter swells into a predictable crescendo of applause for the Blues Brothers' "Soul Man." The glistening instruments shoot up into the air and Effie recognizes a string of television theme songs. *Barney Miller, Get Smart, Hawaii Five-O.*

Across the room Donnie leans against the painted backdrop, his shoulders rising and falling to the beat of the music. Effie, amusing herself, begins counting the heads in the audience. She stops at fifteen, fascinated by a spectacular boater topped with a spray of yellow plumage.

The student turns and Effie sees it is Martha, beside her scrawny Tommy Murphy, his hair a geyser of clumps. Effie stares at the pair, struck by the incongruity. Lady Bracknell and the Artful Dodger. She swallows hard and closes her eyes.

Effie hurries home to work on her Halloween pumpkin, the first she has attempted since she and Garfield carved one Rastafarian style, boiling corkscrew pasta for hair. Later that night they sipped white rum and mango juice and slow-danced to "Colour My World."

She picks up the knife from the table and sets about her business, gutting and carving. She digs out two oblong eyes, shapes an oval nose and a round, toothless mouth. Orange goop clings to her wrists and nails and hangs from her bangs. When she finishes she places the jack-o'-lantern on a stack of books in the living room window, inserts a candle, lights the wick and runs downstairs to evaluate. High above the dusk-lit street the pumpkin hovers, immense eyes and gaping mouth, innocent and afraid.

"That's *hysterical*." Mary's voice sneaks up from behind.

"Oh my God, Mary, you scared me! Your hair—you look like a ghost."

"I hope you're not expecting a lot of kids tonight. They avoid this building like the plague. John and I were thinking of coming down to visit you though, if that's okay." Mary lowers her voice. "We wouldn't want the goblins to get you."

Effie registers what Mary has said: she and John are coming to visit. Together. "Come down if you like," she says, as she hurries back into the building.

Upstairs Effie clears the pulp from the table and wipes the surface with a clean cloth. She washes her hands. After running a brush through her hair, she gathers the strands up into a knot at the nape of her neck. She tidies her books and gathers her clothes from the floor. Changing into freshly washed blue jeans, she slips into her favourite sweater—a grey cardigan with tiny jewelled flowers sewn along the shoulders, the polished shank buttons embossed with green jumping frogs—and marches into the living room and sits down, waiting for children or guests, whoever comes first, the candlelight flickering across the ceiling. She fingers the buttons absently as if they are worry stones. When she hears a knock on her door, she considers before rising.

"Trick or treat!" Batman and Robin hold out two floral pillowcases. A young woman hangs back on the lower landing, smiling. "Trick or treat!" they repeat, shaking their sacks.

Effie snatches two bags of potato chips from a roasting pan that's perched on a stool inside her door. "Happy Halloween!" she says. The boys eye their goodies and wheel around. They hurry down the stairs, elbowing past the woman, who follows them at an easy pace.

Donnie Fitzgerald vaults up the stairs past the threesome, a package in his hand. "Am I too late for candy?" he calls out to the air. When he reaches Effie's door he scans the room behind her and offers her the parcel. "This is from Mom." He stands in the outer hallway, panting. "I ran all the way from the house."

Effie can't remember the last time she received an unexpected gift. She feels the thrill of impetuous pleasure but worries that if John witnesses the exchange he will misinterpret the scene. She pulls back the wrapping paper gingerly, feeling something square and hard under the tissue. A book.

"Gordy was having a fit that I wouldn't see you. Halloween is his favourite holiday and you are definitely his favourite girl." Donnie slides his arms out of his jacket and winks. Effie wonders if he has a tic.

"Mom hopes you'll like it."

"Oh—it's C.S. Lewis. *The Four Loves*." She turns the book over in her hands. "It's beautiful. Please tell your mother I said thank you."

Donnie hangs over her. "*The Four Loves* is one of my father's favourites."

"I've only read the Narnia books." Effie stuffs the tissue paper into the roasting pan.

"*The Four Loves*," he begins. "Affection, friendship, erotic and . . ." Donnie taps the book with his finger, pleased to be sharing his wisdom.

"*Agape*," finishes John from the stairwell.

Donnie smirks. "*Agape*? Including the accents? Or a-gape?"

"Selfless love. Mary knows what I mean, don't you, Mary?"

"Selfless love," Mary echoes, appearing behind John.

Effie makes a slurping sound with her tongue and her teeth that she hates, a resentful sound that always betrays her.

"I know what *agape* means." Donnie shakes his head at his friend and forces a smile. "How very Latinate of you." His smile vanishes. "Of course, timing is everything. Anyway, it doesn't matter because there is no such thing. I might be a good Catholic, as you like to say, but I'm not completely delusional." The light from inside the pumpkin streaks across the ceiling.

"Let's come in and discuss it, shall we?" John holds up a large bottle of wine, and Mary follows, a basket of candy in one hand, a small velvet bag in the other. Golden hair courses over her scarlet pashmina sweater.

Little Red Riding Hood.

Effie wonders if Mary and John have been drinking.

Mary eyes Effie's full roasting pan. "Have you had anyone yet?" A single cellophaned jawbreaker, in symphony with Mary's question, pops out of the pan and lands on top of a dust ball.

Effie retrieves Donnie's jacket, flings it onto a hook, and flicks on the light. She pauses, her back to her guests. "The same two you've had, no doubt."

"I've had no one." Mary drapes the basket over the inside doorknob. "Or if they came, I didn't hear them."

Donnie grabs the wine bottle from John. "Old buildings like this never appeal to children. Too many stairs. Besides, the kids are probably afraid of the old witch upstairs." He ambles down the hall toward Effie's kitchen, carelessly swinging the bottle. "I'll do it, Effie," he says. "Take a load off."

Effie sets down *The Four Loves* and drags the rocking chair closer to the coffee table, aware that Mary and John have snagged the couch for themselves. Mary tucks the velvet bag beside her. "Oh, I forgot something in the basket," she says, jumping up. Effie watches John watching Mary, his liquid eyes following her into the hallway, an artist trailing his muse.

Donnie returns to the living room holding a trayful of glasses. He slides the tray onto the table and plops into the armchair. "I'm not sure if I believe in selfless love," he says. "Does anyone do anything just for the sake of kindness? Isn't there usually an ulterior motive, even if the motive is unconscious and even if it's only to bask in one's own goodness?"

Mary waltzes back to her seat beside John, floating down like a feather.

John hoists the bottle and fills the glasses, resting his free arm on Mary's knee for leverage. Effie recoils. *Like a dog all over hot hamburger*, she thinks.

Mary looks sharply at Donnie. "Look—do we have to talk about this again? You two droning on like tedious Quakers."

"I was a Mormon once," Effie blurts. "It's true," she says, suddenly realizing that she and John have already discussed this. She pulls on one of her frog buttons. It pops off and rolls under the couch. She wonders what's in Mary's little bag.

John reaches over and touches Mary's sleeve. His eyes fire up as he looks at Donnie. "Have you read *anything*?" He sets his drink on the coffee table hard enough that the wine slips and slides, splashing over the top of the glass. "Live harmoniously. Call nothing your own. Abandon pride."

Donnie leans over and wipes off his shoes with a napkin, unable to explain even to himself his degree of frustration. He's used to sparring with John. It can't be that. "Shoulda coulda woulda, John. It's doesn't seem entirely real."

"Jesus, Donnie—which side are you on? And real to *you*, you mean. Plenty of people live loving, holistic lives. St. Augusti—"

"But just not on the island, right?"

"Islands are different."

"So you keep saying."

"Islands are insular, exclusive, sectarian."

"And St. Augustine wasn't? That's a laugh."

"St. Augustine wasn't bound by the dynamic of big fish small pond."

"St. Augustine was hardly urbane."

"How do *you* know?"

"I think you mean urban," Effie mutters.

"He married a twelve-year-old for Christ's sake—after waiting two years!" Donnie roars. "That's not urbane."

"*That* was the Roman Empire."

Mary opens her book. "This is the most ridiculous, convoluted conversation you two have ever had. Can we change the subject?"

Effie, curious, scooches forward.

"The Book of Runes." Mary says, closing the cover to show Effie the title.

John raises his eyebrows playfully. "Is it magic?"

"Okay, Mr. Cynic, try it. Put your hand in the bag—no— first, ask yourself a question—then put your hand in the bag.

When you feel a stone pulling toward you–no–like a magnet, lift it out of the bag. Don't turn it over or flip it. Just bring it out of the bag exactly as you feel it."

"Speaking of convoluted."

"What sort of a question?"

"Anything you want. Is my friendship with Donnie in trouble? for example."

Donnie sinks into the armchair, splaying his legs. "You don't need a magic stone to answer that."

John considers before speaking. "Do I have to reveal what I ask?"

"Not at all. Choose one, and I will show you what you have to read in the book. Each stone has its own page of description."

"Okay, here goes." John dips his hand into the bag tentatively. The stones make a rattling sound as he fishes around. "What does this mean?" he asks, laying a Rune on the table.

"Is that exactly how you pulled it out?" Mary asks. "Okay then, let me match it to its place in the book. This one is called *Perth*, and you've got it reversed. How do I know? Just look at the picture. See? You've pulled it out backwards." Mary flips through the pages searching for the corresponding description.

John sidles in closely and quotes from the heading. "*Initiation. Something Hidden. A Secret Matter.*"

"Here. Let me read it." Mary begins. "*A counsel against expecting too much, or expecting in the ordinary way, for the old way has come to an end. You simply cannot repeat the old and not suffer. Call in your scattered energies, concentrate on your own life at this moment, your own requirements for growth. Perth counsels you neither to focus on outcomes nor to bind yourself with the memory of past achievements. In doing so, you rob yourself of a true present, the only time in which self-change can be realized.*"

Effie wonders what it all means—*the old way has come to an end*. Is Mary the old way? Is it the island? *Concentrate on your own life, your own requirements for growth*. What requirements? Perhaps to see what's—or who's—right in front of his face? *Don't focus on outcomes*. That doesn't sound good. At least not for her.

"You may feel overwhelmed with exhaustion from meeting obstruction upon obstruction in your passage. Yet always you have a choice: You can see this apparent negativity as bad luck, or you can recognize it as an obstacle course, a challenge specific to the Initiation you are presently undergoing. Then each setback, each humiliation, becomes a test of character. When your inner being is shifting and reforming on a deep level, patience, constancy and perseverance are called for. So stay centered, see the humor, and keep on keeping on."

What humiliations? Effie can't imagine John ever being in trouble with anyone. At least not with anyone who counted. Maybe she is the obstacle course—the challenge to his initiation. Maybe she will *be* his initiation. But initiation to what? Effie blushes, appalled by her self-interest.

"It's all Greek to me," John says. "Great advice, but applicable to practically anyone."

"That's how they suck you in. *Tomorrow you will wake up and find yourself alive, unless you don't, in which case you will be dead.*" Donnie swallows down his wine. "Speaking of dead, Mary, what's the newsroom scuttlebutt on Chief Trainor's suicide?"

"His *alleged* suicide," John says. "I, for one, refuse to believe Jerry Trainor killed himself."

"Neither does anyone at the paper." *Neither. Does. Any. One. At the pap-er.*

"He was just in to recruit for the United Way and he was laughing and carrying on like he always does." She bit her lip before correcting herself. "Did."

"His wife does have cancer," Donnie says. "Maybe he felt he had nothing to live for."

Effie swipes the wine bottle from the table and refills her glass. "That's not exactly true. Mildred Rutherford told me—"

"Mildred Rutherford? When did you two become friends?" Donnie wags his finger at Effie and laughs. "Effie's been holding out on us."

"We walked home together a few weeks ago. Mil— *Rutherford* said that Peggy Trainor was going home to recuperate."

"You see?" John pummels the arm of the couch. "I told you!"

"Jeeze, John, that doesn't prove anything."

Mary sits up straight. "I think the best way to look at this is logically. For one thing, why would the Chief kill himself if he knew his wife wasn't sick? Or more to the point, why was his wife's supposed illness used by the police to explain his suicide?"

"Donnie's right. Lots of people appear overly optimistic before they kill themselves," Effie says. "In fact, it's one of the warning signs."

"Wait a minute." John shoots a look over at Effie. "How did Rutherford know about Jerry Trainor's death?"

"She didn't. We were talking about hospital care. Or rather *she* was."

"Peggy Trainor is the salt of the earth." John pushes up on his sleeves. "And so was her husband. He was one of the only ethical policemen I've ever known."

Mary leans back. "Everyone at the paper feels the same way. Peggy must be devastated."

"Are all law enforcement officers suspect in your eyes or just the ones on the island?" Donnie shifts in his chair impatiently. "You know John, not everyone is a bastard or a murderer."

"Precisely!" John shouts. "Use your own logic. You can't prove Jerry Trainor wasn't murdered any more that you can clearly understand *anyone's* motive."

"I have no idea what goes on in your head. Sometimes you're too owly for me John, plain and simple. I don't know a thing about who killed who—or is it *whom*, your Great Dictum—but I'm fed up with you endlessly having your shirt in a knot. There are so many *real* things you could be worried about—like your students, for example. Did you know that Gary Lowther's mother died of alcohol poisoning? Or that Virginia Halfpenny was molested by her uncle? You have plenty to say about the state of the world and yet you seem to miss half of what's going on right under your bloody nose." He clears his throat and heads for his jacket, thanking Effie as he walks past her. "I'll give Gordy your love." Before Effie can say anything, he is gone.

"Oh goodness," Mary says, "I hope I didn't hurt his feelings.

John frowns at Mary. "*You*? I'm the one he's annoyed with, not you. Who could ever be angry with you?"

"Well, something's bugging him tonight. He was making less sense than usual—and that's a piece even for him."

Effie stands in the centre of the living room looking down at Mary and John, fingering the threads where her button has come off. "More wine anyone?" She tips back her glass, draining it.

CHAPTER 14

Effie sits on the floor in front of the coffee table tapping the tip of her pencil monotonously. Scattered in front of her several recently purchased books—secondhand copies of *The Paris Reviews*, John Gardner's *On Becoming A Novelist*, and E.M. Forster's *Aspects of the Novel*; crumpled balls of paper scarcely written on—litter the floor.

In her first year of university a professor had suggested to Effie that she write more (she initially misunderstood him to mean length instead of depth), to fill in the gaps, extend herself. But as hard as she tried, torturing herself with convoluted phrases and synonyms, she could not find a way into a more complex sentence. It all felt like learning to walk.

Spurred on by the Halloween night fiasco, Effie launched into a rigorous campaign to become the sort of woman she most admired, one who would attract the sort of man she most admired. She adopted Jo March from *Little Women* as her inspiration, astounded by the similarities between herself and Alcott's heroine.

Effie writes on a clean sheet of paper:

Similarities
-tall, thin, fair-skinned
-desire to become skilled in an artistic profession
-longing for passion, independence, service and harmony
-teacherly
-imaginative, energetic
-admiration for dependable, industrious, poetic, affectionate, truthful men
-loving mother, absent father
-sacrificial
-thwarted

Clutching her notepad, Effie moves to the rocking chair, hoping the light and the view will inspire her. Slowly, she begins writing.

The woman did not understand what she was intending. She stared through the window at the discrete (discreet?) flakes of snow that blew in horizontal lines across the cracked tarmac, above her head brown-edged bits of curled plaster recoiling from the blasts of the forced air furnace. The drugstore would be closing in thirty minutes, and she would have to change out of her nylon slip and tidy her hair. Make it seem as if she had something to live for.

Effie reads and re-reads her first paragraph. She hates sentence fragments, despite their utility. They hint at a faltering, fragile world that cannot be counted on. Her theme feels childish; her descriptions maudlin and cloying. She picks up her pencil.

She looked down at her bare feet, overwhelmed by an urgent sense of longing. These were the feet of her father: clean to an almost bleached white, toenails trim, proud calluses evidence of an industrious life and nature—a fortifying call to allegiance, she and her father standing alone and stalwart, defiant against the insidious betrayal by the people who once promised to love them.

Effie shivers. It does not occur to her to turn up the heat.

The woman practiced her speech while she dressed. "I know that it says no refill, but Dr. Dennis assured me she was going to call you. Yes, I ~~also~~ know it's too late to reach her tonight, but you're closed all day tomorrow and if I don't get some sleep my boss is going to fire me." She caught sight of herself in the mirror, her lips working in a way that surprised her, sensually, like Marilyn Monroe. Irony is what her father would have called this—the way we keep revealing the opposite of what is true about ourselves, and the way people keep missing the obvious.

Jarred by a sudden noise, Effie stands up and moves to the window. Outside, tiny snowflakes have begun to fall, the late morning sky a twilight shade of grey, ominous and claustrophobic. Down below, a row of yellow school buses rumble past like a string of happy building blocks. They turn the corner and pull over across from the cenotaph.

Effie watches as a line of white-haired and bald-headed men dressed in military greens and browns, artificial poppies stuck through their uniform caps and coat collars, step down from the vehicles, their medals and ribbons visible even from this distance. She imagines her father curled up under the cockpit of a B52 bomber, setting sites on his target. She thinks of the posters at school paid for by Veterans Affairs—a lone airman leaning against a plane, standing in cobalt blue shadows, horizon and sky meeting in a landscape of sapphire, a splash of diamond-white afterglow.

The soldier who had recited the poem about Dieppe had cried on national television. *This was my brother at Dieppe,* he read. *Quietly a hero, who gave his life like a gift, withholding nothing.* A single tear rolled down his cheek—his *withered* cheek—and she wonders how many friends had been laid out before him on the grass or in the snow, staggered rows of crimson carpets. She knows all about blood and arterial flesh—a river of red gushing upward and spattering the walls, a hemorrhagic surrender.

This was my mother at Dieppe.

She grabs the back of the rocking chair then stares out into the street again. She can't make out the features of the people at the monument, they are too far away, but she sees a group of children and knows that some of them have been assigned to lay memorial wreaths. The wind rages fiercely, fit for the day and the occasion, and Effie feels guilty that she has not gone out to stand among the crowd. She lets go of the chair and opens the window so that the lonely trumpet call can come in. She sits back down.

She dropped the keys into her pocket and put on her leather gloves, one finger at a time. As she placed her hand on the door-knob the telephone rang. She knew who it was immediately, the same way ~~anyone~~ a person knows when someone they love is about to be hit by a car [?]. He hadn't called in almost two weeks, not since his wife had come home. And his letter had said it was over. She hesitated, but did not remove her hand from the doorknob, committed to it like a pathologically curious child locked onto an electric fence, perversely amused by the fact that her thin leather glove could not protect her—the way that nothing could stand between the child and that terrifying ~~bolt~~ jolt of electricity.

Effie puts down her pencil. Why hadn't her mother tried harder to stay sober? Done something important with her life? Bisecting insects could lead to propitious discoveries, like the woman who had helped uncover the mystery of the double helix. She had died too, but of cancer, and after how many unselfish years, her eyes pinned to a microscope.

Effie stands up and stretches her arms. She turns back to the window. The streets are clear of people except for two skimpily dressed teenagers walking in the wind holding hands. The couple approach the apartment building, the boy poking the girl playfully in the ribs, his hat lifting off in a gust of wind. Effie recognizes the brilliant orange hair. Tommy Murphy, Martha at his side. *Oh God. What next?* As Effie gathers up her papers she does not see the patrol car edging around the curb or Jimmy Fitzgerald waving to his young friends.

CHAPTER 15

Two years and seventeen days. This is the length of time that has passed since Effie has seen her mother. Social Services has placed Effie with a four-member family on Mississauga Road, people who have more money than they know what to do with.

Mr. Ferris works as an executive for Encyclopaedia Britannica and Mrs. Ferris, a longtime stay-at-home wife and mother, has recently fulfilled a yen for a career in real estate, deciding that her children are old enough to fend for themselves on days when she is late home for dinner. That, she says with a smile approaching a grimace, is what the housekeeper is for. Besides, Port Credit Social Services is in upheaval, the most recent uproar arising from mismanaged funds, and they haven't been by to check on Effie's progress in months. Mrs. Ferris and her husband have taken on a foster only because it seemed like a charitable thing to do at a time when there was considerable neighbourhood competition over who could do the most for the needy, a fervour spurred on by the recent Arab-Israeli War.

The Ferris children, Judith and Walter, attend a private school, so there is no fear of overlap for Effie in her daytime world. She and Kathleen Raminsky have forged a bond, although Kathleen's cryptic home life prohibits what Kathleen's stepfather refers to variously as intruders, outsiders and meddlers.

Effie longs for her mother but tries to endure, reminding herself of Romans 12:12: *Be joyful in hope, patient in affliction, faithful in prayer.* She cannot admit to herself that some part of her consciousness, although utterly bereft, is relieved of the daily anxiety of wondering what, or who, she will be coming home to, or if her mother is even home at all. The most painful aspect is that no one has, or will, tell her what has become of her mother, and Effie, despite her best efforts to locate Mrs. Cambridge, is under strict orders to be back to the Mississauga home within thirty minutes of the four o'clock bell. She and Kathleen ponder and plot, attempting to ferret out ways in which Effie can travel further afield. But now that her foster mother is out and about showing homes to prospective buyers, Effie is in even greater risk of being discovered.

Kathleen, who lives under an equally rigid but more often self-imposed timetable, promises that as soon as an opportunity presents itself, she will venture up Lakeshore Road past the public library and, if possible, ask questions in pertinent places. Kathleen's first concern, however, is for own her mother, who the young girl wants to protect against a raging stepfather, whose 7:30-4pm work schedule creates a tight race home to the finish line.

At night, Effie lies in bed wondering what has become of her family's belongings—the stuffed rabbits and teddy bears, the Raggedy Ann doll her mother surprised her with three Christmases ago, *The Golden Treasury of Knowledge*, the cobalt-blue table, her mother's poetry volumes. Has her mother been able to hang onto her jewellery, the Avon costume rings and bangle bracelets she promised to bequeath to Effie? And what has happened to the summer halter dresses and her mother's beautiful high heels that she kept in a neat row under the bed? Effie imagines these treasured items crying out from a flea market in New Toronto.

Effie's longing eventually turns to fear, a gripping terror that she will never see her mother again. In her dreams she races through crowded supermarkets, empty hotels, deep forests—mysterious places whose names she does not know. Sometimes her mother is visible, but always just out of reach, and Effie attempts to grab onto her trailing scarf or the hem of her vanishing skirt. Once, her mother turns around, arms beseeching, mouth open but emitting no sound and Effie, tangled in woodland overgrowth, watches as her mother fades into ether.

In daylight hours, as Effie tamps down her fear, the lining of her stomach slowly fires, a gentle heat at first but eventually suppurating, and by the time she is fourteen she has built into her routine tri-annual trips to the Peel County Hospital where her barium-coated stomach is examined by a radiologist and she is sent away with a renewed prescription for a brown glass bottle of Diovol. Apart from the initial consultation and the agony that took her there, Effie never mentions her pain to anyone, and she is grateful that the burning in her stomach keeps her away from sugar-laden soda pop and candy, except for those times when a crushing sadness compels her into bingeful gluttony. So much around her feels foreign, a treacherous, mocking lie, but she tries desperately to acclimate, eager to adjust to her new surroundings if only so that one day she can tell, and please, her mother.

But she is young and hasn't figured out the parameters of her foster home. The house on Mississauga Road, spacious and newly modernized, feels antithetical to Effie's character and past, the basement strewn with playthings—Shoop-Shoop hula hoops; two pair of Snoopy roller skates; a trunkful of competitive-sports balls; a four-player badminton set; several tennis rackets, many of their strings warped or unravelling; a right-handed archery kit; an east wall strung with family-sized snow skis; a debilitated rowing machine; a Twist 'N Tone, which Effie mistook as a Frisbee, and, over in one corner and never used as far as Effie can tell, a Vita Master, a massager *cum* weight loss machine that Mrs. Ferris insists she will use as soon as she or the housekeeper finds the sealer lotion.

CHAPTER 16

Effie sits with her hands in her lap, eyeing the women at the table. She has promised herself that she will not let the other teachers spoil the Christmas party for her. Scanning the room she smiles cheerily, but her effort makes her feel like a marionette, shapeless legs and skinny arms strung from invisible wire. She wishes she hadn't gone for demure, her attempts at an Audrey Hepburn style—hair pulled into a low chignon and already loose, her bangs swept to one side beneath a glob of uncooperative gel, and a secondhand knee-length black satin dress wearing out at the back—more Blanche Dubois than Holly Go Lightly. Tragic.

For their part, the Minegoo teachers are mostly oblivious to Effie. They occupy the second floor of the Morning Dove, dootied up and shining, distributed around tables like wedding guests. The women, their eyes glistening, their cheeks plumped and rosy, sit separately from the men. *How Catholic.* Some of the male teachers twitch itchily in chafing collars and holiday ties. Others hold back their shoulders like linebackers.

Tonight Effie wants to be both affecting and unobtrusive, a person who leaves more of an impression than a memory. She was aware of some of the criticisms levelled against her in Toronto—standoffish, disjointed, prim—but these were mostly uttered by people who resented her desire for things intellectual. While she had had minor dealings with pretty much everyone in the room, this is her first actual social occasion with staff and she wants to be part of the fabric, indistinct and harmonious, not some terrible flaw.

Across the table from Effie, Jill, her red tartan skirt falling neatly at her ankles, a creamy cashmere sweater pierced below her shoulder by a jolly holly berry broach, looks exuberantly cheerful, her hair piled in layers hosting rainbow-coloured sparkles that twinkle gaily under the overhead lights. Effie smiles.

Sitting next to Jill, Gemma Weekes, animated, converses with Vickie Myers, whose hands move faster than her lips, her sprightly corsage bouncing up and down on her breast. They are talking about Joe Ghiz, the island's Premier. Effie overhears his name but is not able to make out the crux of the conversation, although the word *Lebanese* stands out because Vickie has said it at least five times.

Effie leans into the table. "You look beautiful, Jill. So Christmassy."

Jill reaches for her broach. "Oh. Do you think it's too much?"

"Oh no, not at all," Effie insists. "It's the time of year to be ornamental."

"Ornamental?"

"I mean decorative. Festive."

"Yes," Jill sighs. "That's what I was afraid of. I look like a Christmas tree."

Effie dabs a napkin to her lips as Patti Page's *Silver Bells* floats up over the balcony railing. She continues to hold the napkin to her mouth, singing along in her head—*it's Christmas time in the city*. She pictures her mother twenty years earlier, poised in the living room on Christmas morning in her circle-cut skirt and white silk blouse, singing sweetly.

"Speak of the devil!" The attention in the room converges toward the main floor entryway and then back over at Vickie Myers as she flaps her hands at the island Premier. "Hello, Mr. Ghiz! Joe! My neighbour!" she declares happily to the faces below.

Joe Ghiz and his wife wave amicably upward, he dapper in a solid, large-pored kind of way—someone who would protect you—and she, smiling warmly. Effie whisks the napkin away from her mouth, smiling back. They make a handsome couple as they stand below, shaking snow off their boots and coats. Someone in the bar shouts, "Kiss her!" and the Premier, glancing up at the mistletoe hanging from the pendant lamp above their heads, dips his surprised wife backward and kisses her full on the mouth. Everyone laughs.

"Dishy, isn't he?" Vickie croons across the table at Effie. "He's my neighbour."

"It's a busy little town."

"*Excuse* me?"

"I just mean the way everyone seems to know everyone else." Effie feigns innocence.

"We don't just *know* one another. Most of us are *related* to one another."

"Oh, are *you* Lebanese? I had no idea." Effie picks up her glass of Ruby Rouge and holds it to the light.

Jill waves her napkin at Effie. "I understand your mother was born on the island." A strand of hair detours across her forehead.

Effie turns, grateful to Jill for rescuing her. "Yes, she was, but her birth here was accidental." Effie glances back toward Joe Ghiz. "My mother's father stopped on the island on his way to a business meeting in the United States. He worked with the railway and arrived the week of the stock market crash. By the time he was able to return to England he had met my grandmother, and when Charlottetown opened the CN Hotel he changed careers and became the hotel steward." Effie reaches for a cracker, aware that she is reciting. "My mother was born two years later, but she left the island at fifteen to pursue a modelling career in Montreal. She had already finished high school, having won the scholastic achievement plaque and the elocution prize. She was a grammarian, you know."

"Your mother was a grammarian?" Jill smiles affably. "I haven't heard that word in a long time, not even at school."

"Oh yes. She could modulate and enunciate better than anyone I ever knew."

"So education runs in the family, then."

"I think of my Uncle Bill as a businessman, not an educator." Effie snags a morsel of cheese. "And do your family come from the island?"

"More or less."

"It's not so bad," Effie consoles.

"So bad?"

"Coming from the island," Effie stammers. "I mean, we all have to come from somewhere."

"Yes, I suppose that's true."

"And the island is so—green. Viridian even." Effie blushes. "At least in the summer."

Jill smiles. "The non-ornamental time of the year?"

"Hey there." John appears next to Effie, smacking snow from his gloves. A few feet behind him, Donnie slouches over and shoves his nose into Vickie Myers' corsage, inhaling deeply. Gemma Weekes stares at Donnie and brays like a donkey—*hee-haw, hee-haw*—while Vickie chastises him with a wagging finger and a fluttering tongue. "Oh Donnie Fitzgerald, you are so bad! I know just what you're up to, don't you think I don't." Without losing a breath, Vicki hauls her skirt up to her knees and heads for the bar. Donnie follows.

John unzips his galoshes, raising his eyebrows at Effie. "Quite the menagerie," he says. He nods toward the coat rack. "I'll be right back."

Effie watches him walk across the room, the outline of his shoulders substantial underneath his camel-haired coat. She senses a shock of longing, the old pull rising from between her legs up through to her throat; feels an urgency to leap up from her chair and run after him, to throw her arms around him and have him turn and look at her, the way Joe Ghiz looked at his wife.

"So, what did you think of the contest?" asks Jill.

Effie creeps back into the moment. "The contest?" She stares into Jill's face, trying to make out her meaning. "What contest?"

John stands at the side of the table. He rests his hand on Effie's shoulder while he loosens the back of his shoe with his finger. "What issue of global importance are we tackling tonight?"

"Remember those fashion photos tacked up on the staff bulletin board last week?" Jill plucks an olive from a serving dish. "The female teachers have to write down what's wrong with each picture and then we have to hand in our answers." She sucks out the pimento before popping the olive into her mouth.

"Yeah," Gemma says. "They're giving prizes."

"And report cards," adds Effie.

"My God." John shifts his hand to the back of Effie's chair.

"Don't you worry, Mister," Jill says. "They're coming for the men in the New Year."

"Joe Ghiz," Vickie oozes. "Tremendous seeing you." She turns back to the group, her cherry-red lipstick greasy under the light. "I'd like you all to meet my neighbour Joe, our *Premier*." Vickie sweeps her arm in a ninety-degree arc. *Ta dah!* The magician's assistant.

"We know he's our Premier, Vickie." John nods warmly at Joe Ghiz. "We don't want you to think we don't vote."

"But neighbour first," says the Premier, winking over at Effie. "I don't think I've had the privilege."

"That's Effie Cambridge," Vickie barks. "She's here from Ontario to fill in at the school. Apparently her mother was born here." She looks down at her corsage, a lonely victim of her own tyranny. "Where's your delightful wife?"

"Over there." His face opens up when he smiles. "Nice to have seen you all. You look wonderful. Very festive." As the Premier turns to leave the small gathering he leans over to Effie. "I know your uncle." He winks at her again, his brown eyes radiating. "But I won't hold that against you. Or the fact that you're sitting with Vickie Myers."

Effie grins like a four-year-old. "Bye bye," she says, and she watches the couple walk arm-in-arm down the stairs. As she follows their descent she is diverted by a sweep of long blond hair flying up the stairs—Mary, radiant in a gold hand-woven caftan.

John stares at Mary from his standing position. "You look like an African queen. Or *the* African Queen."

Effie lunges forward, lodging herself between them. "What are you doing here? Are you covering the dinner for the newspaper?"

"Hi Effie. Wow! You look beautiful." *Bee-yoo-tee-full*. Mary throws her arms around her friend. "It's so good to see you. I haven't seen you in weeks. I've missed you. Haven't I, John?" Her hair smells like honeysuckle. "John and I have tickets to the ballet tonight. His parents invited me along after Donnie said he'd rather have a root canal. And you know how Donnie hates to miss a party. I was beginning to wonder if you'd moved out." Mary shimmers like a bar of gold.

Donnie sneaks up behind the threesome. "Yes. John MacDonald can't waste his evening with his co-workers. He has more cultured things to do."

Pain prickles along the sides of Effie's neck. "You go by my door every day. Why would it seem as if *I* were the one who had moved?" She slides her eyes pointedly, up and down the length of Mary's dress. "Anyway, it's nice to see you too. Your dress is very stylish. Very ethnic."

"We'll be back here afterward, Effie." John touches Effie's shoulder again but she jerks sideways, sloughing his hand away. "It's just across the street and it'll be over no later than ten o'clock. We could all meet later for drinks downstairs."

"Yes, Effie, we could." Donnie slides in closer. "Besides, you don't want to spend your evening with old Mister Sobersides. We'll have more fun without him, won't we?"

"What am I—*ten*? I don't care where John and Mary are going. Have a nice evening. I'm going to the washroom."

Her heart banging at what feels like a dangerous speed, Effie rushes into the farthest cubicle in the bathroom and locks the door. She sits on the toilet and puts her head in her hands, trying to ignore her escalating pulse. As she waits out her panic, she stares at the tiled floor and wonders if Mary and John will hold hands at the ballet, he occasionally squeezing her fingers, she squeezing back, their passion rising with the strains of a sad violin. She pictures a small circle of light illuminating their faces. The floor tiles blur in front of her and mascara stings her eyes, blackening her cheeks. Wiping her face with the back of one hand, she reaches with the other for toilet paper.

As she slips back into the restaurant she spots Donnie standing at the bar, beckoning her over. Alongside him members of the ballet are ordering Perrier water with slices of lime, and chamomile and ginseng tea. Effie recognizes them by their posture and their outfits, many dressed in ankle-length tights that are visible beneath their long woollen coats. They skitter about like characters in a Jacques Tati movie. Some of the women have wrapped their hair up in colourful headbands—shocking pinks and shades of vivid green. Degas.

Donnie holds out a brimming martini glass filled with red liquid. "Have a drink, Princess. It's a Christmas cocktail, made expressly for you by Angus."

"It's red," Effie says. "She reaches for the martini and sets it on the bar.

"It's Christmas." Angus stands behind the counter, offering her a paper napkin, its border lined with fat-bellied Santas. "It's called a Red Apple. I think you'll like it. They're very popular this time of year." He blinks rapidly. "Merry Christmas, Effie."

"Merry Christmas to you, too, Angus. And thank you for the drink." She glances sideways, scoping the room for John and Mary, not knowing whether she is more eager than distressed. They are sitting at a table, having been joined by a middle-aged couple who are evidently John's parents.

John's father is dressed in grey from head to toe, except for his shoes, which are black. His wide charcoal tie lies limply against a mouse-coloured shirt, all of which gives his face an ashen hue. He wears horn-rimmed octagonal glasses and his hair lies flat like dying grass, clipped and grey. He reminds Effie of the father in *Dennis the Menace*. Or an ironing board. He cuts into his pizza with precision.

Effie spins back toward Donnie. She has no desire to watch Mary and John or examine his parents. It is enough to have seen the soft light rippling off of Mary's golden hair and the even softer look in John's eyes as he admired his rare beauty. Throughout the bar, Sting's mellifluous *Gabriel's Message—then gentle Mary meekly bowed her head, 'To me be as it pleaseth God,' she said*, haunts the season. Effie burps acid.

"Excuse me dear, could you move your elbow?"

"Pardon me?"

A tall ballet dancer buzzes around Effie. "Your elbow, dear. It's on the napkins." He flits his fingers in the direction of the countertop.

"Oh. Sorry." Effie had no idea ballet dancers could be that tall and still manage to stay upright. She swerves her arm and leans back. "Break a leg," she says as he resumes his place along the bar.

"And at his great height he just might," she whispers to Donnie.

"Topple over?"

"So gay," Effie mouths.

"Effie, I'm surprised at you. What does that mean—so gay?"

"Oh, I don't have anything against homosexuality. Or homosexuals."

"The world will be thrilled to know it." Donnie slurps his drink.

"Don't be a smartass, Donnie. You know what I mean."

"No, I don't think I do. Why don't you tell me?"

"Well, I think a few things. I think that some of it is choice and some of it design, and not everyone who is gay is born gay. I think sometimes it's genetic and can't be helped."

"It needs helping?"

"Mostly I believe what Kinsey said—that people run on a continuum and that we all fall somewhere along that line. I guess, because I think of myself at least eighty-nine per cent on the heterosexual side, I am more comfortable with my own type of person, that's all."

"Eighty-*nine* per cent?"

"Mock me if you will. I have considered the percentages hard and long. I have even spent some time with paper and pencil on the problem. On the other hand, I don't think heterosexuals are any great shakes. I mean, Jesus—look at the divorce rate." She leers over at John's table. "So many people marrying for the wrong reasons. Sex, religion, superficial good looks."

Angus stands back from the counter observing Effie, ignoring the customers and mindlessly snatching maraschino cherries from a jar. He leans forward and rests his elbows on the sticky countertop. "Effie, are you seeing anyone?"

Donnie winks at Angus. "As in a psychiatrist?"

Effie raises her hands solicitously. "I mean, what's with Charles Nelson Riley, for example?"

"Or Rock Hudson?" Donnie plunks his drink on the bar and looks hard into Effie's eyes. "Charles Nelson Riley *is* gay, for Christ's sake. Effie, you're not making any sense."

Effie looks away from Donnie and sees that Angus is staring at her. "I'm sorry, Angus. Did you say something?"

"You've been standing there forever and you haven't touched your drink. Would you like something else instead?"

"You're so considerate Angus, no thank you. This looks scrumptious."

"Effie," Donnie places his hand on Effie's elbow. "I think it's time we went back upstairs to the party. Angus, we'll see you later." He guides Effie with one hand and holds her glass in the other.

Angus closes the lid on the cherry jar and slowly wipes down the bar.

At the top of the stairs, Donnie scoops up Vickie Myers' corsage from the floor. "Party's in full tilt," he says to Effie. "Vickie's lost her corsage. Happens every year."

The first course has not yet been served and Vickie and Gemma are lurching from table to table, half-drunk. After setting Effie's drink in front of her, Donnie walks back to his section, waving goodbye over his shoulder with Vickie's corsage.

"He's a cut-up, isn't he?" Jill laughs.

"I don't know what to make of him," Effie says. "One minute I like him and the next I think he's a jerk."

"Donnie? A jerk?" Gemma hee-haws from across the room.

Effie hears the disapproval in Jill's voice. "Well, maybe goof is more accurate. Or goofball." She points to the middle of the table. "Look at those centrepieces. Aren't they pretty?"

"Oh God, no, they're awful. When you light the candle it sparks. Last year Gemma set the table on fire."

Effie hesitates then picks up her drink. "I'm not doing very well, am I? I keep saying the wrong thing." She wets her tongue in her martini.

"Goodness no. You're fine." Another coil of hair slips down across Jill's forehead, as if designed that way.

"You're so pretty," Effie says. "My whole life I wanted curly hair. Or at least to look like someone else."

"Hair like this can be had for the price of a curling iron. And look like who?"

"Oh, I don't know—an actress. But not Katharine Hepburn. I felt sorry for her when I read that her brother hanged himself in the barn, but she's too angular. And not June Allyson. She irritates me with those sloping bangs and that raspy '*help me*' voice. And definitely *not* Meg Ryan." Effie gulps her drink, emptying her glass.

Jill laughs. "So who would you like to look like?"

Effie signals to the waitress. "Another Christmas cocktail, please. An apple whatever. I see them lined up like happy little soldiers on the bar down there." She turns back to Jill. "Elsa Lanchester. She is completely mesmerizing. Her eyes remind me of Theda Berra, although I wouldn't choose Theda Berra because she's been dead forever. Or Jessica Lange, mostly because she's odd and a free spirit but I think she has principles." Effie glances down toward the bar. "Or maybe—this is very hard—"

"Too many?"

"Too few. But I think I'd have to say Joanne Woodward. She has strong features, intelligence and a perfect voice."

"And Paul Newman."

"And Paul Newman." Effie sighs, and thanks the waitress for her drink. "So many blonds."

"What's this about Paul Newman?" Gemma hiccups over Effie's shoulder. "He's so hot. And he makes yummy spaghetti sauce." She hiccups again.

As a team of starched waitresses march in with silver serving trays, Effie inhales another long sip of her drink. A burst of pleasant heat streaks from her neck to her upper legs, and her brain spins the way it used to on the Tilt-a-Whirl.

"Sooooo . . . Effie," Vickie slurs from behind her. "What do you think of our little get-together?"

"Now Vickie," Jill cautions her coworker, "don't be nasty."

"I wasn't going to say anything nasty. It's Christmas, for *chrissakes*."

Effie raises her martini glass in a mock toast. "Merry Christmas, Miss Vickie." She smiles around the table. "You, too, Miss Gemma, and you especially, Jill. I am afraid I forget the rest of your names, if I ever knew them. I've seen all of you in the hallways but most of you look the other way when I pass." Effie tosses out a laugh. "Then again, that may have more to do with my uncle than with me. He *is* rather embarrassing, isn't he?" Effie nods into her glass.

During dinner, the conversation wanders between Christmas pageants, January exams and the spring concert. Jill offers up a reminder that Effie will be directing the play, and remarks that many students have shown a keen interest in auditioning, "largely credited to their love for your class, Effie." Vickie snickers and Gemma slaps the back of her friend's hand playfully, but hard.

Some of the teachers comment on the upcoming holidays and their families: who will be hosting Christmas dinner this year, and how much money they will or will not spend on their children. A discussion of hockey equipment arises and everyone concurs that prices have become exorbitant.

Effie is about to drive her dessert fork into her slice of cranberry cheesecake when she glances through the railing and down toward the entryway door. Mary and John are stamping their boots as John dusts powdery flakes from Mary's coat. Amy March and Professor Bhaer. Effie lays down her fork and folds her napkin across her dessert plate. "You know, Jill, I'm not feeling very well, and it's getting late. I think I'll head home now."

"But we haven't had the dancing yet. The men are still stuck on the other side of the room." Jill presses her palm to Effie's forehead. "You *are* a little warm. But I hate the thought of you going. It's early, and it's your first staff party, and I know one man in particular who is dying to dance with you. He told me so last week. *Several* times." Jill appeals to her friend. "Oh Effie, you *can't* go."

"I promise, I'm just going to lie down for a bit and if I start to feel better I'll come right back. I only live a block away." Effie stands up and says goodbye to the guests at the table, including

Vickie Myers. John and Mary are ordering drinks at the bar as Effie slips down the stairs and out into the dark.

She walks home through the churchyard beneath the naked trees, occasionally slipping on the ice, which causes her to laugh out loud despite her distress. *Who does that Mary think she is anyway, sidling up to me and pretending to be my friend, telling me stories about the fixed link and her sick father, the whole time trying to derail what I'm building with John?*

She spots something moving in the tree above her. *Mary thinks she is so special in that exquisite outfit and that stupidly glorious hair. Clothing from Africa, of all places. And in the middle of December. And who keeps their hair like that these days anyway. Crystal Gale?*

A great long caw breaks out above her. *One crow sorrow.* Effie stops walking and holds her breath.

The bird lifts off the branch, shaking down glittering snow and Effie searches briefly for the moon. Snow banks the ledges of the church windows and, except for the footpath, not a mark has been made by a single human anywhere in the churchyard. She remembers the snow angels she made years ago with her mother and pushing the kitchen chair along the frozen river in her black-booted skates.

The cold mixes with the martini in her guts and as she nears the apartment building she looks up at her living room window and wonders how other people see her, *if* they see her, when they spy her sitting on her promontory, overseeing the yard. She trundles across the street and finds Pistachio, plump and purring, lying on the first-floor landing of the apartment building, as if he has been waiting.

Effie runs up the first few steps, picks up the cat with her mittened hands and kisses him on the mouth. "Meow, Puss," she says. "Give me kisses." Pistachio's tail curls into the soft shape of a J. She hugs him close and burrows her face into his woolly neck. "Brrr, Pussums. It's cold." Tucking him under her lapel she fumbles for her keys. "Your mother doesn't take very good care of you, does she? You're coming in with me." Pistachio licks Effie's hand, flicking his sandpapery tongue.

Effie scoots down the hallway of her apartment and into the bedroom, shaking her coat and mittens and hat onto the floor, marvelling at Pistachio, who has jumped like a lithe acrobat onto her bed, spring-boarding from the crook of her arm. She yanks the elastic out of her hair and tosses her shoe bag onto the bed.

"I'm hungry, Kitty. Let's you and me bake." Pistachio meows twice, which Effie takes as approval. "And how about a little milk for Pussums while I pour myself a tiny glass of wine?" Effie hauls down a glass, a bowl, a box of Rice Krispies and a bag of stale marshmallows from the cupboard, pausing to admire the shelf paper of yellow moons.

"Shit, cat. There isn't any vanilla. I wonder if I have butter." Pistachio hops up onto the aluminum table and cocks his head toward Effie, his eyes glowing like emeralds in the refrigerator light. Overhead, the sound of stomping feet alert her to Rutherford. "Pistachio, what do you think of that old woman up there?" Effie nuzzles her face into the cat. "She's a cow, isn't she?"

Standing in her Christmas outfit in the moonlit kitchen, Effie stirs the sticky cereal on the stove singing...*for you and I have a guardian angel on high with nothing to do.* When she arrives at the end of the lyric—*and to give to me love forever true*—Garfield intrudes into the melody. She pictures him sitting on a leather couch next to an emotionally mature black woman, a mohair blanket trailing casually across the back of the sofa, the two lovers ardent in front of the hearth, the taste of rum and mango juice lingering on their full and sumptuous lips. "Love forever true my ass."

From behind, Effie hears a loud knock.

"You Who!" Mildred Rutherford wrenches open the back door and bounds into Effie's apartment. "Would you care to join us for some Christmas cheer, Effie? I'm having a little holiday party."

Pistachio slips between the two women and dashes upstairs.

Effie glares after him and considers the invitation.

CHAPTER 17

Tommy Murphy spins around on an orange vinyl stool, waiting for a hot hamburger platter.

"Doesn't all that spinning make you dizzy?" Jimmy Fitzgerald tugs at his collar.

"Nothing makes me dizzy, not even the Tilt-A-Whirl." Tommy skids his tennis sneakers on the floor and stops rotating. He checks out the policeman in the mirror that covers the long wall behind the counter. "Why are you buying me lunch?"

Jimmy grips his belt buckle with both hands and sits up tall. "Why aren't *you* at the Christmas party? And where the hell are your boots? There must be three feet of snow on the ground."

"Can't afford 'em." Tommy shrugs. "What about you? You always got your sunglasses on, even in this shitty weather."

"Does your father know you swear?" He itches for a cigarette but has promised his wife he would try to quit for at least twenty-eight days. After twenty-eight days it's a habit, she'd said.

"My father's busy. He has more important things to do than worry about my mouth, or my feet."

Behind the counter, soap rings up to his elbows, a middle-aged man dries water glasses with a grimy rag.

"So, what do you think of that new teacher, Miss Cambridge?"

Tommy spins around again. "She's a real douche bag. Stiff as a hunk of peanut brittle. Thinks she knows everything, too. Did you know that her cousin is my girlfriend?" He looks at Jimmy in the mirror. "Why do you want to know about her?"

"You know teachers, Tommy. God's gift to the world." Jimmy points to a waitress carrying two steaming plates. "Hey look—here comes our grub."

The waitress sets their meals on the counter and Jimmy claps Tommy on the back.

"Dig in!"

Tommy attacks his dinner ferociously.

"So what does your dad do for a living?"

Tommy replies between bites of undercooked carrot and hunks of juicy meat, gravy dribbling down his chin. "My dad's been at the same job for near on twenty-five years. They say tradesmen make a lot of money but it isn't true."

"Do you have any plans after graduation?"

"If I graduate at all, you mean. What with teachers like Miss Cambridge and John MacDonald there isn't much hope of those assholes letting me pass."

"What would you like for Christmas?"

"Me? I guess if I could have one, what I really want is a Yankees baseball hat."

"How long has your mother been sick?"

Tommy doesn't answer. Instead, they sit silently through the rest of the meal.

When Jimmy stands up to pay the bill, he leans toward Tommy. "Would you like to come with me on Saturday night to a hockey game out at the arena? My buddy cancelled on me." He dumps some change on the countertop. "I have an extra ticket."

"I'll have to get the okay from my dad first but I'd really like to." Tommy pauses. "I've never done that before." He catches his reflection in the mirror and knuckles his chin hard to remove the gravy.

Over at Minegoo, the end of the year party is in full swing. One of the senior students has taken over as DJ and the Christmas carols have been replaced by Cyndi Lauper. Donnie has broken the ice by asking Martha to dance, and John has followed suit with Virginia. The girls giggle and twitch, Martha hauling on her pantyhose and Virginia sweeping her bangs away from her forehead. Danny Callbeck grabs Gemma Weekes by the waist and swings her out to the centre of the floor, the teacher braying wildly, smacking her hands together and squeezing her eyes shut.

Standing alone near the auditorium stage and holding a broken cookie, Effie sizes up the students and teachers and admires the Christmas garlands that are fastened with duct tape to the cement walls. She speculates whether John will ask her to dance or if she has ruined her chances with him. Still, he seems to be having such a good time. When the song changes to *Walk Like an Egyptian*, John raises his hands flatly like Nefertiti and Effie laughs out loud.

Callbeck and Dalziel are leading a dozen or so students along the basketball sideline, dancing in tandem, knees bent, hands front to back, eyes moving side to side. Martha follows in the rear. She reminds Effie of a young Margaret Mead, a cultural anthropologist finally having some fun.

Effie looks back at John and sees him peering at her overtop of Virginia's head. He smiles, and the moment she smiles back she sees Donnie lean over and say something into John's ear. Then, walking like an Egyptian, Donnie crosses the gymnasium floor, his eyes locked on Effie.

CHAPTER 18

Effie can't believe she accepted an invitation from Mildred Rutherford for breakfast, on Christmas morning of all days, and has little memory of having been in Rutherford's apartment the night of the staff party. She had been drunk when the offer was made and now here she is sitting in the nurse's front living room in a high-back red leather chair feeling, despite her height, like Alice in Wonderland. She fiddles with her hair, brushing it back from her face with her hands, and waits for her host to retrieve tea from the kitchen.

Rutherford bustles down the hallway toward Effie, wearing square-toed shoes, a baggy beige dress splashed with brown roses, and support hose that wrinkles at her knees. She ferries a tray laid out with two china cups and saucers, two earthenware teapots, a covered butter dish, a steel-handled butter knife, two glass dessert plates and a bowl of scones. "I begin every day with a cup of hot tea and a stick of cinnamon. Good for the blood pressure."

Effie's hostess plants herself in a matching high-back chair. Thrusting a plate toward her guest, the older woman looks forlornly at the tray. "Goddamn it! I forgot the napkins."

As Rutherford trots away, Effie removes the lid of her teapot and pokes at the floating bark. Sighing, then shifting her focus, she strains to read the type on the framed diplomas that hang on the opposite wall: *School of Nursing, Dalhousie University. Certificate of Mental Hygiene, McGill University.* A heart-shaped display of photographs surround portraits of graduate nurses, white and sturdy and starched, and to their left a row of medical journals, their spines an assortment of sombre widths and colours. Effie knows some of the titles from time spent researching symptoms—abdominal aneurysms; brainstem abnormalities; ophthalmic injury; skeletal trauma; thymus gland function.

Below these a voluminous and pristine collection of psychology and psychiatry textbooks—Sigmund Freud, Carl Jung, and Johnson and Johnson—many of the other names too faded to read. Dozens of Harlequin Romance novels, immediately recognizable by their size and lurid colours, line the bottom shelf.

In front of a white leather sofa, a company of Royal Doulton figurines sway and swoop on a squat mahogany coffee table, pirouetting around a single hardcover book. The painted flower on its cover gapes tumid and red, a vivid botanic vagina. Not a cranberry wreath or tinkling silver bell to be seen. No little choirboy candle.

Mildred Rutherford tramps back into the living room, the floorboards creaking heavily beneath her. "Do you like my table? Hospital sale." She passes Effie a napkin and places another on the arm of her chair.

"Are those sales open only to staff?" Effie lays the napkin across her lap.

"Staff first, public second."

"As it should be, I suppose. My mother said that people devour life when they should savour it."

Mildred Rutherford nods curtly. "Was your mother some kind of guru?"

"You mean my aunt hasn't told you about my mother?"

"Trying to get information from your aunt is like picking thistles from an Ecuadorian rose. She has enough to say about Jesus, but she is terrible stingy on the subject of family life." Rutherford points to one of her figurines. "I gave her one of those once, for her birthday." She squints, calculating. "At least I think it was for her birthday. Who can remember anything at my age?"

"My mother had many jobs, but she wasn't a guru." Effie pours milk from a tiny porcelain cow pitcher into her tea. "Everyone is a philosopher, don't you think?

"Bullshit. Philosophy's dead." Mildred Rutherford slams down her teacup and attacks her scone. "Nowadays it's all about the libido. Libido *this*, libido *that*." She clunks the butter knife down on her tray. "What do you make of it?"

Effie's face burns.

Miss Rutherford points at Effie's cheeks. "Are you *hot*? You look like a pomegranate."

"I—well, I don't have any opinions about libido," Effie says. "I'm not even sure what it is." Effie lies, imagining Mildred Rutherford in bed alone at night with her Harlequin surgeons and her libido.

"And *you* teach school. Good God Almighty."

"English, Ms. Rutherford. Not sex education."

"*Romeo and Juliet? Lolita? Lady Chatterley's Lover?* Anyway, it's all about the *wanting* of it." Mildred Rutherford screws up her face. "Reduced desire, they say, for portly people." She licks her finger and uses it to pick up crumbs from her plate. "That's *hog-wash*."

"What got you into nursing, Ms. Rutherford?" Effie takes a tentative bite of her biscuit.

"Freud." The older woman's eyes wander over to her book-shelf. "I was reading about steam engines and cathexis and I saw my life as a Cyclopean journey on a train and I knew that I had to dedicate my life to the greater good of man—and Freud."

Effie wonders if this is the longest sentence Mildred Rutherford has ever uttered. She doesn't even try to wrestle with the word *cathexis*. She knows that Rutherford's libido remains close to the surface. "Then why not work in psychiatry?"

"Jesus Christ. There's no full steam ahead in psychiatry." She offers Effie another scone.

Effie shakes her head no.

"Have you ever *met* a psychiatrist? None of them can *touch* him."

"My mother's, yes." Effie squares her shoulders.

"Your mother must have been an odd duck."

"She is nothing of the kind."

"*Is*? I thought you said she was dead. You're a mighty queer girl." Mildred Rutherford smiles, her face sinking like cake batter. "More tea?"

"No thank you. I am afraid I have to go."

"Big plans for the day? You've hardly touched your scone."

"Not exactly big, but dinner, yes."

"With Shirley and the gang?" Rutherford asks, skeptical.

"With friends." Setting her napkin on the tray, Effie stands up and offers her hand. The word *friends* rushes through her like hot wine.

The older woman gapes at Effie's hand. "What's that for? A tip?" She rumbles with laughter and stands up, her napkin caught inside her belt. "I'm baffled that you wouldn't be with family today."

"They're going somewhere out of town for dinner. I think they said Dalvey?"

"Dalvey? *Today*?" She holds the door open for Effie to leave. "Well, you should know."

CHAPTER 19

Except for the trees and the patterns of footprints, the church-yard is empty. Evidence of a Fox and Goose game just beyond the path pulls Effie back into childhood—she and Kathleen Raminsky chasing one another in a field of glistening snow that has broken open to expose soft white powder beneath their boots; cloudy afternoons skating on the Credit River, spinning backward in circles or grabbing a friend's waist in a game of Crack the Whip. At the end of the afternoon, slouched over Sloppy Joes and hot chocolate, Effie listening to stories about curling on Larder River in Northern Ontario after the war, her mother's eyes lighting up as she stands soberly at the sink with a tea towel in her hand.

Effie shivers and swerves away from the path. She crosses Richmond Street, nodding at the porcelain dolls in the window of the Morning Dove. A sign tacked on the door reads *Closed for the Holidays*. "Merry Christmas, dolls," she says, and holding a bulky bag of presents tightly to her chest she turns the corner onto Queen Street and quickens her step.

She can feel the silence in the air, not even the sound of a Seaman's beverage truck rolling up the spindly road, everything shut down for at least two days. The tottering houses seem frozen in time, and she wonders if Gordy will be waiting in the upstairs window.

Donnie said that John would be coming by later, after an afternoon dinner with his folks. *Folks.* A funny word. Murderers and thieves are never called folks. Neither are alcoholics. Folks are sociable people who wear knitted sweaters with guns and ducks sewn into them. *Ducks.* Oh God. She hopes Mrs. Fitzgerald isn't serving duck. The last time—the only time—Effie had eaten duck she had thrown up, also on Christmas Day. The packages hurt against her chest. She glances at the empty upstairs window, her heart beating through her coat.

Gordy answers the door. "Hey there, Effie! We've been waitin' all day for you!" He reaches for her bundle. "Come on in!" Effie dodges a jumble of boots that have been thrown about the front hall and are dripping water across the linoleum floor. Gordy pants ahead of her like an eager puppy, his hair toppling to one side. "Hey everybody—Effie's here!"

Ruth, dressed in casual black pants, a pinafore blouse and a long white apron, sets down a bowl of chocolates. "Dear girl, so happy ta-have-you." Effie catches the welcoming cadence and bites down on her lower lip. Abel Fitzgerald stretches back on the couch next to a boy Effie does not recognize. An older son perches on the arm of the sofa, while two more of the Fitzgerald boys are sprawled on the floor with a younger child, facing the television. Scrooge's sister, Fan, is speaking. "*I have come to bring you home, dear brother. To bring you home, home, home.*"

"How's that for synchronicity?" Donnie catapults out of the armchair and holds out his hand. "Merry Christmas, Effie." He pulls her to him, nudging her sideways toward an empty arm-chair. "We saved this seat for you," he says. "You can bask in the glow of me and the Christmas tree."

Effie stares at the room around her, each corner gleaming with red Christmas lights that have been strung up in bow for-mations, their centres tidy knots of coloured ribbon. On top of the piano, a miniature Santa Claus sits stuffed into a pocket-sized rocking chair, which spins on a silver platform. Beside Santa, a Lilliputian band of elves play real music on tiny drums and tam-bourines—*Marching to Pretoria* the current tune—none of the songs having anything to do with Christmas, which Effie finds particularly funny. Next to all of this, cardboard angels in ascend-ing height stand with open mouths, little hymn books resting calmly in their hands. Effie looks over at the tree, a string of pop-corn and cranberry winding haphazardly around the branches.

"We voted against tinsel."

Effie looks down at the pile of gifts on the floor and silently itemizes: one soccer ball, one football, one baseball bat, a dictionary, three interchangeable sets of gloves, one pair of skates, two books by Robert Heinlein (one of them *Red Planet*, a story Effie loved as a child), *The Joy of Cooking*, an Osterizer blender, a package of white dress shirts, a stack of gift boxes (lids closed), and one parcel wrapped in red reindeer paper.

Donnie stands behind Effie and lays his hand on her shoulder. "Effie, I would like you to meet Jeffrey and Donald, our junior cousins from up Alberton way. Their dad had a bit of an accident at work, so the boys have come to join us for dinner while my aunt is visiting him in hospital."

Effie turns to the boy who is sitting on the floor. "I hope your father is going to be all right."

"Oh yeth, he'll be okay." Jeffrey opens his mouth wide, exposing a gap between his front teeth. "He had a bit of a wrangle with one of hith workmaitht becauth of the hockey game. Thee?" The boy points to his mouth. "Ithz how I lotht *my* teeth."

"A workmate?" Effie smiles at him, hoping to make light of the episode.

"Playing hockey." He smiles at Effie, his face crinkling triumphantly. "My new oneth will be in after the holidayth." The orange cat, purring loudly, sidles up to the boy. The boy buries his face in the cat's fur.

Ruth picks up a plate from one of the side tables. "Here Effie, have a candy. We have jellybeans, humbugs, gingerbread men—"

"—and mussels and cockles, alive, alive oh!"

Abel hooks his thumbs under his suspenders. "Donnie never gets tired of repeating himself, Effie."

"Mom, come sit down with us and talk to Effie while I get her a drink." Donnie heads for the kitchen, calling back over his shoulder, "Eggnog, Effie?"

"When the movie is over, I want you to put on some Christmas music." Ruth appeals to Gordy, who is sitting on the arm of the couch. "I love the Mormon Tabernacle choir." She sits down next to her husband.

Abel snaps his suspenders. "Donnie'll repeat himself until after he's dead."

"Ignore him, Effie," Donnie yells out from the kitchen. "I forget. Do you like rum?"

"And he'll keep on repeating," says Abel. "Like cucumbers."

"Yeah, we'll see how much you miss me after I've taken that job in Halifax." Donnie hands Effie a cinnamon-rimmed mug.

"Ah, they won't want to keep you over there once they know how smelly your stinky socks are," Gordy laughs.

"What job, Donnie?"

"Hey! My socks don't smell!"

"Thanks to Mom, they don't. If it were up to you—"

"What job, Donnie?"

"Oh, likely nothing. I have a friend who teaches over in Halifax and they're opening up a senior position in their science department next year. One of their high schools is expanding." Donnie twirls the ends of his moustache. "It might be fun to try somewhere different."

"I thought you *loved* living here."

"*What's love got to do with it?*" Donnie sings in broken falsetto.

"See what I mean, Effie?" Abel winks. "Not an original thought in his head."

Donnie smiles at his father then looks over at Effie. "I'm trying to talk John into coming with me."

Ruth catches the look of alarm that crosses Effie's face. "John'll never leave the island, not as long as his parents are alive."

"Hell, it was *his* idea." Donnie swallows a chocolate whole. "You could come with us, Effie. If it even happens. Which I doubt."

Scrooge's ashen face fills the television screen, his eyes huge and terrified.

Ruth glances at the clock on the wall. "Dinner's in about an hour. Are we going to do gifts first?"

"Oh yes, I brought gifts." Effie loosens the knot in her bag, hating the false buoyancy in her voice.

"No dear, I meant our gift for you."

"Gifts!" Gordy high-fives the air. "Effie brought gifts!"

"Please, Mrs. Fitzgerald, could I give you your gifts first?" The idea of opening a present makes Effie feel sick to her stomach. She plucks an item from out of the bag, reads the tag, and hands it to Abel.

Everyone watches quietly as Mr. Fitzgerald holds up a pair of red suspenders. Smiling, he unhooks the clasps on the pair he is wearing and fastens the new ones to the waistband of his pants, slipping the straps up over his shoulders. "Thank you, young woman." He grins at the boys on the floor. "What do you think, Jeffrey? Am I handsome?" For a moment Abel reminds Effie of John.

"Oh yeth, Uncle Abel—they look thuper!"

Ruth gently tears the paper off a flat, square package. "It's a record! Oh Effie, I *love* records." She wipes her forehead with the back of her sleeve.

"I wish I had got something more Christmassy," Effie apologizes.

"Marty Robbins! Look Donnie, it's *Marty Robbins No. 1 Cowboy*. Abel, tell Effie how much I love Marty Robbins."

"My wife was the only woman in her high school class who knew all the words to *El Paso*."

Ruth hands the album to her husband and walks over to Effie. Crouching down, she wraps her arms tightly around the younger woman. "Thank you, my dear girl," she whispers. She embraces Effie a few seconds longer and then stands up and laughs. "I hope I didn't get turkey grease all over your pretty sweater." Ruth kneels down to retrieve Effie's gift from under the tree. Effie collects herself and holds out her hands.

Whisking off the paper and crumpling the tissue, Effie gasps, John momentarily evaporating from her thoughts. A small glass box, bevelled on top and plain at the sides, reveals a delicate purple pansy inside its lid.

"It's for your jewelry, dear."

"It's beautiful." Effie turns the box over in her hands. "It reminds me of Narnia," she says. "Like something Mrs. Beaver would have had on her mantel." The instant Effie said *Mrs. Beaver* she regrets it. "You know—the children's books by C.S. Lewis. Like *The Four Loves* that you gave me." She scrambles to make sense, to sound like an adult.

"I am so glad you like it, dear. It reminded me of you."

"Thank you." Effie inhales through her nose, nervous and proud. "You give the best gifts."

"I'll go check on dinner," Ruth says. "I hope you're all hungry."

"Mom—Effie has more."

"Oh goodness, Donnie, you're right. I'm so sorry, Effie." Ruth laughs weakly. "You see? I got my lovely surprise and who cares about anyone else?"

Effie hands Donnie a gift, his name prettily written on a Santa Claus sticker. She waits and watches as he unwraps it, his eyes lit up like a firefly.

"Oh Mum—look at this. Effie, thank you so much." Donnie holds out a copy of Stephen Hawkins' *A Brief History of Time*. "I thought I'd have to go to the mainland to get this. Wow." He makes a play at kissing her cheek but she waves him away.

"Gordy," Effie says, "Would you please come over here?" Effie passes Gordy a large rectangular-shaped gift. "Something for all of you boys."

Gordy transfers the package carefully to his cousin. "Here Donald, you open it. You're the guest."

"Tho am I!" Jeffrey shoots back.

"Jeffrey," Gordy laughs. "You've already said enough."

"Oh wow! It's Risk!"

"Have you ever played it?"

"No, but it's about war so I know that I love it."

"Let's set it up before dinner. Donnie, can you help us?"

Effie stands up and follows Ruth into the kitchen. Abel puts his feet up on the footstool and watches his sons and nephews lay out the game on the card table, Scrooge long forgotten.

"Effie," Ruth says, "Donnie told me you are allergic to turkey, but I made a ham, too. Do you like ham, Effie? The cloves and pineapple needn't be permanent, just in case. You can hand me that sifter if you like, and help me with the biscuits." Ruth kneads a glob of dough on the counter.

"You see that window, Effie? When Donnie was little I bathed him in the sink—I did that with all the kids. He used to look up at the sky and ask me if I could get him some clouds in his bucket. More than anything I wanted to be able to get him whatever he wanted, but that isn't always possible, is it?" Ruth begins cutting out circles in the dough with a flour-rimmed glass. "He's been a dreamer his whole life and when he gets his heart set on something it's just awful for me when he can't have it. Mind you, he only makes sound choices. How many people can we say that about, Effie?"

"How would you feel about him going to Halifax?"

"If it's what he wants, there has to be a good reason for it. I think he wants it more for John, which is reason all by itself. He and John have been best friends since they were boys." She places the uncooked biscuits on a cookie sheet. "You know, I married the *good* Fitzgerald, and thank God the kids have got their father's inclinations. Them poor kids in there—you can't imagine loving them more than you do, but then they grow up and turn into someone like my nephew James and you wonder where all that dearness went. A person could cry."

"Why do you think John wants to go to Halifax?"

Ruth stretches a tea towel over the remaining dough. "Well Effie, some of John's troubles would be better off left on the island, that's for certain. He's a good man, but I worry about him." She brushes the flour off of the counter, into the sink. "I think you like him, don't you, Effie?"

"I think he likes Mary."

"I think Donnie likes you. And, if you want a mother's opinion, you couldn't do better. Although I know there's a lot of talk about chemistry these days and I grant that counts for something. It certainly did in my case." She turns on the faucet, setting the dirty baking dishes into the sink.

Effie smiles. "Do you think that's why Donnie teaches it?"

"Teaches what, dear?"

"Chemistry."

Ruth laughs and sets the oven timer at ten minutes. She reaches for the dish soap then turns to look at Effie. "But I would like you no matter who you cared for." The older woman kisses Effie's cheek then turns back to the sink.

"Why? Why would you like me?"

"Why *do* I like you, you mean. I like you for many reasons." She hands Effie a tea towel. "You see this sink here full of bubbles? That's what you're like—a sweetheart and a mystery and working hard to get things right." Ruth brushes back Effie's bangs. "Your mother must have been so proud of you."

"Mom! Time to do the table?"

Ruth shakes water from her hands. "Effie, follow me."

Jeffrey and Donald push the armchairs and sofa toward the far wall while Gordy wheels the sewing machine in front of the television set. Donnie and John shift the dining room table and Abel ducks into the bedroom to retrieve a wooden insert that is a third as long as the table itself. Ruth pulls a crocheted tablecloth down from the shelf and calls out names as she sets down the dinner plates.

"Jeffrey, bring your auntie the silverware from the box over there on the piano seat. Donnie, could you light the candles, but mind that the cats are out of the way. We don't want another fire like last year." Ruth lays the silverware around the table. "Now let me go do up the potatoes and grab the other batch of biscuits, and you boys be ready to help when I call."

At Ruth's bidding, the family parade into the kitchen and return carrying plates and bowls and baskets of turkey and ham, carrots and peas and potatoes, dressing and mushroom gravy, biscuits and butter. "Someone grab the wine please—there's a white and a red under the sink. Look at me! I've gone and forgotten the V8 again."

"Mom, no one wants V8."

Ruth looks solemnly at her husband. "Abel."

"Ruth, no one wants V8." He glances around the table. "Effie? Boys?"

"Wine, pleath." Jeffrey raises his empty glass.

"Now, hold your cups and forks boys, we have to say grace." Abel bows his head. *"Bless this food to our use, O Lord, and us to Thy loving service. In Christ's name, Amen."*

"Donnie, put on Marty Robbins, would you? No one will mind if we pass up the choir this year."

Effie and Ruth stand in the kitchen washing and drying dishes while Abel hunches on a stool next to the counter, sliding silverware back into its velvet-lined chest. Six boys cram around the table in the living room, facing the game of Risk.

"Donnie, what's the difference between cavalry and Calvary?"

"About four hundred horses and a cross."

"And how do we read these numbers? I know that the X is ten but does the V mean fifty?"

"Does it matter what colour we take?"

"Green matches my eyes."

"More like your *snot*."

"Nice Christmas talk, boys," John interrupts. "Am I welcome, or is this going to devolve into another holiday battle?"

"Oh, that's funny! We're playing Risk. Effie gave it to us."

"So Effie's here, then?" John steps back into the porch and tosses his hat onto a hook. "Great stuff." He walks into the living room and nods toward the stereo. "What happened to the choir?"

"This sure is a funny looking map. See, John? This is supposed to be Canada—Alberta, Ontario, and Quebec."

Effie strolls out of the kitchen followed by Ruth.

"I think they'd agree with that up in Ottawa, don't you Donnie?" John turns and faces Effie. "A Merry Christmas to you," he says, smiling.

Professor Bhaer.

He lifts a gingerbread man from a wreathed plate. "Hello Ruth! Merry Christmas. Give me a big hug."

Effie wonders if he has a present for her. A pretty scarf or a piece of jewellery. A pair of inflatable boot inserts.

"John, you're going to have to help the boys understand the game." Donnie holds out a chair for his friend. "Look boys, John wore his Santa socks. Wow, those are blinding!"

"That's so you can see that I'm well-red." John pulls his chair up to the table. "Okay. Choose one person over the age of fifteen to read the rules, because when you're fifteen these things are easier to understand. You older boys leave out anything that is too hard. The rules were written by Omar Bradley, and he was a General in the Second World War. It was his business to conquer territories. How are you supposed to comprehend the complicated details of war strategy?" His voice is warm, Effie thinks. Avuncular.

"But Effie gave us this game. It's a *present*."

"Of course." John looks quickly over his shoulder at Effie. "I wasn't insulting Effie. I was plainly stating a fact. Risk is a wonderful and exhaustive game, but one that takes patience and practice."

"And Rithk!"

"What's exhaustive mean?"

Donnie calls across from the couch. "He means it tires him." John glides his hand over the surface of the board.

Effie watches him.

"Conquering the world is busy work. What do you say, Gordy?"

Jeffrey grabs a handful of artillery pieces from the table. "Wath Thanta good to you, John?"

"Why yes, Jeffrey. Santa brought me a new camera."

All the boys look up. "Wow! A camera?"

Effie remembers that day they walked to the framing store. The first day of school. She had fallen and he had cleaned blood from her knee with his finger.

"A real spiffy camera." John smiles, and begins sorting out cards and game pieces and dice. "Now, there's a beginning for you, and if you need more help, just ask."

Abel emerges from the kitchen and excuses himself for the night. He walks over and kisses the tops of his sons' and nephews' heads, one by one. "Merry Christmas boys. And don't fight." He winks at John, steps over the armchair and stops in front of Effie. "You, my dear, are a pleasure." He snaps his suspenders again. "I hope you will continue to come as often as you can stand us." He leans over and picks up her hand from her lap.

"Thank you, Mr. Fitzgerald."

"You are most welcome." He straightens up and inclines his head toward his wife. "And woman, don't stay up all night and be hounded by these boys."

"Hey!"

"Not you boys, Gordy. These older ones on the sofa." Abel ambles out of the room.

"So how was your Christmas?" Effie asks John.

"The usual," John says. "And the unusual. I saw Rutherford sitting in her window when we were walking to church. She had her arms crossed like Mary, Queen of Scots trapped in the Tower of London." He puts his hand up to the side of his face and pushes in at his temple. "The sermon was oddly Calvinist—"

"Did you stop by and see Mary?" Donnie sends Effie a sidelong glance.

"No, she came by to see the folks last night on her way home."

Folks.

"I invited her tonight but she won't be back in town until next weekend."

Just in time for New Year's.

"Vacation?" Effie asks.

"Friends in Halifax."

"Halifax is quite the hub it seems." Effie runs her fingers along the stem of her wineglass. "Donnie was saying that you might move there to teach."

"You can come with us," Donnie breaks in. "Come on, Effie. You know you want to."

"That's *my* artillery." Gordy's voice rises above his opponents.

Ruth offers the bowl of chocolates to John.

"Egypt is *mine*!"

"You could come and teach English, Effie—real mainland English. Roight?"

"Look out! Hith army ith invading!"

"Terrible thing about her father. He was a lovely man."

"All of her family are lovely."

"Egypt isn't such a big loss."

John reaches for the wine bottle. "More wine, Ruth?"

"No thanks, John." Ruth tosses a candy back at her eldest son. "Goodnight all. I'm off to join my husband."

"Ere I was Abel."

Ruth smiles and waggles her apron strings at John as she walks past.

Donnie glances at his watch. "Hey boys, isn't it time for your hockey game?"

"You guys comin' skating with us?" Gordy nudges his older brother. "*You* got new skates, lucky dog."

"Next time," Donnie says. "Promise."

"You too, Effie?" Gordy bounds to the side of Effie's chair where he rocks back and forth on the balls of his feet.

"Effie too," Donnie says. "Now, you have to be back home no later than midnight—right? Roight! So let's get a move on! And Jeffrey, watch your teeth."

Jeffrey lets out a gurgling laugh. "I haven't got any teeth!"

CHAPTER 20

Mary sits on the steps that lead up to the first-floor landing. She has been waiting for Effie to arrive home and has already scooched over three times to accommodate an agitated Mildred Rutherford, who keeps returning to her apartment for forgotten items. Rutherford finally opens the front door, holding it wide with one hand and fluffing her scarf with the other. A breath of new snow flies in and lies on the hallway floor. Mary shivers and hugs herself, watching the nurse's triangulated frame disappear across the churchyard.

As Rutherford rounds the corner from Richmond onto Lower Queen Street, preoccupied with her ladies' group luncheon at the waterfront hotel, Effie emerges from Donnelly's Drug Store on Upper Queen carrying a silver bag that contains one compact mirror and a tube of Midnight Moon lipstick.

She accelerates past the shops on Grafton Street, the store windows featuring catchy cardboard placards—*End of Year Sale! Boxing Day Blowout!* She crosses Prince Street, sidestepping the patches of ice, reciting, *two roads diverged in a wood and I, I took the one less traveled by, and that has made all the difference.* As she reaches for the heavy glass door to the apartment building her feet slide out from under her.

Reeling backward, she grabs again for the door and misses, her body swaying momentarily before landing in a cold pile of slush. The door drifts shut. She sits there, mouth open, knees apart, the inside seam of her leotards exposed to Mary, who Effie is surprised to see hurtling down the stairs to help.

Effie clambers up, bucking the dirty snow and water from the back of her coat. She picks up her purchases, the tube of Midnight Moon poking through the silver lips of her gift bag.

Mary holds the door open for Effie. "Are you all right?" She brushes the back of Effie's coat with her bare hand.

Effie starts up the stairs and Mary follows.

Effie keeps her head down as she turns the key in her apartment door.

"May I come in, Effie? I want to talk to you." "

"Could I *please* have ten minutes to get tidied up? Do you *see* the state I'm in?"

"Do you promise to answer when I knock?"

Keeping her back to Mary, Effie steps into her apartment.

"Ten minutes!" Mary calls from the outer hall.

"Screw you," Effie says under her breath.

When Mary returns, Effie answers the door with more equilibrium. "Won't you come in? I'll put the kettle on for tea." Something about Mary's expression reminds Effie of Kathleen Raminský. Puppet faces.

Mary sits down in the corduroy armchair. "Effie, I think this dance between us has gone on long enough." She looks at Effie, who is standing behind the rocking chair. "I really like you." She wonders why Effie won't sit down. "Our friendship started out so auspiciously." *Auspicioussss-ly.* "It's not easy to make friends on the island, even for Islanders. Everyone's either related or too related or wants to be related, and there's a lot—I mean a *lot*—of gossip." *Goss-ssip.* "If you thrive, people resent you, and if you fall down, people deride you. There's no middle ground, especially for people who come from away. Remember that joke about Nancy Reagan—*ladies against women*? The island's a lot like that."

"You seem pretty fortunate to me."

"Do I? Did John or Donnie tell you about my brother Jackie?"

"Why would they tell me about your brother? I didn't even know you had a brother."

"Because they love me. Because they're kind."

Effie nudges the back of the rocking chair.

"When he was four, my brother Jackie was playing in the front yard with his toys."

Effie relaxes her shoulders, hoping to appear indifferent in preparation for what she knows is coming. She pushes the rocker a little harder and feels hot in the room's bright sunlight.

"His favourite was a yellow Tonka truck. He spent so much time playing with it my father thought he was autistic." Mary lets out a laugh. "My father, of course, said autistic the way someone else might say genius, as if Jackie were Einstein or Harry Houdini." A vein bulges angrily beneath Mary's smooth skin. "And who knows?" she says. "He might have been."

Effie's arms itch under the prickly heat of her sweater.

"My mother was standing at the living room window. She watched a truck come around the bend in the highway. Jackie was on his knees in the yard and he let go of his Tonka, thrilled to see another big rig coming down the road." Mary grasps the arm of her chair. "That was the last thing he saw." Her voice sounds far off, as if she is speaking through a faulty telephone line.

Effie walks around to the front of the rocker and sits down. "How old were you?" She takes off her sweater and lays it over the arm of the chair.

"Twelve. My dad got sick a year later, and with Jackie gone—he was the best little kid."

"How awful." Effie wipes her nose with the back of her hand. "I'm so sorry."

"I know you are—that you would be. That's not why I told you." Mary extracts a tissue from her shirt pocket and hands it to Effie.

"You're so different from me," Effie says. She looks at Mary's hair hanging down over her shoulders in rectangular sheets. Summer curtains. "You're beautiful and everybody loves you."

"I thank you for the compliment, Effie, but without my brother what does it matter? And who is everybody?"

"Donnie." Effie stares at her knees. "John."

"Well, yes, they love me. As friends. I have known them forever. They don't love me in any other way, if that's what you mean."

"But you and John—"

"John is not in love with me Effie, I can promise you that. And neither he nor Donnie is my type." She laughs. "But Donnie clearly has his heart set on you."

"I can't imagine why John wouldn't be your type." Effie arches her eyebrows, eyes widening, lips parted. The sun shines down upon her like a benediction, a promise of better things to come.

"In an alternate universe, perhaps, but not in this one. We are good friends, which I think is better. Friendships tend to last longer than romance."

"Donnie's not my type either," Effie says. "To say *type* is so—I don't know—wrong. He just isn't serious enough for me."

"I don't want to convince you, Effie, but Donnie hides behind his humour. Underneath it he's thoughtful and loyal."

"Then why isn't he your type?"

"I have a thing for adventurers. Mountain climbers. White water rafters. Men who sail to faraway places."

Effie laughs. "Sir Walter Scott?"

"Sir Walter Raleigh."

"So you prefer men in tights?"

"Only on stage. I do like men with moustaches, though. Sir Walter Raleigh had a very prominent one."

"Donnie has a prominent moustache." Effie springs from the rocking chair, snagging her leotards on a floorboard. "Would you like a glass of wine instead of tea?"

"The most stirring adventure Donnie ever had was going to Moncton to buy a lamp," Mary laughs. "Did you say wine? Oh, yes please. We could get a little head start." She trails Effie to the back of the apartment. "He turned green on the ferry coming back and the waves were no higher than my hand. I love Donnie, but he's no adventurer. A test tube maybe, but not a rocket."

Mary halts in the kitchen in front of Effie's glass cabinet. "Oh, look at all your salt and pepper shakers. I *love* the Dutch girl and boy. Oh, her little hat's chipped." She points at a lower shelf. "Is that Hansel and Gretel?" She points again. "Oh look—Jack and Jill. Where did you get these? They're adorable."

"Promise not to say anything to anyone? I feel a bit juvenile." Effie opens the fridge and extracts a bottle of wine. "They were my mother's."

"I'll share a small secret with you in return," Mary says. "I know all the words to John Denver's *Sunshine*."

Effie pauses, holding the corkscrew in mid-air. "I can top that one, no problem. I saw the movie. Twice."

"Couldn't have been any worse than *The Other Side of the Mountain*."

"Oh God, I wanted her to keep going right over that hill, didn't you?" Effie grins. "All right. I cried the first time I saw it."

Mary holds out her glass. "And the second time?"

"Same as the third time." Effie laughs and slops wine over the side of Mary's glass.

Mary sets her wineglass down on the table and sits. "I love this kitchen. Everything's so compact but you still have room to sit down. I wish I had an ironing board that came out of the wall. You have so many neat fixtures."

Effie laughs. "Actually, I've got my mother's fixtures and my father's features." She sits down across from Mary. "Have you ever contemplated leaving?"

"The apartment?"

"No, the island."

"Me? Leave PEI? Temporarily, maybe. Permanently? Never. For all my complaints and criticisms, I love it here."

"Okay. Name ten reasons why not."

"Are you *sure* you're not interested in Donnie? He loves these sorts of games." Mary smiles. "First off, I'm a realist. I know all about greener grass, yet nothing else appeals to me."

"But how do you know if you've never lived anywhere else?"

"If you think we've got problems here, and of course we do, have you ever been to Ottawa? John says it's parochial. A cold, cold city. He says they have far too much money up there. A beautiful city, but their entire focus is status." *Stat-usss*.

"Toronto's not like that at all. The rest of the country hates us, but at least the people are friendly." Effie smiles. "Mostly because they come from somewhere else."

"I can name ten things, easy." Mary taps her fingers on the table. "Greenwich Beach. Private. Gorgeous sand." She looks up at the box of Band-Aids on the top of the fridge. "Waves that come in for miles." Her eyes follow the line of yellow-painted cupboards to the curtainless window. "Panoramic." She smiles. "It's incomparable. And there's North Rustico—deep sea fishing, coming in to shore at sunset, seagulls chasing boats looking for food, and after you dock the best maple walnut fudge in the world."

"I'm allergic to walnuts."

"The lobster suppers are a standout, too, and I love to pick out the families. The Howatts from Tryon, just for one example. They all have the same friendly, almond-shaped eyes. You could be in Timbuktu but you'd know a Howatt anywhere."

"Oh yes. Like me and my Uncle Bill. We come from the potato family. Several eyes per head."

"You're too hard on yourself, Effie. You have bewitching eyes and you've got skin like a baby's. Why are you smiling?"

"I love the way you pronounce your words. You hold down on your esses and your cee-aitches."

"I do?"

"Batten down the hatch-chez." Effie says. "I may be a potato head but my mother was gorgeous. When I was a little girl she had a beanbag ashtray." Effie forms her hands into a square. "On Friday nights before I went to bed she would slip a bean under my pillow. In the morning I'd find a surprise."

"What did she look like?"

"Nothing like me. High cheekbones, shapely lips. Full, but not too full. The tip of her nose turned up a little but it wasn't pug. People said she looked like Susan Hayward."

"How did she die?"

"From a brain tumour."

"Your mom had a brain tumour?"

"Susan Hayward had a brain tumour."

"I mean your mother."

"You mean my mother. Of course. She died in a rooming house in Toronto."

Mary slides her hand across the table toward Effie.

"My grandmother wasn't keen on smart girls so my mother was shipped off to an aunt and five cousins—all girls," Effie said.

"Here on the island?"

"No, Nova Scotia. On a pig farm. The cousins were all named after gemstones—Ruby, Pearl, Opal, Topaz—who would name a baby Topaz?—and Emerald."

"I wonder how it is that your grandmother could have imagined that would be a better life for your mother."

"Oh, she didn't. She thought it was a better life for herself. But my mother didn't say this. The stories came from Opal, who used to visit us in Port Credit. She smoked cigarettes out on the balcony and I bugged her for secrets."

"What happened to Opal?"

"She died when she was thirty-nine. My mother and I looked after her son Robert until he got sick with a retinoblastoma—a tumour behind his eye. He died before he was twelve."

"Oh my God, Effie. How terrible."

"I was just a kid myself, so it was much harder on my mother. Anyway, it's no worse than your Jackie, and in a way not as bad. Opal drank, just like my mother, although my mother didn't start seriously drinking until after Robert died. She got a lot worse after that." Effie eyes glisten like a child with a fever.

"You see, Effie? We have more in common than you suspected."

"All my mother ever said was, 'Darling, don't judge all lives by mine. There are many happy families and plenty of wonderful marriages.'"

"Do you believe that's true?"

"No."

"Effie, look at the Fitzgeralds, and my family. We love each other unconditionally. John has a good family, too. There's tension between John and his dad, but they love one another."

"What are you wearing tonight?" Effie asks suddenly. "That outfit you had on the night of the Christmas party was spectacular."

"My mother made that for me. Tonight I'm going casual. Jeans and a nice sweater. What about you?"

"It isn't dressy?"

"It's what John would call eclectic. I was invited by a friend who works over at CBC and he told me it's an odd mix. I don't know. I feel a little uneasy about the whole thing, but when he said I could bring anyone I wanted, I thought it would be an excellent way to ring in the New Year together."

"Safety in numbers?"

"I've been so worried that you and I wouldn't become friends." Mary places her empty wine glass in the sink. She stands with her back to Effie. "For all that I do love about Prince Edward Island, real friends are hard to come by. Was that true in Toronto?"

"I have no real friends in Toronto. The one friend I thought I had moved back home."

Mary turns around. "Don't you think it would be fun tonight if we could hook you up?"

"Me? What about you? Maybe Jacques Cousteau will be there. Or Wayne Gretsky. "

"His wife just had a baby," Mary says. "And Jacques Cousteau must be at least eighty years old."

"That would be more my luck." But the truth is Effie feels a surge of optimism and is glad she has chosen Midnight Moon.

CHAPTER 21

Effie shimmies into a jet-black Donna Karan bodysuit and skin-tight jeans, an outfit designed, as the magazine said, for the lean and the chic. She tries on her mother's silver bracelet, weighing its heft against a patina she worries John might find garish. She removes the bracelet and slips on a black onyx ring that Garfield gave her as a graduation gift, huffing on the silver band and rubbing it across her jeans. She tries to push away the memory of Garfield's tongue in her mouth and making love in the bathroom shower, Garfield singing low in her ear, *as time goes by, I realize just what you mean to me.*

Liar.

The snow continues to fall as Effie, Mary, Donnie and John head for the party in John's car. John glimpses over his shoulder at Mary. "Where are we going exactly?"

"Saint Claire Avenue, just off of Goodwill."

"I know where Saint Claire is, Mary. I mean the number."

Donnie pokes his friend in the shoulder. "What's eating you this time, cranky arse?"

"I got a call from that idiot cousin of yours. He was insinuating that I had something to do with missing money from the band travel funds. Randy Payne already told him that was impossible—the money went missing when I was in Halifax. Payne's wife and I were on the same ferry, for God's sake." John glimpses at Effie in the rearview mirror. "Even your Uncle Bill asked him to let it go." A chunk of ice slides down the windshield.

"You know how he is, John. He likes to torture you because you're nothing like him. He used to hold my head under water when we were kids and honest to Jesus I think he would have happily drowned me. He's got a screw loose. I don't know why you let him get to you. His real problem with you is that you're my friend and he's a jealous prick."

"He's a menace. I wish to hell he'd just leave me alone." John flicks the defroster to high. "He's not going to be at this party tonight, is he, because if he is—"

"As far as I know," Mary cuts in, "it's a bit of a mixed bag. But the party's at Dr. McCready's house and I can't imagine why Jimmy would be there."

"McCready's a gynecologist," Donnie explains. "Jimmy's more interested in manly activities, like porn films and strip bars."

"It seems so unusual, journalists and gynecologists at the same party."

John smiles. "The McCreadys know everyone on the island. One brother is an MP and another teaches at the university—and isn't there a sister?"

"Yes. She works at the newspaper but I don't know her very well. I was invited by a fellow over at the CBC."

"Small world," Effie says.

"Well, I hope everyone's wearing their Sunday best."

John motions to the bag beside him. "I didn't think I'd have much chance to use my new camera before summer, so I brought it tonight. You never know when your best friend might try on a lampshade." John grins at Donnie.

"Summer? What happens in summer?"

"Warm weather. A camera is cumbersome in the cold.

"Make a left here, John."

"Yes, I know where it is. I used to pick up my mother's birth control pills here when I was a teenager."

Mary whacks John on the shoulder. "Then why did you ask for the number?"

"Dr. McCready dispenses contraceptives?"

"He did then."

"I can just picture you peeling over on your Supercycle," Donnie says. "Why not go to the drugstore?"

"You know how Mom is. It was just easier for her if I got it from the doctor. It wasn't a big deal."

Effie scores the ice on the inside of the window with her fingernail, squinching at the brightly coloured houses capped with snow. Her breath comes back to her in crisp bites. You take the yin with the yang, she says to herself, the good with the bad. She suddenly remembers a story John told her a few weeks ago, about Gary Lowther lying under his front porch, his drunken father hollering his son's name.

Elizabeth McCready, Dr. McCready's gap-toothed niece and Professor McCready's daughter, opens the front door and grabs Donnie around the waist. "Hello you old devil!" She waltzes him past an over-stocked martini bar and on out of sight into the kitchen, his scarf dragging behind him. Effie hands her coat to someone she does not know and bee-lines to an empty space on the couch, pulling Mary down with her. John disappears into the kitchen and returns with three cold bottles of beer.

"I didn't think peppermint martinis would be your thing," he says, handing Mary and Effie two bottles of Olands. "Or am I projecting?" He shakes off his coat.

Mary licks condensation from the side of her bottle. "I have to find the bathroom, but I won't be long. Save my seat."

Lacing her fingers around her beer, Effie sits back and surveys the spacious living room—the carpet, the walls, the furniture in varying shades of beige. Not a book, medical or otherwise, in sight. She stares at the bartender in his black-and-white outfit rocking a shaker, his upper back powerful in the mirrored wall. Tangerine Dream's "Song of the Whale" floats above him from a set of wall-mounted speakers, and through the floor-length sheers on the opposite side of the room Effie can see a yardful of pot-lit trees.

John cups his hand beside Effie's ear. "Looks like a Holiday Inn, doesn't it?"

Effie blushes. "Which one is Dr. McCready?" she asks.

"He's not here. Elizabeth said he's in Halifax, tying up loose ends."

"Umbilical cords or fallopian tubes?" she asks, but John doesn't hear her. She eyes a tray of pâté and crackers laid out in front of her and sets down her Olands. "I *love* liver pâté." She picks up three crackers. "Who's that talking to Mary?"

"Which one?"

"The one with the diminishing hair."

"The diminishing hair belongs to Dr. McCready's youngest brother, Michael, Member of Parliament and decidedly aloof if you ask me," John says, "although no surprise that he is attracted to Mary."

"Who isn't?"

"Standing next to him is his brother Kenny, Professor of Political Studies at UPEI. The guy holding the vegetables."

"Does everyone's name end in a *y*?"

"Not always y—sometimes *ie*—or, for the MacDonalds, e-i-e-i-o."

"Kenny, Jimmy, Dougie, Donnie, Willie, Billie, Jerry. Mary."

"Effie."

"If she's so attractive why aren't you going out with her?"

"What are you talking about?"

"Mary. If she's so attractive why don't you go out with her?"

"I'm not interested in Mary in that way."

"John tells me you teach English." Effie looks up. Kenny McCready has the same gap-toothed grin as his daughter, but his voice is less friendly. "Crudités?"

John reaches down and picks up his camera. "Effie, I'll get you another beer."

Donnie and Elizabeth saunter in from the kitchen and squeeze in beside Effie.

"Effie, meet Elizabeth. Elizabeth, Effie." Donnie's eyes sparkle like a miner who has just struck gold. "Elizabeth is a hair-dresser—I haven't seen her in ages."

"Stylist."

"She's going to open her own shop some day."

The rosy-cheeked woman lowers her voice like a courtroom witness. "When my family get over my unforgivable betrayal. I went away to study law but it just didn't take."

"Betrayal?" Effie asks.

"Professor's daughter, MP's niece? What do you think?"

Effie wonders what Elizabeth's family would think of *her* mother and father.

"But it's what I love." Her voice grows louder, more confident. "I couldn't stand most of the class and, besides, my mother was a stylist, too."

Effie notes Elizabeth's use of the past tense. Gulping the Olands, she breathes in its woody smell and closes her eyes.

Donnie nudges Effie. "I know we just sat down but do you mind if we dance?"

Effie smiles. "You and me?"

"Me and Elizabeth." Donnie's moustache wiggles as he speaks. "We need to liven up this party."

Elizabeth claps her hands.

The last house party Effie attended was with Garfield. She counts back the months in her head. Not a word from him in all this time. Punitive bastard. She smirks at the idea of him swaying to gospel music in his Southern-style Baptist church, sallying off afterward to an enormous public feed. Oh, how he'd boasted about the joyful times back home. *Chicken and cheese.* She pictures him flirting with casaba-breasted women in pinstriped pantsuits, their hair slicked back with Ultra Sheen.

Garfield always thought big—onyx rings and corporate level jobs and airplane tickets to Jamaica. But Effie had been unwavering. It wasn't the big things she was after having. Big things had not been a feature of her childhood, and for this she was consciously, profoundly grateful. Her mother, in fact, had been the benefactor of small things: hot water bottles tucked in between cold sheets; diligently polished shoes; summer radishes transformed into miniature tulips.

Even in less sober times, her mother had kept things small. Celery sticks dipped in peanut butter. Triangulated toast. Shot glasses filled with liqueur: white crème de cacao, anisette, sloe gin. Seashell ashtrays. The special vodka glass. Peppermints.

Effie swallows a mouthful of beer and looks toward the kitchen, wondering if John is a man of little things or large. Cameras and nice clothes cost a lot of money. She catches a glimpse of his elbow and hears him laugh, his laughter careful and low. Through the haze of cigarette smoke she can see Elizabeth and Donnie as they loop around the living room, pushing their way through the genial throng. Effie wonders what the doctor, or his housekeeper, will think of Donnie's scuffmarks on the rug. The couple gesture to Effie to come and join them. Effie raises her bottle in return. She glances over at Mary, who is leaning against the wall, her face turned toward the Member of Parliament, her lips moving uncharacteristically fast, his long back arched away from the party guests.

"Effie—you're all alone. I'm so sorry." John sits down beside her. "Here's the Olands I promised you." He sets his camera on the floor at her feet. "God, I'm so sorry. Where did everyone go?"

"Mary's standing over there in some kind of heated conversation with the MP and Donnie's jiving up a storm with Elizabeth." She puts her head back and chugs the beer. "Where were you?"

"Taking my usual combative stance." He laughs. "Are you sure you should be drinking so fast?"

"Beer has been my best and only companion." Effie lets out an exaggerated sigh. "Tragic, but true." Pointing to the label, she says, "Beer is not long suffering. It is kind and is not jealous. Beer does not boast. It is not inflated. It is not discourteous, selfish, or irritable and neither does it rejoice over wrongdoing."

"Corinthians," John says.

"Exactly."

"Beer covers all things, has faith in all things, hopes all things, endures all things. But while it is truly not inflated, it doth bloat."

"Eventually I will have drunk my way through every house in Charlottetown." She lets out a belch. "I think it's a gene."

"Beds Are Burning" blares out from the stereo. John whisks the bottle from Effie's hand. "Let's mambo."

She cautions herself against snapping her fingers or hopping around like a pony.

John moves his feet heavily, the polished tips of his shoes peeking out from beneath his corduroy pants. In this aspect he

and Garfield are aligned. Garfield hated blue jeans, thinking
them the scourge of the twentieth century, and he decried the
onslaught of Doc Marten lace-ups. She tries to remember his
brand of footwear and can't and instead conjures his feet:
cracked soles, long thin toes and pale toenails. Not like John's
feet at all. She has seen John's feet at the beach—square, stub-
by-toed and ineptly manicured—the feet of a man who would
never waste time on anything as frivolous as a pedicure. Samson
the Nazirite.

She stands back from him as the song changes to "Paving
The Highway With Tears," an old country tune her mother had
loved. *You found another sweetheart that's why I couldn't stay, though
I still love you darling I'm only in your way.* John holds out his arms
and Effie steps into them, laying her head on his shoulder, her
body fitting tightly into his. She is keenly aware of his hand graz-
ing the lower part of her back, his other hand warm and firm,
enveloping hers. How soft his sweater. How sweet the smell of
tangerine and pine along his neck. She concentrates on Hank
Snow's sharp vowels and emphatic consonants—*you'll find me if
you'll follow the teardrops on the trail*—and peeks through the window at the fir trees—low-lit sentinels. Like me, she thinks.
Predictable and neat.

"What are you thinking?"

John's words startle her. The song is over and she hasn't
heard it end. She feels like a deaf girl caught out by her infirmity.

"I'm thinking about the trees."

"The trees?" John looks toward the window. "Out there?"

"Yes, the ones out there. The ones that remind us of
Christmas." She pulls back and stares at him hard.

"I think you need to sit down," he says.

"I think I need to sit down."

He pulls her by her fingertips over to the couch.

Effie sinks down and quiets herself, her hands squeezed in
calm little fists at her side, her knees and feet pressed together.
When Mary signals with a worried look on her face, Effie tilts her
head and smiles, letting Mary know that she should keep her
place against the wall with the MP.

When John returns from the kitchen with a plateful of food, Effie trades him his camera for crackers and cheese and then waves him away with a saltine.

Donnie and Elizabeth wheel on through the haze, the other guests having relinquished their gyrations, standing once again in tableaux, holding up long-filtered cigarettes and thin-stemmed wide-lipped drinking glasses.

Effie puts her hand over her mouth, muffling the laughter that curdles upward. She looks over at Donnie, his limber body careening across the room. For the first time since she has met him, Effie admires his persistent pleasantness—his round open face and radiant eyes, the way his moustache moves so agreeably when he grins. Elizabeth moons back at him dreamily, and Effie wonders what percentage of people know, the very instant they meet someone, that this is *it*, that this person is truly the one.

Effie grins. Here on the couch her mind can wander, safe from onlookers, free to hurry away if what she encounters is even minutely unpleasant. She munches her crackers and cheese, catching glimpses of John—a handsome, solid Nazirite—taking pictures of the revellers. She wonders why she can't be more like Mary, able to converse with ease, able to move through the world naturally, magnetically.

Someone shouts, "Ten minutes to midnight!" and Effie searches for John, momentarily distracted by the MP, who is pressed as flat as a flounder against the wall, Mary so close a person can't tell where one of them ends and the other begins.

John pokes his head out of the kitchen, watching and smiling, and Effie hears Bette Davis's voice in her head. *"Oh Jerry, don't let's ask for the moon. We have the stars."*

CHAPTER 22

Effie stares at her mother and tries not to cry, the cobalt blue table blinking at her from the living room, the light from the green glass lamp shimmering across the floor. How can it be true that her mother has been living in the apartment this whole time?

Effie's mother uncrosses her arms, tightening one hand over the other, her shoulders hunkering down. One sleeve of her sweater looks longer than the other. Her hair, once patchy and running to grey, seems fuller; a rich chestnut brown. She tells her daughter that she has been in and out of the apartment; that some of the time she's been away, too. She says this softly, apologetically, relaxing her arms and stretching her hands out.

Effie wants to know where *away* is. Chicago? Paris? She remembers the blood-red cover, *Uhuru,* and she wonders— Africa?

Lavinia Cambridge pulls her hands back, quietly explaining that it was nothing as exotic as all that, calling Effie darling and reassuring her that, were this the case, she would have taken Effie with her. She wipes sweat from her forehead with her palm and insists that she wasn't only at the apartment. She calls Effie *angel,* explaining that she was away, getting better.

Effie shakes her head rapidly in disbelief, asking who paid for all this, reminding her mother that she had missed her daughter's foray into high school, hadn't cared that she had been living with some other family who didn't even know her full name.

Mrs. Cambridge places her hand on her head, primping her hair, hoping to show that she is healthy.

Lavinia explains that the money came from no one Effie would know and she asks her daughter, coaxingly, imploringly, if it isn't wonderful to be back together again, telling Effie she has missed her so much. She steps in toward Effie, lifting her arms and resting them gently on her daughter's shoulders.

Effie continues her tirade, roaring into her mother's face, declaring that she was given a Snoopy doghouse toothbrush for Christmas and that she is practically fifteen. She hardens her lips and narrows her eyes, refusing to cry.

Mrs. Cambridge calls her darling again, and pet, and says that she's sorry and that she hasn't had a drink in six months. She shows Effie her hands as proof, and tells her they aren't even shaking. She explains that Reitman's has taken her on at the Dixie Plaza. That she has a whole section to manage. That she gets discounts. She nods at Effie, entreating her to come on the bus with her so that they can pick out new clothes, gazing at Effie and telling her that she's gotten so thin and that her skin is so pale. She places her hand beneath Effie's chin.

Effie raises one eyebrow, asking what sort of clothes, and her mother laughs, relieved that her daughter is about to forgive her.

That spring, Effie's nightmares disappear. If she dreams at all, she retains only vestiges—hints of fantasies, everything out of proportion, but nothing that Effie can't manage. Kathleen, temporarily freed by a change in her stepfather's schedule and encouraged by her mother, comes by Effie's apartment after school, she and Effie analyzing and commiserating on the day's events while Effie runs the feather duster over the furniture and sets the table for dinner. Her mother won't be home before seven and Kathleen will have gone on her way long before that.

Effie maintains a love-hate relationship with the Port Credit high school. Her locker is located in the technical wing and in the mornings and late afternoons she often finds herself lingering to peer at the boys in shop class, fascinated by whatever car is up on the hoist (she wonders vaguely about insurance and law suits), wishing shop were an option for girls, resenting the enforcement of home economics and the narrowly focused teacher who has no patience for left-handed girls who can't cut on the bias. Effie feels she would have a healthier relationship with pistons and carburetors and mending a broken fan belt with a pair of nylon stockings. The apron she has sewn for her mother in home ec class is pretty enough, but Effie forgot her basting pins inside the waistband until she heard her mother's soft *ouch* in the kitchen one day.

Effie sometimes wants to join the tribe of students hanging about in the courtyard at lunchtime but finds herself too shy and too judgmental of their cigarette habits. She knows it is only a matter of time before Kathleen is lured over to this other side and Effie's not sure what she'll do then: blindly leap with her friend or walk away, abandoned?

She loses herself in most of her classes—deciphering Marcel Pagnol's *Fanny* in French, discovering Shirley Jackson in English, enthralled in biology by the intricacies and possibilities of deoxyribonucleic acid, ignoring the cliques and critics that surround her, either oblivious to or shunning their whispering and hints of mockery, one grade ten boy going so far as to tilt back an imaginary bottle every time he passes Effie in the hallway.

By grade ten, however, Effie and Kathleen's friendship solidifies and Effie no longer worries about her friend jumping ship. At lunchtime, while students gather on the front lawn smoking and discussing souped-up car engines, hairstyles, makeup and clothing and party plans for the weekend, Effie and Kathleen head off to the school's two-storey library, which is ensconced in the west wing of the building. Effie rifles through poetry books— Emily Dickinson, Robert Service, Edna St. Vincent Millay—and Kathleen seeks out tales of high sea adventure, Edgar Allan Poe's *The Narrative of Arthur Gordon Pym of Nantucket* her favourite.

The girls haven't time for leisure after school, each of them now employed in diners on Lakeshore Road. When their shifts permit, they meet after work in a third local restaurant for Cokes and fries, neither of them in a hurry to go home, their conversation taken up with innocuous gossip: will Gretel Gunther marry Hank Hughes if the rumours about the pregnancy are true? Is Maggie Mortimer's mother paid to put lipstick and eye shadow on the dead bodies in the mortuary or does she just do their hair? How much money would Effie and Kathleen have to save to buy a Volkswagen and take a trip to some place far away?

Effie figures that, after her share of the rent money is paid, she will be twenty-one before a purchase is likely to happen, and what about tuition fees for university? Kathleen replies that she is not likely headed to university. Her mother wants her to get into a good secretarial school and take up a career she can depend on, which means that Kathleen might even finish up at the high school at the end of grade ten.

Effie chokes back her fries, devastated.

CHAPTER 23

Effie gathers her coat around her shoulders, trying to keep the wind from blowing up her sleeves. The day has been long and noisy. "Teaching is hard work."

John walks beside her, his thick winter gloves reminding her of bear paws. "What was your first clue?"

She stares longingly at his nose. "You sound like Donnie." A clump of snow plops down in front of her, shaken from its resting place in a tree.

"Oh my God, not these days I don't. Have you seen our lost boy? He's truly smitten." John looks up at the sky and Effie thinks he sounds a little sad.

"Do you think people are truly smitten anymore?" she asks.

"Why couldn't they be? Haven't you ever been smitten?"

"Twice," she replies. "Have you?"

"Now there's a dangerous question." He scoops snow from the top of a hedge and forms it into a ball, packing it in the palms of his heavy gloves. Effie laughs, watching the better part of his efforts blow away in the wind.

"Then you know what it means to be smitten." He runs ahead, his boots sliding in long strides across the snow. "Come on! Let's go have supper at the Dove."

"Is this a *date*?" She calls to him in a teasing way, her voice an octave higher than usual, not sure if she wants him to know she is serious.

John pivots and runs back to her, grabbing her hand and pulling her alongside him in his practical rubber boots. The kind good fathers wear.

"These gloves are unwieldy. And whoa!" He points down at his feet, laughing. "Talk about ugly boots!"

Effie's heartbeat accelerates. This has to be a sign. In a breathless monosyllable she asks, "Would you rather come over to the apartment? I could make us something for dinner." In her head she rifles through the contents of her kitchen cupboards: saltines, dried peas, chickpeas, spaghetti noodles, a can of kidney beans, stale rice cakes. There is nothing in the refrigerator except an apple, a bag of miso and root beer. She had intended to stop at the Co-Op on her way home and pick up a few essentials.

"I'd be glad to do the cooking," John says, "and if you like we could pick up some things on the way."

It is as if he has read her mind. "Yes, let's do that," she says, trying to make her voice sound nonchalant, grateful that the wind can explain away her scorching cheeks.

An hour later John stands in Effie's kitchen, a tea towel fashioned around his waist like an apron. He is whistling "Harbour Lights," a song her mother used to sing.

"So, do you really believe there's such a thing as altruism?" she asks.

"Could you hand me the pepper, please?" He twists the handle of the grinder over the frying pan, the vegetables searing. "What made you think of that?"

"It's a theme that seems to interest you." She watches him stir the red and yellow peppers, the mushrooms and eggplant, admiring his panache.

"Are you all right with some onion?" he asks.

Effie roots through the grocery bag. "Is that a metaphor?"

"Apples and oranges? Apples and trees? I don't know. Maybe," he says.

"Like attracts like?"

"You're judged by the company you keep?" He turns and smiles at her full in the face. "Now, if you would grab the flour, two eggs, that slab of butter and some milk, and set them over there on the counter, I'll dial this down in a couple of minutes and get to work on the biscuits."

Effie lets out a sigh. *What can't he do?*

"Effie, you can't depend on my ability—or maybe I should say my inability—to stop my mood from reflecting my opinions."

"Excuse me?" Effie uncorks a bottle of wine and pours out two glasses, inhaling the smell of garlic that permeates the kitchen.

"On a bad day, I tend not to believe in things like altruism, but on a good day," he smiles at her again, "I tend to be more altruistic."

"That's rather self-defeating." she says. "But at least you're a tidy cook."

"I'm a greatest-good-for-the-greatest-number kind of person. Bentham and Mill."

"Bentham and Peppermill, you mean." Effie smiles at her own joke. "But isn't that a form of altruism?"

"No. I think that's more about survival of the fittest." He slowly rolls out the dough. "I'm being somewhat cynical, but I do think human beings are innately self-preservationist. Then again, in the end, I think self-preservation *is* more altruistic—if you can even specify degrees—because what use can you be to another man or woman if you cannot come to them with a whole—a holistic—heart and mind?" John tosses chicken cubes into the pan.

"Do you think that putting others before you is wrong then?"

"No. But I think awareness precludes the possibility of the act. Or perhaps I mean the integrity of the act. If there is such a thing as altruism, you and I aren't going to hear about it. It will just be. Acts of true human kindness take place every minute of the day and nobody ever knows about them. I think that, in general, an altruistic person can't possibly ask that question, and yet it comes up all the time."

Effie blushes a smudgy red.

"Oh, I don't mean you, Effie. I mean the intellectuals who pose high-minded questions. The postulators." He lowers his voice. "Never you."

Effie sits down. If her face gets any hotter she thinks she might die from malignant hyperthermia. She sees John as a well-intentioned philosopher, like Plato or Nietzsche, but despite his intimate tone she finds it difficult to respond.

John returns to the biscuits, a flour-rimmed cup in his hand. "Ideally these should be baked on top of the filling, but if we do it that way we won't be eating until tomorrow." He holds up the teacup. "Haven't you ever rooted for someone you cared about, willing them to be good, to make right choices? And haven't you ever been surprised, disappointed even, by their inability to be their best selves?"

"Yes, I have. But I have also been surprised the other way around. Like with Mary. I thought she was going to be stuck up and jealous, but I couldn't have been more wrong. Maybe you expect too much of people?"

John laughs. "There's your John Stewart Mill for you."

Effie is mystified by this turnaround, how she is the one on the optimistic side of the argument.

"That wasn't meant to be cynical. I was trying to make you laugh," he says, removing the towel from around his waist. "All I am trying to do is get it right. That's all. Just get it right. Get my life right."

After the biscuits come out of the oven, Effie and John sit down to dinner.

John says, "I am sorry if I'm overbearing this evening. I realize there may be only a thin line separating me from those—what did I call them?—postulators?" He drops his head to his chin. "To be honest, I'm ticked by something I heard at school today."

Effie bristles, wondering if this has something to do with one of her students or, worse, with one of those gossipy teachers. Had they said something to him about her? Did someone find out— from loose-lipped Donnie perhaps? Did someone tell John that she liked him?

John puts down his fork. "They continue to blame me for the missing band funds."

Effie coughs on a mouthful of chicken. "How could anyone possibly think that you, of all people, would have anything to do with missing money?" She bangs on her chest. "I can understand why you'd be upset." She hacks up a chunk of chicken and buries it in her napkin. "Who do they think they are?" She takes hold of the bottle of wine. "More?" she asks, pouring a generous portion into his glass. "Where did you get this information? Who told you?"

John sits at the table quietly, eyes gleaming. "Who knew I had such a fervent ally?" He picks up his fork and pushes it through his pile of vegetables. "Jill told me, but in the strictest confidence. I'm not privy to where she heard it, although she said I should prepare myself for a head-to-head. You've been here long enough to know what that place is like. Everything has ears—the kids, the walls, the teachers—even the bloody toilets."

"A head-to-head with whom?"

"That's just it. I have no idea. Neither does Jill. The school board, I expect. But the more serious problem of course is if there *is* money missing, what will I tell the kids? I don't think we can raise enough cash for the Boston trip in time for spring." He sets his napkin on the table. "They'll crushed." He glances over at Effie's empty plate.

"You see?" she says. "*That's* altruistic."

"Stolen band funds?"

"No. You. Here you are, accused of robbery—why are you laughing? It's true—and yet your primary concern is for the students."

"That hardly defines altruism, Effie. Besides, I want the trip as much for me as for the kids. I've never been to Boston."

"Now that's baloney, Mr. Peppermill."

"Well, I haven't. And in the middle of all this, the principal wants me to arrange passports for all of the kids."

"That's not what I mean and you know it." Effie leans into the table and picks up John's plate. "Do you think," she whispers stealthily, "do you think it could be jealousy?" A string of onion hangs from the underside of her sleeve.

John leans forward, mirroring her. "I don't know. Do you?"

"Now you're making fun of me." She stands up and transfers the plates to the sink. "A charge like that is no laughing matter and if you ask me—and you just did—jealousy is the root of all evil."

"And not the love of money?" John raises his eyebrows, feigning surprise.

"Nothing can come close to jealousy." Effie spins the hot water faucet and squirts the dish soap. "That's all right." She scoops out a handful of bubbles and tosses them at him. "Just keep on making fun of me if it makes you feel better, but I know—"

"I can't imagine how I could inspire jealousy in anyone." John daubs at his sweater with a napkin.

Effie shuts off the tap. "Oh, it doesn't take much."

"Thanks for the compliment." John stands up and pushes back his sleeves, heading toward the sink.

She waves him back with the wet dishcloth. "That's not what I mean. You know that even minor things can rankle someone whose balance is easily tipped."

"Such as?"

"Position. Admiration."

"Doubt that, although the position is small, that's true."

"I thought you loved what you do."

"That's not what we're talking about."

"Then what about talent?"

"Not a worry."

"Liar."

John leans back, his front chair legs lifting away from the floor. "You have onion on your sleeve."

"Okay then, what about intelligence?"

John looks down.

"I said *intelligence.*"

"I heard you. Frankly, a shoe size beyond Neanderthal passes for intelligence around here." John lifts his glass so Effie can run the dishcloth across the top of the table.

She lingers and leans in close to him. "Why do you hate the island?" she asks, running the rag across the aluminum top.

"Who said I hated the island?" John rests his elbows on the table. "You never talk about your family, Effie. How come?"

"There isn't anyone to talk about. I had my mother, but there's no one else except . . . you know."

"Ah yes, the brother from Brighton." He stops abruptly, his eyes so dark she cannot tell where his irises begin and his pupils leave off. "Sit down and tell me about your mother."

Effie returns to her chair. "There isn't much to tell. My mother would be close to sixty if she were alive. She and my uncle had an older brother who was killed in the war. He was barely eighteen when he died. A tail gunner. Did you know a tail gunner's life expectancy is shorter than a rabbit's? At least that's what my mother used to say."

"What else did your mother say?"

"It all depended on how sober she was. "

John is moved by the directness of Effie's admission. "That must have been awful for you."

"Well, I wasn't the one with the hangovers." Effie's face takes on a darker shade, like someone who's been living under a cloud for a long time. "We had good times, too, but alcoholism is frightening."

"I don't think my parents have shared more than two drinks between them." John waits before asking, softly, "Why did your mom's drink?"

"Life, I suppose. But stomach surgery made it worse. She had a gastric ulcer that got out of hand, and by the time she saw a specialist—anyway, after the surgery they told her that brandy would help her sleep."

John's eyes sting and he rubs his forehead, pulling his thumb and fingers toward the furrow above his nose.

"It helped her all right," Effie laughs. She pushes her bangs away from her face with the back of her hand. "When I was really little I used to climb up on her bed in the morning and pry her eyes open to see if she was still alive."

John reaches over and places his hand flat on the table, close to Effie.

"As soon as I saw her corneas I was set for the day. Kids, eh?"

"Yeah. Kids." He hears the catch in his voice and breathes deeply to relieve it. "What else was your childhood like?"

"You mean besides a nightmare?" Effie laughs again. "Not really. We had fun together, too. Picnics down by the river and

Scrabble and lots of talk about school and friends, even boys. My cousin Robert lived with us for a while. We loved him. And no one mocked herself more than my mother. The time she drank rubbing alcohol—"

"Jesus God. Your mother drank rubbing alcohol? That poor woman."

"Exactly," Effie says, swallowed in relief. "But most people don't see it that way. They want to turn her into a villain. Or me into some kind of victim. Which is why I rarely talk about her or about my life."

"No wonder." John's voice is so low Effie can barely hear him.

"She went blind, but only temporarily. When she regained her eyesight the first thing she saw was the picture of the highland dancer on her Export A tobacco can." Effie wonders if John has ever smoked. "You could smoke in hospitals in those days," she says. "Mom laughed so hard she had tears rolling down her face, and the nurse ran into the room to see if we were all right. My mother saw the irony in things."

John slides his hand toward Effie and rests it on her arm.

"She also liked aphorisms. *Let not your heart be troubled, neither let it be afraid. Shame to waste two houses*, which made us laugh because it is so true. *Dog in the manger.* My favourite is *consider the source.* I use that one a lot." Effie feels the weight of John's touch, embarrassed, realizing she has said too much.

John plucks the piece of onion from her sleeve and withdraws, not wanting to alarm her. He smiles reassuringly. "Yes, you'll find that one very useful on the island." He stares into Effie's worried eyes. "Take for example Donnie's cousin Jimmy. He's some piece of work. A real credit to the Charlottetown police force."

"Do you think he's the one pushing the investigation at the school? You know, I've seen him in the parking lot talking to Tommy Murphy."

"You have? When?"

"I can't remember exactly. Last Tuesday or Wednesday. Donnie's cousin was offering Tommy a lift home, which you can't blame either of them for, that neglected boy half-dressed the way he is all the time."

"I noticed a police car out by the side of the school a few weeks ago. Half-dressed or not, that can't be healthy for Tommy. He's got enough trouble in his life as it is. But they certainly seem to like spending time together. This isn't the first or even the fifth time I've caught sight of them head to head. I sometimes wonder. . . ." John's voice trails off.

"Wonder about what?"

"It's probably just paranoia but I wonder if Jimmy engages Tommy in illicit activities."

"Such as?"

"That's just it. I don't know. Gambling, Drugs. Maybe something more—something darker; more nefarious perhaps."

"More nefarious than gambling and drugs?" Effie pulls back in her chair. "You don't mean sex do you?"

"I don't think so. No. But something that can't be good for that kid."

"I wonder if you aren't over-worrying a little. I was thinking of trying to interest Tommy in the school play."

"As who? Faust?"

"At first I wondered about the fool, but then I worried that he would feel insulted."

John touches his hand to his forehead. "He's not savable, Effie. Forget any plan that requires that boy to be reliable. Or sane."

"Wow. That's pretty harsh. Don't you believe in redemption?"

"Hitler loved Wagner." John raises his empty glass. "But what can you expect from a boy whose father is violent, whose mother is done for, and who spends half of his time kibitzing with criminal cops?"

"I expect kindness from people like you."

"Kindness isn't going to help him. It's already too late."

"I could make some tea and maybe even change your mind, if you would be interested in watching a video with me."

John glances at his watch. "A movie?"

"In effect, yes. *Twelfth Night*. I got a copy from the university." She hopes the mention of the university will appeal to John's scholastic side.

.

"You know, Effie, when I was a child, I had a recurring dream about a little girl. She had patches of freckles and straight dark hair and bangs. Her eyes were round and green, and in the dream we were playing together." He grins at her, and Effie can't be sure if it's as a lover or a friend.

"Where?"

"Sometimes at the seaside, other times under a shady tree. I figured the child was someone I'd met and forgotten, a cousin perhaps, or someone from the schoolyard. But you know—" he points to Effie's cheeks—"I think that she was you. In fact," John says, "if I can inspect those freckles a little more closely, I think I'd know for sure."

Effie lets go of the teapot, the pieces scattering across the floor.

CHAPTER 24

"No, not like that!" Effie sets down her script. "Virginia, hand your baby over to Martha and watch Vivian." Vivian Myers juts her chin out like a runway model, turning to face the waiting students. Danny Callbeck rolls his eyes and Martha, annoyed, takes hold of Virginia's baby as if she were lugging a ten-pound bag of Netted Gems.

"Is it like the twelve days of Christmas, Miss?" Bruce Jarvis gazes around the gymnasium as if he were seeing the room for the first time.

Danny heckles, "Yeah, that's right, Brucie. On the twelfth day of Christmas my true love gave to me."

"Why don't you tell us what the title means, Danny, since you seem so certain?"

"Easy one, Miss. It's the twelfth day of the twelfth month. December 12th. Right?"

"Wrong," mutters Gary Lowther.

"But why is this called the spring play, Miss, when it's only January?"

"Bruce, come on. Think." Gary taps the side of his head with his finger.

Effie inhales deeply. "Because today we have tryouts, then after that we select the actors, then after that we have rehearsals, and then after that we put on the play in the spring. Could some of you boys grab those chairs from along the wall and set them in a semi-circle? When everybody is sitting, we can begin."

Students continue walking into the gymnasium in twos and threes.

"Over here!" Effie calls "Come and sit so we can begin." She drums her fingers on the back of a chair. "Although this play is heavily weighted in favour of the boys, the female parts are rich and vital to—"

"Why is that, Miss Cambridge?" Ruthie Acorn's hands rest decisively on her small hips. "Why are there so many parts for boys and practically none for the girls?" She fluffs the back of her skirt as she sits down.

"Yeah," Danny says. "Why did you pick this one and not something everyone could do? Like *Anne of Green Gables*?"

"Anything's better than that awful Anne." Ruthie shifts forward in her chair.

Effie raises her voice so loudly she startles herself. "When Shakespeare wrote *Twelfth Night* only men were allowed to act and so they played all of the parts, even the female ones. To make it up to you girls, I am going to ask some of you to act as my assistants and help with costumes and sets and lighting and so on."

Griffen Dalziel curls his upper lip. "But some of those are *boys'* jobs."

"When I call out the name of a character, please raise your hand if you are interested in that part. In the spirit of Elizabethan theatre I will also consider girls for boys' roles."

"Now that's just weird, Miss."

"Think of it as historical inversion, Griffen."

"Ass over teakettle?" Donnie Fitzgerald strolls into the auditorium. The students laugh.

"Good afternoon, Mr. Fitzgerald." Effie scowls. "Why don't you explain to everyone what I mean by historical inversion?"

"Miss Cambridge, the students are old enough to know that themselves, aren't you kidlets?" Everyone laughs again except Effie. "And I think, just maybe, you mean historical reversion? Or even revision?"

"Yeah, Miss, I'm not so sure we want to go back to them times—"

"Those times, Kenny, not them times."

Donnie swaggers up to Effie. "Although I wouldn't mind havin' meself a servant, poor wee boy that I am."

"Please. Enough silliness." Effie looks sternly at Donnie. "Mr. Fitzgerald, you are welcome to stay but you will have to behave."

"Yes, ma'am. I had best learn to do as I'm told." He winks at the students then saunters toward the gymnasium doors. "Good day, children. Break some legs!" He walks into the outer hallway past Tommy Murphy, who is leaning against the concrete wall, his body angled like a broken pencil. Tommy waits for Donnie to pass by before inching his way toward the auditorium.

"All right, boys and girls, pay attention." Effie begins to read out the names of the characters. When she gets to the part of Maria, Virginia raises her hand.

"Miss, if I have a part in the play would it be all right if I bring the baby to rehearsals?" Virginia looks up at Effie from beneath her bangs. "The day care can't keep her that late."

"I'll ask the principal, Virginia, but I think it should be all right." Suddenly, *boys and girls* sounds ridiculous. "Virginia, wait. Forget the principal. It's fine. Bring the baby along with you. And Griffen, if that snickering happens again, you'll be out. Understand?"

"Yes, Miss." Danny and Gary let go of a uniform sigh. "Can we start the tryouts, Miss?"

Peering through the crack between the wall and the gymnasium door, Tommy watches the cast selection unfold. He runs his hand along his sore arm, bruised from a fist fight he'd had the night before, perspiration drenching his thin t-shirt despite the drafty air.

Three hours later and long past suppertime, Effie dangles her legs from the edge of the stage in the empty auditorium working through her selections. Gary Lowther, the brightest student in grade ten as far as Effie can tell, should probably play Orsino, and Ruthie Acorn would excel in the dual role of Viola and Cesario. Effie will have to purge Ruthie of priggery, but otherwise the girl is versatile and cunning and could manage two parts adeptly. At least that much is clear. No one seems more eager to succeed than Ruthie Acorn. Effie stares out into the vast gymnasium imagining Virginia Halfpenny as Maria. Effie wants to help her but wonders whether Virginia can handle a part in the play as well as tend to a baby.

Making her way through the list, Effie discovers that most of the characters are easy enough to cast. Bruce Jarvis' marshmallow face is perfect for Sir Toby Belch, and Griffen Dalziel will make a credible—if somewhat abrasive—Antonio. To Effie's wonderment, he read the text with more comprehension than any of them. Vivian Myers, daughter of Vickie Myers, has succeeded in outshining everyone for the role of Olivia, which annoys Effie considerably given how hateful Vickie is. Nonetheless, if Effie turns the girl down there will be nothing but trouble. Besides, she has to be fair. And at least this way, with Vivian in a leading role, Vickie Myers will be so busy gloating she won't have room to give Effie, or anyone else, grief. Even Martha is delighted with the idea of being a stagehand. "Oscar Wilde had to start somewhere, didn't he—and I can help Virginia with the baby."

As Effie returns the chairs to their places alongside the wall in the empty gymnasium, she is overcome by the students' enthusiasm, which had erupted in bursts of giddy chatter and elbow nudging. Most had left the tryouts happy, exuberant even. She worries about the disappointment of those who didn't make it and wonders if any will cry—or retaliate.

Effie trudges home, resenting the cold, the ice and the darkness. A loud gurgle roils up from her stomach. She longs for a sticky bun or a curt lemon tart but the bakeries in Charlottetown don't stay open past five o'clock. After six, lugubrious islanders attend weekly meetings of Overeaters Anonymous at Kingdom Hall. Effie laughs out loud.

"What's so funny?"

Effie startles at the sound of Mildred Rutherford's voice behind her. "I—I don't know. I was just thinking about how I hadn't eaten all day."

Rutherford surges forward in lockstep. "That's funny? Well, a good cup of tea with cinnamon would cure that." The older woman's Wallabees crunch purposely along the snow-covered sidewalk.

"Oh, I'm afraid I haven't time—"

"I wasn't offering. Can't you make yourself a good cup of tea? Surely even *your* mother taught you the basics."

"Miss Ruther—"

"A soft-boiled egg can't be too difficult. Or cinnamon toast."

"I grew up over a bakery, Miss Rutherford. I know how to cook."

"How does one obtain cooking skills by growing up over a bakery? Osmosis?" Her words soar ahead of them along the deserted street. "My dear girl, you need to get out and have some fun. I've just come from the hospital and I can tell you that life is far too short indeed. Pancreatic cancer, arterial blockage, tired old worn-out brains. People wetting themselves in their night-gowns, foul-smelling stool and blood pressure that would blow your mittens right off."

They round the corner onto Grafton Street.

"I've heard some rather unsavoury news about your John MacDonald."

"He isn't *my* John MacDonald, Miss Rutherford. Why is everything *my* or *our* around here? Do people actually *own* other people? Is that why they need to know everything about every-one? Or feel they have a right to?"

"A place this size? What did you expect?" The older woman stops walking and grabs hold of Effie's coat sleeve.

Effie yanks her arm back. "Where I come from—"

"They don't gossip above the bakery, Miss Cambridge? Come now. Gossip is universal. In fact, it's healthy to have a little chitchat about your neighbours now and again. They're gossiping this very minute all over the world. In Papua New Guinea, in France, even in India where children are starving. It's a fact of life. If you want to survive here you had better get used to it."

"You make it sound like all of those diseases you were just talking about." Effie wonders what people are saying about her.

"Some diseases are good for you, Miss Cambridge. Just not the terminal ones. Some diseases stretch your limits, make you work for your future. Make you appreciate what you have."

Effie imagines Mildred Rutherford spinning like a top, sucked up into the plume of white steam that is pouring out of the generating station a few blocks away.

The older woman drones on. "Do you think that people don't talk about you? I got an earful from your aunt just the other day. With family like that, who needs enemies?" Mildred snorts.

They cross the lights at Prince Street and Effie sprints ahead. "I think I hear my telephone ringing!"

"From *here*?"

Effie disappears behind the heavy glass doors, the abandoned nurse yelling out to no one, "Libidinous urges!"

When Effie reaches her door she realizes that her phone is, in fact, ringing. She fumbles savagely for her keys but by the time she unfastens the lock the telephone has gone silent. She flattens herself against the door, barring the possibility of further intrusion from Rutherford, half-regretting she hadn't asked the nurse what she meant about John. What unsavoury news? That he's fed up with Prince Edward Island—a sentiment that would be deemed criminal? That he isn't afraid to talk back to people who treat him like he's poison? That he's interested in someone from away?

Effie stops.

Could that have been John on the phone? She enumerates quickly. Her uncle seldom calls and Mary would have come downstairs and left a note. Donnie would have called right back. (Once he told her he'd rung her three times in a row when Ruth wanted Effie to come to dinner.) The students don't have access to her number.

Who else would be calling her tonight aside from John? Perhaps he wants to discuss something with her, confide in her, ask her advice, create a plan. Tell her he loves her. Valentine's Day is only two weeks away.

Of course he doesn't love her. Love this soon isn't possible. Not for a serious man like John. He likely needs something minor, something banal—a book, or an idea for an essay topic. At the start of the winter term he had called her for that very reason, stating emphatically that senior students should be able to write about the musicians whose music they are playing. And then he had laughed and told her how one student, Jillian MacLean, had written an essay called *Schumann: The Sad Years*.

Effie slips off her coat and drops her mittens. Rutherford's Wallabees stop on the landing, then pass by the door.

The phone rings again and Effie tears down the hall. On the third ring she lifts the receiver, nearly dropping it as she raises it to her ear.

"Effie? It's John."

"Oh, hello John."

"I was wondering. I know it's late notice, but would you be free the Saturday after next for a night out? I have tickets to the Confed Centre. Of course, I understand if you're busy."

She puts her hands up to her stinging cheeks. Is it possible? The day before Valentine's Day. She hates Valentine's Day.

"Who said anything about busy? I'd love to go with you."

"Great. I'll come by at six, if that isn't too early."

"Yes, six will do fine. See you then."

"Effie?"

She hears the teasing tone in his voice. "Yes John?"

"I'll see you tomorrow in school."

"Oh yes. I knew that." She hangs up the phone and runs to the kitchen to make breadballs.

CHAPTER 25

"Front Page Challenge? We're going to Front Page Challenge? On Valentine's Day?" Effie's voice escalates on the second *Challenge*.

John stands silently, his hands stuffed in his coat pockets, his feet set apart like a soldier's. The overhead fixture in the apartment hallway lights up the top of his head, his split ends shining.

"Front Page Challenge?" She twists a button on the front of her dress.

"And dinner," he says. "I promised you dinner. And Valentine's Day is tomorrow."

"I'll just grab my coat." She hammers down the hallway to her bedroom.

At the small corner window she reaches out her arm and lifts the sash, sucking in as much cold air as she can without choking, and then, turning sharply, she struts across the room to her closet, banging her knee on the corner of her bed and ripping her winter coat away from the hook on the back of the door. *Front Page Challenge. I should have known.*

She wheels around and walks back toward John, who is still standing stiffly in the doorway, his lit-up hair reminding her of bug lights and fireflies. "Do you think Lee Harvey Oswald was guilty?" she asks. She steps into the outer hall and pulls the door closed behind her.

"Excuse me?"

"Lee Harvey Oswald. Do you think he was guilty?" She follows him down the stairs.

"Effie, is everything all right?" John stops on the first floor landing.

Effie keeps walking. "It's a simple enough question," she says, "Guilty or not guilty?"

"Do you not like Front Page Challenge, because if you don't—"

"Why wouldn't I like Front Page Challenge? It was one of my mother's favourite shows." Effie pushes open the heavy front door and bursts into the street. "When she felt well enough to watch it."

"What was that?" John picks up his pace behind her. "What did you say?"

"Guilty or not guilty?" She stops at the corner traffic lights.

"Do I have to decide before we get there? Experts have debated that question for decades. We're only going one block."

"Everything in this city is one block." The traffic light turns green and Effie forges ahead.

John stalls at the corner. "Guilty," he says, "but not acting alone." He steps away from the curb as the light changes to amber.

"Really?" Effie stops in the middle of the street and watches him walking toward her. "Guilty? And not acting alone? I think so, too." John suddenly looks handsome, vulnerable even. The yellow switches to red, the warm cherry glow a valentine blessing.

"Even the DVA building looks pretty at night," she says.

John brushes against her shoulder. "Let's count our footsteps to the Confederation Centre."

"But it's right *there*."

"That's what makes it doable." He reaches for her hand.

Effie can feel the crush of John's sheepskin glove. "One, two, three," she begins.

Fifteen minutes later, his hand already a lingering memory, Effie shifts in her seat trying to find a way to contain herself. "What a splendid auditorium," she whispers.

"You don't have to whisper. It hasn't started."

"The seats feel so luxurious and the lighting is fantastic."

"You sound surprised. What did you expect from a multi-million dollar enterprise? Anne Shirley has put more money into our economy than lobster fishing."

"You're kidding!"

"Only just. Most of the credit should go to Don Harron."

"I've never seen it."

"Really? I didn't think there was anyone left in the country who hadn't seen *Anne* at least eight times. I'll take you this summer. But oh my God," John smacks his forehead. "That godawful ice cream song will stay in your head until hell freezes over."

"Look at all the people coming in."

I'll take you this summer.

"More than you can shake a stick at."

"They're so spiffied up."

A galaxy of ticket holders cruise in, a long line of velveteen coats and fur-lined hats parading down to the front row. Effie stares past them, below the level of the stage. "Is that an orchestra pit?"

"Are you sure you're from Toronto?"

"Why would they have an orchestra for Front Page Challenge?"

"They'd have an orchestra for the Muppets."

The opening notes of "God Save the Queen" start up, and John rolls his eyes, his *"For Christ sakes"* barely audible. Up they stand in an atmosphere that is as hushed as any Sunday morning service. Effie's eyes follow the sloping shoulders in front of her, and she wonders how many couples are here. Perhaps John wasn't so far off the mark after all. Maybe this is the way Islanders celebrate romantic holidays.

As host Fred Davis sweeps across the stage, the audience sits down amid their own thunderous applause. Effie flattens her dress, assuring herself that dinner reservations indicate some sort of commitment.

She feels a pat on her knee, John tap tap tapping—fondly it seems to her—and she returns her gaze to the lanky Davis, whose gentlemanly comportment and modulated tones remind her of Jimmy Stewart.

The host thanks Charlottetown for its warm reception and delectable seafood, which elicits chirps and titters from the crowd.

John leans into Effie. "Nice suit."

"He can afford it," she whispers back. "But he's too thin."

A hissing "Shhh!" shoots over their shoulders, and John squeezes Effie's hand. "Nice suit," he repeats, and this time when he says it he turns around.

"Oh, hello John. Sorry. I didn't see it was you." The middle-aged man removes his hat.

A rush of "*Shhhs!*" swirl around them.

"I think you mean *us*, Jack." John places his hand on Effie's shoulder.

Effie, rigid in her seat, is afraid that if she moves she might break something—a tiny bone in her foot, or a finger—a counterbalance to elation, like displacement.

The evening's first mystery guest can't be much older than a teenager. Effie wonders what he could have possibly done at his age. Judging from the excited buzz in the audience she thinks he must be a Maritimer—a courageous deep-sea fisherman or an innovative potato farmer. Inside the mystery guest booth, he looks like a framed picture.

At the far end of the judging panel Pierre Berton, his butterfly bowtie peculiarly large, reminds her of Charlie McCarthy.

Effie leans into John again. "I can't *believe* that's actually Pierre Berton."

"And Betty Kennedy."

"Betty Kennedy? Wow—how old is she? And isn't that what's-his-name's wife—the journalist—sitting next to Pierre Berton, glaring? She's *glaring*."

The guest answers the panel's questions perfunctorily. *No, he hasn't done anything groundbreaking in science. No, he isn't linked to the FLQ. Yes, he is from the Maritimes. Yes, he comes from a prolific family, but doesn't everyone who grew up in a mining town?*

"Are you in some way connected with the National Hockey League?" Pierre Berton's question sounds more like a statement.

The young man seems disappointed.

The jounalist whips around, snarling, "The Calgary Flames!" She points her finger toward the man's throat. "Your slap shot split Jimmy Liut's mask. You just about killed him." Someone in the auditorium coughs.

"Remarkable!" Fred Davis glances from the panel to the hockey player and back to the panel again, while behind him Pierre Berton peeks at his wristwatch.

"This has to be a record!" the host exclaims. "But you haven't revealed the name of our illustrious guest."

Pierre Berton fusses with his tie. "Alfred MacInnis. Max Kaminsky trophy recipient."

Davis turns to Berton. "*Allan* MacInnis," he says, ignoring the guest who is correcting them all with, "It's Al."

A cry rises from the theatre, "Go Flames, go!"

John laughs out loud. "How did they get that with so little information? They must have recognized his voice."

"Be fair now, John," comes the voice from behind. "They have years of experience. Haven't you ever watched the show?"

John turns around. "Oh come on, Jack. It's just a Canadian *What's My Line.*"

"No need to be rude, young man."

Onstage, Fred Davis vociferously thanks Al MacInnis, who trips over a microphone cord as he walks off, the orchestra blasting out theme music from *Hockey Night in Canada.*

Tap tap tap on Effie's knee again, and up onstage the cohorts snap black masks over their eyes, awaiting the arrival of the evening's extra special guest. The journalist relaxes her arms, her mouth hanging open, reminding Effie of a skinny-legged child. Not so the no-nonsense Betty Kennedy. A cookie in her mouth, a grenade in her jacket pocket.

Installed in the booth behind them a beaming Anne Murray grins like the Milky Way.

"Do you like her?" John's words disappear beneath an uproarious round of applause.

Hoots and hollers sound around them.

John raises his voice. "Do you like Anne Murray?"

People stop clapping and turn to stare at him.

Effie locks her attention on the panellists.

Another wave of applause rolls through the auditorium.

Effie knows next to nothing about Anne Murray except that she was born in Springhill, Nova Scotia, and once taught physical education classes on the island, which would explain the audience's frenzy. How island-like she is—hair layered from hot rollers, eyelids dusted in fluorescent blue—a pert and cheeky Cabbage Patch doll. The panellists flex their neck muscles like chickens, Anne Murray's tapered fingers seizing the arms of her chair as if she were about to ride a rollercoaster.

"Hypocrites," John says, and Effie wonders if he had read her mind.

The questions and guesses keep coming from the panel—*Rita MacNeil, Kim Campbell, kd lang*—Anne Murray answering in her best Queen Elizabeth imitation, sending Effie into laughter so extreme that people around her begin laughing too. Pierre Berton pushes on the corner of his mask, causing some post-show gossip that he was trying to cheat.

To Effie's surprise, Betty Kennedy comes up with a revealing set of questions, zapping them out with bullet precision.

"Are you, by any chance, from Nova Scotia? Were you a regular on *Singalong Jubilee*?

Did you teach physical education in Summerside, Prince Edward Island?"

The crowd goes berserk. "Snowbird! Sing Snowbird!"

Anne Murray bolts from her chair and lunges toward the microphone before Fred Davis can say a word.

Midway through the song Effie inches up from her seat to catch a full view of the singer. "Stand up," she says to John. "You're the only one sitting."

Looking around, she sees arms waving furiously in her direction—Mary and Michael McCready—the two of them motioning to Effie and John, John now standing with his back to the stage, tears of laughter streaming down his face as Fred Davis bids the audience goodnight.

Jack whisks up his coat from the red velvet chair. "Quite the display." The feather in his porkpie hat points upwards like a fishing lure. He puffs up the aisle, his head raised in haughty resolution.

"Who does he think he is?" Effie asks. "He treated you as if you were an eight-year-old."

"He's a friend of the family."

"Some friend."

Shouldering against the shuffling throng, Mary and Michael inch toward Effie and John.

A woman leaving the theatre touches the sleeve of Mary's coat the way an adoring grandmother might pat a favourite grandchild.

Effie and John sit across from Mary and her date at a table in Peking Palace, the waiter assuring the foursome that it is no trouble at all to add two place settings.

"Effie, are you sure about this?" Mary reaches across the table toward her friend.

"Of course I'm sure." Effie blinks at the centrepiece vase. "I think it was lovely of John to ask you to join us." Her tone, deep-throated and veiled, belies her.

"I tried to make reservations at the hotel," John pulls his chair closer to Effie, "but they were booked, and I figured you'd be tired of the Dove."

"Of course they were," Effie replied wanly. "So—Mary and—" She stares blankly at the MP. "I'm sorry. I've forgotten your name. Oh yes. Michael. What did you think of Front Page Challenge?"

"A marvellous surprise and a perfect delight for Valentine's Day." Mike's teeth glisten, his gums pink and moist.

Effie wonders if he drools on his pillow.

"Egg roll?" The waiter lingers with his pad in hand at the side of the table.

"Pardon me?" Effie eyes his bowtie.

"Would you like egg roll for your appetizer?" The waiter's eyelashes touch his cheeks when he blinks.

"I'll have what everyone else—wait. No. Is there MSG in the egg roll?"

The waiter chuffs impatiently. "You will find MSG in most of the items on our menu." He holds the pen tightly, positioned to write.

"Are you allergic to MSG, Effie?" John asks. "I should have worked this through more carefully."

"Not exactly. It gives me a headache though, and it's a car-bohydrate inducer." Her voice is crisp. Why had John not told Mary and Michael that this was supposed to be a *private* date?

Michael McCready lists in his chair. "We could use you up on the Hill," he says.

"The hill? What hill?" Effie feels suddenly, urgently sick. Because maybe John hadn't intended this as a date at all.

"Parliament Hill. In the kitchen." The MP taps on his cable knit sweater. "I've gained ten pounds in the last six months." He points to his stomach.

The nausea creeps into her throat. "You must have been a stick." Of course. John had probably been given the tickets. Isn't that what he said?

Michael McCready laughs, his teeth shining. "My rakish physique, you mean."

"Effie, excuse me, but the waiter. Would you like an egg roll?"

Effie picks up a menu, a gummy film sticking to the pads of her fingers. "No thank you. No appetizer for me." The nausea passes.

John smiles up at the waiter. "Do you still serve Mai Tais?"

The waiter nods. His nails are bitten down, the ends of his fingers stained a sickly yellow. Effie wonders if there ought to be a universal rule against waiters smoking.

"We'll have four please, or a pitcher if that's easier for you."

Effie girds herself, feeling the hard rim of the chair digging into her spine. He hasn't even asked if that's what she wants. What if the Mai Tai is laced with pineapple and causes a reaction? What if it proves fatal? She imagines the announcement the principal will make over the PA system—*We regret to inform you of the unexpected demise of Miss Effie Cambridge, teacher from away, whose death we would more deeply regret had she been born and raised here, like her alcoholic mother.* Effie has left her allergy kit back at the apartment. How fast can John run? How fast *would* he run? She slides her chair back and peeks down at his feet, checking for his overshoes. No one can run on black ice in Florsheims. She has to calm herself. She knows that. *Expend your energy by expanding your horizons.*

The waiter returns with four Collins' glasses.

"I think we need a few more minutes before we order," John says, "but we'll take the egg rolls whenever they're ready." He rests his arm across the back of Effie's chair. "Have you had a chance to look at the menu?"

Who does he think he is, Effie wonders. Putting his arm on my chair as if we're out on a date. Or worse—does he think he's my father?

"Everything's good here, Effie," Mary says. "It's been a stupendous night so far, hasn't it Mike? I loved Front Page Challenge. You know, I was surprised by how pretty Anne Murray was." Mary's hair shines fuchsia in the pink light, her face bathed in a soft rose hue.

Effie wonders how it happens that some people are so genetically blessed.

John nods. "I agree with you, Mary. She's quite lovely."

"You sound as if you know her personally." Effie ruffles the menu in front of her face, fanning herself. "Was she *your* phys ed teacher?"

Michael McCready laughs. "You should have been a comic, Effie."

"Yes, I've heard that before."

The waiter drops a basket heaped with egg rolls onto the table.

John nods a thank you. "Effie, do you know what you'd like from the menu?"

"Yes, I do." Effie watches Michael plunge his hand into the basket, his long fingers juggling an egg roll. She smiles at the waiter. "I'm going to have the #4," she says. "Sweet and sour chicken balls—with extra pineapple, please."

CHAPTER 26

Lavinia's sobriety cannot and does not last. It isn't Effie's way to complain outright; to speak of hard things and, besides, she loves living here with her mother; loves the charm of the apartment with its tiled bathroom walls and sloped ceilings, the lines and colour and lighting. The rooms feel warm and inviting. Enchanted. She is so grateful to be home, and Lavinia is elated to have her daughter back. It is easy to pretend that nothing bad can happen again.

One stormy afternoon Effie climbs the unlit stairwell, fingers interlaced with Derek's, a boy she met two weeks earlier at the Peel County Public Speaking Regional Finals where Effie delivered a speech called "Juvenile Delinquency: Nature or Nurture?" Afterwards she sat enraptured, stuck to her aluminum chair, listening to this handsome boy pontificate on the colonization of army ants in the Costa Rican rain forest. Later, he introduced himself at the dairy bar, complimenting her superior insights and offering her an ice cream soda.

She looks up at him as they climb the stairs—he is inches taller than she is—and notices the way his chin dissolves into his neck. She can't tell where one feature ends and the other begins. She loosens her hand in his grip and withdraws the house key from the pocket of her sweater.

As she swings the door open she halts at the sight of her mother, who is clad in a sleeveless polka-dot dress and kitten high heels, her hair flattened on one side.

Mrs. Cambridge smiles lopsidedly, a pink peppermint falling out of her mouth. She repositions her hand along the wall, staring fixedly at Effie. The apartment suffocates in an overhang of fried bacon and cigarette smoke. Lavinia hesitates then leers, first at Derek and then at her daughter. Her irises slide up, meeting her eyelids, which is the way she looks whenever she is about to come in for the kill. Casually, as if she is chatting about the weather, she remarks that she has just finished the laundry. Her eyes widen, irises lowering. She tells Effie that her panties were soiled in blood and she pauses, turning her head at a three-quarter angle, almost playfully, waiting for Effie's response. She lurches forward, her leg contorting at the ankle, her high heel turned down into the floor. She waves her hand carelessly.

Effie staggers backwards and heads down the hallway stairs, clutching the railing. Derek walks behind her silently and, at the landing, edges past her. He pulls open the front door and steps into the street, barely whispering goodbye. Effie stares after him and then toward the lake before climbing the stairs.

Later, when the effects of Lavinia's vodka have mostly worn off, Effie listens to her mother's heavyhearted apologies and takes up her suggestion of foot-long hotdogs and vanilla milkshakes and, after that, a game of Scrabble.

For a while Lavinia is able to hang on through her AA meetings and the responsibilities of a new job. Customers in the clothing store love her and appreciate her honesty, remarking to the other clerks how friendly and helpful Mrs. Cambridge always is. She gives her opinions kindly but truthfully, and is not shy to suggest other shops.

Effie learns some of this from another handsome boy, this one in her grade eleven class whose name is Stewart. Stewart comes from a well-off family on Mineola Road. He wears tweed patches on his sweaters and expensive penny loafers on his feet. The girls in Port Credit Secondary all wish that Stewart would ask them out on a date, because he is also intelligent, funny and friendly. At first, Effie wonders why he is telling her stories about her mother, but eventually she comes to realize that Stewart recognizes a good employee when he sees one and truly wants to convey his appreciation to the person who would value it most. Effie doesn't allow herself any assumption that Stewart might be attracted to her or she to him, but she never forgets his thoughtfulness. She has had one almost-boyfriend experience and that was enough.

Effie's mother has in the meantime developed a deep if remote attachment to religion, away from St. Andrew's Presbyterian Church where she feels less and less welcome. Billy Graham and Elmer Gantry have become two of her mainstays, and Effie often catches her mother singing George Beverly Shea's, "Just As I Am" *(I come, I come)*. Lavinia relays anecdotes, too, reminding Effie over and over again that Bill W., cofounder of Alcoholics Anonymous, hadn't had a drink in the thirty-seven years leading up to his death. Effie, who is beginning to understand a thing or two about enabling fictions, and remembering her mother's latest slip, tries to prepare herself for Lavinia's ultimate downfall. And yet, when it happens, Effie is caught entirely off guard.

Hippolytos Houlis, Effie's boss, has sent her home early on account of Effie's having a cold, yelling at her that even a sick person should be able to tell the difference between Javex and vinegar, and demanding to know how he is going to pay for all those ruined takeout fish and chip orders.

Effie trudges up the stairs to the apartment, her head stuffy, sorry and annoyed about her mistake and wishing Hippolytos would label his refill bottles. She is surprised to find her mother not only at home but dressed scantily in panties and bra. Effie senses that something is acutely wrong but, like all traumatized people, she waits quietly to determine what it is.

Lavinia Cambridge is pointing from the second-storey kitchen window to the bank building on the corner and asks Effie why the cleaners, a husband and wife, aren't joining in with the marchers. Like most Port Credit business establishments, the town is shut down on Wednesday afternoons so that people can take their half a day off, mix it with their Saturday half-day and all-day Sunday to come up with a five-day workweek. This is when janitorial staff work—when everyone else is home—and two of these cleaners are in the bank now with their floor polisher and bucket and mop.

Effie wonders what marchers her mother can be talking about just at the point when Lavinia launches into a frenetic description of what sounds to Effie like a full-blown parade, her mother gesturing excitedly, her hands all jumpy and jivey, her eyes wild and wet as she recounts a childhood memory of a pipe and bugle band, declaring how bagpipes always make her cry. She calls Effie to the window to see. Frightened by what she cannot know, Effie considers calling the police. Or an ambulance. She looks down onto the empty street below, the only evidence of life the two workers inside the bank.

Effie asks her mother a series of questions—Who else is in the parade? Why isn't her mother dressed? Isn't her mother supposed to be at work since the out-of-town mall is open all day on Wednesdays?—but none of Lavinia's answers make sense. Effie has no idea who Adeline and Catherine are (or were) or what *doocy beddo* means or why her mother is propped by the window half-naked on a day when she should be walking about Reitmans at the Dixie Plaza helping customers like Stewart.

Effie picks up the phone and calls the police, who come faster than Effie thinks should be possible. Her stomach lurches when they pound on the door, seeing the terror in her mother's eyes, feeling her own Judas betrayal. Quickly she calculates— wages plus tips plus hours per week—assuring herself that the landlady needn't know any of this, as long as no one is home to see the police car. Even then, Effie can lie if she has to.

The officers assess the situation, realizing quickly enough that Mrs. Cambridge is what they will later describe as two bricks short of a load. None of this is fair, of course, but it won't matter to them that the fault of Lavinia's hallucinations lies equally with an over-prescribing doctor—*I guess Librium and Valium don't mix well*, he said, as if this were news to him—and Lavinia's confusion. Why Effie later sneaks a vial of tranquilizers into the hospital inside the toe of one of her mother's high heel shoes, she can't explain, except to tell herself that she hates to disobey and, worse, she can't stand to see her mother feeling trapped. This habit will prove to be something of a hallmark later in their lives, but for now Effie's mother is not only made happy by her daughter's loyalty but she is the most glammed up patient anyone has ever seen in the psychiatric unit of the Mississauga Hospital.

Between school and work and hospital visits, Effie is exhausted. She thinks to herself perhaps it isn't all that tragic that Kathleen has left Port Credit Secondary School for Gordon Graydon Memorial after all, since Kathleen's mother had been so insistent, urged on by a vengeful husband who couldn't bear seeing his stepdaughter taken over, as he said, by her little lesbian friend. He also cost Kathleen her waitressing job, showing up one night after work and making a spectacle of himself, sweeping a cheeseburger platter off the counter and smashing it into a dozen pieces on the concrete floor. Since then the girls have spoken only by telephone, Kathleen hiding in the hall closet, masking the phone cord under the rug and whispering in regretful tones. As the months go on and the phone calls lessen, Effie comes to understand that it isn't only that Kathleen enjoys her new secretarial classes, but that she is also making new friends.

Effie distances herself from the world by moving through it at arm's length, casually lying to the landlady about the date of her mother's expected return; smiling with patience and sometimes disdain at the restaurant customers, always mindful of her dependence on tips; sitting up late through grade twelve assignments, scrawling essays about T.S. Eliot and the Industrial Revolution and glands and hormones of the endocrine system, eyes half open, pages slipping off the kitchen table onto the floor.

Slowly, her diet shifts from scrambled eggs and bacon to soft boiled eggs and cheese, root beer becoming her beverage of choice, an excuse to walk across Lakeshore Road to the grocery store in between tasks.

At school, she no longer visits the library for purposes of reading poetry but rather to complete assignments. She is careful about electives, too, dropping the more challenging physics, chemistry and trigonometry in favour of a sharper focus on languages, history and biology, subjects that entice her with promises of a past, a future, and change, Effie feeling ever more aligned with an idea that she is destined to travel; to be cordial but not revelatory; to swallow up hardship by reminding herself that everyone dies.

The degree of her increasingly anaesthetized behaviour is commensurate with her mother's mental illness, not yet (and as it turns out, never to be) diagnosed, but certainly a pathology larger than simple addiction (which Effie already understands as effect, not cause).

Her teachers worry about her, but keep their distance, not only out of respect but also because of their inability to know how—or perhaps even want—to help this unusual girl. Her landlady avoids her, not wanting to pressure Effie into further lies, and lowers the rent, a gesture she credits to a decrease in property taxes. Some nights, after the restaurant closes, Hippolytos Houlis finds himself wiping his arm across his nose, his face damp from either perspiration or tears. He isn't always sure which.

Except for a nascent relationship that develops between Effie and the young men who take their meals at the diner and work down the block at the funeral home (where Effie finally learns the truth about Maggie Mortimer's roster of duties), Effie might as well be a foreigner, living in a strange land where she neither speaks the language nor understands the customs.

CHAPTER 27

Effie lies on the couch wondering what went wrong. John had walked her home after their dinner at the Peking Palace but left her standing at her door digging in her pockets for keys. She wanted to invite him in—had expected to invite him in—but he had hurriedly said goodnight, turned and walked down the stairs before she could find the words to call him back. He pulled open the heavy entryway door and set off into the night. Effie's *thank you* trailed after him down the stairwell.

She had run across the living room to the window, her boots leaving traces of dirty snow on the wood floor. She watched him cross the barren street and make his way into the foggy churchyard. Where is he going, she wondered, although she had a fairly good idea. He was headed to the Dove to meet up with Mary and the MP for a nightcap, without her.

When Michael McCready had suggested this at the end of their meal, Effie creased her brow at John, expecting that he would take her home and stay for a drink or two at the apartment. An unopened bottle of Boutari and two polished wineglasses were sitting on her kitchen counter, waiting. But now, instead of coming in, John is walking briskly toward Richmond Street. As he passes like a ghost through the fog, the church spire sounds its uniform chimes, marking midnight.

"Goddamn bells!"

Effie wallops her chest and leaps up.

Mildred Rutherford hovers on the threshold. "Nice room," she says, her eyes scanning the furniture like an x-ray machine. "Didn't mean to scare you." She shrugs. "Spare, but homely. Wouldn't expect that from a girl like you. I anticipated more chrome. Clarice Cliff sort of thing."

Effie wonders who Clarice Cliff is and stares back at her neighbour. "Your boots are on," she says.

"Yours are, too. I figured it was *de rigueur*." Rutherford chuckles. "Hmm," she says, her eyes darting from one item to the next. "Passive-aggressive."

"Pardon me?"

"Green and red. Unpredictable seas."

Effie closes her eyes. "So you're telling me that *Christmas* is passive-aggressive?"

"You mean to say that it *isn't*?"

"Not everyone can afford Georgette O'Keefe, Miss Rutherford. Beggars can't—"

"Oh yes they can." Mildred Rutherford's face crinkles into a smile. "Secondhand furniture comes in all colours. What we inherit is a choice, you know. Even Georgia O'Keeffe—if you go in for all that labia." Her eyes follow the length of the piano keyboard.

"Is there something I can do for you, Miss Rutherford?"

"Is there someone you were watching for? It's mighty late to be out. Hate the evening shift myself, although it's quieter than the insanity that rolls in after midnight. Tonight we had a full-blown appy. Chap had a mud-green face." Miss Rutherford's eyes light up. "Peritonitis."

Effie takes off her gloves and stares at her hands.

"Not much time after *that* sets in." The older woman unfastens the buttons of her coat and slides it off of her shoulders. "You know, you remind me of one of those dolls—those Holy Hobby dolls."

"*Holly* Hobbie."

"The ones made out of rags. With the bonnets and the queer eyes." She heaves her coat onto the back of the rocker, setting the chair in motion.

"Don't do that! It's bad luck!"

"What's bad luck?" Mary pokes her head into Effie's apartment.

"What are *you* doing here?" Effie unzips her boots. "I thought you were with John."

"John? What are you talking about? I just saw him passing through the churchyard, but he didn't seem to see me.".

Effie looks up. "He didn't? But I was sure—"

"Whatever you thought," Rutherford booms, "you thought wrong." She sits down in the rocker, the wood heaving and creaking beneath her.

"Didn't the MP walk you home?"

Mary steps out of her boots and into the hallway. "Is it all right if I come in?"

Mildred Rutherford picks up her speed. "What MP? Not Michael McCready! Sweet thundering Jesus, you've not gone and—"

"Miss Rutherford, do you mind? Mary is a guest in my home and your question is grossly impertinent."

"You're the one that spilled the beans, Holly."

"I can take care of myself, Mildred, thank you." Mary smiles at Effie, the highlights in her hair sparkling in the hallway light. "And thank *you*, Effie." Mary closes the door behind her.

"Rude smude! It can't hurt to warn a favourite girl that—"

Effie breathes in deeply. Was there someone else—some secret lover hidden in a duplex down on Dorchester Street? Another teacher? Or someone Donnie knows? A friend of Elizabeth McCready? And is Mary *every*one's favourite girl?

"Could I offer you both some wine? I know it's late but since we're all here."

"Effie, that would be lovely." Mary settles down into the couch. "Thank you."

"So, the MP, eh? On the eve of Valentine's Day? Just the four of you? And how long has Effie been seeing our John?"

Effie turns on the cold water tap in the kitchen, dipping her head for a drink so she can relieve her tightening throat. She splashes water on her cheeks with her fingertips and dries her hands on a tea towel. Retrieving a third wine glass from the cabinet, Mildred Rutherford's words harden like a pit in her stomach. Who does she think she is? Effie plunks the third glass onto an enamel tray and walks steadily back into the living room.

Rutherford's jowls jiggle. "Mary says you have a fondness for art." She stares at Effie. "You seem more of a maths and science type to me . . . and there's the question of Georgia O'Keeffe."

"What about her?" Effie sets the tray on the coffee table.

"You called her Georgette."

Effie picks up the wine bottle, her hands trembling. "I most definitely did not."

"Oh but you did. Just a few minutes ago, right before our girl came in." *Our girl.*

Mary reaches for the bottle. "Have you never made a mistake, Mildred? Here Effie, I'll do that."

"Most indubitably I have." Mildred scrutinizes the label. "But I always own up to it. Indeed, when I was a fledgling nurse I once wrote *ephemeral cast* in a patient's chart. That's what the doctor said and that's what I wrote. Even saw the damn thing right there on her leg and, regardless, I wrote *ephemeral*. They laughed about that one all right. So did I. Not much point in letting your own jokes fly right over your head, if you take my meaning. So be it, as they say."

"My mother used to say that. *So be it.*"

Rutherford's chair creaks. "Ah yes, your mother the guru. Lover of Dickens."

Effie bristles. "No, *you* said that Miss—Mildred. I didn't. My mother had innumerable talents, and she was often wise, but she was not a guru and wouldn't have wanted to be one."

"What about Gandhi?"

"She felt that anything in the extreme was unhealthy. Even in herself."

Mary smiles, brushing an eyelash from her sleeve. "Your mother sounds like John."

"Gandhi is dead. He died in my time, you know." Mildred Rutherford smiles proudly. "I was too young to remember. I'm not *that* old. But I was working in Emergency when JFK died. A woman had been brought in by ambulance—car accident— hit her head hard—a double retinal detachment. We didn't know that right away of course, but I remember thinking, later, which would be worse—having your brains blown out in the back of a convertible or losing your eyesight—bang! Just like that!"

"Bang!" Mary says. "Right in the back of the head."

"Those Kennedy boys had a hand in other gardens, if you take my meaning." Rutherford unleashes her arms and swoops up her glass. "I think Marilyn Monroe had a lot to do with that side of things. She was a viper. Adam himself would have been tempted!" Rutherford rocks forcefully in her chair. "Why couldn't Michael McCready have followed in his father's footsteps and become a gynecologist? Done something valuable?"

"Miss Rutherford, must you always be rude?" Effie glances at her watch, then at Mary.

"Young lady, when you have had the benefit of my years and experience you'll think twice before calling me rude."

"Young lady? Do you have any idea how old I am?" Effie places her hand on her chest. "I'll be *thirty* in two years."

Mildred Rutherford's eyes pop open. "Good God Almighty! I took you for twenty-three. Twenty-four tops."

Mary uncurls her legs and lays her head on the arm of the sofa. "Effie has ravishing skin."

"Skin? It's got nothing to do with skin." Mildred studies Effie's face. "It's that you *seem* so young." She clears her throat. "Granted, I ought to apologize. I'm usually much more up on my facts." She exhales. "But that explains a few things. Either way, you'll thank me when you're fifty." The nurse pitches out of her chair like someone prodded with a stick.

At three in the morning, after the bizarre but not entirely unpleasant nightcap with Mary and Mildred, Effie, braced against the pillows on her bed, the wind rattling her window, continues to wonder why her evening with John had gone so terribly wrong.

One floor above, Mary lies twisted up in romantic meanderings—late night flights on week-long jaunts to Whistler, camping in New Brunswick by a silky stream, a leisurely fishing trip on the Miramichi.

Across the hall from Mary and above Effie, Mildred Rutherford snores on, her head filled with Lytton Strachey and

Sigmund Freud, the two men sitting in lawn chairs, smoking their Meerschaum pipes, charmed by the lithe recumbent dreamer circling before them, a lissome Isadora spiraling under the elm trees.

A few blocks away John stands in his living room, pulling two snifters from the sideboard. He gently unscrews the cap of a Jameson bottle, calling out softly over his shoulder, "I'll be there in a minute." He glances up, catches his reflection staring back at him from a glass-encased painting on the wall. For a second he wonders who that man is—dark-eyed, drawn, sinister. He pours from the bottle and notices that his hand is shaking.

CHAPTER 28

"Beware the Ides of March, Miss."

"Why, Griffen?"

"I don't know, Miss. It's just what my mother says."

"Do you know that March is not the only month containing ides?"

"No, I don't Miss. I don't even know what an ide is."

Effie sits down, her eyes sunken, her skin whiter than usual. "That's all for today, class. For those of you with play rehearsal tomorrow, please don't be late. Bruce, could you please erase the blackboard?"

On her way home Effie stops off at the Confederation library, wondering if a change in reading material would lighten her mood. She is beginning to feel ground down by bucolic tales of rural tragedy. And her students, mired in contrast-and-compare essay assignments and multiple-choice tests, seem listless and lost. Since childhood she had been told that self-discovery was healthier than spoon-feeding; that independent seeking and non-assertive authority were more rewarding; that in the end, the most meaningful things were those we come to on our own. Effie believes that her job as an English teacher requires her to convey these things in significant ways, but she isn't sure she knows how. While *The Wars* had clearly touched Gary Lowther's heart, she couldn't take any credit for it.

She pulls back the handle of the library door and walks in, heading past the desk toward the shelves of books. Perhaps they have a pedagogy section she can plunder.

"Can I help you?"

Effie jumps.

A woman whose nametag reads *Aida Lynn* steps out from behind the counter. "You're John MacDonald's friend, aren't you?" She speaks confidently, like someone used to being in charge.

"Shouldn't you lower your voice?"

"I'm almost certain we're the only ones here. Besides," Aida Lynn pauses to look at a chickadee scrambling in the wind outside the tall strip of window, "I'm head librarian. Who's to chastise?" Her eyes follow the bird's path away from the glass and up toward the branches of a tree. "Would you like a cup of tea? I just boiled the kettle."

"Here? In the *library*?"

"I was just about to close up. I would appreciate the company." A set of brass keys dangles from her hand. "I spend hours of my day staring at the stacks." She turns a key in the front door lock, drops the set into the pocket of her skirt then steps back behind the desk. She smiles, exposing a row of square, oatmeal-coloured teeth. "I love my work, but some days the books become mildly irritating. Like one's children, I suppose, were a person to have too many of those." She steps toward Effie, extending her hand. "Pleased to meet you. I'm Aida."

"How do you know I'm John's MacDonald's friend?" Effie releases her school bag onto the floor and briefly grasps the librarian's hand.

Aida Lynn retrieves a ceramic teapot from a shelf behind the counter. "Do you like your tea weak or strong? I like mine steeped but there are some people who prefer waving the bag over the top. Usually I make it by the cup. I hope you like peppermint."

Effie speaks preemptively. "Sometimes we—John and I, I mean—spend time together."

"Please, sit down." Aida Lynn points to one of two stools that sit behind the desk. "I've known John for years." She opens a small drawer, exposing packets of sugar, a spoon and a tangle of paper clips.

"I'm not his girlfriend, if that's what you mean."

"I made that assumption."

"That I was?"

"No. That you weren't." She pours out the tea into two mugs, each one marked *Ad Fundum*. "I hope I haven't hurt your feelings. I am not a romantic in that sense. It doesn't suit me and I certainly intend no unkindness."

"My feelings aren't hurt in the least." The pain in Effie's upper chest reminds her that her options are shrivelling. "That's not true. My feelings are hurt, but not by you." Effie stares at the teacups. "Oh look!" She tries to make her voice sound light and carefree. "Bubbles in your tea. That means money."

"Does it look like a lot of money? Because I could use a vacation."

Aida Lynn is what Effie's mother would have called homely. The lines around the librarian's eyes and mouth show her age, and her eyebrows sprout above startlingly blue eyes. Her hair, a hard grey, sits on her head like a hat. She reminds Effie of a faded, unpainted barn—the one you hope to come upon at the end of a long drive in the country.

"I've come in search of some help," Effie sputters. "In the library, I mean. From the books." She feels like an idiot. "I'm having some challenges."

"What is it you're finding difficult?" Aida Lynn blows across the top of her mug, disintegrating the bubbles. "The curriculum? The students? The grammar?"

"Yes," Effie laughs. "I asked the class the other day what a participle was and one of the students said I should save that question for the science class."

"Some of the staff here are very lazy—more lazy than incompetent, frankly. A person never knows where a book will be misshelved. Yesterday morning, I found James Joyce next to Joyce Carol Oates. Lazy. But then, of course, one has to locate the source of that—or any—laziness. Is it rooted in boredom or disillusionment or something more systemic? It can be very difficult to engage hormonal teenagers, but that may be your key."

"They do seem interested in the play we're putting on, but they complain about the novels we're reading. Most of them seem to have trouble relating to setting and characters, let alone understand theme and story arc."

"What about encouraging them to write? Perhaps you could run an essay contest. Make it competitive. Offer year-end prizes." Aida Lynn's eyes brighten. "There's nothing like a prize to lure an audience. Sometimes a little brainstorming works, too. Do you brainstorm? You could divide the class into groups. Put the students in charge. Make them understand they have power, a voice. But do that without telling them. Show them." She dips her head toward a metal cart piled high with books. "I think the reason the library staff misshelve is because their minds have drifted out the door. Too often we choose careers for ourselves when we love the work involved in *becoming* those things. Think of a pharmacist. All those years studying physiology, medicine, chemicals and outcomes, only to end up counting pills in a drugstore and changing banners on chocolate boxes."

"I don't know if I have the personality to inspire in those ways." Effie peeks at one of the book titles. *Out of Africa*.

"Oh, but you do. I can tell that you're passionate. John MacDonald wouldn't have chosen you as a friend if you weren't. He is a stellar individual with impeccable taste."

Effie eyes Dostoyevsky's *The Idiot*, which is teetering weightily on top of Dinesen's memoir. "If you were stranded on an island—a desert island, I mean—and had to choose ten novels to read for the rest of your life, what would they be?"

"Oh glory. I've been asked this question before, and every time I answer I seem to have a different list. Let's see . . . *The Wind in the Willows*, *The Secret Garden*, *Black Beauty*—"

"Those are all children's books."

"*A Tree Grows in Brooklyn*—"

"I love *A Tree Grows in Brooklyn*!"

"How many is that? Five? *House of Mirth*, *Madame Bovary*, *To Kill a Mockingbird*, *Anna Karenina* and, let's see . . . *The Canterbury Tales*. And *The Mill on the Floss*."

"Did you know that Betty Smith left school in grade eight to work in a factory? It's why she chose an industrial theme. Like Dickens, but in Brooklyn of course. Mostly I love the empathy that Mary Frances, who is clearly speaking for Smith, feels for her father. So many people deride alcoholics when they might instead have sympathetic understanding."

"I'm not sure I hold out a lot of compassion for alcoholic parents. It seems to me the worst kind of self-indulgence." Aida Lynn empties another sugar packet into her mug.

"Self-indulgence? How do you figure that? Who are any of us to decide what makes a life tolerable?"

"Men and women have walked away from fascist governments, ghettoes, even holocausts, and managed to raise children in loving, sober homes. When friends fail and life disappoints there are books, art, music and one's own company. You needn't have money or any of those—*these*—things."

"It isn't that simple." Effie is beginning to feel the weight of Aida Lynn's observations.

The librarian smiles. "It isn't that complex. We make choices. When we make the wrong choices, we make new ones. Most people I see have problems. It's written all over their faces and in the books they choose. We all have moments—good ones, bad ones, some that are so-so. It's up to us to at least try and make the bad ones better."

"Madame Bovary poisons herself and Lily dies of an overdose. How did they make their bad choices better? By dying?"

"There is no worthwhile book—or life—without tension. Viktor Frankl writes that in *Man's Search for Meaning*. Who can enjoy the beauty of a sunset if she has never felt the rain?"

"You sound like Kahlil Gibran." Effie pours more tea into her mug. She nods toward the long pane of glass that faces Richmond Street. "Who's that woman? She's been standing there watching us."

Aida Lynn turns around. "Oh, that's my friend," she says. "That's Jane. I had best see what she wants." The librarian steps soundlessly into a pair of winter galoshes, pulling the keys from her skirt pocket at the same time.

Effie stands up from her stool, feeling exhausted. "I should be grabbing some books and getting home."

"Oh—wait just a moment, would you please? I'll be right back."

The librarian and her friend stand in the snow facing one another, from this distance virtually mirror images. The visitor is shorter and wider than Aida Lynn, but to Effie these female figures hail from the same tribe: pragmatic (what her mother called dutiful), reliable and discreetly plain.

She studies the nuances of their faces, the upward curve of their smiling cheeks, the downward slope of their lashes. Is it possible in this small town of small minds that two women can so freely express their romantic feelings for one another?

"It's cold out there."

Effie has not seen Aida Lynn move away from the window or heard her turn the key in the lock.

"My friend—Jane—and I are meeting for dinner but we forgot to say where."

"I should be going. It's getting dark." Effie picks up her school bag. "I'll come back another time. Thank you for the tea."

Aida Lynn smiles. "You're right. It's getting late and I've kept you long enough. But I want to help you with your selections. Could you come by tomorrow? I used to teach, you know. Library science, which of course isn't English, but the methodology's the same."

Effie traipses the long block home, vexed by the proximity of everything, kicking at the ground in small petulant steps. What had Aida Lynn meant by *friend* exactly? Gossip was an intoxicant in this town. Too often since she had arrived on the island, the biddies from *The Music Man* had sung like chickens in her head— *pick-a-little talk-a-little pick-pick-pick*. Although, to be fair, Aida wasn't like that at all.

"Hey you!" Mary is outside the apartment building waving a book in the air. "I have something for you."

"What is it?"

"John's annotated version of *Twelfth Night*—with John's comments in the margins."

Effie wonders why John hadn't given it to her himself. "Why? Does he think I need it?"

"Obviously, goofball." Mary laughs. "Second set of eyes sort of thing."

Effie has never heard Mary talk so freely.

"Can I come visit? I'm dying for some tea, and I've run out."

"I have a lot of schoolwork to catch up on and I've just had some tea." Effie tugs on the heavy door, catching her reflection, and remembers Aida Lynn standing in the snow with that woman. "Yes, of course you can come up. I'm kind of sick of school."

"I am so excited! Mike and I are going to Whistler. In *B.C.*"

"I know where Whistler is, Mary." Effie runs up the stairs ahead of her. "Isn't skiing season over?"

"Effie, it's only March. Do you know how high Whistler is? They ski right into June on Blackcomb." Mary's face sparkles. "Hey—wait up!"

Effie shoves her key in the door and pushes through in one motion. She walks straight to the kitchen and piles her coat on the table. "I'll be out in a couple of minutes," she yells. "Make yourself at home." When she returns she finds Mary curled up on the couch.

"Is that your family in the photo?"

"No," Effie replies impatiently. "You know my entire family except for my mom, and she's dead of course."

"Effie Effie Effie, you have to stop being so defensive. I am sorry about your mom—really sorry. But we all have losses."

"Did *your* mother wash down a month's worth of sleeping pills with forty ounces of vodka? Did *your* mother slit her wrists and ask you to take care of her when you got home from school? Did she? Do you know what fatty tissue looks like Mary? It's white and slides out like bay scallops. That's what happens when you cut the wrong way." She feels a tremor in her legs and steadies herself by levelling her knee into the side of the coffee table. "I wanted to tell her at one point that if she wanted to die all she had to do was slice along the artery, but that's almost never what people do, is it?" She does not see Mary's mouth fall open. "What kind of a mother does that? How dare you tell me to stop being defensive? Who do you think you are?" Fat tears roll down Effie's cheeks and into the knitted fabric of her jumper. "Does everyone live their lives here running around in circles? Is this island just one fucking endless triangle of tedium? It *never* stops." She puts her hands up to her face, unaware of Mary abandoning the couch and raising her arms protectively toward Effie.

Effie drops her head, rigid in Mary's embrace. She feels only the dry ache in her throat as she sobs. She doesn't notice her rapid heart rate or feel the rivulets running from her crimson nose. She doesn't feel her fingers grasping at the edges of her sweater, or see the inward turn of her foot, or sense the soft curls that hug the back of her neck. She feels Mary's arms around her in a distant way, as if Mary were standing in another room. "My moon is in Pisces," she says, stepping back.

"Yes, you told me that before."

CHAPTER 29

Effie snaps on a pair of yellow rubber gloves preparing to scrub the toilet bowl the way her mother had taught her: on hands and knees. How many people use these anymore, she wonders. Surgeons? Hairdressers? Serial killers? She found an orphan pair hanging in the hardware store on Grafton Street. The manager said he didn't have much call for them anymore.

Effie had grown up with an appreciation for industry, which was partly rooted in her love of Charles Dickens—smoke-filled skies, dirty factories and well-intended people toiling under cruel masters. Effie doesn't believe that perseverance always brings salvation—it certainly hadn't saved her mother, despite her menial jobs—but the rigours of manual labour compel her.

She scrubs at the rust rings, smelling bacon, picturing Mildred Rutherford upstairs in her kitchen bent over a sizzling pan, hot grease smattering her face and chest, slices of pumpernickel carved up and stacked on the breadboard waiting to be toasted. Effie thumps the back of the Comet can, sending mint-green powder beyond the toilet's perimeter. She wonders what style of apron the nurse is wearing. Plain or print? *Kiss the Cook* or *Carpe Diem*?

A rush of shoes and boots ascends the staircase, converging like a force field overhead.

The geese.

She'll have to make quick work of things. With all the windows shut their voices will be muffled, although vents and aging plaster are always advantageous.

Effie flushes the toilet, stands up, yanks off her gloves and runs to the refrigerator, grabbing a late-morning root beer. She wishes she smoked.

Heading off to the back hallway she hunkers down in a corner of the curved stairwell, inserted between the two apartments.

She can hear the women settling and wonders if her aunt is among them. Chair legs scrape across the floor. Maritimers sure have a thing for kitchens.

And so it begins.

"April Fool's Day? I never bother with those pranks. Besides, they're only kosher in the morning. What does short sheeting a bed mean?"

"Who made up that morning rule anyway?"

"Who made up April Fools' Day?"

"It has something to do with the Julie calendar—New Year's moving up from the end of March to January."

"Isn't there anything more interesting we can discuss? Mmm . . . bacon. I hope it's not peameal."

"Julian."

"Like the salad?"

"No, that's julienne. E-N-N-E."

"Jesus! You don't have to yell at me!"

Effie holds her breath trying not to laugh, imaging a Julienne calendar, thin strips of ham, carrots and celery falling from its edges. She nurses her drink, longing for bacon with white toast and egg yolk for dipping.

"Guess who I saw in town the other day? Pulled up right beside me at Ken's Korner. And no—it wasn't Don Harron so don't even go there, please. It wasn't his fault. *She* was *jealous*."

The voices grow suddenly louder, Mildred Rutherford's proclamation rushing down the stairs. "I won't leave it open for long. I'm letting the smoke out."

Effie looks up, afraid to be found lurking like Uriah Heep.

"It was Colleen Dewhurst. Right there beside me!"

"What's so shocking about that? She's lived at the Inn at Bay Fortune for years."

"What's-his-name is doing all that work out there. Has any-body been by to see it?"

"She stays there in summer. That's not exactly the same thing as home."

"Colleen Dewhurst is sick. It couldn't have been her."

"It was her, I tell you. She looked just like Marilla."

"How do you know what Marilla looks like?"

"I mean she looked just like Marilla the actress."

"Marilla the actress?"

"The actress who played her. Jesus!"

"Jesus played the actress Marilla?"

"Now you're just being mean. I mean the *actress*—Colleen Dewhurst—who played Marilla."

"I saw Kris Kristofferson at the airport."

"What is she sick with? How do you know she's sick?"

"Yes, but he has a home here, too. A *real* one."

"Where do you get all of your information? *The Book of Lists*?"

"From my cousin who works at the airport. She says he's in and out every other week."

"Your cousin wouldn't know Kris Kristofferson from Lenin."

"Do you like him? I find him greasy. Unkempt."

"Shirley, you would call Jesus unkempt."

"Undeniably He was. Can you imagine conditions in the Middle East in—"

"Twenty BC?"

"Kris Kristofferson was engaged to Barbra Streisand once upon a time."

"Does that make him a homosexual?"

"Raggedy clothes and no proper bathing facilities. I wonder what they did without showers and running toilets and shampoo."

"That's right, Shirley. The mere lustre of the Mediterranean Sea."

"Good God, next thing you'll be wondering how they disinfected their knives and forks without dishwashers!"

Effie hugs her shins, wondering what it is that she misses—if anything—in friendships. These women are just like any clique or sorority or those back-biters who chum around making trouble for girls outside their circles. All they talk about are movies, sex and make-up. No one wants to have an intelligent discussion except for the women who spend their crowded hours in women's studies classrooms sneering at you if you so much kick back with a root beer.

No. The groups Effie wants to join—the subjects she is interested in—are overflowing with flakes and blowhards. Pottery, astrology, creative writing, yoga, glass blowing—they are all off her list, and they'd all come off the hard way.

"Speaking of homosexuals"—a fork pings loudly against the side of Rutherford's stove—"has anyone heard any more about that New Year's Eve party?"

"What party?"

The hair on the back of Effie's neck stands up.

"Where all the homos—homo*sex*uals—attended, and what went on after the party was over?"

"Who told you that?"

"My brother."

Effie clamps her hand over her mouth.

"Your brother? What would he know? Doesn't he make picture frames?"

"He was there."

"If a few gay people show up at a party, so what?"

"Well, we need to know if there are gay people taking over our town."

Idiots.

"Taking over the town? I don't want to be the first one to break it to you, Shirley, but gay people have been on earth since the beginning of time. There's at least one homosexual in every family, I'm sure."

"I always did wonder about your brother."

"Here we go again."

"Or in every closet."

"Enough about the gay people."

Effie yawns.

"A *what*? Does your mother know you use words like that?"

"That's what you get for going into the Grafton Pub. That and head lice."

"Not that this matters, but your husband was in that bar with some of his friends. If it's handier for him to be there . . ."

"Enough about the gay people. Please."

Effie looks up through the window at the sky. A burly cumulus cloud, unexpected on a winter's day, has broken away and pulled itself up into the shape of a witch's hat.

She lowers her gaze and sees a shadow fall across the hallway wall. She keeps her eyes down, her hands slipping on the perspiration of her pop bottle.

"Your door was open. Front *and* back." Mildred Rutherford has never looked larger. "What are you doing out here? Listening in?" She teeters on her Wallabees. "Why not just come up and knock, if that's the case?"

"I wasn't listening to your jibber jabber. In fact, I often come out here for a break. If you must know, I was thinking about witches." She stares up into Mildred's disbelieving face. "I am allergic to Comet—the dust fills the apartment—and I came out here until things settle down."

"Oh I see. Taking a breather."

"Something like that."

"You're more than welcome to bacon and eggs if you want some. Your aunt hasn't had a chance to polish them off yet. You needn't sit out here feeling sorry for yourself—conjuring up witches."

"I can cook for myself, thank you just the same."

"Good enough, then. Shall I depart the way I came, or should I return on my broom?"

Effie storms through her apartment, clomps loudly up the front stairs to the third floor and knocks hard on Mary's door.

Mary comes running on padded feet.

Speaking as loudly as she can, Effie projects throughout the hallway, "Do you think you might have some time to help me?"

"Are you on fire?"

Effie points cryptically to Rutherford's door. "I'd like some input on the play. I have to map it out before tomorrow but I'm afraid I'm going to muck it up."

"Half an hour okay? I have to shower and feed Pistachio."

"Perfect!" Effie roars. "See you then."

She hammers back down to her apartment, gathering up a row of markers from her pencil box. She sets them on the coffee table one by one, mumbling. "Green for Gary, red for Ruthie, blue for Bruce, violet for Virginia, gray for Griffen, and putrid yellow for Vivian." She sits down on the couch, imagining the kids onstage on opening night, joining hands for the curtain call. Her gaze trails through the living room window beyond the church and the Department of Veterans Affairs, scanning the tops of the low-rise department stores on Grafton Street.

Before long all the trees will be in bloom again and an entire year gone by since her arrival on the island. And what has she accomplished? A classroom full of kids who, if they don't exactly dislike her (except of course for Tommy, who probably still calls her a cunt behind her back) have not moved ahead in leaps and bounds. Martha has developed a passion for Oscar Wilde and totes his plays faithfully under her fleshy arm, but like most of the students she continues to wrestle with iambic pentameter and blank verse. *Miss, am I supposed to feel blank when I read it? Because that's what's happening.* Far too many of the grade tens had barely made their way up to C+ on their winter exams.

As for the other teachers, even the ones Effie likes aren't exactly inclusive, talking on and on in the lunchroom about *up home* this and *up home* that, never thinking to invite her *up home* anywhere. In the end, despite any idea of birthright—and this is the worst part—the island is not her home.

"Ta-pocketa-pocketa-pocketa." Mary stands in Effie's living room, her hair wet and combed out from her shower.

"Excuse me?"

"You know. Walter Mitty. He was like you—always fantasizing about something." Mary sits down on the sofa next to Effie. "What are the markers for?"

"I can't half remember who got what part in the school play. So green is for Gary, red is for Ruthie, blue is for Bruce—"

"You're kidding, right? You're *not* kidding?"

"I have a weird memory. If I don't put it all down on paper in an organized way I'll forget. Have you ever seen me try to make tea? I practically need a recipe."

"What if we discuss the play and see if that helps lock them in your mind? Don't you think that would be a lot easier than—"

"Putrid yellow for Vivian? Yes, I do."

"Vivian? *Vickie's* Vivian? Oh no."

"Oh yes." Effie scratches her cheek with a marker. "See why I need help?"

"That priggish Josie Pye gets her nose stuck into everything."

"It could be me, but I don't remember kids being as yucky when I was that age. I want to throw a pie in her face every time I look at her."

Mary laughs. "Her whole family's like that. Her father comes from up our way and I can tell you there's no bigger fish in a smaller pond than Clarence Myers."

"The big fish from Little Pond? Ha! But I wonder, how does a person move outside herself to become bigger?" Effie glances up toward the ceiling.

"What do you mean—bigger?" Mary follows Effie's gaze. "You can't get much bigger than Rutherford."

Effie snorts. "No. Bigger. More encompassing. Magnanimous. For example, rather than me sitting here sounding like the women upstairs, if I were better able to access—who knows what, but something—I might become a bigger, and better, person. Someone who wouldn't care about small-minded people like Vickie Myers and her daughter."

"Effie, you're living in Cassandra land. Perception without power. Take the Myers family. They're a hateful lot. Pigs, if you want the truth of it. But the thing is, you see, *I* can call them pigs—I can even say that outside of this apartment—at my work, or in a bar—as long as I don't say it to one of their relatives. But you—people who are from away—can't. It makes me embarrassed and ashamed, but there you have it."

"But why do people persist in it? Surely not every islander is an asshole."

"Surely not." The pigment deepens along Mary's neck. "But there are just as many who are tired of people who come from aw—other places and blow around big puffy ideas like a lot of hot air, treating islanders as if we are backward or inferior."

"Oh. You mean like my Uncle Bill? My uncle who *is* an islander?"

"No. I mean people who you would expect to know better. I don't—"

"That's just snobbery. And simplistic. Why do you expect someone to know better because he's from Vancouver or Calgary or even Toronto? We come with the same problems and limitations that everyone else does. In fact, we don't have the luxury of all this cozy insularity."

"Oh Effie, it's not cozy at all. It's incestuous and nepotistic and supremely disappointing. How would you feel having to live in a fish bowl with a lot of people you can't stand? It isn't pleasant having to—every single day, mind you—smile and say hello to two hundred people you marginally know and like even less, and just as many of them talking about you as if they know you better than you know yourself."

Effie swallows. "What do you think about sex?"

"Sex? Did you say sex? You sure know how to switch topics."

"No really, I mean sex. Sexual activity. What do you think about it?"

"I guess I think it's pretty great altogether."

"Or *in* the altogether." She shifts closer to Mary. "When I was a kid my mother took me to hear some man—in our church, of all places—give a talk about sex. It was radical at the time and I'm still not sure what my mother's motives were."

"Elmer Gantry meets Dr. Spock?"

"I couldn't wait to go home and talk to my best friend about it. Maybe that's what my mother knew—that she was incapable of being consistent, of setting things straight. Maybe she trusted that I would talk to Kathleen and that Kathleen and I would work it out. Maybe that's what my mother wanted for me. But it didn't make much difference because I'm still at a loss to figure it out. How to get it, want it after I get it, and hang onto it."

Mary grabs a highlighter. "You hang onto it like this." She lengthens her arm, demonstrating.

"Not if it's *that* small I don't." Effie rounds her mouth in mock surprise, her face alight with glee.

Mary laughs and winds a lock of hair around her finger. "I don't think you have any idea how beautiful you are."

Effie chokes on saliva. "You think I'm beautiful? You're not mocking me, are you?"

"You are beautiful, Effie. You have an ethereal quality about you. Like Audrey Hepburn."

Effie crosses one eye, a habit she perfected for her mother. "I don't look anything like Audrey Hepburn." She thinks back to the Christmas staff party, relieved.

"It's the quality of you, not just your features. The whole look of you—the way you move and even the way you're uncomfortable with yourself."

"Confidence is supposed to make people alluring—not self-consciousness."

"That's hogwash. I bet men fall all over themselves when they're around you. Women, too."

"Are you out of your *mind*? The last time someone fell over me he was walking with a seeing eye dog." Effie stands up. "What if I bring out a copy of the play along with some notes I've made and we can have a gander?" She slips away from the living room calling behind her, "I won't be long. I have to dig up the notes from my bedroom."

Mary sits back and closes her eyes. She thinks about Mike McCready and their weekend cross-country skiing up at Harmony Junction. She had stumbled over a snow-covered tangle of surface roots and he had fallen on top of her, the two of them kissing, warmly knotted on top of the cold ground, skis crossed. "Someday," he said, "I am going to marry you. You are the girl who will *not* get away." Mary had laughed and accused him of stalking her.

Effie sneaks up behind her. "You're all lit up like a Christmas tree. Does Shakespeare excite you that much?" She cradles a pile of papers and a copy of the play. "I know he does me, especially once I was prepared to understand him. I had to read the words out loud, that's all."

"I saw *Romeo and Juliet* at the movies with my mother. I didn't need to understand all the words to take his meaning." Mary eyes the stack that Effie has dropped on the table.

Effie shrugs. "If Franco Zeffirelli were directing this play it wouldn't be a problem. Or if Bruce Jarvis or Virginia Halfpenny could convey anything the way real actors do, I'd be all set."

There isn't even time for a breath. Had the windows been open, the crash would have been heard the length of the block and into the churchyard. As it is a flight of cooing pigeons that were resting on the living room window ledge are flapping their wings vigorously and flying away.

Clouds of white dust pour out from the bathroom, a momentary sound of nothing followed by broken coughing, fitful at first then gathering steam, a steady staccato rising and cascading down the hallway.

As the particles disburse, Effie is able to make out a silhouette where her toilet used to be—the toilet she had only an hour earlier scoured so strenuously. Propped in the corner of Effie's bathroom, on a toilet of her own, Mildred Rutherford, her beige hose pulled down around her Wallabees, her flesh a creeping yellow, sits like a phoenix in the ashes.

"For Jesus sake," she snipes. "I knew those bloody pipes were leaking."

Effie inches into the room, slack-jawed, and reaches forward to grasp Mildred's hand, not knowing where decorum ought to take them. She pauses, unsure, looking upward to the snow-white faces staring down through the ceiling, the plaster settling like confetti in their hair. "Hello Aunt Shirley. Ladies. Now, would someone please go call an ambulance?"

CHAPTER 30

Tea kettles percolate in kitchens all over Charlottetown—a utilitarian baked enamel cauldron in the hospital kitchen, overlooked by long-legged spiders hanging from dusty ceiling corners, unreachable except by extension ladder, the kitchen a hallway away from the room that Mildred Rutherford shares with three other islanders, all of them recovering from assorted injuries and operations: an osteotomy for an improperly healed fracture, a double bunionectomy from a stubborn commitment to high-heeled shoes, multiple stitches incurred by a fall from a barn rafter, and Mildred, from emergency surgery the night before. Dr. Bob himself had come in to see her, reassuring her that he would be getting at the pipe problem promptly, and *whoa ho ho ho* that must have been quite some landing! Mildred, swooning in an anaesthetic haze, waved him away, a tiny river of spittle oozing from the corner of her mouth onto the starched pillowcase.

And on the small white stove in Mary's apartment kitchen, a red Paderno kettle—made in Prince Edward Island and given to her as a Christmas present—simmers on medium-high, Effie waiting patiently in her bathrobe and bare feet, wandering through the other rooms, examining: watercolour paintings that Mary has hung on her walls; diminutive glass pyramids filled with pretty gemstones that have migrated onto shelves and end tables in the bathroom and bedroom; sunlight bursting through the windows and splintering the ornamental glass; a Canon Starwriter 80 sitting on the polished rolltop desk in Mary's spare bedroom where Effie has slept overnight on a comfortable Depression-era cot and now, back in the warm kitchen, waiting for the kettle to come to a rolling boil the way her mother had taught her, Effie sidesteps furry mice, miniature baseballs, and cheerful cloth birds lying about the floor, Pistachio for the moment asleep on Mary's double bed.

And plugged into the wall in the newspaper office, a Black and Decker kettle comes to a slow boil while Mary, catching up on leftover work and leaving Effie time alone to get used to her temporary home, pores over a news article, oblivious to the chattering keyboards, the hum of the fax machine, the coffee slurpers, the intermittent tapping and clicking of pens and pencils, and a rogue blue jay that has made its way onto the branch of an oak tree that is rooted next to the building, the bird's mechanical clicks punctuated by short-lived, piercing screams.

And in Donnie Fitzgerald's family kitchen on King Street, Ruth pours scalding water into a Pyrex teapot—a metal spoon slants against its insides to prevent cracking glass—calling out to the boys to stop goofing around and get themselves ready for Sunday service, and to mind that their socks match, that they pick up their collection plate money from the bedroom dresser, that their porridge will be ready in five minutes, and that if they want toast they'll have to help themselves, while Abel, biding time in the living room in his white shirt and loose suspenders, laments the itchy wool pants that wait for him.

CHAPTER 31

"Mildred Rutherford is Dr. Bob's *cousin?*" Effie sounds like a child who's been invited to the circus but has been passed over for popcorn. She rubs her forehead, aware of a gathering tightness, a festering septic pestilence aimed at taking her life.

"She's my cousin, too, you know," says Donnie, laughing.

"Come on! This has to be a joke. You're kidding—right? How can she be your cousin too?" Effie scrutinizes Donnie's face.

John pulls his chair closer to the table, bringing the musky scent of Zino Davidoff's Cool Water for Men with him. "Donnie's aunt—Ruth's sister—is married to Mildred's brother. That is, they *were* married. You can imagine what life with a Rutherford would be like."

"How does that make you cousins? You're not cousins! You're not even related except through distant marriage."

"Yes," John says. "She's more like an aunt once removed."

Donnie sighs. "I wish *someone* would remove her."

"Someone almost did."

Effie massages her fingers into her temples."Oh God. Wood smoke!"

"Effie, are you okay?" Mary reaches out to Effie and touches her arm. "This isn't much of a way to celebrate your birthday."

"What I want to know is who is going to drive us all home from Hunter River?" John leans back in his chair. "Mike drives that two-seater micro-car so that takes care of Mary, but who can trust the rest of you to stay sober?"

"Don't look at me," Donnie says. "Elizabeth and I are staying overnight. In case it snows." Donnie grins like a boy at camp.

Effie sneezes. "How did they get a licence for this place? This doesn't look like any bar I've ever been in."

Donnie digs into his pocket for Kleenex. "Here's what John would tell you: The Three Brothers' Ale House, a favoured and out of the way hall, was converted to a tavern after a quick sale coincided with the arrival of a Westphalia vanful of west coast hippies who were in search of a low-key bohemian lifestyle that an influx of foothill serial killers had made impossible to maintain."

Effie laughs.

"I hope it snows," Elizabeth says.

Donnie nods. "Me too. Y'know, I think I've got a sliver in my ass." He pulls his wallet out of his back pocket and slams it down on the table. "Effie, you're not paying a red cent for anything tonight."

"Therefore if thine enemy hunger, feed him. If he thirst, give him drink. For in so doing thou shalt heap coals of fire on his head." John squints at a rafter.

"Thank you, King James."

Effie slouches in her chair, her eyes cast down on her wine glass, the dishwasher stains shamefully evident. Her mother would have been appalled. She moistens the edge of her napkin surreptitiously with her tongue then briskly runs the cloth around the rim of the glass. The noise at their table seems far away. She looks at John who is fixed in his chair, his eyes now roaming, taking in parameters, dimensions, making mental configurations that she cannot penetrate.

At the far end of the room a trio of musicians wearing corduroy caps and bib overalls corral, one of them kneeling to unlock his guitar case, chromatic labels slapped across the vinyl. The taller musician—violent red hair corkscrewing around his ears like a comic book character—rifles through sheets of music while the third unties a knot in his bootlace.

"Wynken, Blynken and Nod," John says, not fully under his breath.

"I'm with you there," Donnie agrees, and the five friends scuttle their chairs forward like co-conspirators planning a quick getaway from a religious revival. "And what's with the cable knit sweaters?"

"It's always like this," John grumbles. "At least until the music begins."

"What happens then?" Effie asks.

"Then," says Mary, "we're all doomed."

"Overtaken," John corrects, "by maudlin sentimentality, our ancestral roots calling out to us from beyond blackened fields of rotting potatoes and the barren tenant farms littered with sad little thatch-roofed cottages."

Donnie laughs. "You won't need a car to carry you home. You can glide back to Charlottetown on a river of tears."

"Precisely," John says, mashing the heel of his hand into his head. "You see what I mean, Effie? Nothing ever changes. Get out while you can."

Effie winces. "You'd have to be *in* to get out."

"Oh Effie," John says, "you're as in as they come. As welcome in the collective as any Scotsman's or Irishman's son or daughter. Look at your skin and the shape of your eyes. Look at the set of your brow. Even your hair colour betrays you."

"Effie looks more Irish than Scottish, at least to me." Donnie lifts his pint of beer. "Be careful, John. You're sounding dangerously Yeatsian."

"Thereby illustrating my point. There are some things we cannot escape and others we can. Even Halifax seems too close to home these days."

Halifax.

"You can't leave," she says.

"Beg your pardon?" Donnie sets down his beer.

"Halifax. You were going to Halifax but then...well, then you met Elizabeth, and I just assumed.... I haven't given much thought to it but it seems to me—"

"I'm just a stylist, Effie. I can work anywhere."

"*Just* nothing." Donnie drapes his arm around Elizabeth's shoulders. "I wouldn't take you away from your friends and family. Besides, you've just got your first bonafide job. That's nothing to sneeze at."

"Wild horses," John says.

"Exactly."

"Wild horses?" Effie asks.

"Couldn't drag him away."

Donnie turns to his friend. "What about you, my man? Thinking of fleeing the scene?"

"That's odd phraseology," John says. "I've committed no crime."

Donnie chuckles. "Unless it's misappropriation of fun."

"Are you leaving the island?" Effie plants her elbows on the table, her heart skittering.

"It's either that or spend my life wondering." John reaches over and grabs Effie's hands away from her face. "Want to come with me?"

Effie, stunned, disengages a hand and waves at Michael McCready, who is striding into the hall looking like the fourth musician. When he spots Mary, his head brightens like a light bulb.

John nudges Effie, putting his lips close to her ear, "Look at all this happiness."

"That's just what I was thinking. We should have brought sunglasses."

John smiles, nodding. "We, you and I, are Dorothy and William Wordsworth, rowing across the lake admiring the daffodils."

Effie warms and cools in rapid succession. She wants to be seen as the kind of woman John needs: level, generous, humble, gracious and smart. But she feels like an ungainly swan, battering her wings against a prickly shoreline.

The band bleats out a medley of Irish folk tunes—"Black Velvet Band," "The Maid Who Sold Her Barley," "Whiskey in the Jar"—the rowdy notes accompanying a delivery of baskets—deep-fried mushrooms caps, zucchini sticks, potato skins stuffed with melted cheddar and bacon bits. Tortilla chips buried in hills of Monterey Jack rise in a great heap on a fleet of round silver trays.

John has switched from malt beer to Irish whiskey and hovers on the edge of tipsy. He repositions himself in his chair, gesturing to Effie to do the same, occasionally plucking a mushroom cap or tortilla chip and dropping it onto a folded napkin.

He hands the morsels over to her, commanding her to eat. "It's your birthday. We'll pretend this is cake."

Cake.

A corner slice of white cake, ribboned in pink icing, a tiny candy rose curled into the corner, a hand—her father's hand—holding it out to her tenderly.

"You know, Effie," Donnie is saying, "April 20th is also Hitler's birthday."

"Donnie—you're horrible!" Elizabeth laughs. "Isn't it the Queen's birthday, too?"

"Age before beauty," Donnie protests. "Besides, I'd rather share my birthday with Hitler than with the queen. At least with Hitler you know where you stand."

John sets his empty glass on the table. "You sound like an anti-Semitic asshole."

"Jesus. I didn't mean anything like that. My comment was really only about the Queen. It had nothing to do with Hitler." Donnie looks over at Mary. "Say—does Queen take an upper case Q when a person is being descriptive?"

John stands up. "Effie, would you like to catch a little night air? This whiskey and Donnie's stupidity have gone to my head. I think a walk would be just the thing."

Back in the heart of Charlottetown, Mildred Rutherford yanks the hospital sheet up over her breasts. An itinerant latex glove drops down from the box above her like a punctured balloon.

"Jesus God," Mildred moans. Pain sears through her upper leg, which is suspended in traction. "Nurse Murnaghan! Get in here!"

A willowy woman wearing a starched uniform breezes into Rutherford's room. "Are you in pain?" The young nurse extracts a small glass bottle from her pocket.

"In pain? Am I in pain?! What do *you* think? Of course I'm in Jesus pain! This goddamn rig hurts every time I suck air." She points to the traction mechanism. "Get that needle into me NOW."

The nurse does as she is told, knowing that to react in any significant way is to incur the wrath of her superior, which could mean anything from a reprimand to dismissal. Nurse Murnaghan draws back on the needle. "This might sting a bit," she says.

Mildred Rutherford lets out a heaving exhalation. She lays her head back on the pillow, fighting relief from the injection, clicking her tongue against her teeth as she racks up the room's imperfections: one disposable cup sitting on the window ledge (set there yesterday by a visitor who had only stopped by to shore up her Christian duty, which wasn't as much in danger of lapsing as collapsing); a full laundry cart parked in the hallway, its lid gaping open; a layer of dust coating the hanging television set, and a tear in the upper gauze portion of the privacy curtain that allows the glare from the hallway's overhead light to kindle the shadowed bed.

If it weren't for the hospital gossip that accompanies the routine visits from staff, Mildred doesn't know what she would do. Traction has rendered her vulnerable, even in the eyes of the doctors and nurses, whose empathy, or prurience (or both), bleeds into idle chitchat at the senior nurse's bedside.

While in hospital Mildred has learned that Dickie Watts has only one testicle; Penelope Windwater has had an affair with the gas station attendant on Fitzroy Street while her husband was having dalliances with Caroline Crockett (to which Mildred replied, "I think I'm the only one *not* having sex with Caroline Crockett); John MacDonald is planning a sudden move to Halifax; Dr. McLean has a brain tumour, and Chief Trainor's death last year is impossible to classify as suicide given the bullet's trajectory.

She waves her hand in the air. "*You say below-knee and I say baloney, you say a femoral and I say ephemeral . . . below-knee, baloney, a femoral, ephemera . . . let's rip the whole thing off.*"

As the young nurse glides down the hospital hallway she can hear the finale of Mildred Rutherford's tortured solo, "*But oh, if we call the whole thing off then we must part, and oh, if we ever part then that might break my heart.*"

★

Effie shakes her arms against the cold. "It was a lot warmer earlier today."

"Yes, such is the nature of weather and night. The sun disappears and, with it, the heat. Here," John says, "take this." He winds his houndstooth scarf around Effie's neck, knotting it gently at her throat. "Which way shall we walk?" They stand outside of the hall, a gust of wind scooping up late-winter leaves that are black from mould.

"This land is your land," Effie says. "You choose." She turns her head away from the cemetery, which she hadn't seen until now. She and John walk silently along the road, heading northward at the corner.

"Over that way we have Saint Patrick's, and up over there just above us is Rustico—do you feel like a fishing expedition? We could go out as midnight pirates. No?" John aims his gloved hand at the other side of the road. "And not too far that way is Wheatley River, which is not to be overlooked—well, yes, to be somewhat overlooked, I reckon. And if you want a fine lobster supper, New Glasgow is the place to be." He guides Effie's shoulder. "All too far to walk to unless you're a Bronte, but there nonetheless."

"How do you keep it all in your head? I get lost in the supermarket." Effie looks up shyly, hiding part of her face beneath her coat collar and John's scarf. "I do know one thing about Hunter River." She sniffs discreetly at the cologne embedded in the fibres of his scarf.

"Is it a secret?"

"Hunter River is Bright River in Lucy Maud Montgomery's Avonlea." Effie sighs. "I hate movies that begin that way."

"What way?"

"The way a character will give out a lot of information, the way you just did, but really it's designed to get the audience up to speed. It's so lazy." Effie trundled along, trying to keep pace.

"I thought you might like to know a little about your surroundings."

"Oh, I do. I didn't mean it that way at all. I was only going off in my head. I do that all the time."

"Yes, I've noticed. It's one of the things I like about you. You're like a rocketing tangent sometimes, spinning off in all directions. I think it's wonderful for your students. They do, too, you know."

"Spin off in all directions? They certainly do."

"Yes, that too, I suppose. What I meant was—they like that about you."

Effie stiffens.

"In fact, sometimes when I'm passing by your classroom I stand in the hallway and listen." John stops walking. "You are so passionate. I wish more teachers cared about what they teach, the way you do. Students would be more advantageously served."

Effie stands beside him, staring at his profile, wanting to touch him. "You sound like Norman Vincent Peale."

"It seems I can do no right this evening."

Effie walks on ahead, the hill challenging her lungs. "I think I'm embarrassed because you said you listen to me. But I'm not sure if it's because you said it, or because you do it." She wants to ask him what he means by passionate.

"Every summer in North Rustico, on the first of July, there's a boat parade that comes in along Cavendish Beach." He loosens his step. "The population swells beyond all probability. Only a smattering of people live in Hunter River—this place hasn't been a cohesive community for all that long—but you should see the traffic come through here once the warm weather sets in."

"Do you think you'll really leave?"

"I don't know, Effie. Apart from my friends and family—"

"And the students—you can't forget about the students."

"True. But you see, despite all this, it's probably time for a change."

"Do you know how lucky you are to have family and friends? Why would you want to leave them behind? It just doesn't seem charitable—not at *all*."

"What if I told you that it's also because I'm tired of living alone? That I would like some companionship. That I would like to be sharing my life with someone."

Why not me? Effie wants to ask. "You could get a dog," she says instead. She can hear the panic in her voice.

"I already take care of the family dog most weekends. My father as you well know drops him off every Saturday night, like a houseguest. And while Barkley would miss me, I don't think he would throw himself off a cliff if I were to move away." John laughs.

"I would miss you, if I didn't come with you."

"Oh Effie. You wouldn't want to come with me. Not really. You've just got here and are beginning to make friends and develop relationships at school. And you have a fantastic apartment." He shuffles in closer to her. "Which is even more avant-garde without a bathroom ceiling. Anyway, it's just like me to fantasize and do nothing about it." He hangs his arm around her. "If you knew all the things I have said I was going to do and—"

"Name two." Her eyes follow the outline of the thinning road that climbs ahead of them. She feels lost.

"Okay. Name two. One, I nearly got into real estate with a cousin of mine. He's a carpenter and he wanted me to invest in a row house over on Pownal Street. It was tempting but I couldn't come up with the cash. And then there was the time I thought I would become a photographer. I even took a class over at the college, but I wasn't as gifted as I'd hoped. Apart from all that, I have had more than my share of seminarian moments."

Effie presses herself into John's ribcage. "Do you know one of the things I like most about you? You keep a direct line open to the person you're with. I like that. And you make me feel brave. I say things to you I would never say to anyone else."

"Not even to Mary? Or to your mother?" John halts. "When your mother was alive is what I ought to have said."

"My mother and I talked about a lot of things—politics, children, religion. People assume because someone is alcoholic they're a mess in every way. I was the only kid in my class who had lunches made with homemade bread. I don't have a fraction of her talent or energy. Well, what used to be her energy."

"Did she always drink?"

"All of my life." Effie smiles thinly, like a child who has just lied about not wanting more cake. "Sporadically the first years, and then later all the time. She hated herself for it and became punishing in her hatred. But even when she jabbed, I knew it wasn't about me, and that's something, isn't it? To know you're loved and valued—how many children can say that?"

"Yes, Effie, you're right. Many of us are taken care of yet cannot be sure how loved we are. Or how loved we would be if we were removed from—if we removed ourselves from—the status quo."

Effie looks at John, alarmed to find him so close. She can feel his breath on her face. Her clothing suddenly tightens, her sweater confining; her underwear squeezing the breath out of her, sucking her back into herself. She wills herself to keep looking at him, their matching height intimidating.

"This is something quite new to me," he says. "This feeling as if I want to kiss you." He touches her nose with the tip of his gloved finger. "I wonder how you would feel about me kissing you."

Sweat drips down the underside of her sweater, the material itchy, irritating her skin. A cut on the inside of her fourth toe begins to sting. She regrets her tight-fitting boots and her obstinacy about relinquishing them, wondering why she is always so lax about trimming her toenails. She longs for a tree to lean into.

John's breath feels warm on her face, the whiskey lingering around the edges. "I am not going to ask again," he says, his voice low. "Speak now or forever hold your peace."

"But—"

He places his lips on hers, pressing himself lightly into her, the sleeve of his coat nuzzling her shoulder. He pauses. "This is nice," he says. "Quite lovely." He opens his eyes and looks at her.

Effie kisses John back tentatively. His tongue, unlike Garfield's, is thick-tipped and round. His kiss feels subtle, more careful.

Dorothy and William Wordsworth row their way through Effie's imagination, Dorothy lying back in the boat with her eyes closed, William roving the hillside. Effie lowers her head.

John steps back and lifts her chin with his hand, the leather of his glove pleasantly cool. "Are you all right?"

"They were brother and sister," she says. "Oh my God." The wind whips around her.

"Who were brother and sister?"

"William and Dorothy Wordsworth. They weren't husband and wife. They were brother and sister."

John laughs. "Yes, I know. Not all love is sexual, Effie. And not all sexual love is ideal." He takes her hand and they continue to walk along the side of the road. "Romeo and Juliet—dead at half your age. Heathcliff and Catherine lost to pneumonia and the moors."

He stops walking and squeezes Effie's hand. "Listen. Did you hear that? A snowy owl. Do you hear that barking?"

Effie speaks into the night air, her words carried away by the wind. "Daphne DuMaurier died two days ago," she says. "The day before my birthday."

"She couldn't wait?"

Effie rushes at John, happy to be laughing again. "You are so sacrilegious. Daphne du Maurier was a preternatural writer. Saintly."

"She was a plagiarist."

"Who said so?"

"Everybody."

"Could you love a plagiarist?"

"If she were you, maybe I could." John throws back his head, his laughter sailing across the pitch black sky.

CHAPTER 32

Effie hurries into the library and heads directly for Aida Lynn, who is standing behind the counter stirring a cup of tea, her keys hanging from her pocket like Christmas ornaments.

The librarian reaches down and retrieves a small box labelled *Wuthering Heights*.

"I'm so glad you've got it." Effie pats the top of the video with her mitten, a magician procuring a genie. "I thought I'd have to go all the way out to the university."

Aida Lynn continues to stir. "This one's from my personal stash. You sounded so anxious over the phone—is this for a school project?"

Effie senses a note of concern in Aida Lynn's voice. "No, I'm merely in the mood for a grand passion. But don't worry," she says. "I know how it ends."

"You mean unrequited?" Aida Lynn watches Effie carefully, waiting for her reply.

"At least," Effie says. "Did you know that Emily Bronte died the year after she wrote the novel? Tuberculosis."

Aida Lynn lets out a quiet sigh. "There are some things even more harrowing than death."

"You're awfully cryptic today," Effie laughs. "I'm just going to watch a movie—not hang myself."

"How are things with John?" Aida Lynn lifts the spoon gently from out of her cup and lays it down on a paper napkin. "Someone told me that you're dating?"

Effie doesn't know whether to be affronted by Aida Lynn's boldness, touched by the intimacy of her question, or thrilled by the assumption. "We spent my birthday together." She squints at her new friend. "Who told you we were dating?"

The lines around the librarian's mouth deepen as she tightens her lips. She pauses before speaking. "A little bird," she finally says.

Effie wonders if Aida Lynn's friend, Jane, has relayed the information. Aida Lynn doesn't seem like a person who would listen to gossip from just anyone.

"Well, I like little birds." Effie smiles warmly. "Little birds in their nests agree," she says, waving goodbye over her shoulder.

Aida Lynn cradles her teacup, her eyes tracking Effie as far as she is able to see her.

Effie emerges from her bedroom wheeling the metal TV cart across the sitting room and plants it in the corner. She shoves the video into the deck of the VCR and hits the play button. A bowl of potato chips and a bottle of Seaman's root beer sit on the table beside her and Effie, piqued, listens for the movie's opening strains.

The early shots of the Yorkshire moors are so reminiscent of her Hunter River walk with John that prickles of excitement feather her arms. Height differentials exist between one set of hills and the other, but the general sense of the wide open spaces, the wild, menacing wind, the isolation are all there.

Laurence Olivier is brutally handsome as Heathcliff, his strong features, his sideburns and prominent nose—his beautiful hands—even his mesomorphic frame. The actor might be taller than John, or Merle Oberon much shorter than Effie, but other than that the similarities are uncanny. Heathcliff, angry, brooding and ostracized, stands out as singularly passionate, determined at any cost to ensure that Catherine Earnshaw is undyingly his.

Effie rifles her hand through the chip bowl, eyes enormous as Olivier pulls Oberon to him, gazing down at her with palpable devotion.

Effie feels faint with emotion. She closes her eyes. *That kiss, that kiss, that kiss.* She runs her tongue softly across and around her lips, wetting them as she probes, feeling for the tips of her teeth and then more deeply, barely touching the inside of her cheeks, wishing John's lips were on hers again, on her mouth and her neck and beyond.

"Oh my heart's darling, my own," Heathcliff cries, and Effie opens her eyes as Laurence Olivier lunges into the night and the storm, following Cathy's ghost high up into the moors— Heathcliff shunted aside by others who hadn't the kindness or the perception to appreciate his vulnerability or his strength of character.

Effie sits upright, stricken. *Of course* John is completely misunderstood in a place like Prince Edward Island, his intensity and deliberate actions in such contrast with this careless, loose-lipped culture. His intelligence isn't valued and he is criticized, even ridiculed as pompous, smug, intransigent. People don't want to acknowledge his carefulness, his incessant drive to be good, instead wilfully assigning his social awkwardness and worry to arrogance and pride. *Mr. Darcy.*

He had talked on in Hunter River after they kissed, a little shy, it seemed, and deconstructing; transitioning from William Wordsworth to William Godwin, the father of Mary Shelley, explaining that Godwin, an atheist, had married Mary Wollstonecraft, the mother of a little girl, the child a result of an ill-fated romance that had prompted the bereft woman to attempt suicide. John expressed how difficult it was to let on, even now, that he did not believe in God, certainly not a benevolent God, and that people would judge him if they knew—even Donnie.

Effie had argued that this was not true; that even on the island times were changing—she knew this from discussions in the classroom—but she could see his furrowed brow, even in the dark, and she wondered what unspoken doubts still plagued him.

Effie is drawn by the music back to the TV where a flickering Catherine stands on the moors, the sun and wind all about her, as Heathcliff runs his fingertips slowly across her cheek, her arms laden with heather. He leans into her and kisses her.

Effie fights off a feeling she can't quite name—foreboding mixed with an uneasy, but curious, anticipation. She watches Catherine intently as if the heroine can give her some kind of clue.

"I dreamt I was in heaven, but it didn't seem to be my home."

Effie waits for more, aware of outcomes but forgetful of the sequence.

"He's more myself than I am," Catherine cries.

Pushing away her discomfort, Effie laughs at how much Edgar, Heathcliff's rival, reminds her of Donnie, so boyish and eager to please. She wonders why Catherine chooses money over love when all the time her words are so expressly insistent on her oneness with Heathcliff. Is this why Heathcliff loves her so devotedly—because he cannot have her?

But Catherine's ominous words persist. "And I broke my heart with weeping to come back to Earth. And the angels were so angry they flung me out into the middle of the heap, on top of Wuthering Heights."

Effie sees the face of her mother in that rooming house bed, choking to death on sleeping pills and vodka, her brain compelling her lungs to stop their breathing. Effie wonders if her mother hangs over the world; had hovered above that bed and watched herself grow purple-grey, her body decaying for three days as she laid there, her absence unnoticed.

Effie puts her head in her hands and cries. She would ask her mother's forgiveness for not having saved her, or for not having loved her well enough to convince her mother to live, except that she cannot expunge the image of the angry angels flinging her mother about and chastising her wickedness.

And Heathcliff from the corner of the room replies, "I could as soon forget you with my own life, Cathy, if you die." And Effie wonders—could John ever love me this way? Is it enough to run a steady course, like Melanie—not a Scarlett or a Catherine—and have this be enough for him?

"Oh Cathy, why did you kill yourself?"

And John's voice comes back again to Effie.

"Think of Mary Wollstonecraft, so lonely and betrayed. People have no business deciding what is possible, or never possible, for others." And Effie realizes that what he was saying was something about Effie and her mother: that no one has the right to judge; that Effie had no more caused her mother's death than Heathcliff had caused Catherine's.

"What do you know of heaven or hell, Cathy, who know nothing of my life? Only do not leave me in this dark room alone where I cannot find you."

A cable cord swings in the alleyway behind the window, casting its shadow across the sitting room wall, and Effie watches it, an umbrous pendulum, back and forth, back and forth, like Catherine's love for Heathcliff; his love for her never wavering—his worship of her a blind fanaticism.

And throughout the sitting room, her root beer now gone flat beside her, Effie hears Heathcliff's final cries: "I cannot live without my life! I cannot die without my soul!"

She swipes her hand across the bowl of chips and watches as they fly across the room.

CHAPTER 33

Effie lies flat on her back in bed, pillows shoved up against the wall, cotton sheet draped over her calves. Surrounding her are the plays that Aida Lynn recommended when Effie returned the video, newly terrified that she and the school play were both doomed. The librarian laughed, accused Effie of overreacting, and squired her toward the stacks.

With the end of the term approaching, Effie worries that she should be busier with schoolwork, more committed, less preoccupied with John, and she blames the students, in part, for their mounting and protracted excuses about lost homework, late essays and missed tests.

"Miss, I had to help my mother at the restaurant all weekend. Honest."

"Oh—I heard you say read about Margaret Laurence, not write about her. I read a good five hundred words, maybe more!"

"We can't have a test today, Miss Cambridge, we just can't. I have a dentist appointment this afternoon and my mother says if I don't go this time my teeth are gonna rot right out of my head."

Instead of marking essays with detailed corrections, Effie had fallen into a pattern of tick marks and rubrics, reassuring herself that these methods were more efficient for most of her students. Were Effie more experienced she might have understood that she amply supplied what her students needed: a persistent nudging and a belief in themselves. She might have appreciated the greater measure of her success, and recognized her achievements.

As a student, Effie had never been lax. To have been lax would have left her alone in an ordinary world. She had habitually kept her nose in her books, shutting out memories. Pink peppermints rolling from her mother's mouth like little tumblers, falling into the crevices of polyester negligees and tired brassieres; smouldering cigarettes teetering on shallow glass ashtrays.

Called *studious* and *diligent* in high school, these words had angered her. Effie wanted to be brilliant, special, prodigious and remarkable, and she blamed her shortcomings on her circumstances and on the teachers for missing the compensatory greatness that poetic justice would unfailingly mete out. What she wanted was reverential infamy, where people lowered their voices and their heads when she passed by. What she wanted were raised eyebrows as she lectured on her specialty topic, followed by modest to moderate to deafening applause that prompted her cheeks to redden and the soles of her feet to tingle. She pictured herself sipping ginger tea and nibbling powdered sugar cookies, lolling in the sun-drenched library attic of a Victorian house.

Effie is not sure why she asked Aida Lynn to recommend plays instead of books on stagecraft. Time is running out. Glancing at her meagre bookshelf, Effie wishes she had had more of her collection shipped to PEI instead of leaving them boxed in a storage locker in Toronto. Shakespeare's plays, her Riverside edition of Chaucer, the modern poetry publications, her Norton anthologies—all too heavy, she had gauged at the time, to load up and take on the train. Her stomach is a tangle of knotted balls. She misses her books. She misses their smell, the weight of them in her hands, the heft of them straddling her arms. She pictures them lonely, their pages hardening, mould spores mottling their edges.

Instead she had chosen to bring the rudimental: *Funk & Wagnall's* college dictionary; a worn *Roget's* paperback thesaurus; her name-engraved Gideon Bible with a chocolate chip cookie stain dotting Jesus' face, and the dog-eared copy of *Anne of Green Gables.*

Effie sighs and reaches blindly for a handful of plays. She rifles through the collection, searching for inspiration. That she cannot, despite multiple readings and rehearsals, remember the plot of *Twelfth Night,* sends her into paroxysms of panic. Aggravated by the anagramming confusion of *Olivia, Viola* and

Malvolio and irritated by Sir Toby Belch, who she sees as a Falstaff wannabe, she needs to find a key, a mnemonic method of memorizing: some trick to keep the characters separate; a link between Shakespeare and hormonal teenagers. She cannot let her students see her fumble.

She has seen all but one of the plays at the movies except for *A Raisin in the Sun*, which she and Garfield had watched on his aunt's black-and-white television set.

One by one, Effie fingers her way through the volumes— *The Glass Menagerie* (crazy mother); *A Long Day's Journey into Night* (addicted mother); *A Streetcar Named Desire* (schoolteacher Blanche alcoholic *and* crazy); *Death of a Salesman* (suicide); *'Night Mother* (suicide); *Who's Afraid of Virginia Woolf* (everyone alcoholic and crazy), and *Our Town* (everybody dead). The only play free of insanity, substance abuse or self-injury is *The Crucible*, and even that one has hysteria as the driving force.

She pulls the top sheet up over her shoulders and slides under the coolness of the cotton. She misses her mother: what her mother was, and wasn't; what her mother could have been. So many reminders and lessons, so many moments of checks and balances. That her mother should die prematurely was inevitable. How could anyone feel everything so poignantly and not be pulled under. Survivors learn to turn away from feeling, supplanting it with aphoristic whimsy. *It was meant to be. What goes around comes around. Fate. Karma. Curse.*

Her mother's aphorisms were weightier, Biblical; platitudes that applied pressure. *Do unto others as you would have others do unto you. You are to be perfect, as your heavenly Father is perfect. I tell you truthfully, the man who does not welcome the kingdom of God like a child, will never enter into it.*

She can hear her mother singing—*praise God from Whom all blessings flow*—her voice hoarse yet melodic. Effie finds herself standing in an unfamiliar house. A brooding house. Tree branches snake their way in through the open window and she turns to see—to seek out—her mother, who is partly hidden behind a vertical beam, her shoulder pushing into the wood, her frail form thinly veiled in a see-through nightgown.

Women filter in through the open door, their feet brushing across the floor, their heads lowered; clandestine. Wide-brimmed caps and capes conceal their faces and the intimate contours of their bodies. Effie's mother keeps singing. *Praise Father, Son and Holy Ghost.*

A wisp of smoke coils upward and whorls around the beam as a rush of breath tickles the fringe of Effie's hair. "Goody Behrens, have you told Goody Brown about the pond?" Soft lips kiss the nape of her neck.

Outside, a child bounces a basketball, stopping abruptly when a man's voice—a distinctly Southern voice—calls out, "Young man, this ain't no place for violatin' women."

The women begin to chant in low voices and Effie's mother, laughing, drops her cigarette onto the timber floor as she turns to face her daughter.

Effie stares into the enormous sockets where her mother's eyes had been, the whole of her mother's face a wreck of bone and cavity. As the smouldering cigarette sparks into flame, the Southern man thrusts his head through the open window, his face framed by the gnarled tree branches. He points a crooked finger. "You can always depend on the kindness of strangers," he says, and all of the women nod. As Effie opens her mouth to scream, John's face replaces that of her mother, his aquiline nose the only feature intact.

CHAPTER 34

"They have a bowling alley in the Basilica?" Effie snickers. "What sort of church has a bowling alley? Mind you, they have one—a bowling alley I mean—in the White House. In the basement. I knew someone whose grandfather worked in Veteran's Administration in Washington and he took his son to lunch in the White House cafeteria. Can you imagine? Sam Rayburn showed them. I'm not sure if they actually bowled, though—it doesn't seem likely, does it? Mostly when it comes to bowling I think of those Port Credit girls walking around with their hair in curlers as if they were in an Elvis Presley movie."

John holds his umbrella over Effie's head, the rain not much more than a sprinkle. She can't see him smiling and he is glad. He is afraid that at any moment he might laugh out loud and he doesn't want to hurt her feelings. "The bowling alley isn't in the church, Effie. It's in the recreation centre owned by the church."

"See? That's exactly what my mother would have said. The Catholic Church gets its hands on everything." Effie stops walking and looks at John. "She didn't say any of this in a mean or prejudiced way, just in terms of pragmatics."

"I see," John says. "And *that's* not dangerous."

"Well, it wasn't as if she was standing on a balcony on Lakeshore Road screaming it out to everyone." Effie stalls. "Unless she was drinking, and then things could get a bit tricky."

As soon as they walk into the recreation centre Effie can smell the wall of bowling shoes. Even in the low light, she is surprised to see a span of a dozen lanes or more, the dark wood absorbing rather than reflective. Effie labours through a momentary fantasy—opposing teams of monks and fisherman vying for a championship trophy, Pope John Paul II holding a raised bowling ball high above the folds of his cassock. Small-town sectarianism. Effie craves an Orange Crush.

"Do you come here often?" she asks John, who is shaking water off the umbrella. *Open close open close open close.*

Effie watches the droplets splash against the glass door and wonders whether he is obsessive. "Do you know Don Carter?" she asks.

"From the pig farm in Winsloe? I know some of his family, yes. Why?"

"No, no, the bowler. He looks like Bing Crosby, only toothier. I saw him once on TV."

"Was he a good bowler?"

"He was fantastic. So professional." Effie looks around the alley again, this time searching for students. She spies two middle-aged women several lanes over who are laughing hard, one of them on her knees with her hands over her face. "I wonder if anyone plays in a league anymore," Effie says. At the far end of the room a ball rolls into the gutter.

They walk toward the counter. "Shall I keep score?" John asks. He lays down a twenty dollar bill and nods hello to the attendant. A customer sits a few feet away, a plateful of fries and gravy at his elbow as he works on the daily jumble in the newspaper. He looks up and smiles at John.

Effie smiles vacantly. "I think Martha comes here."

"How is she? I've noticed a change in her lately. She doesn't seem so wanton." He sets his wallet on the counter. "What size shoes do you take, Effie?"

"Eight and a half, please. I think it's the play, although I hope it's not Tommy Murphy. Mind you, anything to get her away from that mother."

"They don't carry half sizes."

"Nines will do." Effie admires the saddle shoes hanging on the wall. She hopes her feet don't stink. "Shirley Cambridge is a zealot and a *bitch*. I nearly fell over when the school renewed my contract." She longs suddenly for Kathleen Raminsky, remembering the Saturdays when they bowled in Port Credit, Kathleen's mom sneaking them cheeseburgers and cokes from behind the counter, the girls teasing her about her uniform and the paper hat her boss insisted she wear.

"You can't think Martha is the only student you have reached at the school. The kids love you. And the ones that don't love you respect you, which is even more valuable."

Effie stiffens, wondering which of her students don't like her. "Do you have any idea what you're going to be doing next year? Now that Donnie and Mary are both in love—" She realizes her mistake and stops herself.

"Things are a little up in the air." A whoop rises up behind them. John carries the shoes and the scorecard over to a dimly lit lane. "Maybe I just need a break or summer vacation. Are you ready for the play?" he asks.

"As ready as I'll ever be." *Up in the air? What does that mean?* "Although the principal might want to renege on my contract once everyone sees it. Some days it feels as if we're putting on the Three Stooges. Between Virginia's baby—do you know there are kids that call her Vagina? Within earshot? It's disgusting. And with Bruce's faltering speech and Griffen Dalziel, it should be a busy little night." Effie unties her Oxfords, sniffing the air like a puppy. "I miss the rain," she says.

John rubs his forehead. "It's raining today. Right now. Remember?"

"Of course I remember. I just mean I wish it would rain the way it rains in Ontario." Effie laces up her bowling shoes, coveting them.

"Do you miss home?"

"Not exactly," she says. "I miss the lake."

"Only the lake?"

"What's to miss? My mother is dead, my best friend has disappeared and my boyfriend is long gone. Too many people see me more as the tragic daughter of an alcoholic rather than a hardworking student, and the friends I made at university, if you can call them that, are off having their own spectacular lives."

She picks up a bowling ball. "Like this?" she asks, holding the ball in front of her, cupping it in her hands.

"It may not be compensation but we do have an ocean, and you have new friends with spectacular lives *and* rising prospects." John winks at her.

"It's not the same thing. At the lake you don't have to worry about jellyfish and wasps. Or rip tides." Effie strides down the lane, smiling. "How's my form?" she asks, hoping to sound both serious and flirtatious.

"Are you going for the pig farmer or the bowler?"

Effie lets go of the ball, arms leaden as she watches the defeated pins topple in a thundering cascade.

John laughs out loud. "A strike—first time around. You're giving Mr. Carter a run for his money. I'd say your form is world class."

"Beginner's luck," she says, pleased with her accomplishment and fearing her inability to repeat it. She glances around to see if anyone else is watching, but the women have disappeared and the remaining bowler is in the far lane focused on improving his game.

Between frames John wants to know what Effie meant about Martha and Tommy Murphy, and Effie explains that she has seen them holding hands.

"How do you feel about that?"

"Not good. I wish Martha could see all that is wonderful about her. She's clever and funny and thoughtful. Children need-n't be lifelong victims on account of their parents."

"You understand that, do you?"

"Yes I do," Effie frowns. "Do you?"

"I haven't made up my mind," John laughs. "If I were a bank account how much money would I have earned in your vault?"

"What are you talking about?" Effie blushes, thrilled by this novel approach.

"Have I appreciated or depreciated? And if I am in the red, how much of that is on account of my genetic makeup and therefore cannot be changed?"

"Are you saying that my mother is responsible for my defi-ciencies?"

"Who said anything about your mother? Or deficits? I only mean to say that some of our worth is based on genetics. I agree that as adults we have choice—there are reasons, but no excuses—but I don't think that's true for adolescents. Take Tommy Murphy. If you could examine his DNA I would wager that the odds are not in his favour. As mad as I can get—and you know how he can infuriate me—on better days I cannot find fault with this angry kid whose parents send him to school in ratty jeans and skimpy t-shirts. I never thought there was enough love to shore that boy up, but maybe he and Martha can help one another. Guide one another out of their reckless homes. Martha's like an old sheep dog just waiting to be led away from the farm."

"My family, you mean."

"From where I sit they aren't your family at all. They are nothing like you, and they should feel very sorry for that."

Effie sloughs off the compliment. "What does all of this have to do with your, as you put it, bank account?"

John smiles at her transparency. "Your feelings for me matter a great deal. I would never want to waste your time, or mine, on frivolous friendship."

Effie doesn't know what to make of him. She can't get at it, at him, and she doesn't know why. She can feel him crushing in on her like weighted steel, sensing that to give it, give *him*, release could be disastrous. She is a risk-taker, but only as long as the risks are statistically in her favour. And she knows unmistakably that John is the type of risk that falls far outside the boundaries of arithmetical safety.

"Have you ever had Frito Casserole?" John asks. "Corn chips and tuna?"

"That sounds horrible."

"Mixed in with cream of mushroom soup."

"Yuck. Who eats that?"

"My Dad and I, every Thursday. We don't have the heart to tell my mother how much we hate it. The tuna was her invention. It's her surrogate for ground beef."

"I think I'm missing your point."

"Today is Thursday. What if you and I sit at the counter and order up cheeseburgers and fries, and then I'll have a reasonable excuse to squirm out of dinner?"

"Can I have an Orange Crush?"

John laughs. "You, Effie Cambridge, can have anything you want."

CHAPTER 35

Lavinia is administered a muscle relaxant prior to her electric shock treatments. The doctor says that the shot will help her relax. As far as Lavinia can tell, neither the medication nor the shock therapy helps her with anything. The most she says afterward is that her brain feels confused, although she states this without blame or even regret.

When Effie visits her mother, she boards a bus heading east to the Humber streetcar loop. There she transfers and rides along to Kipling Avenue before disembarking and making the trek south along the winding drive to Lakeshore Psychiatric, Building J. Once there she is let in through a door out of which a small upper section has been cut and replaced with a wire-mesh peek-a-boo window. Effie feels an absurd desire to laugh whenever she sees a nurse staring back at her, a free-floating head hanging in limbo. But once inside, Effie's inclination abruptly vanishes. This is a place made for monsters, even if the buildings' inhabitants—staff and patients alike—were not.

Making her best effort to relegate the other asylum dwellers to a bilateral fraction of her peripheral vision, Effie imagines the room a kaleidoscope, her mother its beautiful, fragmented feature, the singular focal star. Sometimes Effie finds it necessary to step over a patient who is flailing on the floor, and the odour of urine is impossible to ignore. But Lavinia acts as her daughter's guide, not so much by invocation as by position, seated as she always is on the edge of her bed, smoking a cigarette.

Lavinia is not resentful toward Effie, who signed her mother in for an initial three-month stint after the Mississauga Hospital social worker said that Lakeshore would be a better facility. But considering that Effie is not yet old enough to legally commit her mother to any institution it is clear that the system that put Lavinia there, and not only Lavinia herself, is out of joint.

Years later, Effie will tell you truthfully, if you ask her, that she has almost no memory of these Sunday visits, and what she retains has more to do with the outside than the inside: the lake, the deciduous trees, snow scuffing across tarmac, a day patient who feeds baby rabbits on the front lawn through dandelion stems. She keeps her mother in a secret compartment of her brain, a little snow globe queen, tragic but immortal.

Had Effie understood that these were among the last hours she is to spend with her mother, she might have made the trip more often—or chosen to stay at home completely. While Hippolytos does not chastise his employee about forfeited shifts, she needs the extra money for her university fund, and she is not hopeful that she has put in enough effort to qualify for a scholarship. She knows she is helpless to save her mother and, for now, when Effie is away from her she is, mostly, not thinking of Lavinia at all.

Saturday nights after work, when she isn't too tired, Effie walks to the end of the block and visits with the boys at the funeral parlour. Dressed in their suits, the men still on duty, they invite Effie to sit with them in the anteroom where they eat take-out pizza and drink Coke from the can, Effie glimpsing in at the satin-lined casket lying in the void. In between peeks and sub-dued conversation, she occasionally measures her life against her mother's, who, like the corpse a few feet away, lies helpless—her mother behind the barred windows of a psychiatric hospital, liv-ing out her life under the changing phases of the moon.

Effie isn't sure in those moments whether to feel angry or cheated or vaguely abused, but she is no longer comfortable with sadness, not since she discovered that poetic justice isn't just at all and that sadness is a waste of time.

A few years later, when *One Flew Over the Cuckoo's Nest* plays on late-night TV, Effie clicks off the remote the very second Jack Nicholson is being ushered into the electroshock treatment room.

CHAPTER 36

"My father says that this is a very confusing play." Bruce pats his velvet vest and smiles.

"Your father is correct," Effie says. "But you're in high school now and I'm counting on you to get it right. We have one more day to iron out any wrinkles before tomorrow night, so let's get started. Vivian, you're going to have to remove that lipstick. I told you that before."

"Yeah!" Kenny shouts. "You're supposed to be in mourning. Who's going to believe it if you look like a model?"

Vivian smiles, showing her teeth. "I look like a model? Wow." She throws back her shoulders.

Martha, shapeless in a sweatshirt and overalls, stands off to the side. Tommy skulks behind her, limply holding a hammer. She looks imploringly at Effie. "I said he could help."

Tommy puffs up like a proud soldier. In the back of his head he stores a small hope.

Onstage, Ruthie Acorn enunciates loudly in a posh upper class accent, "*Sew* many love triangles—Violah and Orsino, Orsino and Oliviah, Oliviah and Sebastian, Malvolio and Mariah! *Sew* re-ah-listic."

"Those are pairs, Ruthie, not triangles." Gary slides her a look of indifference.

"Hey, Mr. MacDonald!" Bruce Jarvis's eyes disappear into his face as he greets his favourite teacher.

"Hey there, Bruce." John bee-lines from the hallway to a front corner of the auditorium waving a piccolo in the air, three students marching in behind him.

Overcome by the impending performance and imagining the after-party sandwiches, Bruce's excitement mounts. "You guys look terrific!"

Effie twirls around to face the approaching troupe, their wadding and doublets and black-feathered hats provided by hard-working mothers.

"Thank you, Bruce," John says. "Think of us as the magi plus one."

Effie turns her attention back to the class, determined not to lose control at this pivotal juncture.

Tommy and Martha shuffle up the auditorium stairs and disappear offstage, Vivian spouting bitterly over their heads, "I am a wealthy countess, Danny! You can't talk to me that way!"

Danny tosses Vivian a withering look. "Listen—you and I are going to be husband and wife so you better get used to me telling you what to do. And my name is Sebastian, not *Danny*." He can't decide if Vivian is a girl he wants to love or hate.

Kenny calls across to his friend, "Is Her Majesty displeased again?"

"Apparently so." Danny rolls his eyes in Vivian's direction.

Effie, irritated by the diversions, flings her hands in the air. "Listen. It's time to get with the program. John—are the musicians ready? Clear the stage, everyone. That means you, too, Ruthie."

In the background, strains of piccolo, oboe, flute and recorder begin wafting across the gym. Gary strolls onstage with a quiet flourish, his wrist rising gently upward. "*If music be the food of love, play on.*"

Laughter erupts backstage followed by the rhythmic *ping ping ping* of a hammer. Gary stops, his ears hot with anger, then, with two of his fellow actors, delivers the rest of the opening scene. As he exits the stage he tugs on the cuffs of his billowing sleeves, creating a small tear at the shoulder.

"That was lovely, Gary," Effie calls after him, "but if you could add a smidge of passion next time."

Passing Gary in the wings, Ruthie moves to the centre of the stage and lifts her hand to her brow as if she is about to collapse. Instead, she belts out her lines, the boy playing opposite her rearing back as if he has been blasted with a blowtorch.

Effie wishes Ruthie could look more tragic than smug. "Ruthie, you believe that your brother is *dead*. You're as good as drowned and you don't know where you are. Could you try to appear—to sound—more lost? And it's pronounced Ill-EAR-ee-uh, not AL-ur-yuh."

"Isn't that what I just said?" Ruthie's hair bounces as she tosses her head from side to side, indignant.

"Go on," Effie says, watching soundlessly through Ruthie's, "*I thank thee. Lead me on*" and her end-of-scene walk toward the front edge of the stage like someone possessed, eyes riveted on the far wall, arm outstretched, hand crooked demurely.

John's small band stops playing.

Effie looks over at him, sees his hunched, shaking shoulders, and knows he is trying to tamp down an outburst.

Bruce walks onto the stage. "I keep sayin' it, Miss Cambridge, but Belch is a funny last name."

"Beats Sir Toby Bendover," Danny bawks from the side-lines.

Kenny widens his eyes in apish innocence. "Bendover, I think I know you?"

John stifles his laughter and addresses the students sternly. "You do want to make your parents proud, don't you? You wouldn't have signed up for this if it wasn't important to you. And most important, Miss Cambridge has worked so hard."

Bruce glances over at Effie. "Sorry, Miss." Danny and Kenny stop posturing. The girls look at their shoes. The smell of cafeteria pizza sneaks in from the hallway, reminding everyone that today is Friday. No one can see or hear Martha and Tommy backstage, Tommy's clumsy advances, one hand on his hammer, the other undoing the strap of Martha's overalls.

"*I'll drink to her as long as there is a passage in my throat,*" Bruce's pronouncement is cut off by Ruthie's metronomic, "*I'll do . . . my best . . . to woo . . . your wife.*"

"Ruthie," Effie interrupts, "remember in this scene that Viola is attracted to the Duke—do you think you could portray that more believably?"

"But I still find it creepy, Miss Cambridge. I'm supposed to be a man."

Here we go.

"And what does *rubious* mean? My mother and I looked it up last night and the closest we could come was red."

"Yes, that's correct, Ruthie."

"So shouldn't *I* be the one wearing the lipstick?"

A small smile plays at the corners of Gary's mouth as he gazes intently into Ruthie's face. "*Diana's lip is not more smooth and rubious: the small pipe is the maiden's organ, shrill and sound, and ALL is semblative a woman's part.*"

Ruthie does not know whether he is teasing or mocking her.

Virginia flits behind them, her eyes glistening with happiness.

Effie forges ahead. "And Vivian, could you please stop talking to Virginia as if she is your servant?"

"But she *is* my servant, Miss Cambridge."

"That's not what I mean. Olivia is not domineering."

"It's no different than how my mother talks to our cleaning lady."

Effie is about to volley back when a series of throat-generated burps precede Bruce's re-entry onstage. "I'm a pretty good belcher, aren't I, Miss?"

John laughs out loud, Bruce's voice undercutting him with "*A plague o' these pickle-herring!*"

John excuses himself from the auditorium, shoulders heaving again, making a noise that sounds to Effie's ear like a child's squeaky toy.

Ruthie, resenting their disregard, calls out, "*—for he's in the third degree of drink; he's drowned. Go look after him.*"

Effie glances toward the hallway searching for John, then returns her focus to the bedlam onstage where Kenny is hopping about in borrowed tap shoes, his legs as thin as chopsticks.

Effie isn't sure whether he is mimicking Ruthie or whether he is basking in some kind of Elizabethan reverie. "Malvolio is supposed to be a prig, Kenny, not Danny Kaye." The top of her head begins to hurt.

Kenny looks over at his best friend. "Who's Danny Kaye?"

"He's the fa—guy who dances with a mop in that movie about the rain."

John, reentering the room, shouts across the gym, "I hope you were going to say *fellow* and not anything else."

"Yes Sir." Danny lowers his eyes.

As the Viola/Olivia scene approaches, Effie understands why Lucy Maud Montgomery had been plagued by migraines.

Ruthie and Vivian stand boldly facing one another, their initial unease overtaken by a feeling of something kindred, Ruthie won over by Vivian's sense of style, Vivian intrigued by a classmate who isn't afraid to stand up to the teachers. Their stares turn into smiles, their eyes indicating a newfound respect, the hatching of future plots more than a promise.

And in the back room, his hammer abandoned, Tommy has made his way to Martha's left breast.

Effie looks over at John, watching him conduct the musicians, his fingers moving at a furious pace along the shaft of the piccolo. She sees herself sitting beside him at the piano in her living room, fire logs crackling, the scent of rosewood permeating the intimate space, the piccolo caressing his lips.

Maybe a guitar would be better, she thinks. Or a violin. Or a cello. No. He will play the piano. And I will sit on the bench beside him, turning the pages of sheet music.

Effie feels the wool from his jacket brushing against her arm, his Florsheims tenderly pumping the brass pedals (*press and release, press and release*—the very act of it making her weak), the creak in the wood floor, her wine glass skating imperceptibly toward the edge of the piano lid.

"*Nay, pursue him now, lest the device take air and taint.*"

Griffen Dalziel breaks into spasms of laughter, clutching his sides in pain. "He's playing the part as if he wrote it himself. If the shoe fits. Or the tutu."

Handing his piccolo to one of the musicians, John walks steadily across the floor, stopping directly in front of Griffen. "Antonio's character is compassionate. His love for Sebastian is strong and, in the end, unrequited." He speaks quietly. "He is gentle, not someone who would ridicule others."

"Are you saying Antonio's gay, Sir?" Griffen leers.

John stares at the boy, unflinching. "You're deflecting my point. You would do well to absorb some of Antonio's humane spirit. It will take you further in life than the direction in which you seem to be headed."

The students stand mutely, eyes shifting between Griffen and John.

John walks back to his waiting musicians, the heels of his shoes clicking rhythmically.

For the remainder of the day the play moves along, subdued and with some of the humour missing, but increasingly eloquent, crystallized, the performances charged with a new vibrancy and understanding.

In the back room, hidden behind a galley of props, Martha lies on the dusty floor, Tommy heaving on top of her.

CHAPTER 37

Tommy stares through the dark at his alarm clock, cold air whistling through the crack in the window overhead. He bundles under the covers, wide awake and worrying. Despite all of the promises he has made and the meals that have been paid for, Tommy hopes there will be time to back out. More than anything, he wants Martha to accept him as her boyfriend. There is something reassuring about her, something familiar.

First of all, she comes from the same shitty kind of home he does, where weak parents make up ridiculous rules when they bother to notice you at all. Second, Tommy can't stand the teachers at Minegoo, and he knows Martha can't stand most of them either. And when he and Martha have sex, she doesn't make cruel faces or tell him to get off the way the other girls had. Instead, she looks at him with those big eyes and says, "You're a really sweet guy." No one has ever said anything like that to him before. He knows there aren't many girls who'd say that to him again.

He scuffs his feet together to keep warm, imagining him and Martha sitting next to each other at the play, the way they have planned. He has already finagled two seats so that no one can interfere. And after they finish school they will leave the island together, go out to Alberta where he will work in the oilfields and she can run a daycare. The pay is good out west. Two of his cousins went out there to work and came back loaded.

For the first time in his life Tommy falls asleep with a sense of the future.

John wakes up with a nagging headache, which he blames on air pressure despite the cloudless sky. He brushes his teeth using warm water (a trick he had taught his own dentist) and gargles with mouthwash before letting the dog out in the backyard. Grabbing the newspaper, he enumerates the spelling and grammar mistakes in the first paragraph and laughs out loud over the social events calendar. *Mrs. M O'Meara of Crapaud fell on the sidewalk Sunday and splintered her foot.* He wishes more of the reporters were as conscientious as Mary, and he wonders if the island will ever catch up to the rest of the country.

Back in his bedroom he opens the top dresser drawer, choosing his red wool socks, knowing that Effie will be amused and irritated all at once, saying something like, "It's May, John, not December," or "Elizabethan musicians wouldn't have worn these!" His costume, hanging on a hook on his bedroom door and preserved under dry-cleaning cellophane, will please her, however, and he will point out that the red cap goes perfectly with his socks.

After a quick breakfast of soft-boiled eggs and toast he intends to walk leisurely to school. He is looking forward to the long summer off, knowing he has some time to decide on his next move, if there is to be a move at all. After calling in the dog he heads for the bathroom and his morning shower. He will pick up a coffee and a Danish at Ken's Korner for a treat.

Martha festers through her first class of the day, sweat beading her forehead and cheeks, eyeglass frames dotted with moisture. She and her mother have had one of their fights. On no uncertain terms—these were her mother's words—would her daughter be sitting anywhere that night except between her mother and her father. Shirley Cambridge didn't care if Jesus Christ himself came down from heaven and asked her to make an exception.

"We are a family and that is how we will present ourselves." She dried her hands on her breakfast apron. "Ever since your father gave you that godforsaken car you've been strutting around like you're the Queen of Sheba. Well let me tell you, young Miss, you'll do as you're bidden as long as you live under this roof so help me God. And I forbid you to see Tommy Murphy. That boy's a pariah."

Instead of figuring out her workbook geometry problems Martha twirls her pencil, wondering how she will let Tommy know. She'll reassure him that they can meet up after the play when everyone else is celebrating. Her father and mother will be so busy putting on the dog that no one will even know that she and Tommy are gone. They could go for Chinese food or take a walk down by the Hillsborough River or maybe even hide out in the props galley. It would be fun to sneak back there with him, with everyone so close by. Or they could make love again, although she feels silly saying this to herself. She stills her pencil.

Fuck my mother.

Donnie calls Elizabeth on his lunchtime break. "You're coming tonight, right? Yes, I know, but I thought I would phone in case something else had come up. Whoa! Stop it. It's too early in the day, even for you." He wrings the phone cord around his finger. "Yes, you can wear whatever you want. It'll be dark. No one will be able to see you. Ha!" He presses his forehead into the staffroom bulletin board. "That's why I love you," he says. "No one finds me as funny as you do. Of course I will. Yup. Nope. Uh huh. I'll pick you up at 6:30. Is that too early?"

Jimmy Fitzgerald yanks at his crotch, aware that his uniform is cutting off his circulation. He wonders if his wife blames their lack of fertility on underproductive testicles. A man can't win.

And now he'll have to tell her he'll be late home again. He'll have to lie. She might want to go with him, and this isn't the night for that. Besides, there would be no end to her ranting about babies if she gets stuck in a roomful of kids. And he couldn't easily explain why he was meeting Tommy Murphy for dinner. Her head would go off in the wrong direction. He smiles. People are such idiots.

Mildred Rutherford drains a cup of lukewarm tea, considering whether to wear her regular Wallabees or break out the new brown pair. The backs of her legs stick to the red leather chair and her girdle pinches. She has told the women she will meet up with them at the school; that she feels like walking despite the cane. But her leg hurts and she might call a taxi.

The late afternoon sun glimmers through her living room windows, lighting up the Royal Doulton figurines as they prepare to minuet. They remind her of childhood Christmases when her mother made coffee table holiday scenes, little round mirrors for lakes and cotton balls for snow. Sometimes she let Mildred help her, but this was a project her mother usually preferred doing alone. Mildred would come home from school to the sound of humming, her mother sitting on the floor, cutting and pasting and shaking out glitter.

The cinnamon stick clings to the bottom of her cup and she wonders, not for the first time, why more people don't follow her helpful dietary hints.

Across the hall, Mike kisses the back of Mary's neck. "I love you, you know. I want to marry you."

"I know you do, and I love you, too. And I will marry you just as soon as my mother has had a little more time to get used to the idea of me living that far from home."

"Oh, I wasn't pressuring you. Just reminding is all. Ottawa isn't so bad. Conservative, yes, but so's the whole country. And there's a lot for families to do. Your mom could come and stay with us as often as she likes. She could even come live with us if you think that might suit her. And you'll love the canal."

"Is it true that people skate to work?"

"Briefcases and all. In fact, I've done it myself. I promise you, you won't be disappointed. And writing for the *Citizen* would be invigorating. Hell, writing for the *Ottawa Sun* would be more inspiring than writing for an island newspaper. I mean, how many times can you report on Gentleman Jim's sponsoring the local hockey team or who's misplaced their diabetic cat?"

"You're a real snob, Mike. Just because we're a little more folksy here doesn't mean there aren't important things to say. We just don't have as many murders, that's all."

"You don't report the murders you do have. Speaking of, isn't Effie going to kill you if we're late for the play?"

Mary laughs. "Shut up and hand me the potatoes."

Effie leans against the gymnasium wall. Too late now to change things, but she isn't worried. John looks heroic in his costume, even with red socks. He told her these were his holiday socks and he had worn them in honour of this special occasion. He had that look in his eyes that she loved. The look that said *I will be seeing you later.*

The room is jam-packed, not a seat to spare, although Effie doesn't know if this is a testament to her skills or a test of them. Mildred Rutherford and her crew have planted themselves in the first row in front of Mary and Mike—Effie wonders if Mary will find the proximity comical—right next to the Cambridges, who are lined up like decoys. Effie can tell from Martha's rounded back that she is upset, which is a shame given all of the hours she has committed to the production. Mind you, could anyone ever feel happy sitting between Shirley and Bill? Effie sighs with relief, grateful that she has sprung from her mother's egg and not from her uncle's sperm.

Onstage the play is proceeding as it should. Thank God, Effie thinks, thank God. She is glad that no one can see the tears on her cheeks. *Enjoy your achievements as well as your plans.* The students are holding up remarkably well. Bruce has fumbled only once and Vivian's lipstick is barely discernible. The musicians are playing with precision and gusto, and Danny has abandoned his eye-rolling, as Effie had advised him the night before. She can feel her shoulders relaxing, her feet sinking comfortably into the floor. She spots Virginia's baby sitting on her grandmother's lap, cooing at her mother onstage, Virginia looking unexpectedly grown-up.

Tommy Murphy stands inside the gymnasium doors. *Bitch*, he says to himself, obliterating Martha's noontime pleas, offered up under an oak tree in the schoolyard.

"I just can't, Tommy. I can't help it. She's nuts, just like your mother."

"Don't talk about my mother that way. You haven't got a clue about my mother."

"You know what I mean. You've met my mother. You know what she's like. She'll make my life hell if I disobey her."

"So our leaving the island is worth nothing?"

"Who said anything about leaving the island? Of course I'd go anywhere you ask me to, but we haven't decided anything yet. Didn't last night mean anything to you at all? Do you think I just lie down and spread my legs for all the boys? For anyone else, ever? We can sneak away after the play. My mother won't notice. She'll be too busy doing God's work. We could take my car, go somewhere out of town if you like—maybe up to Brackley. We could talk. Or whatever." Martha shifts her shoulders, trying to look seductive.

"I have something else to do. I have to talk to someone about other plans. I wasn't so sure they interested me. But now you've gone and fucked everything up, so why not? Why did you have to go and do that?"

"For frig's sake, Tommy, it's just a two-hour play. Calm down. We have our whole lives to be together. You've just got to trust me."

"Trust a person who hasn't got the balls to tell her mother she wants to sit with her boyfriend? *Screw you, bitch.*"

Martha stood under the tree and cried, not caring who saw her blotchy face.

Tommy stares at Martha's stooped back and abruptly leaves the gymnasium.

As the curtain comes down on the final act, Effie scans the room carefully to see who is standing. Amid the furious applause, the only person still lodged in her chair is Mildred Rutherford, but she has a bad leg. John waves at Effie from the corner of the stage, his eyes lit up with enthusiasm. A flat-out victory. Her mother would be proud.

CHAPTER 38

"Well, Bruce, how did we do? Did you bring any frogs with you today?"

"As it happens, Miss, I didn't. But it was a great year. I've learned heaps," he beams, "and I loved being in the play. I can't believe I might be going to grade eleven!"

Danny Callbeck yawps, "You'll never get old, Bruce my boy."

Effie laughs.

John steps into the classroom. "Ready for exams?" he asks.

A chorus of boos bounces around the room, and John nods sympathetically. "I remember it well."

"No offense, Sir, but you teach music," Danny says.

"And everyone knows there's nothing to that." John winks at Effie and turns back toward the hallway. "I just came by to wish all of you the best of luck on your exams. Miss Cambridge," he adds cheerfully, "I will see you later."

Oohs and aahs circle the room and Effie laughs again.

"I want you to remember this year's syllabus," she says, suddenly serious. "I have not in any way tried to trick you on the exam, but I do want you to invest your answers with imagination. This is about you and what you bring to the subject matter, not merely about what you take away. Emphasis will be on the novels—most of you did your Shakespearean duty with the play—and there will be some poetry. Frost and Vincent Millay are featured, for example, as is Whitman. But this isn't about memorization. A chimp can memorize."

Danny hoots, clapping Bruce on the back. "And a smart chimp can do Shakespeare."

"Before we end for the year, I'd like to know which parts of the course you liked or didn't like. Which authors you are now more interested in. You all remember how Gary was affected by

The Wars. What about the rest of you? What mattered to you? What moved you?"

Effie sts on her desk facing the students, thrilled by the simultaneous replies.

"I would really like to meet Alice Munro. She's smart enough to be a psychologist." Ruthie sounds authoritative but conscientiously polite.

Vivian shoots a thumbs-up at her new best friend. "I agree. With Alice Munro you get that she is writing about where she lives and the people she knows."

Danny rolls his eyes. "You make her sound like a peeper."

Gary laughs. "I learned that Walt Whitman wrote some phenomenal stuff about love and friendship and how you can apply that to the individual. I also learned that he was probably gay but that he kept his personal business to himself."

"That's because he didn't feel safe to do otherwise," Vivian chimes in. "No one would have looked at his stuff, as you call it, if he had been out of the closet."

"I really liked *Lord of the Flies*. It felt so real to me."

"Yeah," Griffen says. "Kind of like PEI without adults."

Bruce gazes fondly at his teacher. "Did you like *Lord of the Flies*, Miss?"

"I did. I saw it performed once by an all-boys' school at the St. Lawrence Centre in Toronto. The staging was spectacular. They used metal bars and ramps for props—the drama was more potent that way. All action and feeling."

"Do you think Tolkien felt bad about killing off—"

"That was *Lord of the Rings*, goof ball."

"Before you go getting all cocky," Effie says, "they are easy themes to cross. Both can be regarded as allegorical—you had better know that word and its meaning for your exam, by the way—one dealing with Christianity, the other primarily with war. But how and to what degree I cannot say because some of you might want to explore this theme over the next week as you study."

"I'm not so sure I liked *Twelfth Night* all that much." Griffen looks up at Effie, friendly but defiant. "I enjoyed being in the play but it wasn't my favourite."

"No? Why not?"

"I found it too silly and confusing. I think Shakespeare was trying to say something more personal but he chickened out." Griffen buffs his fingernails on his shirt.

"I don't agree with you at all," Kenny pipes up. "I think he was real brave, even for all they got away with at that time."

"What do you mean—all they got away with?"

"Elizabethan England was crawling with prostitutes and pornography."

Effie resists a laugh. "How do you know that, Kenny?" she asks.

"From my mother. My father was giving her a hard time about being a prude—he told her she should have lived in Shakespeare's day—and she told him that there was lots going on in Shakespeare's day, just as there could be at home if only he would pay more attention."

The class roars with laughter.

"I am not completely sure what it takes to be a writer," Gary says after the noise dies down, "but after taking your class, Miss Cambridge, I wouldn't mind being one."

Effie stands up from her desk and walks down the aisle toward Gary. "Thank you," she says. "That means everything to me."

"I wish we were allowed to bring you gifts, Miss, but a bunch—a group—of us would like to buy you a hot dog and an Orange Crush from the stand." Virginia Halfpenny's bangs are pinned to the sides of her head. She looks up at the clock on the wall. "It's a bit early for lunch, but maybe you could meet us outside around noon?"

Some of the students applaud in a haphazard, embarrassed way.

Effie feels herself go red from her neck to her hairline. "Why, thank you. That would be lovely." She tries to keep her voice steady and strong. "Now, are there any questions before you leave?"

The students shake their heads, eager to get on with summer.

"Then I want to thank you for giving me a particularly wonderful year. You know, when I first came to this school I wasn't sure how I would manage, but you have been a terrific class and

I am proud of each and every one of you. I wish you the best holiday possible, and I'll be seeing you in the hallways in the fall. But not before our hot dogs."

As the students gather up items from their desks, Tommy Murphy cuts across the schoolyard. Martha glares sharply through the window until she thinks her eyes will burn out of her head.

CHAPTER 39

Lavinia returns to Gerrard Street like a carrier pigeon flying home, the apartment on Lakeshore Road relinquished by Effie when she enters her first year of university and moves into a roach-infested rooming house on Bedford Road in Toronto.

She believes her mother has come to the city to be closer to her, but Mrs. Cambridge, who is as detached from the present as any sufferer of short-term memory loss can be, is hearkening back to a time when she first lived with Effie's father. The "fresh start" that Effie's mother offers her doctor is enhanced by a commitment to a new sponsor at the Gerrard Street AA and the fact that no one is familiar with the assorted bridges she has burnt behind her in Port Credit. No one can know, not even Lavinia herself, how impossible trying to recapture the past will be.

While Lavinia attempts to settle in, subsisting on tomatoes and small bits of Colby cheese, Effie is forging a path at Victoria College. Undaunted by clubs and cliques, she puts all of her effort into her studies, grateful to the first-year grant unexpectedly provided to her by the university, who deemed Effie's accomplishments unusual to the point of exceptional, especially after the principal of Port Credit Secondary School sent along a confidential letter outlining the particulars of Effie's home life.

Eventually, inevitability thrusts Effie onto the path of a young man named Garfield, a student at York University who lives with his Jamaican aunt on O'Connor Street. He is five years older than Effie and has come to Canada to earn a degree in Economics, after which he intends to study law and right what he calls the egregious wrongs of Montego Bay. He and Effie see one another sporadically because, as Garfield quotes routinely, time waits for no man.

★

On a grey November afternoon, Effie and her mother sit in the kitchen of a ranch-style home in the Bridle Path, a tony neighbourhood that Effie finds difficult to navigate. The house is enormous—tennis court, Olympic-size swimming pool, three living rooms—and on the television set, which has been muted, preparations for the Santa Claus parade are in order, a pack of elves stamping their feet and blowing on their cold hands, little brass bells attached to the soft green felt of their hats.

Lavinia seems proud of her new job as housekeeper, even if the daily trek is long and complicated, and she boasts playfully about a television set in the kitchen. Some of the vigour has returned to her hair, and her face is no longer sallow, but Effie observes the worried lines etched into Lavinia's forehead and the nervous way she scratches herself, a habit her mother attributes to an allergy to flour.

The house smells of industrial cleaner and gingerbread, and Effie looks around for any sign of the homeowners, wondering what they would make of an interloper sitting at the white lacquer table, eating a sugar cookie and sipping a cup of Red Rose tea. This is Effie's first, and as it turns out, only visit, and she startles when Lavinia leaps up to attend to her responsibilities, nervously advising Effie to relax and make herself at home.

Effie's eyes follow the long line of cupboards and she wonders just how many dishes a family of three actually require. Judging by the size of everything else around her, the number must be extraordinary. She compares the house to the one on O'Connor Street, which is stately but reasonably sized, and wishes she were there with Garfield, not worrying about causing her mother trouble or finding her way back.

A week later, when she is at Garfield's, he feeds her wild rice and salmon (she does not tell him that the brown-grey underside turns her stomach), and instead of sending her off home on public transit before his aunt's hospital shift ends, he invites her to go for a stroll, which seems an odd word to Effie given Garfield's aversion to late autumn chills.

They walk east before heading south on Greenwood, past a battalion of post-war homes that expand into something taller and gloomier, saved only in Effie's eyes by the bountiful trees.

Near Danforth Avenue they hop on the subway before transferring onto a bus at Woodbine that takes them down to the Beaches. At Queen Street they walk south toward the lake, the monolithic silhouette of the Olympic swimming pool etched in black, a concrete edifice against the grey-black sky. Effie can hear the water lapping against the shoreline and her heart accelerates.

She remembers how the heels of her shoes clicked toward the Port Credit pier when she and her mother strolled behind the Dominion after church, the ribbon of Effie's velvet hat whipping her cheeks in the wind, the seagulls picking apart day-old dough-nuts that had been discarded late yesterday by the grocery staff. And how once she had slipped on the gravel outside of Building J, cutting open the skin on her knee.

In the spring Effie makes her way to her mother's apartment on Gerrard. From there the two woman walk up the street to attend an AA meeting, where Effie is introduced to a well-known Canadian folksinger whose name she cannot repeat. He is handsome, his plaid scarf coiled around his neck, a fedora tipped at a cocky angle over one eye. Playful is how people who don't know him well describe him.

As Effie stares at him she imagines she sees reflective stars in his eyes, an image she finds suddenly very funny. She notes his particular attentions toward her mother, Lavinia smiling under an umbrella of protectionism, which will inevitably snap shut the second they all step away from the building. It is for this reason alone that Effie hopes the dapper gentleman will direct his atten-tions toward someone more savvy and better suited emotionally than Lavinia Cambridge.

Walking back to the apartment, mother and daughter decide to pop into a local grocer's where they pick up items fit for a pic-nic—eggs for hard boiling, sweet mixed pickles, a packet of Swift Premium salami and a brick of mild cheddar cheese.

As the women settle into the sofa, their shoes kicked off onto the floor, Effie takes note of the plastic curtains, their little orange flowers as sweet as any she has ever seen, the long sheets blowing in and out, guided by the soft wind, their faint crinkling the only indication that they are not made of cloth.

The curtains will stand out in Effie's memory for years to come, a hallmark of heartache. The last time she sees them is a day when she and Lavinia have planned to go to the movies. They have chosen *The Eyes of Laura Mars* (which Effie has taken to calling *The Eyes of Laura Mars Bars*, mostly to make her mother laugh) over *The Deer Hunter* or *Coming Home*, citing the war movies as too dated and depressing.

But when Effie arrives her mother does not answer the door. Effie has not thought to ask for a key and she sits on the porch stairs curled in on herself, contorted and small. Where could her mother be? Effie fantasizes the folksinger swinging by unexpectedly, whisking Lavinia away for a cup of coffee, promising that he would have her back home in time. Mrs. Cambridge had hinted over the telephone that she had engaged in one or two pleasant conversations with her new friend, but she was vague and the absence of detail unnerved Effie for reasons she did not fully understand.

Fifteen minutes pass before Effie, stirred by a scurrying squirrel, stands up and steps back onto the porch. A tail of one of the flowered curtains is stuck on a small nail that protrudes from inside the window frame and, as Effie leans forward to release it, she sees through the narrow opening her mother lying sideways on the sofa in front of the flickering TV, a vodka bottle empty on the floor, propped against the leg of the coffee table. Lavinia's right arm extends itself over the edge of the couch, her hand flaccid and open, no sign of the sleeping pills she had ingested several hours before.

Effie whispers loudly through the crack in the window, beseeching her mother to wake up. But even from this distance she can tell that the colour of Lavinia's face is shadowed and dark and that her fingers look tenderly bruised.

Effie pushes herself back carefully as if she might break, before making her way down the porch stairs. Heading toward the pay phone at Carlaw she digs in her purse for a dime, her hands frantic and trembling. Awash with panic and dread and a

numbing sense of relief (a feeling that will dog her forever), she
dials the number for the Port Credit funeral home where her
friends will break with protocol and drive the ambulance into
Toronto.

Chapter 40

Effie hops onto the Rod 'n' Reel, immediately enchanted by its cut-out windows and the turquoise trim that runs stem to stern along the top edge of the white oak frame. School is over, and it is apparent to Effie that any intention John and Donnie may have had to leave the island has been kiboshed. Effie, excited to move forward, tamps down her fear of drowning and steadies herself on deck. Mary and Mike are already aboard chatting with Jill and her husband, Roddy. John strolls along the pier toward the dock, in easy conversation with Elizabeth and Donnie.

On the last day of the term Jill proposed that the eight of them head out for a late-morning south shore tour and then anchor near Fort Amherst to enjoy the rest of the day. Roddy, a seasoned fisherman, would provide the lobster dinner and sobriety so that the rest of them could sit back and enjoy their first free day of the break.

Jill greets Effie with a hug and an introduction. "Effie, you know my cousin, Mike."

"Michael McCready's your *cousin*?" Effie asks, hugging back. "I know Mike. I know you. Wow, everyone on the island really *is* related." Effie smiles and mutters through her teeth to Mary, "How did I miss this bit of information?"

"So many cousins, so little time."

John, Donnie and Elizabeth clamour onto the boat amid a rush of hellos, everyone remarking on the sultry day and their eagerness to be out, as Donnie puts it, *to sea*. Sunlight shimmies across the surface of Charlottetown Harbour towards Southport and beyond.

As Roddy stands in the wheelhouse easing the boat out of the harbour, the guests accept Jill's offer of beer, wine and lemonade, and relax on cushioned bench seats that are fastened to the perimeter of the deck. Effie feels her blood pressure drop as she listens to the chug-chug lull of the engine, her cheeks and fine hair brushed by the ocean breeze. Low-hanging clouds scud by, a clear blue sky above them. She wishes her mother could have met John, who today appears singularly robust. At regular intervals Roddy calls out to them like an airline pilot, unable to keep the facts of his work to himself.

"Our top speed today will be 25 knots per hour."

"When you stand up, you'll notice how comfortable the deck is. It's designed to go easy on your back."

"If we had to, we could make about 300 miles before needing to refuel."

"You can see that the interior trim is varnished front to back."

But when he wanders into "cleats and chocks" and "seacocks," Jill cautions him to be quiet.

"That was beautiful, Rod. Like a Wordsworth poem." John shoots Effie a look.

After dropping anchor near Fort Amherst, Roddy comes out on deck and squints into the sun. "The fishing season is about to end in this part of the water." He holds a folded map up over his eyes.

"I have never understood how that works," Effie says. "Do lobsters migrate?"

"The lobsters here on the south shore are the largest and most delicious." He points at the water, as if speaking to the lobsters themselves. "They feed on rock crab, which is high in protein. It fattens them up. And the warm water doesn't stunt their growth either. Do you like lobster, Effie?"

"I'm allergic to shellfish." She pauses. "At least I think I am."

Donnie's mouth drops open. "You mean you don't know?"

"No, not exactly. But lobsters make me nervous."

John grins, unsnapping the strap of his camera case. "Is it their beady little eyes?"

"I have trouble with so many things I figured shellfish would have to be at the top of the list. But I've never been tested for it.

Or even tasted it. You know," she laughs, "come to think of it, it was probably the wine and not the turkey that put me to sleep that time."

"*That* time?" Donnie shakes his head. "You know, Effie, I think you could use more days like this, out in the sun."

"Or perhaps that's her problem," John teases. "Too *much* sun." He peers through the viewfinder of his camera, playing with the settings.

"That—and genetics." Effie grins back at John. "Some of the things I react to bothered me the first time I ate them. You don't need testing for those. It only takes once."

Roddy stares at her, worried.

"Oh, it's all right. I have an Epi-pen. One stab and I'm good to go."

"Well then, who's ready for lunch?" Roddy asks, almost satisfied with Effie's pragmatic answer.

"It's kind of an all-day spread." Jill stretches her arms and stands up. "Designed to sop up alcohol. But we're saving the lobster for later in the day."

Jill and Roddy carry out Melmac snack trays and colourful cloth napkins and set them down on a portable table with foldout legs. Marinated cucumber, an assortment of pickles, hummus from Cedar's Eatery, pita bread, crackers, sliced French bread, a basket of strawberries, a bowl of cherries and, stashed under the bench seat, two cases of beer, a bottle of Yukon Jack and a magnum of champagne. Effie wonders how much all this cost.

Donnie snatches a pickle and wraps his free arm around John. "This is the philanthropic side of the island," he says. "A more common occurrence than *some* people would have you believe." He squeezes John tightly and winks at Effie.

"Are you insinuating I'm a curmudgeon?" John asks. He flings Donnie's arm away affectionately and leans toward the table, eyeing the strawberries.

"Insinuating?" Donnie and Mary speak in tandem.

"All right. I can be stern—"

"Oh, a pun!"

"I can be stern, but—"

"But not after a glass of port."

"Donnie, shut up."

Donnie laughs. "I bow to your authority," he says.

"But I think I'm fair." John grabs a plate and balances it on his knee. "I have never said islanders aren't generous. However, do I think they can be intolerant? Yes, I do."

"Yes, we know. You're the best example of that." Donnie passes an unopened beer to John. "Is there something we can discuss other than this?" He picks up the bottle opener from the table and flips off the cap.

"Did anyone here see *Jaws*?" Mike asks.

"Nice segue, Mike," Donnie drawls. "Are you expecting company?"

"The closest you'll get to Jaws out here might be a tiger shark." Roddy straightens the waistband on his Bermuda shorts. "We've had more than one of them circle back to the island."

"I was thinking more along the lines—hey, another pun!—of scars. Remember that scene when the men compare their injuries?"

Jill points to her husband's shirt with a dill pickle then tips back her head, shooting the pickle into her mouth like a sword swallower.

Roddy smiles at his wife, unbuttoning his shirt. A thin white scar snakes from the crest of his tanned chest down toward his navel. "It's not what you think," he says. "Nothing very exciting. I mean, it's not Orca."

"Heart?" Effie guesses.

"Heart's not exciting?" John asks.

"Only to the patients," Roddy says. "But yes, heart, and well over ten years ago. I'm good to go. Set for another fifty years."

Jill raises her beer. "God help us all. Here, John. Put down your camera and try the hummus."

"Hang on a minute, Jill. I need to take a picture for the Rod 'n' Reel's new brochure—*Captain Roddy's Wild Sea Adventures*." John focuses the viewfinder on Roddy's bare chest, his olive-brown skin clean of any hair. "Hold steady, Roddy my boy. I'm going to make this last one look like the San Andreas fault. You'll be famous."

Effie sits back, breathing in the wind and salt spray, wishing she could stay here forever, bobbing gently in this boat with all of her friends around her, safe from the intrusions that make up the hard parts of a life.

Donnie tips his head forward and parts his hair with his fingers, showing off a jagged silvery line that tracks across the top of his head.

"It wasn't brain surgery," John deadpans.

"If it was, it didn't work." Elizabeth kisses Donnie on the cheek.

"Nope. A shovel. Frigging cousin Jimmy caught me in the head with a shovel when we were out playing hockey one night. The team was goofing around on the rink and for punishment the coach made us clear out his driveway."

"That's abusive and inappropriate," Mary says.

"That's hockey. Anyway, Jimmy was pissed off—he's always been a lazy arse and he was some mad when I told him he wasn't doing any of the work. He hauled off and whacked me over the head."

"Did your parents call the police?"

"They threatened to but in the end he got away with it. The little bastard didn't even say he was sorry. There's genetics again for you, I guess, because I'm not so hot at apologizing myself. It was kind of funny, though. Blood all over the snow in Coach's driveway. He never made us do that again." Donnie lifts a corner of Elizabeth's shorts. "Show them *your* scars, sweetie."

Elizabeth flutters her fingers in the air. "You probably can't see them, but I have tiny little nicks all over my hands."

"From cutting hair?" Effie asks.

"Yes. I'm not so adept with a razor, which might not say so much about my other abilities."

"Come on," Donnie says. "Look at my hair. And Mum's. You're the best stylist in Charlottetown. And when we get married and have all those kids we'll buy a bowl for each one of them."

"You're what? You're getting married!? When?"

"Not tomorrow." Donnie grabs Elizabeth's hand. "But probably before the end of next summer. Hey, we could have the wedding on a boat. Whaddya say, Roddy? Can't sea captains perform nuptials?"

John sniffs. "With all those Catholics in attendance—"

"More than you can shake a stick at?" Donnie asks, squeezing Elizabeth's hand and laughing.

"—you'll need an ocean liner. The Queen Mary was docked here not that long ago. Maybe they'd give you a dispensation discount." He licks hummus from his fingers.

Effie, confused by the mix of happiness, jealousy and trepidation she feels, sees herself walking down the aisle with John who will, undoubtedly, be Donnie's best man.

"It's not earth-shattering news, except for us," Donnie says. "But it would be wonderful if we were all together. Anyways, enough!" He gulps down the remains of his Alpine. Elizabeth giggles.

"Enough of scars and onto weddings," Mary interjects quietly.

"Or close enough," Mike says.

A vagrant cloud stalls overhead, leaving Effie in half-shadow.

Mary looks over at Effie. "We haven't worked out the particulars, so I'm not handing in my notice just yet, but I'm going to join Mike in Ottawa. For now, with a husband in the offing and a new best friend—who could ask for more?"

Effie blushes with embarrassment and shock.

"That leaves only you two," Mike says, staring at Effie and John.

"Whoa!" Donnie interrupts. "Let's not tip us all into the sea at once. Right, Effie?"

"This is turning into a Samuel Goldwyn movie."

"Or the Love Boat," adds John.

Mike smiles goofily, his teeth stained red from cherries.

Effie, still stunned by the news that Mary is leaving, wonders why no one else seems surprised. "Is this something else you all knew that I didn't? Why is it you all think I can't handle anything?" She smiles bravely, feeling sick at heart over losing her friend, who had once assured Effie she would never leave the island.

"Can I get anyone another drink?"

"Pop your cap and sit down, Donnie," John's eyes seem small in the sun. "Does everyone have a drink?" He reaches over, his skin more olive than it had been that morning, and hoists a wine bottle, filling Effie's glass.

"To my best friend, Donald Reginald Fitzgerald, and to his sweet-tempered bride-to-be—the woman who will divert us from the annihilating path of Ruth and Abel's eldest son."

"Here, here!" everyone yells, and Roddy steps into the wheelhouse and sounds the horn. "Here, here!" he calls. "To Elizabeth and Donnie!"

A pleasure boat gliding by toots back.

John turns away from his friend and faces Mary. "And to Effie's best friend and the fearless MP—to Mary and Mike. May they cohabitate in political union for years to come. Although with Mulroney—"

"Here, here!"

The boat sways gently in the mid-afternoon sun. Donnie explains the world of jellyfish to Elizabeth, advising her that of the more than fifty species only five are harmful to humans. He talks about moon jellies and Lion's Mane and the less prevalent Portuguese man-o-war. He says that he knew a man who went swimming off the north shore who was stung by a jellyfish that got jammed in his swimming trunks, leaving a pattern. He switches topics to currents and tides. "The tides," he says, "can last anywhere from two to eight hours. At least here in the strait. And you don't want to get stuck swimming in a harbour current because that would be that. When we were kids, John and I used to jump in down by the pier and come up covered in leeches. Not so much a girl's thing, I guess. We knew enough to skirt the currents further out, but Jesus, it was cold." Elizabeth sits enraptured, not once reminding him that, as an island native, she also knows a thing or two about currents and tides.

Jill and Roddy sit in the wheelhouse discussing mooring techniques, Jill comparing it to ballet and Roddy arguing that it is more complicated than that, which leads to a dispute about fly fishing versus deep sea fishing and whether one requires more skill than the other. "It's all about the tension," Roddy says. "Isn't everything?" Jill retorts, and then she kisses him.

Mary curls up on the bench seat like a cat, facing Mike who is describing Ottawa's various neighbourhoods and advising Mary that although the Glebe has some of the grandest homes, he thinks she will prefer Sandy Hill or Lower Town, which turns into a debate about the English and the French and whether Brian Mulroney really is the worst prime minister ever.

At the back of the boat, sitting side by side in two deck chairs, Effie and John face the water. Effie has reverted to lemonade and John is experimenting with his camera and nursing a beer.

"Do you think sex is critical to a marriage?" John asks. "Does it take precedence?" He turns around and shoots a close-up of Donnie and Elizabeth. Effie, flummoxed by John's sudden intimacy, skims bread out to a group of seagulls. John captures the scavengers in flight.

"I've read that if sex is satisfying so is everything else," she says. "Even when you are poor. But I don't know. I think the most important part of a marriage is friendship. I would rather live with someone who loved and respected me than someone who was only hot for my body."

"So would I. If the sex goes—which it seems to in most marriages—"

"What does that mean?" Effie tightens her grip on the heel of the bread.

"Oh, that could be to their credit," John says a little fuzzily.

"Who's *their*?"

"Heterosexual couples." John's camera dangles from his neck.

Effie stares at him. "It sounds as if you are saying that gay couples have an easier time maintaining a physical relationship."

"Not all gay couples. Gay men. I meant gay men. You know what men are like. Just imagine two of them together."

"Do I have to?" Effie asks.

"You know what I mean."

"Ah yes—the virtuous female. Another fringe benefit for women. You do know we vote, don't you?" Effie hurls the remainder of the bread into the water. "I think you're being simplistic. Lots of people like sex." Effie lowers her voice. "In fact, nearly everybody likes sex, unless they have troubles."

"Limpid libido?" John laughs.

"Careful, you're sounding like Mildred Rutherford." Effie pauses, hoping to seem unaffected. "No, not necessarily. Or not directly. Trauma, exhaustion, apprehension, anxiety, abjection. Lots of things happen to dull people's desire." Effie closes her eyes. "Is that what happened to you?"

John laughs again. "It isn't that I don't like sex. But I'm not wasting it—well, that's not exactly what I mean. I mean I am not wasting marriage on just anyone."

Effie grasps the arms of her chair, hoping she won't stutter the way she sometimes does when taken off-guard.

John raises his camera and takes a picture of her. "I'm not talking about you. You are precisely the sort of person a nice man—and I *am* a nice man, aren't I?—would want to marry. But I don't want to rush things. A person can't be too careful. We have to be careful."

We? "Yes, we have to be careful. And thoughtful," she says. "It's better to savour than to rush." She lets go of the chair. Before her, the sky opens up and the ocean shimmers a wild blue. She follows the vanishing seagulls, her head buzzing. She wonders if she can risk one more question.

"What about children?" she asks.

"What about them?"

"Do you want children?"

John stares off into the horizon. "There are many things I am cautious about, but having children is not one of them. Nothing would make me happier."

Effie holds her breath, waiting, wondering if anyone on deck has overheard them.

Donnie stands up, pulling Elizabeth with him. "Before I drink too much and forget my manners," he says, "I've been out on plenty of boats, but this one is the best." Donnie locks arms with Elizabeth. "You know sweetheart, you and me gots to get ourselves a boat." He turns his head away, his eye caught by a series of specks dotting the shoreline.

"What are all those people doing over there?" Elizabeth shields her eyes with her hand.

"Fort Amherst. The national Boy Scout Jamboree. Remember, Donnie?"

Effie thinks John sounds wistful.

"How could I forget. I sure miss those days of scavenger hunts and lighting farts after midnight."

"Boy Scout Jamboree?" Effie jumps up from her chair and swings around to see. "Like the Flintstones?"

"Like every time they have a jamboree, wherever. Those people are probably laying down the plans, marking out tent sites, digging latrines and so on. They're expecting ten thousand boy scouts this year."

Effie claps her hands. "It *is* like the Flintstones!"

Donnie crosses the deck and rests his hand on her shoulder. "Effie, how old are you?"

"Laugh if you will, but when I was a kid that episode made me cry. All those children, all those countries. Everyone getting along. Where else does *that* happen?"

"Only in Bedrock," Donnie declares.

"It's symbolic, Donnie," Jill interjects.

"Exactly," Effie says. "I bet the same thing will be true here, at the real one."

John fits a longer lens onto his camera and pulls the tiny figures closer. He pauses, glancing back at Effie. "Would you like me to take you?"

"Me? You mean we can visit? When the boy scouts are here?"

"Sure we can. In August," John says. "I'll take you."

"Oh, I'd love that! Thank you." Effie laughs at herself. "They sang *Old MacDonald*," she says. "On the show. *Old MacDonald had a farm.*"

"I can't promise you that, but we could hum a few bars if you like. *E-i-e-i—oooo.*"

"Speaking of bars," Donnie ogles the cooler of beer, "anyone else ready for another one besides me?"

The boat rocks in the harbour, all eyes on Effie.

"If I can eat this without dying, I vow to give up all superstition." She stares at the lobster as if it were going to leap up and bite her. "Poor thing."

"Where's Nurse Rutherford when we need her?" Donnie asks. "I bet she would just love to stab you—or anyone—with a big long needle." He watches Jill as she twists a cork screw into a bottle of red wine.

John stands up and ties a red-checkered napkin around Effie's neck. "If you're going to go," he says, "it might as well be in style."

"How does my hair look?" she asks, grinning up at him.

"Fit for a laying out, my dear."

"Jesus. You guys are too morbid, even for me," Donnie laughs. "What say you, Mike—are you ready for a true Maritime feast? I bet they don't serve you lobster up on that big hill."

Mike shakes his head. "Hell, no. It's feast or famine there, but never like this, no." He sighs. "Mary, are you sure you'll be all right in Ottawa?"

"It won't be forever," she says. "Unless they make you Prime Minister, in which case I'll be divorcing you, so it's a moot point."

Effie extracts a sliver of pinkish-white meat from a cracked claw, takes a deep breath, then bites down on the muscular flesh.

Seven faces stare at her.

"For all the talk of richness, it's kind of bland." She chews a little more. "I'll need a few minutes before we know if it's going to kill me. I hope I brought two Epi-pens so I can have another bite. It's actually quite delicious." She hesitates before raising her glass in the air. "Salut!"

"Salut!" The guests lift their glasses toward Roddy and Jill, who insist that everyone return the following weekend to watch the Canada Day fireworks from the water.

At sundown, as Effie and John walk up the pier, Effie is so elated she doesn't even mind when he tells her he will be dropping her off but won't be coming upstairs. "I'm a little too tipsy, my girl," he says, slinging his jacket and camera carelessly over his shoulder. She can tell from the slur of his words that he isn't looking for excuses. "But you and I could attend church next Sunday. I'd like my parents to meet you." He leans into Effie and she weaves her arm through his, bolstering him. He squeezes her elbow with his own, before relinquishing her grip.

Effie laughs. "You need a week to prepare them?" They walk along Great George past the Basilica and stand outside her apartment building falling into one another, his breath plummy from wine.

"Actually," John says, "there is something I would like to discuss with you. It's personal, not conversation for the street." He lowers his voice to a near-whisper. "And I need to be sober." His eyes moisten, and Effie thinks—hopes—she understands why he seems overwhelmed.

"A man of mystery," she says, her body suddenly weightless. "It's okay, I can wait."

His voice becomes buoyant again. "Yes, you're absolutely right. It can wait."

Effie shivers and John, thinking she is cold, slips his jacket around her shoulders.

"No need for you to go further," she says, nodding toward the front door. "Unless you would like me to call you a cab. I'm not sure you're in any shape to walk home."

John kisses the top of her head. "Art's Taxi is just up the row if I need a lift but I think I can make it from here." As he saunters up the street, Effie stares at his receding outline. John calls back over his shoulder, but what he says Effie can't make out.

She climbs the stairs to her apartment, repeating calmly to herself with each step, *Effie MacDonald, Effie MacDonald, Effie MacDonald.*

CHAPTER 41

The knocking is soft but persistent, the noonday sun beating in through Effie's bedroom window indicating the lateness of the morning. She shuffles down the hallway barely awake. She opens the door, relieved to see Mary on the other side.

Behind her, Effie's telephone starts to ring long and loud, exaggerated, like the sound in a cartoon.

"It's probably Donnie," Mary says, her voice close to a whisper. She guides Effie back into the apartment and over to the couch. "He called to tell me. To ask me to let you know. He'll be on his way over soon, so if you can't answer the phone, don't worry. Oh Effie," Mary's eyes flood with tears. She stands frozen, as if she wants Effie to find the words she herself cannot say.

"Is this about John?" Effie asks.

"Oh Effie," Mary repeats. "John's dead."

The church bells peal out the hour.

Effie's eyes droop and she is suddenly struck by the smallness of Mary's feet. She says, as if she's known all along, "What happened?"

"The police will want to ask you questions, Effie, since you might have been the last person John saw last night." Carefully, she goes on. "But there'll be time before that, and we can talk it over with Donnie."

"The police? What does this"—she can say neither the name John nor the word death—"have to do with the police? What happened?"

"John—" Mary halts.

"What happened?" Effie repeats.

"Effie, he was murdered. John was murdered."

Effie is prepared for an accident, a drunken stumble, a mishap, an error in judgement, but not this. "Murdered? How is that possible? We stood outside this very building last night and made plans for church next Sunday. With his parents. It was going to be a wonderful weekend. Remember? We were going to go out on the boat again and watch the fireworks. We were going to go to church.".

Mary's head drops and she starts to cry. She takes Effie's hand. "Effie, I am so very sorry," is all she can get out between sobs. Effie sits rigid beside her.

Donnie arrives within the hour, breathless and blazing. He paces Effie's living room. "They left his door wide open. Barkley was out in the yard, beside himself, just about deranged. Oh my God, that poor dog." Donnie stops moving. "The bastards choked him to death, but—God forgive me for saying this out loud—they stuck a knife in him. In his fucking backside. And no blood anywhere. Except...except where they bashed him in the head. And even then. . . ."

Mary looks bewildered. "Why would they do that? Why would they need to do that? How do you know that he was choked to death? How do you know that the knife didn't kill him?"

"No. That's right, Mary." Effie speaks coldly, clinically. "There would have been blood."

"Don't you see, Mary?" Donnie implores. "The knife was symbolic. Or at least where they shoved it."

"I don't understand. What do you mean by symbolic?" Effie sounds less sure of herself, less in control.

Mary opens her mouth silently, grasping something important. "Oh my God," is all she is able to say.

"Effie, sooner or later the cops are going to show up here asking you all kinds of questions. Where you were last night. What you were doing when you last saw John. What *he* was doing. That sort of thing."

"I was standing out front with him watching him walk away. He was thinking about getting a taxi at Art's. He invited me to church to meet his parents. Next Sunday we were going to church." She turns and faces Donnie, speaking evenly. "Donnie, tell me what you seem to already know."

Donnie hesitates and then lets out a breath. "Effie, John isn't straight." He looks over at Mary.

Donnie's words shock Effie almost as much as the news of John's death. She stares at her friends, incredulous. "How kind of you all to tell me. John most especially. Was anyone ever going to tell me?" She feels an impossible ache in her chest as she pushes back sobs. "And here I had convinced myself that he had fallen in love with me. How could you not tell me? How could you let it go on all of these months and never say a word? Why did he not tell me? I wasted all that time on a man who could never love me."

Kneeling down in front of her, Donnie speaks quietly but firmly. "He did love you, Effie. He told me that he did. But he had other desires and that wasn't his fault. It's just the way it...he was. He hoped that if he found the right person—if he found you—he might be able to have a different sort of life. And lately, the way he was with you, I figured he'd found his way through to something. He did love you, Effie. Maybe not entirely in the way that you wanted, but you're not a conventional girl." Donnie attempts to smile.

"I am hardly a girl." Tears splatter her cheeks, her face regaining a painterly appearance, a fragile figure distantly removed.

In the outer hallway a crush of shoes sweep by her door, making their way up to Mildred Rutherford's apartment.

Mary and Donnie sit with Effie all afternoon, but the police do not appear. They wait through two pots of tea, uneaten toast and the lingering gossip upstairs. Mary offers to fetch something for dinner, but no one is hungry. She calls Mike and speaks to him briefly, promising that she is okay and that she will see him later. She holds Effie's hand for long periods and cries into Donnie's shoulder.

Later, with Donnie and Mary gone, Effie becomes lost to the world around her. She finds herself walking along the lake, brewing hot tea after church. She stands in the front yard of her Port Credit apartment building, pulling the rake through a helpless toad, not knowing what it was—that it was—not meaning to kill it. She tastes toasted Westerns at the diner and sips sweet Coca Cola. She sees vodka in peanut butter glasses, pink peppermints, the train engineer lying without his cap or his boots on the frozen embankment.

The ambulance comes from Port Credit and Effie speaks in a whisper. "I'm so sorry to tell you, but my mother. . . ." All those false alarms and, now, barely believable. She sees her mother all those years earlier, standing in high heels, snow falling in slow motion around her, lipsticked and smiling, blowing kisses up to Effie who stands at the frosted window, her bare feet cold on the linoleum floor.

The pain, which comes in the evening, begins in the pit of her stomach, radiating through her back then driving down into her bowels, her upper thighs, and into the soles of her feet. The tentacles reach back up through her stomach and shift into her left breast, unforgiving, rolling on into her upper arms and joints. The pain comes in waves, sharp at first then more rhythmical, undulating like the hills of the island countryside where she had walked, too briefly, with John. She laughs out loud at her hackneyed imagery.

She pictures his hands, once thick and inclined to redness, now limp and edging into blue. She looks at her own hands, the veins popping up like a network of tributaries, fingernails wide and flat, the crosshatch lines on her palms indicative of what a psychic called *repair*. Her heart, so used to racing out of control, beats steadily in her chest, no murmur of arrhythmia or atrial fibrillation, pulse strong and regular, his heart no longer beating.

Her cheeks, perpetually pink from flushing, are as white as China clay, freckles standing out like pinhead dots. His cheeks, devoid of oxygen, sink like hollow craters, the cartilage of his monumental nose rising defiantly.

Effie stares at the playful beams of twilight sun that bounce in through the window, bands of light showing off plaster and dust. Twice in the evening she hears a light rapping on her door, distant and surreal, the ghosts that have haunted her for years bandying about, attempting a feeble, half-invested entry.

She does not hear the chimes ringing out the hours, or feel the breeze that blows the curtains into the room. The summer roses that call up to her from one floor below, their sweetly redolent blossoms intimating a balmy summer love, remain unfolded, the streetlights blinking, ushering in the dark.

And still she sits, shoulders back, spine tall, the way her mother had insisted, upright and unexpectedly elegant, her breathing imperceptible, body temperature slightly below normal, blood pressure favourably low, pupils marginally dilated: a proper girl sitting in a secondhand chair, hair clean, bangs evenly cut, fingernails painted in clear polish, lips faintly parted, nostrils flared, eyes dry.

CHAPTER 42

Mary and Effie walk to the church beneath a leaden sky, a blanket of thick cloud folding across the horizon. Mike will meet them there. The wake, which had taken place over two nights, seemed more like a cocktail party than a memorial, teachers and students flooding out of the funeral home chatting in small groups, framing the edge of the parking lot and spilling onto the sidewalk. So quick, people said, for a murder investigation. *Expedited.*

Donnie and his five brothers are serving as pallbearers. "John would have loved that," Mary says. But Effie wonders how anyone so young could love anything about being dead.

Mary tries to smile, but her face is streaked with tears, her eyes puffy, vertical lines of grief etched between her brows. "Are you all right?" she asks Effie.

"I'm not sure I'll ever be all right again," Effie says evenly. Her shoes click along the cement and she can see her mother bending down to buckle up her Mary Janes, straightening the cuffs of Effie's Sunday socks. "What about you?" she asks Mary, and without waiting for an answer, "You see, the thing is there will never be anyone like him. You could walk from here to Kingdom Come and never find anyone like him. I would have married him. Gay or not. I would have married him." Effie amends her pace, aware that she is walking too quickly.

"I know," Mary says. "There were clearly some things he kept hidden, but he was the most principled person I knew." A small leaf sails down from above, landing on Effie's head.

"It's a sign," Effie says, trying to bolster herself for the long day ahead.

As Mary and Effie approach the church they fall in with streams of mourners: a profusion of students and teachers; the

Fitzgeralds accompanied by Elizabeth; Shirley and Bill with Martha, Willie absent; Mildred Rutherford with her gaggle; Peggy Trainor; Jill and Roddy; Aida Lynn and Jane; the friendly man from the framing store; Angus from the Morning Dove; the man from the hot dog stand—more people than Effie can count or know. A battery of police officers stand off to the side of the entrance.

Inside the church, John's parents sit waiting for the Fitzgerald boys to carry in the coffin. Effie, eyes on the ground, follows Mary, guided by her hand, Mary's other hand clenched in Mike's. The air feels saturated.

Jimmy Fitzgerald slips into the church behind them. "I've got some questions for you, Miss Cambridge," he mutters. "I'll be calling on you next week."

"That's good," Effie says loudly. "Because I have some questions for you." His head is huge. Encephalitic.

Mary propels Effie forward, and Mike steps in between Effie and the policeman, crunching down on Fitzgerald's shiny shoe. "Forgive me," Mike says, his voice filled with contempt. He waves his hand toward the back of the church. "Hadn't you best join your fellow officers?"

An usher guides the three friends to a front pew, Effie taking the aisle. She lowers herself slowly, the scene surreal. She presses her knees together and folds her hands.

White lilies border the nave, their trumpet-like petals mirroring the lips of the choir, who sound to Effie as if they are appealing to God, their voices ascending upward.

When I survey the wondrous cross on which the Prince of Glory died, my richest gain I count but loss, and pour contempt on all my pride.

She closes her eyes, afraid to find herself transfixed by the casket and John's body lying inside. The flickering candle at the head of the coffin seems pointless, bringing neither heat nor comfort. He will be cold, she thinks.

John's mother fans her fingers across the top of her husband's hand, he tunelessly uttering the words of the hymn, she singing strongly, her clarity a revelation to the congregation who expected her to be too bereaved (or ashamed) to sing.

Her voice soars.

Were the whole realm of nature mine, that were a present far too small; love so amazing, so divine, demands my soul, my life, my all.

John's father isn't able to finish the hymn.

The Rector stands. His words circle airily. "When we speak of death we are, in effect, talking about a period of contemplation; a time when we must sacrifice in order to observe, cleanse and repent. Only through reflection can we be prepared to understand the sufferings of Christ: what He sacrificed for us in order that we should live. Today we will turn to the words of Daniel, Job and Samuel, and, with these men, realize that without death and mourning, a rich and meaningful life is impossible."

Ruth Fitzgerald's sobs cut through the sermon as she watches her sons lined up together in the front pew, their wheat-coloured heads bowed. Abel, august in his black suit and red suspenders, grasps her knee, his heart heavy with guilt because all of his boys are safe while Ed and Elmira MacDonald's only son is gone. Abel had known for years that John had *worries*, but Ruth and Abel weren't concerned. John was a dear man, just as he had been a dear boy—another son; a member of the family.

Effie stares up at the round window full of Jesus, his arms outstretched, his robe the colour of Saharan sand, his hair looking as if it had been ironed, the way she and Kathleen Raminsky straightened their hair when they were girls. Ashes to ashes, she says to herself, tears beginning to form and swell, threatening at any second to give way. She pushes them back. For long months after her mother died, Effie felt numb, detached. But this is different. John is different. John is raw. Ripping.

She looks up at Jesus, her eyes running along the colossal organ pipes and following them up to the ceiling. God's gold-plated pencils. She pictures Jesus sitting at an imposingly large desk writing out scriptures. Her eyes wander back to the Rector, who is speaking confidently but dispassionately, guiding the congregation toward the hymnal. Everyone stands for the singing of *Guide Me, O Thou Great Jehovah*, and Effie sees with dazzling clarity how painful these rituals must have been for John; how hard he must have railed against the futility of a bland God whose platitudes were easy and narrow-minded, and whose congregation fell in with protocol.

She wants to run from the church; to run and keep running. But she has nowhere to go. The life she has built in the past year will not be enough to sustain her. Not now.

John's dead. *John's dead.*

Ruth's crying continues, and Jimmy Fitzgerald rocks nervously on his heels, not knowing what to make of his aunt's grief; not wanting to make anything of it at all.

Effie takes some comfort in the Gospel of St. Matthew, ignoring the monotone delivery, letting the words come to her in the consoling voice of her mother, who first read this passage to Effie when Effie was only five.

> *Blessed are the poor in spirit,*
> *for theirs is the kingdom of heaven.*
> *Blessed are those who mourn,*
> *for they shall be comforted.*
> *Blessed are the meek,*
> *for they shall inherit the earth.*
> *Blessed are those who hunger and thirst for righteousness,*
> *for they shall be filled.*
> *Blessed are the merciful,*
> *for they shall obtain mercy. Blessed are the pure in heart,*
> *for they shall see God.*
> *Blessed are the peacemakers,*
> *for they shall be called sons of God.*
> *Blessed are those who are persecuted for righteousness' sake,*
> *for theirs is the kingdom of heaven.*

She touches her fingers to her cheek, remembering her kiss curls and the scotch tape that held them in place through the night. She squeezes Mary's hand. Mary sobs quietly beside her. Effie feels ashamed, unable to cry in front of all these people, most of whom she does not really know; most of whom aren't fit to sit at the feet of John. The mouths of the lilies gape.

The Rector delivers a final message conveying what he calls John's essence. Effie wants to ram a spear through his skull. How does *he* know what John's essence was? Had these sentiments been delivered to him by way of John's parents, or did they come from personal experience?

"—he was a brave man, denying his worldliness in place of the common good. Like all of us, his struggles will be those things for which he will be remembered, for in God's house it is that which challenges us that will move us forward into a higher realm of understanding—"

Effie holds her breath, listening. Tears slide down her cheeks, channelling around the contours of her mouth, dripping helplessly onto her jacket. Donnie turns his head, locking eyes with her, his crestfallen features promising her that, for all their sorrow, better days lie ahead. He nods at Elizabeth, who is sitting beside Ruth holding her hand.

As the congregation rises for the final hymn Effie remains seated—*the darkness deepens, Lord with me abide*—afraid to stand, afraid that she will walk out or that her legs will buckle beneath her.

Help of the helpless, oh abide with me.

Mike and Mary guide Effie out of the church. They gather under the grey sky and wait for Donnie and his family, drifting a few feet away from the legion of mourners and hoping to stave off conversation, each for his own reasons. Mike is expected in Ottawa early Monday morning and Mary assures him that she will be safe with Donnie and Effie. Soon they will be making their way to the graveyard. Mike kisses Mary goodbye, promising to call her later that evening. As he walks away, Effie understands why Mary has chosen him.

Effie scans the approaching horde, searching for John's parents, wanting to convey her condolences but unsure of what she'll say or if they'll even know who she is.

Donnie emerges with Elizabeth and his family, holding his mother's hand. They walk together over to Mary and Effie. Ruth lets go of her son's hand and enfolds Effie in her arms. "I am so sorry, my girl." Effie shivers in the damp air. Gordy, who is standing shyly next to his mother, twists his legs into a knot. "We're sure going to miss him, Effie." Effie leans over and kisses him, grateful to this boy who has always made her feel as if she, too, was one of their family.

Effie and Mary say their goodbyes and depart to Donnie's waiting car, Elizabeth insisting that Donnie ride with his friends. The trio head through town and up St. Peter's Road, not waiting for the procession. "Do you think this is right?" Mary asks, and Donnie replies, "What do you think John would want us to do?" Effie laughs, remembering the first time she sat in this car heading up this same road to the beach, John and Donnie squabbling (about what, she has long forgotten).

"This might not be the best time to talk about this," Effie says, "But given that Jimmy Fitzgerald has started menacing me—"

"He what?"

"He stopped Effie in the church today," Mary says. "He thought Mike and I couldn't hear him."

"He said he has some things he wants to talk to me about. He shoved his face into mine and all I could think of was that day on the beach when John called his head a television."

"That cocksucker." Spit flies from Donnie's lips.

Effie turns her head toward the window. "He says he's coming to see me next week."

"Oh really? Is he? Well, you won't be alone for that."

Effie avoids looking down John's street. "I can handle him, Donnie. But I'd like to tape record him. Do you think that would be safe?"

"I wouldn't trust that piece of shit as far as I could throw him," Donnie fumes. "Jesus, I hate him. I bet he had something to do with this, that fucker, or knows more than he's saying."

"Whether he's privy to details or not—he's a cop, Donnie, after all—you can be sure he isn't sorry to see John gone."

"They're going to make this about John's being gay, you can count on that." Donnie's words settle around them awkwardly.

Effie suddenly remembers what she'd found. "Last Saturday, when John walked me home, he left his jacket with me. There was something in the pocket. I forgot I had it." Her heart thrums like a hummingbird's. "And now I don't want to let go of it."

Donnie eases the car over to the side of the road. "No one need know you have his jacket, Effie. His family wouldn't mind."

"There was a roll of film in his pocket." She brushes off the front of her skirt. "From last weekend."

"Our last day together," Donnie says.

"Not to be mystical, but doesn't that seem odd?" Mary asks. Her voice brightens. "He left pictures for us of last Saturday."

Last Saturday. The words puncture Effie's heart. "He said he was afraid of getting his camera wet, but he brought it with him anyway." Effie struggles to continue. "He said he was more interested in experiencing the day than seeing it through a lens. Even so, he couldn't pass up the opportunity to take pictures."

"Effie, what did you do with the film?" Donnie asks.

"It's here in my purse." She taps on her bag. "I've been afraid to tell anyone about it. I didn't want to lose this record of how he saw us."

"Give me the film, Effie, and I'll see that it's safe."

Effie grips her bag. "That's okay, Donnie, I'll look after it. John took me into the store last year and the owner was so nice. He won't mind if I take it in to be developed. He really liked John. I saw him today in the church and he looked devastated."

"Everyone looked devastated," Donnie says. "Except for those cops."

"John took so many photos. Once I get the prints back I think we should see them together." Effie hesitates. "If I can stand to look at them."

"We'll look at them together, Effie, whenever you're ready."

"Look, Donnie," Mary says. "There goes the procession."

Donnie flicks on his blinker. "I guess we'd better join them." He waits until the tide has passed and then steers his vehicle back onto the road. Turning on his headlights, he hooks onto the end of the line.

★

All of her life Effie has loved wandering through graveyards, daydreaming about visiting Paris's Père Lachaise where Édith Piaf and Abelard and Héloïse are buried, imagining herself eating orange slices under a cluster of trees, which is a ludicrous thought because she is allergic to oranges. In her fantasy the day is windy, the sky low and threatening rain.

But today Effie wishes that the sun would push the clouds aside. As it is, she has no idea how she is going to make it through tomorrow or the day after that. John had become the hinge for her; the pivot. Effie remembers her birthday—she and John walking the dark island hills, John holding her hand. "*Hansel und Gretel*," he'd said.

Mary watches the car doors opening and closing one after another, like a flip chart. "Are you ready for this? Because I'm not."

"Maybe if we think of it as a scene in a movie we can stand back from it." Donnie runs his hands through his hair. "I can't imagine what John would think of all this."

Mary inhales through her nose. "Perhaps that a lot of people loved him." She points to the gathering circle of mourners. "Look at all the students. Look at them, Donnie. Oh my God."

Mary, Effie and Donnie step out of the car and walk toward the ring that is forming around the gravesite. Donnie smiles reassuringly over at this mother, who is standing across from them with Abel, Elizabeth and the boys.

Donnie speaks in a low voice. "Effie, what movie does this remind you of?"

Effie pauses. "*The Children's Hour*. And you?"

"*The Conversation.*"

Effie laughs out loud then clamps her hand over her mouth.

Mary gestures at the policemen hovering on the fringe. "Breaker, Breaker 1-9," she says, tossing her hair over her shoulders. "Or how about *Magnum Force*?"

"*Magnum P.I.*," Effie shoots back.

"Magnum *P.E.I.*," Donnie stammers.

Effie looks up. Many of the mourners have turned to stare at them.

"Got something of yours on?" Effie says loudly, staring back.

"Good for you, Effie!" Donnie squeezes her shoulders.

From out of the swarm a contemptuous voice jeers, "Sure is mighty queer over there."

Donnie stands upright and begins making his way forward. The congregation sinks back, leaving Jimmy Fitzgerald standing alone. "What did you say, asshole?" Donnie's face is blood red. "Is that what you said to John? What the fuck are you doing here? Why don't you crawl back into that hole you slithered out of!" Donnie strips off his jacket. He raises his right arm, his hand forming a fist. His hair flaps in a gust of wind.

Jimmy rears back and rolls his shoulders forward, his arms thrust out in front of him, his fingers splayed.

"James, Donald! Stop now!"

Donnie looks back toward his mother then whisks up his jacket from the ground.

"Listen, you son of a bitch. You have no business being here. You've been gunning for him for years. Couldn't stand who he was, could you?"

Jimmy lowers his arms and glowers, as if bolstering for a fight, his complexion deepening; lizard-like.

"Uncomfortable in your own skin, aren't you?" Donnie sneers at his cousin. "You're not fit to tie his shoes."

Ruth breaks down again but this time she cries for her son. Her son who is angry. Her son who has lost his best friend. She strides over to Jimmy Fitzgerald and grabs his corpulent chin. "I have tried all my life to love you because you need love more than anything. But that's not going to happen."

Abel gazes at his wife proudly, having relinquished his nephew years ago. He braces his arm around Elizabeth, squeezing her tightly.

Mr. and Mrs. MacDonald stand helpless in the background, hidden by the crowd.

Mary and Effie hold hands, watching the scene. Mary is crying again, too, and Effie feels the familiar pain return to her left breast. As the Rector commences with the burial service and Donnie rejoins Elizabeth and his family, the business at hand carries forward. The coffin is lowered, earth sprinkled onto the rich mahogany. Effie catches sight of John's stricken parents, their tired hands sifting remnants of red dirt into his grave. "From ashes to ashes," they chant in unison, stepping back slowly. Effie is relieved to see Abel and Ruth slide in on either side, supporting them.

Dizzy, Effie views the tableau before her, the lines of a D.H. Lawrence poem floating in her head. *And at the foot of a grave a mother kneels with pale shut face, nor either hears nor feels the coming of the chanting choristers between the cypresses, the silence of the many villagers; the candle flames beside the surplices.* She latches onto Mary's arm, afraid that without support she will collapse.

CHAPTER 43

Effie stands outside the newspaper office waiting for Mary. She watches the shadows of the leaves play on the side of the building, remembering these same shapes from her childhood— Miss Kitty hiding behind overturned chairs, Matt Dillon standing in the line of gunfire and the horses, helpless, tied up to the railing outside. And she wonders why she cannot remember John's exact words to her on the boat, yet the nightmares that tormented her twenty-five years ago remain indelible.

Mary flies out the door, her kitbag slung over her shoulder. She stops to give Effie a kiss on the cheek. "So, did you get them?"

Effie takes hold of Mary's shoulder strap and manoeuvres her toward Grafton Street. "We'll talk at Donnie's."

Mary looks puzzled. "But did you get them?"

"About ten minutes ago. The owner couldn't have been lovelier. But there were a lot of people around so I haven't looked at them yet."

Effie and Mary cut through the churchyard, the cawing crows flying low above their heads. Richmond Street patio diners ogle the women with curiosity. Some speculate that Mary and Effie are lovers. Others debate which of the women had loved John more. A few note their contrasts and their symmetry, the one woman fairytale blond, the other bookishly dark and beguiling. One man, jamming a bratwurst into his mouth, pronounces, "Wouldn't kick them outta bed for eatin' crackers."

Effie hugs her purse to her side, trying to ignore the onlookers. The crows are everywhere—perched on the library wall, lining the rooftops on Sydney Street, colliding with seagulls at the bottom of Queen. "I feel like we're in a Hitchcock movie. Gawking people and shrieking birds." Mary links arms with Effie and they continue on toward King Street and Donnie's lopsided house.

Donnie stands waiting at the front door. He ushers his friends inside and guides them toward the couch, glancing at Effie. "Are you sure you're up for seeing them?"

Effie spirits the packet from her purse, opens the envelope and spreads the photos across the coffee table.

An uncomfortable silence settles into the room.

Donnie speaks first. "These aren't from the boat. These are from the New Year's Eve party. See, there's Effie on the couch and one of me cutting the rug with Elizabeth. And look, Mary, here you are making eyes at Mike." In the picture Michael McCready is backed up against the wall, confined by Mary's flailing arms.

Effie covers her mouth with her hand, stifling a painful laugh. "Here I was steeling myself and these aren't even the pictures we thought they were. But why would this film have been in John's pocket? The New Year's party was months ago. And where are the pictures from Jill and Roddy's boat?" Effie points to the corner of the table. "Who are those men standing in Dr. McCready's kitchen?"

The threesome bunch together, examining each photograph in minute detail, the act a deferral against what is most painful.

"That's odd," Effie says, tapping one of the pictures. Two uniformed policemen stand kitty-corner to a third who is dressed in Calvin Klein blue jeans and snow-rimmed Gucci loafers. A pastel blue jacket lies across the back of a kitchen chair. Liquor bottles litter the counter behind them, the three men glassy-eyed and laughing, bathed in a haze of cigarette smoke.

"You mean those two policemen—or their friend?"

Donnie snorts derisively. "Yes, those two and the Chief Justice."

"Is that who he was?" Effie asks. "I saw him come in. Nattily decked out but he seemed shifty. I thought he was a lawyer." She examines the picture again. "What would John want with them? And why are they wearing their uniforms? I don't remember seeing them at all. They look really drunk."

"They had just gone off-duty," Mary says. "I know because Mike and I had a brief run-in with them. They made some asinine comment and seemed disappointed when Mike just smiled at them. Imagine—right there in his brother's house." Mary studies the photo. "They stayed in the kitchen all night as far as I know. At least they were there whenever we went in for a beer."

"But why would John take all of these photos and not get them developed?"

"Effie, see that man's hand? Where is it?"

Effie looks closely. "Oh, I see what you mean. It's in the other man's back pocket." She settles into the couch, unable to shift her disappointment. She wants to see evidence of their last day together. She wants to see how John had seen her. "Why would John take a picture of that? Of them?"

"Think about it, Effie," Donnie says. "A man spends the sum of his life trapped in a place where he doesn't belong, hounded by these bastards. Bastards with their own secrets."

"The same would be true in Toronto."

Donnie shakes his head. "You can't tell me that being gay is the same on the island as it is in Toronto."

Effie smiles wanly. "Now you're sounding like John."

"They burn down people's houses here. They beat people into unconsciousness. Ostracize them forever—make them feel as if their only option is to leave."

"You know," Mary says slowly, "there have been rumours swirling about corruption for years. But how does Jimmy Fitzgerald fit in? You seem so sure that he's involved in what happened to John. Why hasn't he followed through on his threat of interrogation? Effie hasn't heard a word from him."

"Oh come on, Mary," Donnie erupts. "Jimmy hated John. Always did. Why do you think that is? John's sexuality hit cousin Jiminy a little too close to home. He couldn't stop talking about it, insinuating, and yet John was so private." Donnie shoves the coffee table back with his feet, confined by his fury.

"What are you saying?"

"I'm saying that Jimmy Fitzgerald is a psychopath and that unscrupulous people do heinous things. They hate people who they see as intelligent and honourable. No one wants to be measured against that long a yardstick. Think how threatening Jimmy must have found John." Donnie watches Effie, who is soothing a cranky housecat, Donnie's vigor restored by his wrath. "And let's face it. To their way of thinking, John was dispensable. Who is going to fight for a man who spoke better than all of them put together? A man who was willing to get at the truth, who they knew might someday reveal the truth, no matter what it cost him, and them?"

Mary's face crumples. "It cost him his life."

"Martyred," Effie says, realizing that Donnie and John were configured in surprisingly similar ways.

"That is entirely my point." Donnie hauls himself up from the couch and moves toward the window. "Rather than seek out the culprits who did this, people can mourn his loss from a safe distance. Conjecture about how he must have brought this on himself. Where's the outcry over the lack of a suspect? A prodigious man they all say, but one—and this part they will tell only to themselves—who isn't in any way like them at all. Fucking hypocrites." He looks out through the window, momentarily distracted by a Seaman's truck rolling down the street. "And what a conundrum," he says. "Ennobled and degraded at the same time."

Mary watches Donnie unruffling the folds of his mother's hand-stitched curtains. "Do you think Chief Trainor knew there were gay men on the force?"

"The irony in that," Donnie says without turning around, "is that Jerry Trainor wouldn't have cared about anything except the deceit."

"Yes, but people lose their jobs for being homosexual. And those guys have families—wives and children and uncles and aunts and cousins, and you know how it goes. Imagine what these kids would suffer if the truth came out."

Donnie whips around and walks back to the table. "The truth about men who called John a faggot, you mean. Good fathers who would cut someone's balls off before they'd risk being honest." His eyes fill with hot tears. "How much self-loathing does it take to ram a cigarette butt into a dead man's body?"

Donnie points at a blurry picture of a man pinned against Dr. McCready's refrigerator. "See this guy here? His wife is a teacher at Minegoo. Bet you a thousand bucks he planted that band fund rumour in her head and it took off from there. Frigging good way to try and drive John off the island. Two birds, one stone. It was all a deflection. Except John wouldn't leave. Couldn't leave."

Effie sets down the cat. "Do you think they were worried that John would say something about them?"

"It's not what he would say," Mary spouts. "It's about what he wouldn't say. John was a constant reminder of who they were—and who they could never possibly be."

"You mean straight?"

"No Effie, ethical."

"Remember what Mildred Rutherford told me? Chief Trainor knew all along that his wife was going to be okay. It was never Trainor who said it. It was everyone else." Effie's face clouds over. "Like those men I told you about in my Uncle Bill's house on Martha's birthday."

"Yes," Donnie says. "Like that. And do you remember who discovered Jerry Trainor's body?"

"Your cousin Jimmy. I heard them say so."

"Or so Fitzgerald said."

"What do you mean—so he said?"

"All bullies are cowards, Effie. And Jimmy is no exception—all talk and no guts. I would be shocked if Jimmy himself had pulled that trigger, but I'll bet he was there." Donnie walks back to the window. "But we'll probably never know. They've got this thing sewn up tighter than Sister Shannon's habit."

Effie and Mary look at each other and laugh. "What does *that* mean?" Mary asks.

"I have no idea," Donnie says, "but it sounded right to me."

"John said all along that Chief Trainor's death was suspicious and that your cousin had something to do with it." Effie hesitates. "Oh my God. If only John had gone to Halifax, the way he had wanted to."

"I thought he was running away from himself," Donnie said. "Then I got so involved—I am so involved—with Elizabeth, I should have talked to him more."

Effie looks stung. Mary jumps in. "It wasn't only that, Effie. He must have been confused by his feelings for you."

"Do you think so?" Effie asks hopefully.

"I've told you all this," Mary says softly. "You've got to trust me." She glances over at Donnie. "Trust *us*," she tempers. "I think it was one of the reasons John didn't develop those New Year's pictures. He was trying to work it through, see if his future held more possibilities than he once imagined."

"I'll tell you what we're going to do," Donnie says, picking up steam. "Tonight, after sundown, we're going to John's. I've got a key."

Effie catapults from the couch. "Are you out of your mind? They've got his house lassoed with yellow tape."

"Listen. Mom's going to be home soon with Dad and I don't want to upset them. So why not let's meet over at your building, say ten o'clock?"

"I've just got one more question," Effie says. "If Jerry Trainor really didn't kill himself and if Jimmy Fitzgerald didn't kill Jerry Trainor, who did?" She doesn't dare ask Mary what she had meant by *work it through*.

Effie and Mary wait outside their apartment building, pacing from the front door to the corner gas station and back again, trying to look natural.

Mary hugs her sweater to her body, staring in the direction of the churchyard. "There he is, Effie."

Donnie darts across the road, his hand balled into a fist around John's house key. He joins the women and they exchange discreetly nonchalant hellos, setting off up Prince Street and speaking in low tones.

At the corner of Euston, Effie puts her head down. "Jesus Christ—look across the street. It's my aunt."

"What's she doing out here at this hour?" Donnie hunches his shoulders before turning around to peek, hoping that Shirley won't see.

"Probably coming from choir practice." Effie raises her voice, in this way daring her aunt to confront them. "Aren't they usually held on Thursdays? I can't believe she hasn't crossed the street to harp at us. She must have seen us walking from the get-go."

"Maybe she thinks you're tainted," Donnie says. "You know, by the homosexual lifestyle."

Mary breaks in. "Actually, I was surprised to see her at John's service."

"Shirley?" Effie's eyebrows shoot up as she lowers her voice. Her eyes are as round as half-dollars. "Are you kidding me? Funerals are like television for her. If it weren't for the church ladies and funerals, she wouldn't have any fun at all."

"Well," Donnie says, "she's turning the corner so she must be on her way home. Isn't it late for her to be out walking the streets, even on choir night?"

"She once told me that fresh air was God's cleanser. Still, I'm surprised she didn't let on that she saw us. Usually she can't resist interfering."

Mary knows this is true and she nods. "Effie, I have to say that on the family side of things I think you got gypped."

"What I lost by way of a family I have more than made up for in friends." Effie draws in a deep breath before going on. "John dead means more to me than any of those people alive."

Donnie nudges Effie playfully. "Well it shorely weren't me that you wanted." He puffs out his chest. "Not even with all this *machismo.*"

Mary snickers. "Yes, Donnie, you're a regular Harrison Ford."

As they approach John's street their levity drains away. The fragrance of lupins infuses the air and a solitary dog barks incessantly, as if he is about to be attacked by a bear.

"I have never been in here before." Effie is impressed by the ease with which Donnie has let them in and terrified by what they will find—what John hadn't wanted her to see and what she would be forced to understand. She gropes her way to the couch with Mary while Donnie feels his way around the house and closes all the blinds.

"There's no police tape in here at all," he calls back to them, his flashlight guiding him through the front room. "And—" his voice breaks, "they seem to have scrubbed things down."

Mary digs her fingers into her cheeks.

"I know this is hard," Donnie says, edging toward the couch. "But this house could give us information." He turns and faces Effie. "Effie, are you sure—?"

"I'll be fine," Effie says. "I just need a minute. But I don't know what we're looking for." With that, she stands up and turns on her mini flashlight, making her way over to a series of pictures that hang on the wall. Mary remains seated and Donnie follows his own beams, little circles bouncing across the floor into John's bedroom.

Effie appraises John's collection of artwork comprised mostly of framed copies of Eugene Smith photographs. Black-and-white subjects, spectral and gaunt, stand beleaguered against Dickensian backdrops. These are the things John had cared about—inequality and injustice.

Aiming her flashlight at the wall, Effie looks closely at the faces in the pictures. So many men, so much desperation. Were these the faces that John loved? Beardless helmeted soldiers, dusky coal miners, weary physicians? Was this the world he had dreamt about, sought after, longed for?

Mary comes up behind her. "Look at this one," she says, pointing to a print of two children, a boy and girl, the inscription beneath. *The Walk to Paradise Garden.* Emerging into the light from a leafy enclosure, the pair—four or five years of age—hold hands. He is a step ahead of her, her chubby legs keeping up with him just the same, both of them tousled as if they had been taking a long nap beneath the arching trees.

"They remind me of my salt and pepper shakers," Effie says. "The ones you like so much on my fridge."

"Hansel and Gretel." Mary places her hand on Effie's arm.

Effie's shoulders begin to heave, tears teeming from her eyes, salty little rivers dripping over her nose.

Donnie careens back into the room, oblivious to the dark. "Look what I found!" He holds up John's camera. "Here," he says, pointing. "The back's been taken right off!"

Mary and Effie stare at the camera. "Do you think they were looking for film?" Mary asks. "Or do you think John left it open?" She considers the options. "John was so meticulous. He wouldn't have left this open for any reason."

"That's true," Effie says, wiping her eyes. "He used to go into the print shop, take his film out as if it were made of glass, and then wrap the camera back up and tuck it into his case, like it was a baby." She laughs.

Donnie laughs. "I used to tell him that a bomb squad didn't take care of things as rigourously as he did."

"Funny, though, that he took the New Year's film out and kept it in his jacket pocket."

"Haven't we been through this already?" Mary says. "That roll of film was a transition, that's all. A symbol. You're making more of it than you ought to."

"And yet not as much as the cops did." Donnie runs his hand lightly along the drywall. "Obviously they thought it was worth looking for."

"I don't see anything else unusual." Donnie sighs heavily. He shines the flashlight onto his watch.

"I think we should go. How about a beer or a coffee? What do you say?"

"Yes," answers Effie, suddenly anxious to be out of John's house. "Or even better, why don't we stop off at Ken's Corners and pick up some junk food? We can take it back to my apartment."

"If you stop calling it Ken's Korners you've got a deal." Donnie slides his hand off the wall. "I could do with a Twinkie," he says. "What about you, Effie?"

"A Joe Louis and a root beer. And maybe some chips."

"You girls go wait by the door while I open the blinds."

As Donnie feels his way across the bedroom, John's telephone sounds throughout the house. The three friends wait breathless past seven strident rings until the answering machine clicks on. A man's voice, casual yet cautious, issues pleasantly, "Hey John, are you there? I thought I might drive over to the island on the weekend. Can you call back and let me know if you'll be home?"

Effie covers her mouth, afraid she will cry out, and Donnie shouts from the bedroom.

"Son of a bitch, Effie. I'm sorry about that."

Mary takes hold of Effie's hand. "Is he the only man in the free world who doesn't know that John is dead?"

"I was just thinking the same thing. You don't think anyone saw us coming in, do you? Could it be a warning of some kind? That we're being watched?"

"Or someone trying to taunt us? Maybe that bastard's been watching the house the whole time we've been in it."

Effie laughs. "I don't know which is worse. To hear John's boyfriend call or to think we're being spied upon. Maybe my aunt is even more of an interloper than I imagined. Maybe she called Jimmy Fitzgerald and let him know."

"That fucking prick!" The flashlight slips from Donnie's hand and clunks onto the floor.

"Better him than *him*, if you know what I mean. Besides, Jimmy wouldn't dare arrest us. He's too much of a coward."

Donnie picks up the flashlight and props it under his arm. "Yeah. Too afraid to draw that much attention to himself."

As they ease their way out of the house and into the night, Effie realizes that losing John feels worse than losing her mother, and she is both angry and ashamed.

Light from a streetlamp arcs across the curling club parking lot. As soon as Donnie spots the idling car he raises his fingers to his lips, nodding first to Effie and Mary and then in the direction of the vehicle. "Wouldn't you fucking know it?" he rasps.

"Quiet or he'll hear you," Mary cautions. They watch from across the street as Jimmy Fitzgerald opens the back door of his cruiser and a skinny figure emerges, hoisting a duffel bag, heavy against his bantam weight.

Jimmy Fitzgerald reaches into his back pocket and pulls out an envelope. He crams it into the boy's hand. "Here's your ticket," he says, his words threatening, distinct. "Now get lost. Permanently."

The slender boy shifts under the pack, his limbs poking out like Pinocchio, the artificial light glancing off of his Yankee's baseball cap.

Jimmy Fitzgerald disappears into his vehicle and drives off, leaving the boy alone in the dark, three sets of eyes watching him stumble away.

"Oh my God. It's Tommy Murphy. That poor stupid boy."

CHAPTER 44

Jimmy Fitzgerald sets his walkie-talkie on top of the piano and scrapes Effie's piano bench across the floor, plunking himself down on the seat. His gut hangs over his belt buckle.

Effie, sitting across from him in the rocking chair, glimpses at the walkie-talkie, its small green light staring back at her.

"I'd like to know what you've heard," he opens, the policeman aiming for a tone midway between friendly and formal.

Effie looks at him, her lips curving upward. "Such as?"

Jimmy fumbles for his belt loops with his thumbs, prompting the buckle away from his belly. "Rumours? Gossip? Perhaps your uncle said something?"

Effie thinks back to Martha's birthday party. To the men on the stairs. "What would my uncle have to do with this?"

"Isn't he the one that got you your job in the first place? I mean, without him you'd still be back in the big city, right?"

"Is it true that someone wrote on John's wall?"

Fitzgerald lets go of his belt. "Who told you that?"

Effie gazes into his eyes, unblinking. "Why are you recording me?"

"What makes you think I'm recording you?" Jimmy turns his head slightly as if to look over his shoulder, then jerks his attention back toward Effie.

Effie inhales deeply, feeling a rush of cool air in her nostrils. "Did someone write on John's wall?"

Jimmy Fitzgerald stands up and ambles toward the window. He looks down at the street. "It seems that some of the kids at school weren't too fond of Mr. MacDonald. Wasn't your niece—Martha?—wasn't she in your class?"

Anger surges through Effie's stomach and up into her chest, but she remembers what her mother has taught her: *Be dignified.*

It drives people crazy. "Your approach feels very menacing," she says evenly. "What are you insinuating?"

Jimmy turns around and faces Effie, not moving away from the window. "Do you know anyone who had a grudge against John MacDonald?"

"Besides you? Why don't you ask your cousin? Or your aunt and uncle?" She modulates her tone. "They loved John like family. Maybe they can tell you what their suppositions are."

"Suppositions? That's a might fancy word, even for a school teacher. You've been reading too many mystery novels." He begins walking toward her, slowly. "I think you and your friend Mary are getting a little paranoid. You seem to have a lot to say to one another."

Effie glances over at her phone. Rage seeps up into her neck. Using her hands as leverage, she straightens herself in the chair, planting her feet on the floor and beginning to rise.

The policeman whisks his walkie-talkie away from the top of the piano. "We have our ways of finding things out. And we wouldn't want any of your newspaper pals getting too jabbery. The less said the better until we have more leads." He attempts to stuff the device into his pocket before resuming his seat on the bench, but the tightness of his pants makes the manoeuvre impossible to complete. The walkie-talkie clatters to the floor, lying mutely like a broken toy.

Effie sees that Fitzgerald is beginning to sweat, dark patches appearing under his arm pits, his face bathed in an oily slick. "The less said the better? Do you ever follow your own advice?"

"Your dead friend was a homosexual, Miss Cambridge. Lots of people wouldn't take too kindly to that."

"Unkindly enough to kill him? Weren't you the one who gave him the most grief?" She listens for sounds from upstairs—Mildred walking about—or Pistachio on the landing. "Weren't you the one hanging out with Tommy Murphy at the school? I've seen the two of you together more times than I can count."

Jimmy Fitzgerald swoops down and recovers his walkie-talkie. "That's none of your fuck—that's none of your business."

"You look very hot, Officer Fitzgerald. I'm friends with a nurse if you're having trouble with your blood pressure. Mildred Rutherford? You probably know her, too. She lives right upstairs. Shall I go get her?" Effie makes a move toward the front door, stopping under the archway, turning to gauge his response.

Shaking his head side to side, sweat now ringing his collar, the policeman focuses his eyes on a spot on the floor. His hands are taut, his fingers clenching and unclenching like the legs of a spider.

"You sure have a lot to say for someone from away."

Effie leans into the archway wall. "All I know is that a remarkable man was murdered—strangled to death in his bed."

Jimmy raises his eyebrows at her, the movement of his fingers now almost imperceptible. "Who tells you these things?"

Effie turns around and walks to the door. She opens it wide. "This isn't a courtroom, it's my apartment. And you're not a judge."

Fitzgerald doesn't budge. "So much fancy talk. Mike McCready teaching you that?"

"I can see where Tommy Murphy gets his manners."

"What did you say?"

She raises her voice. "Isn't it *your* job to protect *us*?"

"And that's just what I'm doing. Setting things straight. Although in this case that's part of the problem, isn't it? Nothing straight about John MacDonald. Most likely killed off by another pervert in a lover's tiff."

"You know Jimmy, there's a theory that people who exhibit pronounced hatred of homosexuals often feel that way because they themselves are gay. It's about self-hatred. Have you ever heard that theory, Jimmy?"

He sits there rooted, sweat running off his forehead.

Effie speaks clearly. "I think it's time for you to go."

CHAPTER 45

Pistachio lies on the third-floor hallway, his body flat, as if he has been sucked in by a vacuum. Blood trails from behind his ear, dribbling over the edge of the top stair and down onto the runner. His eyes stare ahead, reflecting no light.

Mary kneels beside him, her hair falling down over her eyes, her fingers gently separating strands of the cat's limp fur. She sweeps the palm of her hand across his face and closes his eyes, her shoulders leaden with the weight of her grief.

Mildred Rutherford flings open her door. "What's all the ruckus?" she bellows. "I'm trying to sleep!" She hobbles over to Mary, whose genuflecting frame has been hiding the cat. "Son of a bitch!" she crows. "What's happened here?"

Mary raises her head toward her neighbour. "Someone has killed my cat." She speaks in little gasps, as if she has been punched in the stomach.

"Killed? How do you know that?" Rutherford sniffs. "I'm sorry to tell you my dear, but cats don't live forever."

"You're a nurse," Mary says. "See for yourself."

Rutherford grips the railing and inspects Pistachio then hoists herself upright. "Poor pet," she says, putting her hand on Mary's shoulder. She shakes her head. "Dead people. Dead cats. What's a person to make of it?"

Mary, sliding her hands under Pistachio, lifts him tenderly, bending her head to kiss him. "I can't believe this. My darling boy," she whispers. "My darling boy." Only then does she wonder how Pistachio had been taken from her locked apartment. She scans the floor, spotting smaller drops of blood leading up to her door. They are scarcely perceptible, like speckles of paint. "Mildred, did you hear anything unusual this afternoon?"

Mildred Rutherford lengthens her spine, indignant. "I can tell you I did not. I would have been out here in a shot! As I said to you, dear girl, I have been *trying* to sleep. And my bed, last time I investigated, was in the back of my apartment, not out here by my front door." She waves her cane about as she speaks.

"It was only a question."

The older woman softens. "Let's get him inside," she says. Without waiting for Mary to reply, she limps toward the apartment door and lets herself in.

Mary, cradling Pistachio, speaks with only a trace of surprise. "My door was locked."

"We have to call the police," Mildred says, hobbling toward Mary's phone. She lifts the receiver.

"Put that down!" Mary's voice echoes across the room. "We're calling no one. This is my business not yours." Mary lowers Pistachio into the armchair, covering him with a sweater that had been hanging on a hook in the hallway.

Rutherford puffs, "Anything that happens in the hallway is my business, too."

"If you make a move for that phone—for any phone—you are putting my life at risk. And Effie's and Donnie's and God knows who else's."

Mildred Rutherford forces herself down into a chair. A prism of light shoots through one of Mary's glass pyramids, highlighting the age spots on the older woman's hand.

"It doesn't matter anyway because at the end of the month I am leaving this place."

"But Dr. Bob—"

"Dr. Bob already knows. I gave him my notice a week ago. So it shouldn't matter to you or the Charlottetown police because I won't be here."

Mildred stares unblinking. "You're leaving? Why wouldn't Bob tell me you were leaving? Why wouldn't *you* tell me you're leaving? You don't trust me. You think I'm a fool. You think if you tell me I won't believe you."

Rutherford rises unsteadily, thumps her way to the door, then turns on her heel. "One day you will realize that Mildred

Rutherford is a far smarter woman than you take her for. And far kinder. And decent!" she calls out over her shoulder. As Mildred opens the door to leave she nearly collides with Effie.

Effie, rattled, walks into Mary's apartment.

Mary weaves across the room and hugs Effie tightly. "They killed Pistachio, Effie. They killed him."

Effie holds on, compelled to look over her friend's shoulder at the small mound in the chair.

Rutherford's door slams, breaking the silence.

Effie turns her eyes away from the cat. "You know, when I first saw you I was so envious. Not just because you were—are—beautiful, but because of the way you were with Pistachio—so loving and sweet-natured. You will always be this way, Mary." Effie goes to the armchair, carefully lifts the sweater and smooths the cat's tail. "No one understood that better than your beautiful cat."

Her eyes suddenly widen. "Oh my God. Jimmy Fitzgerald came to see me this afternoon. He could have easily come up here before you got home. He said some terrible things. Oh my God. I wonder if I'm the cause of this. Oh Mary, I'm so terribly sorry."

"Effie, I'm leaving the island." Mary's cheeks are dappled from crying. "Sooner than later, I mean. Before the month is out. There's no reason to wait."

"I knew that even before you said it. And I think you should. After what that imbecile said today—and now your precious cat—this place isn't safe. Fitzgerald is paranoid and he's not going to stop until he drives us away. You wouldn't believe some of the things that he said—and threatened. Mary—they've been tapping our phones."

"John was right about him all along."

"For all of my pessimism, I wouldn't have believed this was possible—until today. Do you know what else he said? He asked me about our day on the boat, and about you—looking at birds. And then he made some crass comment about John liking Roddy Hannebury's chest and waiting for boy scouts."

"He what? What was he talking about?"

"The photos from the boat. Jimmy must have taken the film from John's camera, which was why the camera was empty." Effie tries not to stare at Pistachio. "Have you talked to your mother?"

"About my leaving?" Mary falters. "Or about—this?" Mary's hands look translucent in the afternoon light. "She knows that I'm leaving but I won't be telling her about any of this. She is so proud of me, Effie, and she thinks Mike's a wonderful guy. I don't want to spoil anything more for her. The less she knows, the safer she'll be."

Effie feels a stab of envy.

"But here's the thing," Mary says. "Mike and I talked things over and we would like you to come with us."

Effie bites down on the inside of her cheek. "Go back to Ontario?" She exhales. "I don't mean to be ungrateful, Mary, but I don't know if I can. And Ottawa is so . . . so . . . parochial."

Mary laughs awkwardly. "Now who's sounding like John. Did you ever once use that word before you knew him?"

"I don't know if I even thought of things in those ways."

"C'mon, Effie. It can't possibly be as conservative as Charlottetown." Mary continues to stroke Pistachio.

"Trust me, Mary, I've been there before. Ottawa's an architect's dream, but you can't have a certain kind of past there. It will work for you—you have Mike. But it's a couples' town." Effie pulls her knees up to her chest. "But maybe you're right. Maybe I should be leaving, too. You know, there are things you can do—we can do—with some distance."

"If they're capable of killing Chief Trainor and John—my *cat*—who's next—you?—my mother?"

"They found a way to shut us up, that's all."

"But that's everything."

"It's only temporary. But there are rumours, Effie, over at the paper. They're bringing in the RCMP because there's talk of an inside job. People are pretending they're not scared—that it's only a homosexual murder—*only*—and you and I both know they're right."

"But that's a good thing, Mary, isn't it? It will mean someone will solve this. That there will be some justice for John."

"Right. Look at your face and tell me that you really believe in that kind of justice. And the thought of leaving you here, of you staying behind, makes me sick." Mary lifts Pistachio and sits in the armchair, supports the lifeless animal in her lap.

Effie pretends to Mary that everything is okay; that she can take care of herself; that Mary's leaving won't make her desolate. Effie smiles serenely, the way she had after her mother died. Her mother's psychiatrist had once told Effie that she would have to safeguard against the treadmill of trauma. When Effie asked what that meant, the therapist explained that children who grow up surrounded by trouble often keep looking for it. "It's all that you know."

Her friendship with Mary, Donnie and John had changed that. But now John is dead and Mary is moving away, and here, sitting next to her friend, Effie has no idea how to proceed.

"You know what else Fitzgerald did?" she finally tells Mary. "He left his walkie-talkie standing up on the piano—turned on—trying to intimidate me. And have you ever heard that Neanderthal laugh? *Huck-uh-huck-uh-huck.* God, I hate him. I wish he'd have a big fat heart attack and drop dead on the floor."

"Do you think we have any recourse at all?" Mary continues to stroke Pistachio, trying to convince herself that the cat isn't dead. "Is there nothing we can do to vindicate John? They've rendered him worthless, dirty."

"Mary, if we bide our time there are ways. You wait and see. You're a journalist and Mike's an MP. And I can write," she laughs, before adding *sort of*. "We can go to the RCMP when we get off the island."

"They won't pester Donnie, I know that. First off, he's a man. Second, he and that monster are cousins. Third, he's heterosexual. Fourth, his cousin's a coward and Donnie might kick the crap out of him yet." Mary lowers her voice. "But if you won't come to Ottawa with us, what will you do? Where will you go?" She looks toward the apartment door, wondering if anyone is listening.

Effie stands up and crosses the room, opening and then closing the door quickly. "I was so looking forward to next year. I even made myself brave enough to ask Aida Lynn for help creating course outlines." She shivers. "Oh Mary, the kids. I can't imagine not seeing them again. I'd feel as if I was abandoning them."

They sit with Pistachio for the rest of the afternoon, Effie relaying Jimmy Fitzgerald's prying questions: *How long have you known the victim? What was your relationship to him? What can you tell me about his personal life? Did you know that he was stealing from the school band?* (At which point Effie came close to laughing out loud.) *How long do you intend to stay on the island? There is only so much room for employment when you're from away. That's a powerful hot body on your bird-loving friend. I bet they have more than their fair share of John MacDonald types up where you come from* (to which Effie had replied, coolly and pointedly, "If only.").

Across the hall, Mildred taps her cane steadily into the kitchen floor. My favourite girl, she says to herself. My favourite girl and now she's going away. The aging nurse sits in her kitchen as the sun moves slowly across the room, illuminating the stove and the porcelain sink, eventually crossing her face like a shadow puppet.

CHAPTER 46

Effie rests her hands on the balcony railing, the lunar eclipse unfolding across the cloudy sky. The moon makes her feel protected—*Goodnight Moon* and the cow that jumped over the moon in *The Friendly Giant* and, later, in high school, Robert Service's poem, "Premonition." *A year has gone and the moon is bright, a gibbous moon, like a ghost of woe; I sit by a new-made grave tonight, and my heart is broken—it's strange, you know.* Effie inhales deeply and then exhales into the night.

She thinks of the Gold Cup and Saucer Race and how the horses had pounded around the corner, hoof beats loud and louder, the hush of the spectators, the red soil stirring up little clouds behind the horses' feet. Effie's heart bangs, remembering how she had held Mary's hand and whispered, *Come on Black Beauty! Come on, Ginger!* as if somehow she could restore all that had been lost.

She steps back and presses her shoulder into the clothesline wheel, looking through her binoculars up at the moon, frightened, remembering a time when she would lie in bed and try to imagine infinity...world without end, amen, the cool night air dusting her shoulders, an evanescent kiss blowing down from Hermes, messenger of the gods and conductor of souls. Chilled, she retreats inside and begins planning her move, deciding that the heavier furniture will stay—Dr. Bob said this was no problem—and that the rest of the items could travel with her or be shipped: the braided mat from Zellers; the scarves; the French lace table cloth (she removed the candle wax with a hot iron), the framed photographs and the binoculars.

She stares up at the glass chandelier and at the roving, indifferent foxes and wonders who David was, his name etched into the dresser. She is afraid to look at the piano for fear she will cry.

Craving the analgesic effect of wine, she walks into the kitchen and opens her fridge, empty except for a root beer and a small block of cheese. She confirms the time on the clock, relieved that she can head up to the taxi stand and purchase a bottle of Boutari. On her way out the door, she decides to give Mary the salt and pepper shakers as a going-away gift.

The street is deserted except for a man and a woman who stand in their doorway gazing at the moon, and the shadowy figure of a young woman walking toward the apartment building. Effie is not surprised to see Martha.

"Are you waiting for your mother?" Effie asks.

"My mother?" Martha's overall strap slips off her shoulder.

"Isn't she at choir practice on Thursdays?"

"That's why I'm out. I knew she wouldn't miss me."

"Miss you from what?"

"I was coming to talk to you," Martha says. "To see if you would talk with me. But you're going out—"

"Only for a short walk," Effie replies. "Would you like to come with me? We could look at the moon as we go. See what we can figure out about eclipses." At the sound of a car engine her eyes dart nervously, expecting to see a police cruiser, as has been happening with increasing regularity.

Martha seems equally nervous. "Could we just go back to your place? We could look at the moon from there if you like. I really don't want to run into my mother."

Effie turns back toward home, the wine forgotten. "Where does your father think you are?" And she remembers with chilling clarity, "*Wasn't your niece—Martha?—wasn't she in your class?*"

"As long as I'm not out late with the car, he doesn't mind. Not now that Tommy has gone." Martha stutters on the word Tommy.

"Martha, did Tommy ever tell you anything more about his plans? Before you split up, I mean? Was he going to be leaving the island?"

"He didn't tell me noth—anything. Not anything real or anything that mattered."

Effie puts her arm around Martha's bulky shoulder and leads her back to the building. When they are safely inside, Martha sits down in the rocker. "I heard *you* were leaving the island," she says. Her sandals slip off her feet with the movement of the chair. Martha stops rocking and looks hard at her cousin. "Were you just going to go and not say goodbye?"

"Sometimes the most painful things are the hardest to muster. But, no, I would not have gone without telling you." Effie stands over Martha. "I want to take you to lunch, if you think that is something you'd like to do."

Martha seizes the arm of the chair. "I *would* like to go some-where," she says.

"Where would you like to go?"

"With you." Martha's knuckles turn white. "Wherever you're going. I'd like to go with you."

Effie steps back and sits down on the couch. "I don't even know where I'm going. It wouldn't be right, and I don't think I have enough money for two."

You've been reading too many mystery novels—isn't that what he had said?

Martha begins rocking again. Her face opens up. "Oh, money's not a problem. I have bonds to cash in whenever I want."

"But your mother—"

"She doesn't know. My father never told her."

"But what about school? You haven't even begun grade eleven."

"I could do school anywhere—somewhere in another city with you or by correspondence. You're a teacher, aren't you? I could even go to technical college. You only need grade ten for that. I asked the guidance counsellor. You know, Effie, it isn't as if they're going to miss me. Life's really weird over there. My mother's like that mother in *Carrie* and my father isn't crazy but he gives into her because it's easier that way. He's mostly nice to me but I know he's not a good person. And my brother just sits around eating cheese sandwiches all day and glaring. He scares me."

Effie frowns. "What would you do in technical school?"

"Lots of things. I like drafting and printing and carpentry."

Effie remembers the rhythmic sounds of Martha's hammering backstage at the play. "You could study set design," she says, more to herself than to her cousin.

Martha stops rocking again. "You mean I can come with you?"

"With one provision," Effie says, taking in a breath, feeling reckless but free. "That you don't tell your mother until we are well away from here. I absolutely mean this."

Martha slips on her sandals and walks over to the couch toward Effie, throwing her arms around her cousin's neck. "Oh, thank you! You won't be sorry—I promise."

Effie feels Martha's necklace pressing into her skin, a tiny pattern imprinted there momentarily. Effie stands up. "Let's watch the eclipse."

CHAPTER 47

Effie inspects the rooms of her apartment, making sure everything is in order for the new tenants who are moving in on Labour Day. She pauses at the living room window, missing the nights when she sat on the ledge eating breadballs and sniffing for worms when it rained.

It is raining today, more drizzle than downpour, as Effie watches for Donnie's approach along Prince Street. Martha, who had parcelled up her belongings when no one was home and hidden them in the trunk of her car, would be coming from the opposite direction later in the morning.

Effie has packed essentials in a shoulder bag—her green-handled comb; cassette tapes (hoping that Martha likes Eddy Grant); a tube of Midnight Moon lipstick; her glass jewelry box; *Anne of Green Gables*—and stuffed her favourite items of clothing and other cherished books into her old paisley suitcase. Donnie will send along her boxed-up household odds and ends, school things and the rest of her clothing once they settle somewhere, whenever or wherever that might be.

Effie has not told Mildred she is moving for fear that any information will go lickety-split to Shirley. Only last week Rutherford said to Mary and Effie in the hallway, as the younger women were carting boxes and crates down to a rented car, that Mary was acting in haste; that corruption existed wherever a person lived, although Mildred could see—even irrefutably say— that big fish in small ponds were better fed. "Gossip is one thing, revealing a secret entirely another," she added, her cryptic tone belying the sentiment of her words. And Effie knows that actions speak louder than words, and that Mildred, given all of her prurient connections, is not to be trusted. As it turns out, Effie's plans were revealed anyway. How could it be otherwise?

Effie spots Donnie's car pulling into a parking space. She watches him step out into the street, his hair dishevelled, the lines around his eyes visible from the second-storey window. She realizes how tired he is, how much he has lost and is losing. She opens the door as he is mounting the stairs.

He holds a bottle of uncapped root beer in one hand and a coffee cup in the other. When he reaches the landing and sees her, he stops cold.

Effie smiles. "Well—are you coming in or not? That root beer's getting cold."

"Scarecrow," he says, "I think I'm going to miss you most of all."

"I think that's my line," she says, turning her back on him so he can't see her face. "You know," she says, dragging her sleeve across her nose, "I've cried more in the past two months than I have in my whole life put together. In fact, a year ago, I didn't think I would've been able to say the word *weep*, and now it's all I seem to do."

Donnie hands Effie the bottle. "Seriously Effie, I don't know what I am going to do without you."

"Me?" Effie demurs and then marshals him in and closes the door.

Donnie cradles his coffee. "You're leaving and you don't even know where you're going. I'm worried about you out there, all on your own."

"I have a bit of a secret," she says, "although you must not tell a soul until I give you the go-ahead, even if you don't approve."

"Ever the mystery woman." He puts his lips to the rim of his cup.

"Martha's coming with me."

Donnie sputters. "Martha Cambridge?"

"No. Martha Washington. Of course Martha Cambridge."

"Have you gone insane? She's *sixteen*."

Effie puffs up her cheeks and blows hard. "That's right, the age of majority in Ontario. Leave her with Bill and Shirley and in two years we can commit her to Unit Nine. And please keep your voice down. These ceilings have ears."

"You have a point. Does Bill know?"

"Martha wrote him a letter that she'll mail en route, after we've got some distance. She doesn't want to be followed, and I don't want that for her, either. Besides, I'm taking her under my wing as my responsibility. Bill loves her at least that much. He has to hide things from his wife to protect his daughter."

"And Martha's brother?"

"I can't say with certainty. He's in league with his mother, which doesn't bode well."

"You can't afford this on teacher's wages, Effie. Do you even have a job lined up?"

"Martha has money of her own. But I'd find a way if she didn't. She needs me. One plus about living on the island has been that there was nowhere to spend my money. You and John took such good care of me—and Mary and your family, of course. And what with the cheap rent—in part thanks to Mildred's crashing in—I've saved at least half of my salary."

"You mean you didn't blow it all on wine and bowling?" Donnie looks small in the foyer. "You know you're breaking Angus's heart, leaving like this. Who's he going to dootie up his drinks for now? All those little umbrellas and cherries gone to waste."

They walk to the back of the apartment, Effie pointing into her bedroom. "Everything's in there," she says. "I can't thank—"

"Oh go way with ya. Mom's so upset that this is all you'll let us do. She is terribly disappointed that they're in Halifax this weekend. She wanted to say a proper goodbye." Donnie passes his cup over to Effie and lifts a compact trunk from the floor, hoisting it onto his shoulder. "Back in a minute," he says. The sleeve of his jacket snags on a nail and he laughs.

Effie can't imagine how difficult saying goodbye to the Fitzgeralds would have been. They were the closest she had ever come to having a family. Even their cats were more loving than most people she'd known. She was going to miss feeling special. Perhaps, eventually, she and Martha will adopt a stray or two. One for each of them.

She thinks of Pistachio buried in a backyard in Little Pond—one of the many island places she'd never visit—and Mary in Ottawa, catless, but safe with Mike. Effie and Mary had bawled like babies on parting, promising visits and making future plans.

Two trips later, as Donnie makes his way toward the door with the last load, Effie grabs hold of the back of his jacket. "Please say goodbye to Jill and Roddy for me." Her face contorts into a grimace of longing and regret.

Donnie puts his hand on the nape of her neck, kissing her forehead. "You haven't seen the last of me, Effie. As soon as you're settled—"

"As soon as Martha and I are settled." Thinking of Martha gives Effie courage.

"Yes, or even before, Elizabeth and I are coming to see you. And who knows? We might lure you back here some day." He can see by the worried look on her face that this is not likely to happen, but he continues. "With Shirley Cambridge *not* on your side, anything's possible."

Effie watches at the window as Donnie drives away, turning right onto Richmond at the Rec Centre and disappearing into the sombre distance.

Swinging her car into the space left empty by Donnie, Martha lumbers out of her father's old Pontiac, hauling on the strap of her overalls, a look of jubilant victory on her face. She glances up at the window and smiles easily at Effie.

At the top of the landing Effie greets her cousin. "Come on in and have a seat," she says quietly. "I'll be ready in five minutes." Effie lifts her suitcase and shoulder bag, and sets them on the end of the couch. She hands her root beer to Martha. "Have some," she says.

Martha laughs. "Breakfast of champions?"

"You're too young for champagne." Effie makes her way from room to room, verifying that she's left nothing of value behind and saying a silent goodbye. She runs her fingers across the kitchen table and peeks out through the window one last time. A cobweb trails from the corner of the ceiling. Effie retrieves the broom, sweeping the web down with ferocity. Over her head, the sound of Mildred's three-legged gait hammers across the hardwood floor. Effie follows the footsteps back into her living room, toward Martha.

"Are you ready?" Effie asks. "We'll have to leave fast. Rutherford doesn't miss a thing." The second she speaks, a flurry of footsteps fly up the stairs, past her apartment. Effie listens against her door, waiting until the shoes have piled into Mildred's living room. Trailing behind, a lone pair of pumps clip-clop their way up the stairs. They stop on the landing outside Effie's door.

Effie touches her finger to her lips, cautioning Martha into silence. A quick series of sharp raps follows and Martha, dependably hypervigilant, slips into the bathroom.

Effie opens the door.

"What is my husband's car doing outside of your building?"demands Shirley Cambridge.

"First of all, Shirley, it's not my building. It belongs to Dr. Bob. Second, how would I know what that vehicle is doing outside?"

Shirley snaps to attention, her hair coiling around the frames of her eyeglasses. "If you're harbouring my daughter it is my right to know!"

"I'm not a pirate, Shirley. This isn't an Errol Flynn movie. Maybe Martha has something to do in town—perhaps at the church," Effie stalls. "Or over at the Rec Centre bowling with friends."

"That girl has no friends, unless she's taken up with that creature again." Shirley grunts. "If you see her, tell her to hustle her buns back to the house and put that room of hers in order. I'll not have her gallivanting all over Charlottetown when there's work to be done. I pray to God that without you filling up her head with nonsense she'll settle down. When are you—"

Effie closes the door in her aunt's face. How fitting that Shirley calls it a house and not a home.

After delivering a round of thundering blows, Shirley descends the stairs. Effie crosses to the window and watches her aunt heading down the block.

Martha creeps out of the bathroom, fidgeting with the buckle on her strap. "Is it safe for us to leave?"

"We'll have to be careful. The group meet in Mildred Rutherford's kitchen and we'll have to be gone before your mother gets back." Effie turns and faces Martha. "Thank God you aren't like her."

"I'm not?" Martha lets go of the buckle. "I'm not like my mother?"

Effie shakes her head no. "I'll take my bags down to the car—may I borrow your keys?—and peek up first to make sure no one is looking."

"The car's open—I don't ever lock it—but wouldn't it be better if we leave together so we can hightail it if we have to? She's not going to run after us."

Effie wonders if John had left his door unlocked. She runs her knuckle across her lower lip, resisting tears. "No, she most likely wouldn't, but she'd call Jimmy Fitzgerald in a heartbeat if she sees us driving away."

"What's he got to do with it?"

"I mean she'll call the police, and they could come after us. You're a minor, after all."

Martha grins broadly. "What are they going to do—arrest me for driving you to the ferry?"

"But I've already lied to her, and you know your mother."

"Yes, I know my mother."

Effie feels energized. "Okay then. Let's go together. You take the root beer and I'll grab my bags and we'll sneak out like Bonnie and Clyde."

"I'll be Clyde," Martha laughs.

As Effie opens the door to the landing, she hears the *tap tap tap* of Mildred's cane overhead. She throws Martha a look, warning her with her eyes to be careful. Waving her ahead, Effie eases the door closed behind them. As she gathers up her belongings, her shoulder bag slides to the floor and thumps its way down the stairs, cassettes scattering everywhere. Martha bursts out laughing and Effie freezes.

Mildred Rutherford's door flies open. "What's all the ruckus out here?" The older woman flashes a look over the railing at Effie and Martha on the stairs. Mildred glances back over her shoulder, calculating swiftly. "Get back in the apartment, ladies. It was nothing. Just some noisy boy delivering flyers." She turns her back on Effie and Martha, hastening them away with the back of her hand. "Ladies!" she hollers in to her guests. "Into the kitchen! The biscuits are burning!" Effie and Martha hurry downstairs and out to the waiting car.

"Don't speed, Martha," Effie warns her. "We don't want to be stopped."

Martha grins. "Oh, I never speed."

Effie and Martha remain silent as they drive through Charlottetown heading for the highway, Effie relieved that Martha is proving to be a capable driver. They snake through the downtown core, curving around the old hospital and up along North River Road, Martha driving on past her own street, her face unchanging.

They are ten miles past Cornwall when Effie speaks. "This part of the island is hillier than I remember," she says. "That graveyard over there is so beautiful."

"I love graveyards," Martha echoes. Her eyes roll over the gravestones, their names a running script that quickly fades into a blur. "It must be hard for you without Mr. MacDonald. Life is surprising, isn't it, and not always in very good ways. Sometimes Tommy and I—sometimes I would take the car when my parents weren't around and go wandering through them."

"Do you miss him terribly?" Effie asks. She knows she will never tell Martha what she and Donnie and Mary suspect. The girl is heartbroken enough. Effie can't even muster any rage against him. Rage feels so pointless. He is, in his own way, a victim. And yet a part of Effie recoils because she knows she ought to be angrier; ought to have been more responsible. She has no idea what species of monster they have unleashed, setting him free that night into the world. In the end, though, it is Jimmy Fitzgerald she wants punished.

Effie rolls down her window as they drive by a herd of speckled cows. "Do you know Vermeer?" she asks Martha.

"Veneer?"

"Close," Effie says, shivering in the wind. "He was a painter." She rolls up the window. "Do you think you'd like to see Paris and London? I could take you next summer."

"Are you serious?"

"We could stash our belongings with Mary and Mike in Ottawa, then go see where Charles Dickens lived. Visit the museums and art galleries. And in Paris we could go to Père Lachaise Cemetery. You know who's buried there, don't you?"

Martha lets out a squeal. "Oscar Wilde!?"

"And Abelard and Heloise." Effie closes her eyes. "And Edith Piaf."

Effie opens her eyes and looks at her cousin. "There are scores of genius writers and musicians buried there. In fact, we could challenge ourselves to read some of their books and discover their music, which will give you a head start when you enter grade eleven."

"But I told you already—I want to go to technical school. I don't need a high school diploma for that."

"Let's just see how things go and, in the interim, we'll plan our home-schooling from away. I am a teacher, after all, as you so rightly pointed out. For now, we'll go where the wind takes us."

Martha loosens her grip on the wheel.

When Martha and Effie drive up to the dock in Borden, a long line of cars have already formed in front of them. Effie is worried they won't make it onto this ferry, but Martha reassures her that there is plenty of room.

The Abegwit floats before them, for Effie a remembrance of things past, for Martha a symbol of freedom. Waved aboard by an orange-vested man holding a baton, they park and climb out of the car. Before making her way up the metal stairs, Effie watches the last vehicle glide onto the boat. The ramp lifts with a groan and a shudder.

Martha hands Effie the car keys. "I'm going to buy us some snacks."

Out on deck Effie holds onto the railing, scanning the Northumberland Strait, glad she has worn a warm sweater. How many weeks since she had been out on the water with John. What she would give to be back on Roddy's boat, unravelling time.

John balances against the taut rope that frames the bow, focusing on her face, his eyes squinting into the sun. "If you could have one thing in the world, Effie, what would it be?

"To be loved." Effie had answered boldly. "And to love back."

John laughs. "That's two things." He adjusts his gaze out to sea. "And you? What's the one thing you'd want?"

"To be loved is a wonderful thing." John stares at the waves, entranced by their textures, which are contoured and altered by light. "But if I could have only one thing, I would want not to be misunderstood."

"I don't get it," she teases.

"To be known," John says, his voice dropping low.

Effie is taken aback by the simplicity of John's answer. "So that you have clarity?"

"So that everyone is included—not loved or unloved, but equally known."

"Oh, but John, love is a much wiser choice because love is more possible."

"Just because something feels unattainable doesn't mean it's not worth seeking. Whole lives are built on unlikely premises, Effie. Rich lives."

Effie bites down on her lip. "And yet," she begins, "sometimes love feels like the unlikeliest premise of all."

"I know you," John says, a seagull swooping perilously close to his head. "That seems like the perfect place to start."

Effie smiles at the lattice of silver rippling across the tips of the small blue waves.

Martha comes up behind her, holding an open packet of cherry licorice. "Would you like one?"

EPILOGUE

Effie picks up her pen and begins to write.

PROLOGUE

I WILL KILL AGAIN, *six inches high, red ink, not felt pen, not blood (barely enough anyway), scrawled out on the white vertical slats of the bedroom wall, and the Labrador retriever whirling around and around, frantic.*

His master hardly looks disturbed, at least not from this distance. You can see him through the opened front door, beyond the living room and straight across into the privacy of his bedroom. He is lying on his bed facing the wall, fetal position, not dreaming and soon to become famous in a way that will make his mother inconsolable and the rest of his family angry and confused.

The howling dog has alerted a neighbour (well, three or four neighbours, but that is the way on Prince Edward Island), and before long a spirited competition arises over the layman's duties of this insurrection. Who will phone the police? Who will examine the body to determine if it is indeed a body and not, after all, a shallow-breathing victim of... what?

Some, of course, are more privy than others to the tales of greater gore, but all in all the quality of the details proves satisfactory to almost all who hear them:

Male, thirty-three, five feet eight inches tall, brown hair, brown eyes, school teacher, immaculate, reserved, infectious laugh. Dead. Murdered. Bashed over the head with a baseball bat and choked with the sleeve of a size fifteen SC Walker blue-and-white striped dress shirt, although many contend that a dress shirt doesn't have enough strength, which causes a whole other argument about silk worms and fibres that has nothing to do with science or shirts or with anything related to his death at all.

Following the choking—the absence of substantial bleeding supports this—a wooden-handled nine-inch knife stamped "Old Nick" was shoved up his rectum, the blade wide enough to slice muscle and fat on either side, separating the buttocks and creating an asymmetrical Betty Boop protuberance. What many never learned, however, is that the butt of a du Maurier Special Mild cigarette had been jammed into the dead man's navel.

ACKNOWLEDGEMENTS

Thank you to Chris Needham of Now Or Never Publishing for taking on a story that has been years in the making, and for doing so with calm assurity and trust. And to Helen Humphries, without whom I might never have completed this book, and whose overview proved invaluable. Thank you to my friends Sheila Mortimer Gibbs and Paul Coccia, for reading the early manuscript, asking pertinent questions (or kindly remaining silent), and for always believing I could do this. Especial gratitude to the late Fran Frazer, whose unwavering faith in me served as steadfast reminder, and to the late Frank Ledwell and the passionate creative writing class at UPEI. I am also grateful to every member of the Charlottetown, Ottawa and Toronto writing groups, whose mutual support and laughter provided hours and pages of inspiration, and to family and friends who replied to my relentless sets of email questions asking, "Which do you prefer?" And to Ian Singer, for his generous, ceaseless encouragement. Finally, to Mary, for her wisdom, perspective, patience, editing skills and love.